EVERY STREET

EVERY STREET

Jeremiah Every is the head of the family. He establishes businesses for his five sons and expects his grandsons to follow in their father's footsteps.

Granddaughters, however, have no part in Jeremiah's schemes, but his rebel granddaughter Jessamy becomes absorbed in her father's pharmacy business and from an early age has a knowledge of herbs and their curative powers.

Her dream is to become a doctor, but she falls in love with the dynamic sea captain, Fabian Montague. But Fabian, like Jeremiah, expects a wife to fall into the traditional mould. When Fabian's interests wander, Jessamy's do too and she is forced to make a choice which will shape the rest of her life and the lives of those around her.

EVERY STREET

by
Mary Minton

MAGNA PRINT BOOKS
Long Preston, North Yorkshire,
England.

British Library Cataloguing in Publication Data.

Minton, Mary
    Every street.

    A catalogue record for this book is
    available from the British Library

    ISBN 0 7505 0349 1

First Published in Great Britain by Random Century Group Ltd.,
1990.

Published in Large Print 1992 by arrangement with Random Century Group Ltd., London.

Printed and bound in Great Britain by
T.J. Press (Padstow) Ltd., Cornwall, PL28 8RW.

To dear Jeanne Minton-Morse, our intrepid
traveller in the family. With love.

'Sigh no more, ladies, sigh no more,
Men were deceivers ever;
One foot in sea, and one on shore,
To one thing constant never.'

Much Ado About Nothing
William Shakespeare

Saint Cade and Saint Peel are figments of my imagination, but are real to me.

CHAPTER ONE

In the early 1800s the only sign of habitation on the road that linked the two small villages of St Peel and St Cade was the Highwayman's Arms, which offered food and shelter to men and horses travelling between the north and the south. The hostelry lay in a hollow protecting it from the open moorlands, where the wind blew strong from the sea. However, in the middle of the nineteenth century, when Jeremiah Every bought a parcel of land which included the hostelry, a colleague declared he could see no sense to the deal.

'Why, Jeremiah? Time won't bring any more trade to the Highwayman's Arms.'

Jeremiah tapped the side of his nose and gave a knowing wink. 'It will when a port is built at St Peel. This was only a rumour a while ago, but now I know it to be fact. Yes, I know there are docks at Newcastle, but this will be built mainly for stone boats. The output of the quarries here is increasing every month. There's a demand for stone from many countries, for dams, piers, buildings...'

He explained his plans. He would enlarge the hostelry and put his eldest son Edward in charge. For his next son Albert he would build a warehouse, suitable for a ship's chandlery business. Jeremiah paused then added, 'And for my other three sons there will be a business each: a wheelwright and saddlery for James, a drapery store for Digby and, of course, a pharmacy for Chadwick.'

Whenever Jeremiah spoke of Chadwick a softness would come into his voice, this youngest son having cured him once of a fever when all other physicians had failed.

'My sons will prosper,' he concluded. His colleague shook his head and said he very much doubted that a port would ever be built.

But it was built and it brought a constant stream of traffic, wagons, carriages, carts, horses. The hostelry seldom had an empty bed and Jeremiah's other sons all flourished. They married, had children and before Jeremiah's grandsons were christened he had plans for them, too. When they grew up they would all be absorbed into the various businesses.

With the coming of the port the area between St Peel and St Cade, once sparsely inhabited, began to develop. Derelict homes were restored and new ones constructed. Cottage industries sprang up and farmers round about increased their stock. A church and a school came into being. On the moors large houses appeared, occupied by shipowners, sea captains and their families.

Jeremiah, who was always preaching that to

accumulate one must speculate, decided to invest in several more shops: in 1890 he installed five of his nephews individually in a bakery, a butchery, a general store, a shoemaker's and a clock and jewellery business. None of these nephews and their families were liked or tolerated by the rest of the family, but because they all bore the Every name, that part of the road in time became known as Every Street.

Four of Jeremiah's sons had sizeable families, but his youngest son Chadwick had only one child, a daughter named Jessamy. But although the child was a joy to Chadwick she was a thorn in the flesh of his wife Esmeralda, who declared that someone must have put a curse on her in denying her sons and, although she was never unkind to Jessamy, she showed little interest in the child. However, Jessamy had so much love from her father, her Uncle Albert (nicknamed Bertie) and his wife Verity, that it made up for the lack of affection from her mother. In fact, Jessamy spent most of her life with her uncle and aunt and their family, and the rest of it at the shop with Chadwick.

The trouble with Jessamy was she was so full of energy, always on the go, wanting to be either in her father's shop, running away to explore the moors or trying to get to the docks to see the ships. The road that turned right past the pharmacy led straight to the wharf, and once Jessamy could be free she would run down the road as fast as her little legs would carry her. A hill barred the view from ships and river and she was always caught before rounding the hill.

Chadwick sympathised with the child's frustration but knew the time had come for her to be disciplined. He always spoke quietly, even when angry, but people recognised the authority in his voice and respected him. When he told Jessamy she would be banned from the shop if she ever ran away again, she too recognised the authority and heeded the warning.

Verity tried to make up to Jessamy for her scolding by promising to take her and her daughter Louise to the warehouse the following morning. As seeing her Uncle Bertie in the chandlery was a special treat to Jessamy she was all sunny smiles again.

The warehouse was always a hive of industry, with men shouting instructions to one another over the clatter of chains being moved, the sawing of wood for the making of crates, hammering and goods being loaded on to drays to take to the ships. But no matter how busy they were Uncle Bertie, big and genial, would always come to greet them, welcoming Aunt Verity first then turning to the girls and saying, 'And where have my lovelies been to this morning? I hope you've been good.'

And the girls would beam up at him and say, 'Very good.'

They would each receive a sweetmeat, then

Verity and the children would walk around the warehouse where the men, in the midst of their labours, would touch a forelock to them. Jessamy always left with a mingled smell of paraffin, varnish and hemp in her nostrils.

They never visited any of the shops run by Jeremiah's nephews, the nephews having made it plain they had no time for children, but Verity would take the children to see one or another of their uncles while they were visiting the warehouse.

On that particular morning they called at the drapery store run by Digby. Small, dapper and tight-lipped, if one of the girls touched any of the goods he would say, 'Now then, young ladies, look but do not touch.'

Sometimes his wife Dorcas would come in. She was tight-lipped, too, and wore her hair screwed back into a bun. The pair were known in the family as the 'Dismal Dees'. Despite this, Jessamy liked looking around the shop —with her hands clasped safely behind her back. There was so much colour in the bolts of materials, the cottons, linens, brocades, satins, velvets and in the skeins of embroidery silks. When Aunt Verity was buying cotton to have dresses made for the girls she would finger the material with ungloved hands, but if she wanted brocade for an evening gown for herself she would pull on a pair of spotless white gloves to feel the quality. Digby insisted, pointing out that if a thread was pulled a piece of material would be wasted.

Verity once said to her husband, 'I notice that Digby doesn't ask the wealthy ones to wear gloves when fingering the brooches, but then they are *ladies*.'

Verity was smiling as she spoke. Uncle Bertie picked up her right hand and kissed the finger-tips, saying softly, '*You* are my precious lady and I want no other.'

Jessamy thought this quite beautiful and hoped when she had a husband he would say wonderful things like this to her.

From the drapery they would go on to the hostelry, but only Aunt Verity went inside to have a quick word with her brother-in-law Edward and his wife Grace. They were always too busy to entertain the children but the girls never minded, for there was so much to look at outside. The building, with its diamond-paned windows and courtyard with a gallery conjured up for Jessamy days gone by, when highwaymen used to rob the wealthy and kid-nap young ladies, carrying them off to secret hiding places.

Jessamy's older cousin Louise, who told these stories with great drama, had no idea what happened to these abducted young ladies in the secret hideouts, but Jessamy would listen wide-eyed and shivery with excitement. And even her other cousins—shy, quiet girls who exclaimed with horror at such happenings—would beg for more if Louise offered to stop.

There was always as much activity outside the hostelry as in Uncle Bertie's warehouse, with carriages arriving and departing, ostlers running to collect the baggage and others ushering the guests inside. From the Highwayman's Arms they would pass Uncle James' wheelwright and saddlery business, where the smells of wood mingled with the lovely tang of leather.

Last of all they would enter the pharmacy, where ribbons of light from the narrow-necked, pot-bellied bottles on the shelf in the window, containing red, blue, green, purple and orange liquid, were reflected on the floorboards.

Chadwick, like Bertie, came to greet them with a smile. Taller and much leaner than Bertie, with his clean-cut features, fair hair and kindly grey eyes, to Jessamy he was the most attractive man she knew.

From an early age she had learned simple cures from her father, like how to make warts disappear from her cousin Luke's hand by squeezing the juice from the stem of a dandelion on them for five days in succession. On the third day the warts had blackened and on the fifth, they were gone. Jessamy said to her father, awe in her voice, 'Are you God, Papa?'

'No, Jessamy dear, I'm not. But God provides all the flowers, plants and tree-bark that ease and sometimes cure people's ailments.'

From then on she thirsted for knowledge.

Chadwick was in the habit of buying many of his herbs, quite a few from abroad, but he would take Jessamy and those of his nieces and nephews who were interested to pick plants from the hedgerows, moors and fields, so that in time they would learn to recognise them and know the value of them as a medicine.

To create more interest, he asked the children to try and find out who, among the elderly people in the area, were housebound and what medicine they took. They were to write down the name of the person and their complaint, and bring it when they next went plant-picking. Two days later, they arrived at the field waving their slips of paper.

Rupert, Louise's youngest brother shouted, 'Mrs Joby says she wants something for her waterworks!'

There were sniggers from the boys at this and Louise muttered to Jessamy, 'I bet he couldn't wait to get here to say that...'

Chadwick's lips trembled in a smile. 'Yes, Rupert, I think some borage might settle that. There's some right behind you in the hedge— see those clusters of blue flowers?'

Rebecca, Edward and Grace's daughter, said that Mr Benson had a grumbling stomach and Chadwick nodded. 'I think some agrimony for that. It's a little further along—those lovely yellow flowers on long stems like church steeples.'

The next request was for a pick-me-up and

16

Chadwick waved his hand towards a field with large patches of yellow Gentians saying, 'Take your pick!'

Yarrow was suggested for a Mr Pettifer with sore gums then one of the boys said with a broad grin, 'Mrs Fuller, who's ninety, wants something for her bloody wind.'

The other boys shouted with laughter. Some of the girls stifled giggles while the rest looked embarrassed. Chadwick said calmly, 'I think that a ninety year old lady who does all her own housework and washing and who bakes cakes for other people deserves to be applauded. Now, who is next on the list?'

There were five 'patients' who wanted relief from rheumatic pains, requesting a herbal tea to drink.

Chadwick looked around him thoughtfully. 'Well now, we have a wide choice of plants but I suggest nettles and they are certainly plentiful. Make sure you wear your gloves, but if you do get stung, rub the sting with a dockleaf.'

Three hours later the children, dishevelled, sun-warmed and chatting happily, walked with their net bags to the big shed at the back of Chadwick's shop, where they helped him to lay out the plants on wire-meshed shelves to dry. Then he said, 'When they are dry you shall help to cut them up or pound them into a powder, but in the meantime I shall give you medicine for each of the people you've sponsored. You've all worked hard and I'm very

17

pleased with you.'

The children were enthusiastic at first but when the first novelty wore off their number gradually lessened so that towards the end of the summer there was only Jessamy, her cousin Louise and her shy, pale-faced cousin Anne who still went collecting the plants. Even then, Louise was half-hearted about the task. 'Why bother,' she said, 'when Uncle Chadwick can buy the herbs.'

'Because this way you learn,' Jessamy said earnestly, repeating her father's words. Then she gave an impish smile. 'And it keeps you out of mischief.'

When customers came in for medicine Jessamy would listen to advice offered by her father or Mr Blackwell, his assistant. 'Yes, comfrey is good for rheumatism,' Mr Blackwell said one day, 'but you benefit by including other ingredients.' He then insisted that the medicine should be taken for several months to have any benefit.

'That's the trouble with most people,' Chadwick said sadly. 'They're so impatient. They'll take the medicine for a week or a fortnight and expect to be cured of a complaint they've had for years.'

To Jessamy when she was young there seemed to be bottles of medicine for hundreds of complaints: to cure coughs and colds, chest problems, nervous troubles and painful kidneys, gout, migraine, heart trouble...the list was endless. Then there were the ointments, to heal chilblains, sores, boils and several creams, the cosmetic kind, which the ladies always asked for a little sheepishly, as if they ought not to need anything to improve their complexions.

The shop was large, with the whole of one wall taken up with drawers of herbs labelled with the abbreviated Latin names, and a ladder that ran on a rail so one could reach the top row of drawers. Jessamy preferred the common names for the plants such as betony, periwinkle, meadowsweet, goldenrod, mignonette, heartsease...

Although many people made their own medicines some would still come to Chadwick, aware that he always added an extra ingredient known only to himself. One very secret item, *Chadwick Every's Elixir of Life*, was much sought after by the more wealthy people. The elixir took a year to concoct, with various herbs being added at different seasons. In March, acorns, betony, orris root, cypress and sweet scabious would be ground to a powder. Later, powdered mace, yellow sandalwood, juniper berries and coriander seeds were added. The peel of six oranges followed, and the whole went into a stone jar containing a gallon of spirits. After being well shaken and corked, the jar was stored in a cool place for three or four weeks.

Finally, the late-spring flowers would go in,

followed by others as they became available. With the last in, the infusion was allowed to stand for nine days more until it yielded two quarts of aromatic spirits. Chadwick would then say with a smile, 'And now for the final touch.' But no one was ever allowed to see this last ingredient being included...

When customers who had never tasted the elixir asked if it was worth all the work, Chadwick would say with a twinkle in his eyes, 'Buy some then tell me,'—and it always meant new customers to be added to the list.

As Jessamy grew up she showed signs of becoming a beauty. She was not tall but like her father, she stood tall. She also had his fair colouring. Her hair shone with a silvery sheen and her eyes, large and widely-spaced, were a deep amber. Most of the time she wore her hair tied back but for parties it was swept up and when she danced, her curls danced with her.

At sixteen Jessamy not only had a wide knowledge of herbs but of people, too. Although she could still be hurt at times by her mother's indifference, she would have said that she had never known any real unhappiness. However, two days after her sixteenth birthday a cousin she had always disliked made a remark that shocked her to the soul. Unable to mention the matter to either of her parents or her cousin Louise, with whom she had shared many girlish secrets, Jessamy decided to confide in her Aunt Verity. Unfortunately, Verity was away visiting relatives for three days so Jessamy had to keep this awful thing bottled up inside her.

She forced herself to try and act naturally but on the third day was beginning to feel the strain. During the afternoon, when her father asked her, with concern, if she was all right, she pleaded a headache and said she would take a walk on the moors. It was here that her aunt found her. It was not unusual for Verity to meet Jessamy on the moors, for they both enjoyed walking, but Verity was shocked when she saw the disconsolate figure of her niece sitting on a slab of rock staring into space. She paused then walked up to her.

'Hello, Jessamy. Louise said I might find you here. I'm glad to be back—I've sat in the houses of so many relatives it's a treat just to get some fresh air.' She sat down on the rock. 'How are you?'

'All right. I—I had a headache, I thought a walk might clear it.'

'It's been a lovely day, lovely for January that is, but it's quite chilly now. Jessamy, is something wrong?'

When Jessamy looked at her aunt her eyes were brimming with tears. 'Cousin Lillian said something that upset me.'

Verity's eyebrows went up. 'Cousin Lillian? She's not the sort of person to upset anyone.'

'Oh, but she is.' There was bitterness in

21

Jessamy's voice. 'I know everyone in the family speaks of her as an angel, but she's evil. I thought so when I was younger but I know now it to be the truth.'

When Jessamy was silent again, Verity prompted her gently. 'Tell me, Jessamy, what did your cousin say?'

'She told me that I was...illegitimate.'

'*Illegitimate*? Your cousin Lillian said that?' The disbelief in Verity's voice had Jessamy shaking her head in despair.

'I knew you wouldn't believe me.'

Verity took her niece's cold hands in her. 'Jessamy dear, you must have been mistaken.'

'I wasn't, I wasn't!' She snatched her hands away. 'She told me that I was just one of Papa's *many* by-blows.'

Her aunt stared at her. 'I can't believe I'm hearing aright.' After a pause she added, 'Do you know the meaning of by-blow, Jessamy?'

'Yes, Louise told me once.'

'And you believe your father capable of such dastardly behaviour? He's the soul of decency, a gentleman.'

'I didn't know what to believe,' Jessamy wailed. 'I thought it could be a reason why my mother dislikes me so.'

'Jessamy.' Verity spoke softly. 'In the first place, let me tell you that I was there the day you were born. I *saw* you being born. So did the midwife and the doctor. What more proof do you want than that? Secondly, your mother does not dislike you.'

'She does! She's always telling me I'm plain.'

'Oh, Jessamy, you have only to look in the mirror to know you are a very attractive girl. Your mother just happens to belong to that category of people who won't praise their off-spring, thinking it will make them vain.'

'And Lillian? Can you explain why *she* should say such a dreadful thing?'

'That I can't explain and I shall certainly speak to her about it.'

'No! You mustn't. She would only deny it. She denied punching me when I was about ten years old.'

'Punching you?'

'It was at one of the family parties. There were bowls of sweetmeats on a side table. Lillian told everyone to help themselves, but when I took one later she grabbed me by the arm, dragged me into the hall, called me a thief and started punching me. She was really vicious, my arms were black and blue. I told Nanny that I had had a fall.'

'I know you are telling the truth, Jessamy, but it's so difficult to believe that Lillian would do such a thing. She's so—'

'So beautifully innocent-looking? Yes, I know.'

'Jessamy, if you won't allow me to tackle Lillian about the dreadful thing she said, then you must put it from your mind.' The afternoon sky was closing in and as a sharp gust of

23

wind swept across the moors Verity gave a little shiver. 'I think we had better go, my dear. I promised to look in on your mother when I got back. We can talk on the way.'

Lights began to appear in the groups of cottages, farmhouses and in the widely-spaced mansions. Usually, this scene gave Jessamy a lovely warm feeling but now she had an ache of melancholy. Why should people be so hateful? They walked on in silence for a while then Jessamy stopped suddenly. 'Aunt Verity, I want to know the truth about Mama.'

Verity looked at her, startled. 'The truth?'

'You went to school together, but you avoid talking about your schooldays. You've always told me the nice things, about going to parties, spending lovely family holidays together in summer and about the wonderful picnics you had.'

'We did.'

'What were the nasty things in your lives? We all have faults, so what were Mama's faults? I heard her telling Aunt Dorcas the other day that she was never really happy at school. Why?'

'She suffered because the girls were jealous of her. She was lovely, fragile-looking, and clever at most subjects.'

'Aunt Verity, I refuse to believe that my mother did not have one flaw in her character.'

'We were never really close as most friends are. For instance, although her drawings at

24

school were average, the ones she did at home were excellent, and showed great talent. I would never have known about them had her mother not shown them to me. Even then, I was sworn to secrecy.'

'Why the secrecy?'

'I did think about it a lot and came to the conclusion that she was treating her drawings like other people treat their journals. I don't suppose you would want to show anyone *your* journal, Jessamy?'

'I would not. But then, it doesn't take talent to do some scribbling.' After a pause she added, 'I've never seen any of Mama's drawings in the house.'

'Don't mention them, Jessamy, *please*, not ever.'

'They are the sort of things I *want* to know, Aunt Verity, so that I can understand Mama's attitude. Was Papa her first love?'

Verity hesitated before replying. 'Your mother had many admirers, Jessamy, but she must have given her heart to your father because she had no hesitation in accepting his first proposal.'

Jessamy pushed her hands into her pockets with an angry gesture. 'She doesn't act as if he meant much to her. I get so cross at times the way she speaks to him.'

Verity smiled. 'Don't worry about your father, Jessamy. He will only stand so much and your mother knows it. He *is* the master.'

Jessamy nodded slowly and gave a deep sigh. 'If only they could be as happy as you and Uncle Bertie.'

'We do all have our faults. Take Lillian, for instance. She is a lovely person, who, as far as I know, has only once stepped out of character.'

'Lillian did not step out of character, Aunt Verity. That is the way she is.'

A silence fell between them as they approached the Every homes which were blocked from view by a natural wall of rocks. Jeremiah had built a house for each of his sons on the moors and charged them rent. All were sited at strategic positions to protect them from the winds. Three were sheltered by natural outcroppings of rock, one by a double belt of trees and Chadwick's was tucked in the shelter of bracken-covered slopes. Although Jessamy loved the setting of the house she was never happy in it and yet it was well-furnished, with fires always blazing in the hall and sitting-room in colder weather. Now, three lamps were lit in the sitting-room, the red-globed one near the window casting a warm glow on the paved forecourt. There was a light on, too, in the hall and an upstairs window—the window of her parents' room.

Before they reached the front door Eliza, the middle-aged, rather dour woman who ran the house, opened the door. 'The mistress will be down in a moment,' she said. 'I'll bring tea and cake. Shall I take your coats?'

With coats divested and hats removed Verity and Jessamy went into the sitting-room, Verity making straight for the fireplace and holding out her hands to the blazing logs. 'My hands are frozen, I came out without my gloves.'

A voice from the doorway said, 'That was very foolish of you, Verity dear. Your skin will get chapped.' Esmeralda came into the room and going straight to Verity kissed her on the cheek. 'How did you enjoy your visit? You must tell me all about it.'

They sat down and while Verity talked about the relatives she had visited, Jessamy studied her mother. She looked really pretty with her cheeks slightly flushed. Her dark gold hair was simply dressed, looped over her ears and caught up at the back with a comb. Her dress was a deep blue brocade, also simply styled but somehow Esmeralda always managed to look as if she were setting out for some social occasion.

Verity was laughing and Jessamy switched her attention to her aunt. Verity always looked as if she had overslept and dressed hurriedly. She had an abundance of dark brown hair with tendrils forever escaping the pins, and her white shirt blouse had come adrift from the waist of her brown tweed skirt. Uncle Bertie teased her often about these things, but he never tried to persuade her to alter, and Jessamy was glad. In contrast with Esmeralda,

27

Verity could be called plain, but she exuded a warmth that the other woman lacked. At the moment her hazel eyes were twinkling.

'If you had seen the faces of the aunts when Cousin Alfred presented me with a single red rose. Shock was not the word! I had a job not to burst out laughing.'

'It's just as well you didn't, Verity. It was rather rash of Alfred doing such a thing. After all, he is a bachelor and you a married woman.'

'It was his fun, Esmeralda. He knows how happy Bertie and I are together. He only did it to shock my straight-laced relatives.'

Jessamy, thinking she heard a movement overhead, looked up, but when her mother made no remark she presumed she had been mistaken. Eliza came in then with the tea and cakes and after the tea had been poured, Verity resumed her narrative of her visit. A moment later another sound was heard above, this time as though something had been dropped on the floor. Verity looked up at the ceiling and asked if Chadwick was at home.

'No,' Esmeralda said. 'It's a friend of his, a Captain Montague. He's resting for a while.'

Jessamy sat up and her mother answered her unspoken question, explaining that the Captain had suffered a blow to the head from a crate being unloaded from his ship.

'A crate?' Verity repeated. 'It's a wonder he was not knocked unconscious.'

'At the time he apparently felt no ill-effects,

28

but when he delivered some seeds to Chadwick which he had brought from abroad, the poor man became dazed. Chadwick decided to put him in a carriage and sent him here to rest. He himself will be home soon.'

This incident was recounted quite calmly by Esmeralda and Verity laughed. 'A strange man in your bedroom, Esmeralda, and not even a blush! Is he young and attractive?'

Colour did come to Esmeralda's cheeks then. 'Don't be foolish, Verity. The man is a stranger —he was ill and I was only concerned in getting him to rest. He must obviously be feeling better. He may be down soon.'

After that there was a feeling of anticipation and conversation became desultory. Verity had just asked what country Captain Montague had sailed from when there was a tap at the door. Esmeralda called, 'Come in,' and rose effortlessly to her feet.

The man who came in was tall and well-built and seemed to dominate the room. To Jessamy he had the stance and arrogance she associated with a Viking. Then he smiled and he became a rogue, a pirate, so completely fascinating that she drew in a quick breath. What eyes! Never before had she seen such a vivid blue.

The man's gaze went from Verity to Jessamy and then to Esmeralda, who introduced her sister-in-law. He bowed over Verity's hand. 'Delighted to meet you, Mrs Every. I had the pleasure of meeting your husband on my last visit.' He gave a quick glance at Jessamy and Esmeralda introduced her daughter.

'Ah.' The Captain's face was alight with pleasure. 'Miss Jessamy, your father has told me so much about you I feel I already know you. You are quite an authority on medicine, I'm told.'

'Oh, no, sir, I'm just a novice really. Papa is a patient teacher but I have a great deal to learn.'

'But you are a dedicated pupil which is so important. I remember my father saying to me once—'

Esmeralda interrupted. 'Captain Montague, do please sit down. I'm sure you must still be suffering from the effects of your accident.'

'On the contrary, Mrs Every, I feel splendid. Quite a fraud, in fact, for taking advantage of your hospitality.'

'Not at all, Captain Montague. You looked really ill when you arrived.' She motioned him to a chair but he insisted that Verity be seated and drew a chair forward for Jessamy.

While the three adults conversed, Jessamy heard only the deep, rich tones of the Captain's voice. Although he had the blue eyes of the Scandinavian race, his hair was dark and curled at the ends. She found herself thinking how wonderful it would be to have such a man pay attention to her, and the thought of being held in his arms brought a sudden throbbing to her body. Jessamy had been in the company of many men in the past, for she had numerous male cousins and met their friends, too, at parties. Some, a little bolder than others, had touched her cheek or dropped a light kiss on her face. This had roused a response in her, but the feeling now was different, stronger—a quickening in the secret parts of her body. For a few moments she was lost in a fantasy world, then her father arrived, bringing her back to reality.

'Fabian, my dear fellow, how are you feeling?' Chadwick came forward. 'I'm so sorry I could not accompany you here myself, but I had just received an urgent message from a farmer to say he thought his wife had been poisoned. She hadn't, fortunately.'

Esmeralda, her lips tightening, remarked, 'People treat my husband as if he were a doctor, he is not qualified to be one.'

The Captain delivered a gentle rebuke. 'But surely, Mrs Every, the important thing is that the people have faith in him.'

'Yes, yes, I suppose so.'

Jessamy was surprised at the gentleness in Captain Montague's voice, and found herself comparing him with her father. Not that they were alike in looks—her father was fair and his eyes grey, but he too had an air of authority about him, as well as a gentle manner when dealing with his customers.

Before the Captain left, he accepted an invitation to dinner the following evening.

Jessamy felt she could hardly wait to tell her cousin Louise all about this wonderful man who had entered her life. A man to dream about...

CHAPTER TWO

After their visitor had gone Jessamy said to her father, 'Captain Montague must have some very interesting tales to relate about his sea voyages.'

Chadwick nodded. 'Yes, indeed. He's visited so many countries and he is an excellent raconteur. No doubt you will hear some of his tales tomorrow evening at dinner.'

Esmeralda's head went up. 'Jessamy will not be sitting down to dinner with us. She's just a child. Bertie and Verity will be with us but that is all.'

'Jessamy is not a child.' Chadwick spoke gently. 'She is sixteen, a young lady, old enough to be married.'

'Married?' Esmeralda's face showed horror. 'Are you actually suggesting the Captain as a suitor for your daughter's hand? He's a seaman!'

'And what are you implying by that?' Chadwick's manner had changed, become cold.

'That the Captain is uncouth because he goes to sea? For your information, he comes from the aristocracy. Jessamy will sit down to dinner with us tomorrow evening and I think that Louise could be invited, too.' He turned to Verity, who had sat silent during this altercation. 'Verity, do you agree?'

'Yes, I—' she glanced at Esmeralda. 'I'm sure Bertie would agree too, knowing that Louise would be company for Jessamy.'

'Good, then that is settled. We live in a very close family circle, after all, and I think an evening spent in the company of Fabian Montague will widen the girls' horizons.'

'I'll say only one thing,' Esmeralda said icily. 'If the girls become besotted with the Captain's extraordinary good looks and charm then the onus will be on *you*.'

Chadwick drew finger and thumb over his chin. 'I suppose the fellow is rather attractive and he certainly does have charm, but then that is all part of growing up. Jessamy and Louise must learn to be selective.'

'Selective? At sixteen? I feel sorry for you, Chadwick. It is *you* who lives in a closed world of your wretched plants, trees and flowers.'

Verity got up to leave then and after a moment Jessamy asked if she could go with her aunt.

'Why do you ask?' Esmeralda asked. 'You practically live there anyway.'

'Only because I know you don't want me

here, Mama,' Jessamy replied quietly.

Esmeralda made no reply.

There was pain in Chadwick's eyes when Jessamy went over and kissed him on the cheek, whispering, 'I'll see you in the morning, Papa.'

While they had been taking tea, the wind had strengthened. When Verity and Jessamy reached the open moor it came at them at force, taking their breath away and it was not until they reached the shelter of the tall formation of rocks protecting Verity and Bertie's house that conversation was possible.

Verity stopped and took Jessamy by the shoulders. 'Try not to be upset by your mother, Jessamy. None of us knows what is in her mind. This evening I think she was jealous at your father permitting you to be with us when Captain Montague comes to dinner. She thrives on admiration and would not want competition.'

'Oh, Aunt Verity, I would be no competition.'

'Yes, you would. The Captain has an eye for an attractive girl—I noticed him glance at you once or twice.' Verity laughed. 'To be honest, my dear, I wouldn't mind being a stowaway myself on the Captain's ship.'

'He would probably hang you from the yard-arm. Isn't that what they do with stowaways?'

They went in together, laughing.

Although the house was comfortably furnished it was never tidy, but this to Jessamy was what gave it such a homely air. Bertie lay sprawled in an armchair, a newspaper covering his face, while Louise was studying a piece of lace. She looked up as Verity and Jessamy entered then came over to them. 'Mama, you're late. The dress I am going to wear for Cousin Andrew's birthday next week needs altering and I want your advice.'

'Oh, there's plenty of time for that. What you *will* have to think about at this moment is a dress to wear for tomorrow evening. We've been invited to dinner at Aunt Esmeralda's and Uncle Chadwick's house, with a *very* special guest.'

'The most attractive sea captain you have ever seen,' Jessamy enthused. 'Already I'm in love with him and so will you be when you meet him.'

A smile spread over Louise's face. 'Sounds interesting!'

'It's more than interesting—he's been all over the world and Papa says he has some wonderful stories to tell.'

'I bet he has if he goes to sea!'

'Who goes to sea?' Bertie drew the newspaper from his face and stifled a yawn. Then, seeing his wife and his niece he got up and came over. 'Hello, Jessamy dear. Verity, my love, I've missed you.'

Jessamy never failed to be moved when her uncle and aunt greeted one another. It might

35

only be a touch on hand or cheek, but the gesture conveyed so much love. It was something she had never witnessed between her parents. There were some evenings when her father returned from the shop and her mother wouldn't even turn her head or address him. Not that he ignored her. He would always say, 'Hello, Esmeralda, how are you? Have you had an enjoyable afternoon?'

Verity said to her husband, 'We've been invited to dinner at Chadwick and Esmeralda's tomorrow evening. And, there's to be a *very* special guest. A Captain Montague.'

'Oh, I've met him, a fascinating fellow. I could listen to his stories all night,' said Bertie and then added that he must go upstairs and wash. Verity followed him out.

Louise then turned eagerly to Jessamy. 'Heavens, what's happened? Your mother would never normally have us there when she was entertaining adults.'

'I know, it was all due to Papa.' The story was told, then Jessamy added, 'And I'm glad he had his way. I wanted you to meet the Captain, Louise. You will be as captivated by him as I was.'

'How old is this paragon?'

Jessamy raised her shoulders. 'It's difficult to tell. In his early thirties, perhaps.'

'He's too old for you.'

'Age doesn't matter.' Jessamy's eyes took on a dreamy look. 'He's everything a girl could wish for. Strong, virile...he's like a pirate, or a Viking.'

'And possibly married.'

'Possibly,' Jessamy sighed. 'But isn't it lovely to have someone in one's mind to dream about?'

'Not for me, it isn't. I want a flesh and blood man I can see every day, not a fantasy creature who's away for months at sea.'

'But think of the homecomings, the excitement, the joy of waiting on the quayside for his ship to come in.' Jessamy's voice lowered. 'Think of the meetings, of having his arms around you... Every time he came home it would be like another honeymoon.'

'Rubbish.' Louise, who was still holding the piece of lace, held it out, measuring the length with her eyes. Then she dropped it and turned, a broad grin on her face. 'I'm looking forward to meeting this wonderful Captain.'

'Oh, I'm glad. It makes it more interesting. What a pity Christian couldn't be here. You know how much he longs for a seafaring life.'

To this Louise replied, a tartness in her voice, 'My brother will have to get used to the idea that Grandfather has the life of every one of his grandsons mapped out and going to sea does not feature in his plans.'

Jessamy nodded. 'I know, but Christian is stubborn and will fight to have his own way. Just as you do, Louise.'

'The difference is that my brother has the

patience to wait. I go at my problems head on and, more often than not, I succeed.'

Louise was a strange mixture. Although she had the plumpness of her father and his fair colouring, and could be genial like him if she pleased, she was also a tyrant when angry. Bertie never became angry. Neither did his eldest son, Christian. Jessamy was very fond of her cousin and longed for the holidays to come around so that Christian could tramp around with her over the moors, along the country lanes, and also accompany her on rare visits to the docks. Rare, because they had to be kept a secret from Esmeralda, who thought the place a den of iniquity.

The girls then moved on to the subject of what to wear the following evening. They were teased by Bertie when he came downstairs. 'What would women talk about if it wasn't clothes?'

'Men!' Jessamy and Louise replied in unison.

Bertie chuckled. 'You *are* growing up, the pair of you. It seems no time at all since you were toddlers. Isn't that right?' he questioned Verity, who had just walked in.

'Yes, it is. By the way, girls, you must visit your grandparents tomorrow. Your grand-mother was especially asking about you, she so enjoys your company.'

'She enjoys seeing Jessamy,' Louise retort-ed. 'I think she probably knows that I find her boring. She always wants to hear every little bit of gossip.'

'Of course she does, she's tied to the house. But there's never anything malicious in her gossiping. She's very dear to us, so please be pleasant to her, Louise.'

'Oh, very well. I'll do my best.'

Bertie said, his tone light, 'Make it better than your best, my love. It's so little to ask.'

'I will, Papa, I will, I promise.' Louise then turned to Jessamy and said under her breath, 'Heaven give me strength!' which was her favourite expression when impatient at being given orders.

Jessamy loved her grandmother, but was a little wary of her grandfather who was always so stern-looking and who seemed to rule the family. Most of the men denied this, but they never crossed Jeremiah if they could help it.

Before the girls settled for bed that evening Louise had decided to wear a favourite, dark blue velvet dress with a ruched neckline.

'I know the bodice is a little tight for me now, but it gives me more of a figure.' Louise grinned as she said it.

Jessamy, who had chosen a pale green silk with a darker green velvet trimming, laughed. 'As long as the buttons don't spring off after you've eaten.'

'A lovely thought. I can just imagine the Captain's face.'

Jessamy giggled. 'He might end up kidnapping you and taking you to China.'

'What a dreadful thought. I want to be here when Joseph Masterson comes home for the weekend.'

'Joseph Masterson?' Jessamy drew herself up in the bed. 'I didn't know you were interested in him.'

'I don't tell you everything! I have to keep some secrets to myself.'

'Right! In future I shall keep *my* secrets to myself.' Jessamy flung herself back on to the pillows.

After a few moments' silence Louise said in a slightly apologetic voice, 'I was only jesting, Jessamy, I like us to share our secrets. It was just that—well, I'm not quite sure about Joseph. He wrote me a note two days ago, simply saying he was looking forward to seeing me at the weekend when he came home. Why? He could have any girl with his looks. And don't flatter me and tell me that I'm beautiful, because I know I'm not.'

Jessamy took time to reply. 'Once when I was visiting the grandparents I had a chance to browse through Grandfather's books in the library. In one I read a piece about one of the mistresses of a king. One person said she was unable to understand why the king should be attracted to this woman, that she was really quite plain, and a man replied, "Ah, but she has a charisma that draws men to her. And nothing will ever take that away".'

'Jessamy, it's highly unlikely that I shall ever

be the mistress of a king, or any other man for that matter. What I want to know is, why Joseph Masterson, who could have any girl he chose, is interested in me. You mentioned charisma—what is it?'

Jessamy pursed her lips. 'I think it's something a woman has that makes a man want to take her to his bed.'

'Oh, thank you very much, so I look like a whore!'

'No, no, it's something...mystical or intriguing, I think.'

Louise grinned. 'That's better, I like that. So when I see Joseph I can start flinging this mystical thing around.'

'You can practise on Captain Montague tomorrow evening,' Jessamy replied, a twinkle in her eyes.

A discussion followed on young men, including the attractiveness of some of their cousins and the friends of the cousins, then Louise, stifling a yawn said, 'I'm getting bored, I want to sleep.'

Jessamy thought she would dream of Captain Montague, but her dreams were of her mother, instead. Esmeralda had changed into a witch and was chasing her daughter across the moors. Jessamy awoke feeling jaded and worried that it might be a premonition that her mother was going to prevent her from meeting the Captain that evening.

However, nothing untoward happened and

she was full of excitement when she dressed for dinner. Her uncle, aunt and cousin had arrived by the time she came running downstairs, but once in the hall she paused then walked sedately into the sitting-room.

Her father and Uncle Bertie were standing talking. Her mother was looking into the mirror above the fireplace while Verity tucked a strand of hair that had escaped the comb at the back of her sister-in-law's hair. Esmeralda was wearing a striking, turquoise brocaded dress, patterned in tiny triangles of rose and violet. Verity on the other hand was clad in a sand-coloured satin, that did nothing at all to flatter her. But while she looked happy, Esmeralda was grim.

Jessamy went over to Louise, who grumbled that she had done nothing right that day. Before she could give an explanation there was the sound of a carriage drawing up and Chadwick exclaimed, 'Ah, that must be the Captain. He is certainly prompt.' He went out of the room to welcome him.

By the time the men came into the room, Esmeralda was a changed person, with a welcoming smile. At the sight of the Captain, Louise gripped Jessamy's elbow and raised her eyebrows. When she was introduced to him and experienced his courtesy, her expression showed just how impressed she was by the guest.

Jessamy was the last to be greeted by the

Captain but when smiling blue eyes looked into hers and he said, 'We meet again, Miss Jessamy,' all sorts of tremors went through her body.

The adults chatted for a few minutes, while Louise whispered to Jessamy, 'He even beats Joseph in looks.' Then the young maid came in to announce that dinner was ready, and they all went into the dining-room.

The predominant colour in the sitting-room was brown. In the dining-room it was dark green, with a deep-piled carpet and matching velvet curtains and pelmets. A number of lamps were placed at strategic points around the room. The circular walnut table was laid with silver and crystal on a fine hand-crocheted lace cloth. All this looked very elegant, but Jessamy preferred her aunt and uncle's home with its red turkey carpets and rugs.

The table could be extended to seat eighteen, but this evening it was the right size for seven people. Esmeralda had the Captain seated on her left. Next to him was Verity, then Bertie. Chadwick was on Esmeralda's right, with Louise next to him and Jessamy seated between her cousin and uncle.

Surprisingly, Jessamy came in for Captain Montague's attention almost as soon as they were all seated. 'Miss Jessamy, your dress matches the colours in the room—how fetching.' Hot colour rose to Jessamy's face, especially as she saw her mother's lips tighten.

Verity said, smiling, 'Yes, it is a lovely dress. I think it's one of Jessamy's favourites.' To Jessamy's relief further talk was temporarily stemmed by the sirloin of beef being carried in by the maid. Chadwick stood up to carve it.

'With so many awful things happening on the high seas,' Esmeralda remarked, 'I wonder that any man wants to set foot on a ship.'

'The sea is my life,' the Captain answered quietly. 'Our biggest worry is the elements—they're so unpredictable. One can come off the night-watch to find the sea like a millpond and then a typhoon can spring up and we're battling within minutes against waves fifty feet high.'

This brought exclamations of dismay. 'Fifty feet high?'

Bertie said he had been out on rough seas, but had never encountered waves of that height.

Captain Montague popped a piece of potato in his mouth, chewed on it, then a beatific smile appeared on his face. 'This potato fritter is excellent.'

'My cook's speciality,' Esmeralda said, smiling. 'She is always receiving praise for them, but even I have no idea of the recipe.'

Chadwick laughed softly. 'Who would have thought the simple potato could be considered a delicacy. Cook does make them seem so, yet at one time they were considered by certain people to be as dangerously poisonous as the mandrake. Fabian, you know a story about

44

that, don't you?'

'Yes, I do. The tuber came originally from Peru, but because it resembled the mandrake no one in Europe would touch it. When potatoes were introduced into France, the king had them served at a banquet and the guests were delighted, because they were something new. However, the peasants still refused to try them because of the mandrake superstition.'

The Captain took another portion of potato and after swallowing it continued, 'The king, determined to overcome this opposition, planted a field of potatoes and placed a troop of soldiers to guard it day and night. This, of course created a great deal of speculation. Whatever was it that was so valuable? The king then withdrew the guards one night and the peasants helped themselves. After that, the potato became their staple diet.'

Although Jessamy had heard the story from her father she laughed with the rest. Bertie requested more such stories and although Esmeralda protested that they must let the Captain get on with his meal, he seemed agreeable enough and said he could manage to talk between eating.

Fabian spoke of places and sights he had seen, like the beautiful and romantic port at Bastia in Northern Corsica, the froth of cherry blossom in the spring in Japan and the sun glinting on the snow-capped mountains of Fiji. He talked of the wonderful gold

45

of the Incas; the exquisite ornamentation, the gold lace they made as fine as cobwebs.

Then he spoke of Egypt, describing the pyramids, the massive figures carved out of stone, so huge that it had taken hundreds of slaves to pull one on a wheeled platform to get it into place. He described the desert, its vastness and silence, the beauty of the sunrise. In the hushed stillness of the room the low vibrant tones had them all spellbound.

Then he began talking of the sea, comparing it to the desert, that feeling of being the only one in the world. He was silent for a few moments and when he looked up there was a faraway look in his eyes.

'Sometimes, if the sea is calm in the middle watches one can feel a great aloneness, for the sea and sky seem to stretch into eternity. Images arise of places, experiences, people. Not all are beautiful. One sees poverty, sickness.' He fell silent again and Jessamy, glancing at her mother, saw a softness on her face she had never seen before. She herself felt an ache of tears in her throat. This big, virile-looking man, who would no doubt roar orders to his men on the ship, had a romantic streak in him and was compassionate.

The Captain gave a sudden glance around the table then said with a sheepish smile, 'Please forgive me, I was carried away. Here I am, getting melancholic, and melancholy has no place at a dinner table.' He turned to Bertie. 'How is business, Mr Every? Flourishing, I hope.'

'How could it be otherwise, with such a busy port? Our father, Jeremiah, wants me to extend the business, open up on the quayside. He has bought some property there and wants all of us to expand.'

Chadwick said, 'I have no wish to do so.'

'Why not?' This was from Esmeralda, who appealed to Captain Montague. 'My husband has no ambitions whatsoever, Captain. I think he is apt to forget that but for his father he would not have a business at all.'

The Captain smiled. 'I'm afraid I cannot agree with you on that score, Mrs Every. Your husband is so eager to help those who are sick he would have managed to find some premises, even if it were only a hut.'

Esmeralda looked taken aback at the rebuff, but she quickly recovered and put on a coaxing air. 'But don't you think, Captain, that a man must always do his utmost for his wife and family? He owes it to them.'

Chadwick reached out and touched his wife's hand. 'I agree, Esmeralda, but I don't think that taking another shop would increase my business. Extra staff would have to be employed and I feel I can cover whatever is required in medicine from the premises I have now.'

Verity spoke up. 'I think the important thing in Chadwick's business is that people trust him. They know he will give endless time to them for the most simple of complaints.'

'And in many cases, he will refuse payment,' Esmeralda retorted. Then, obviously realising she had put herself in a bad light, she started to make excuses. 'I know I must sound the most terrible person, but we have a daughter who is coming up to marriageable age.' She gave a helpless shrug, as if she had only her dear daughter's welfare at heart.

Furious, Jessamy said, 'I won't be getting married for years. I want to be a doctor.'

Captain Montague's eyebrows went up. 'Is that so? I applaud you, Miss Jessamy.'

To this Esmeralda replied with a forced smile, 'Jessamy has some very strange ideas. She'll change her mind before she is very much older. Just wait until she falls in love.'

Jessamy opened her mouth to answer, but noticing her father shaking his head at her she closed it again.

Bertie chuckled. 'I don't think it will be very long before some young man steals my lovely niece's heart.'

'I agree.' The Captain's all-embracing smile made Jessamy's limbs go weak.

The pudding was brought in and Esmeralda looked relieved. Conversation after that was mainly among the men, who discussed politics and world trade.

Louise stayed with Jessamy that evening and later, when they were alone and Jessamy talked dreamily of the Captain, saying what a wonderful man he was, Louise was disparaging. He was nothing more than a woman chaser, a charmer—it was an act he put on.

Jessamy was outraged. 'How can you say such a thing? He's a lonely man, you could tell by the way he talked about the sea and stars.'

Louise gave an impatient sigh. 'How can you be so gullible? But then so is your mama, *and* mine. I watched their faces, soulful, feeling for the man.'

'And our fathers were, too,' Jessamy retorted. 'And they are not taken in by an act.'

'Uncle Chadwick is. He's too soft-hearted, listens to all the hard luck stories.'

'You are wrong there,' Jessamy spoke firmly. 'Papa is never taken in and he does know when a person is telling a hard luck tale. The other day a man came in for some medicine and he pleaded he had no money. Papa said, "Mr Jones, stop supping ale and you'll have enough money to pay for the medicine to help your complaint".'

'But he still weakened and gave him the medicine free?'

'No, he did not—Mr Jones paid up. Anyway, Louise, you are easily taken in yourself. Look at Joseph Masterson! He's had dozens of girls, and soon drops one when someone new comes along.'

'But he doesn't pretend to be otherwise. We all know what he is, not like the Captain who pretends to be so goody-goody. I repeat, you are a fool to be taken in by him.'

'Well—what about Cousin Lillian? You, like all the rest of the family, think she's an angel! I know she isn't. Some day you might learn that I am the discerning one.'

'So!' Louise stood glaring at her, hands on hips. 'All the family are wrong about Lillian and you are right? You were a child when you said how rude she was to you.'

'Not rude—cruel.'

'I think you exaggerated the incident. You probably took two sweetmeats and rightly, she scolded you.'

'I took one and I do not exaggerate her behaviour to me.'

Louise picked up her dress from the floor and flung it onto the bed. 'You are so smug. Well, I could tell you things that would wipe that look off your face. All our family are rotten, all of them have their little secrets. Yes, your parents as well as mine.'

Jessamy felt a coldness stealing over her. 'What secrets are my parents supposed to have?'

Louise unfastened the tapes of her underskirt, and let it drop to the floor. 'Do you think I'm going to tell you? You can find out for yourself.'

'I think you are making it up, just to hurt me.'

Louise stopped, picked up the underskirt

50

and flung it on top of her dress. 'I don't make things up. You think you are so clever and have so much knowledge. Well, you are a babe in comparison to the knowledge that I have about people, not only our family but those who live in the big houses on the moor. They're all rotten, all of them!'

Jessmay felt a dull ache in the pit of her stomach. Her cousin was seventeen to her sixteen and she had always thought of her as an elder sister, they had shared so much. True, she had behaved strangely at times but...

Louise said suddenly, her expression stormy, 'Stop staring at me like a hurt puppy!'

'Why do you say things like that, Louise?' Jessamy spoke quietly. 'There has to be a reason.'

'Yes, I have a reason! I would crawl to your *wonderful* Captain if he looked at me the way he looks at you. But no, he only has eyes for you. I hate you, hate you!'

Jessamy stared at her, appalled. What had happened to her cousin? She had been sharp at times, spiteful even, but never ever had she been vicious. She stood, helpless for a moment then seeing tears in Louise's eyes went over and made to put her arms around her. But Louise pushed her away. 'Don't play the good Samaritan with me. I don't want your pity.'

'It's not pity, I—'

'Just leave me alone, will you. *Leave me alone.*'

51

It was a situation that Jessamy had never previously faced and she had no idea how to cope with it. She started to undress, her fingers fumbling with the buttons, tears not far away.

CHAPTER THREE

Jessamy spent the most wretched night she could ever remember. It was dreadful to be sharing a bed with Louise, both of them so stiff with tension it was almost a tangible thing. At night, they were used to chatting about things that had happened during the day but now, although Jessamy longed to break the silence she felt she could not stand another rebuff. Who would have believed that such a situation could arise over a dinner guest, a man neither of them really knew?

Worse than the friction over the Captain, of course, was the statement that Louise had made about the family. They were all rotten, she had said, they all had secrets. It raised once more for Jessamy the question of why her mother disliked her. What could the secret be? And of what possible indiscretion could her father be guilty? He was such an honest, open-handed man.

It was not until Louise was breathing deeply

and regularly in sleep Jessamy's commonsense took over. How could her cousin know all these awful things about the family? Who would have told her? Secrets of a whole family were not likely to be bandied about. No, her cousin had wanted to hurt her, simply because of an imagined slight from Captain Montague. If she had been watching him closely Louise would soon have realised that he had paid no particular attention to anyone. He had been lost in himself, reliving his journeyings. Perhaps Louise would realise this in the morning. Jessamy prayed so, not wanting the present rift to widen.

When she awoke the next morning Louise had already gone downstairs, or perhaps she had already left the house? But when Jessamy went into the breakfast-room Louise was helping herself from the hot dishes on the sideboard. She looked around. 'You went off to sleep again after Eliza called us, so I thought I would just let you sleep. I was wide awake so decided to have breakfast.'

Although Louise was not her usual self, she was talking, at least. Jessamy felt a sense of relief. 'I was a long time getting off to sleep.' She lifted the lid from one of the silver dishes and took a piece of bacon. Usually she had a full breakfast, but she did not have much of an appetite this morning. She brought the plate to the table then, for the sake of making conversation, which was never necessary in the normal way, she said, 'It's certainly cold this morning.'

'Yes.' Louise cut a piece of kidney, speared it on her fork then looked up. 'About last night. I behaved like a pig. I don't know what got into me. I don't hate you.'

Although it was said in a grudging way Jessamy felt as though a shaft of sunlight had lighted up the dark morning. 'I know you don't.'

Louise popped the piece of kidney into her mouth and chewed on it. 'But I don't take back a word I said about the family. Not *one* word. You'll find out in time what they're like.'

'But Louise—'

'I'm not going to discuss it. I said too much last night.' She waved her fork. 'But I'll tell you one thing—if I had any chance at all with the devastating Captain Montague, which I know I haven't, I'd go all out to get him and I wouldn't give a tinker's cuss if I hurt you, or anyone else in the process.'

Jessamy sat studying her cousin. There was a fierce light in her eyes which gave an odd beauty to the rather plain features. Was it this that drew men to Louise? She was never coy with any of them, in fact, just the opposite. She would be quite short, make sharp retorts. Perhaps men saw it as a challenge. She was a female to conquer. Men *had* to be the masters.

Louise spent some mornings at the warehouse. This was after she had offered to help

54

out when two of the staff in the office were away ill at the same time. Bertie had to admit she was competent, very competent, and always found jobs for her to do. Esmeralda had complained bitterly at one time about Jessamy working in Chadwick's shop. It was demeaning, she said, it lowered their standards. Jessamy ought to be sent to a finishing school. Chadwick, knowing how much Jessamy loved working in the shop, laid down an ultimatum. Jessamy either came to the shop or she stayed at home with Esmeralda. He knew as he said it that the battle was won.

When the girls were ready to leave Eliza, as always, brought them their coats, knitted hats, scarves and gloves and told both to wrap up. In turn Jessamy would say, 'Thank you, Eliza. Will you tell Mama when you see her that Louise and I have gone and that I will be back with Papa at midday.' Then Eliza, without a word, would go and open the front door for them. Once they were outside, Louise would mimic the whole procedure. This morning, as she tossed the end of her emerald green scarf over her shoulder, she complained, 'Doesn't it make you squirm? It never varies. Oh, the monotony of it all—sometimes I think I'll scream.'

Jessamy laughed softly. 'And Eliza would say, "Just a moment Miss Louise, I'll go and get the sal volatile".'

'She would, yes, she would! At times like this

I feel like running away. We'll go to the shop and your father will say, "Oh, there you are, girls, I'm glad to see you're well wrapped up." And when I go to the warehouse *my* father will say, "Oh, there you are, Louise, all ready to lift an anchor this morning?" '

'Well, what would you want them to say?' enquired Jessamy. She gave a little shiver and buttoned her coat at the neck.

'Anything but what they *do* say every time. It would be a change if your father said, "I poisoned a man this morning, gave him the wrong medicine on purpose. I didn't like him." And if my father were to say, "Louise dear, Captain Montague wants to marry you and take you on a long voyage." '

Jessamy was silent for a moment, realising how close the Captain was in her cousin's thoughts.

'Well, don't you think it would make a change?' Louise demanded.

'Oh, yes, definitely. Papa would hang high on the gallows on Tucker's Rise; the Captain's ship could possibly flounder in a storm and the two of you could end up in a watery grave. *Quite* a change.'

To this Louise replied, 'What could be more satisfying than ending up in one's lover's arms at the bottom of the ocean instead of living a deathlike existence in this—' she flung out her arms, 'this dreary expanse of nothingness?'

Jessamy stopped. 'Oh, Louise, for heaven's

sake, stop being so melodramatic. Just look at the scene in front of you.'

The morning had not yet begun to lighten and the lamplight from cottages and houses put a sparkle on the overnight frost. 'Look at the beauty. Think of the moors in the changing seasons. You don't know how lucky you are. You could have been born into poverty, into the black hole of a town.'

Louise gave a low chuckle. 'Why are you getting so upset? Yes, I could have been born into poverty. I could also have been born into wealth and been travelling to foreign places.' She linked her arm through Jessamy's. 'Come on, we are standing here getting frozen. You should know by now that I need dramatic things happening in my life in order to exist.'

'So all that talk about the family having secrets was just a dramatic outlet?'

'No.' Louise spoke firmly. 'That was the truth.' In the next breath she added, 'I wonder if we could sneak away to the docks and see if the Captain is on his ship.'

Jessamy gave a sigh of despair. 'Really, Louise, you think yourself so knowledgeable and clever. Don't you know that the last way to get a man interested in you is to chase him?'

'Clever, clever Cousin Jessamy.' The sarcasm in Louise's voice made Jessamy wonder what had happened to her cousin to have wrought this drastic, unpleasant change in her.

They walked on in silence, their breath a mist

in the frosty air. Looking around her, Jessamy said, 'How could anyone think of the moors as a nothingness?' There was such a grandeur about them, a vastness, with their colours constantly changing. Even the shades of the rock formations changed with the weather. Clouds drifted by, making beautiful patterns. Then there were the tarns. Dark, fathomless and mysterious on grey days, when sunshine and a playful breeze put ripples on the water, they were fairy lakes. There was a magnificence in a storm on the moors, when great crashes of thunder reverberated across the whole expanse, and lightning zigzagged from sky to earth. And then in the aftermath would come tentative animal calls and birdsong. Oh, no, the moors did not deserve to be called a nothingness.

After a while the ground began to level out. The road came into view and with it, Every Street. There was the usual cacophony of sounds, the posthorn from a vehicle arriving at the inn, a hammering at the wheelwright's, wagons, barrows, men shouting.

Jessamy glanced at Louise and said, 'The boys will be home at the weekend, so you'll see Joseph Masterson and next week it's Andrew's party.'

Louise raised her shoulders. 'All so very boring.'

As they neared Chadwick's shop Jessamy found herself saying sarcastically, 'Then I don't suppose you'll want to see Papa, who

58

will bore you further with his regulation greeting.'

Louise pushed past her. 'Now who is being stupid? Your father is never boring. And anyway, isn't there a new assistant starting today?'

'Yes, there is. His name is Alistair MacKay and according to Papa, he's an elderly, dour bachelor who never has more to say than ''Is that so'' and ''I ken what you mean''.'

Jessamy opened the shop door and as the bell above it tinkled Chadwick looked up and smiled. 'Hello, girls. I thought you would both have still been under the eiderdown this frosty morning.'

Jessamy glanced at Louise, her eyebrows raised, as though to say 'No regulation greeting this morning', then she said aloud to her father, 'It's a beautiful morning, so invigorating.'

Louise unwrapped her scarf from her throat. 'It's freezing, I'm icy cold. Is that cocoa I smell, or some concoction of medicine you're busy with?'

'It's cocoa to drink—Mr MacKay has just made it. Come in the back and meet him, he's an interesting man.' There was a twinkle in Chadwick's eyes and Jessamy understood why when they were introduced to the new assistant.

There was nothing elderly or dour about Alistair MacKay. He was a personable young man with a mop of curly dark hair and a smile bordering on a schoolboy grin. He bowed to each girl in turn. 'I'm delighted to meet you, Miss Jessamy, Miss Louise. I've heard a great deal about you from the master. I understand you lead him quite a dance.'

Jessamy eyed her father with mock reproach. 'How can you say such a thing, Papa, when you know we are two *very* well-behaved young ladies.'

Alistair laughed. 'And I know that's not true by the look of mischief in the eyes of the pair of you.'

Louise, exaggerating his Scottish accent, said, 'Ye've a lot to learn about the two of us, Mr MacKay, and when ye do, ye'll be changing your mind.'

Chadwick suggested they sit down and have their cocoa. They settled around the fire and when the cocoa was poured, Chadwick explained that Alistair came from the Highlands of Scotland and was the eldest of eighteen children.

'Eighteen?' Jessamy echoed, her eyes rounded in astonishment. 'Are they all living?'

Alistair nodded. 'They are, and my parents are hale and hearty. My mother is a wee thing and still bonny.'

Jessamy, who had imagined his mother to be worn out with so much childbearing, could only sit and wonder. Eighteen children! Chadwick then revealed that he was a friend of

Alistair's uncle, who had suggested that his nephew write to him about a position as his assistant.

When the men had gone Louise said to Jessamy, 'And what is your mama going to say when she knows that the new assistant is young and quite attractive?'

'I doubt whether she'll ever know. She hasn't set foot in the shop for over a year.'

'She doesn't have to, cousin dear. There will be plenty of gossipers to impart the news. I should imagine she will know by the time Uncle Chadwick and you go home at midday.'

Jessamy's head went up. 'I know only one thing, I am not leaving the shop. After all Mr MacKay and I will work together and that is all, we are not about to start an alliance.'

'But it could happen,' Louise said softly. 'Strange things do occur.'

Jessamy laughed. 'I can read your mind, Louise. You think if I was paired off with Mr MacKay, it would leave the way clear for you to work your wiles on Captain Montague. Well, let me tell you that you will have me to contend with.' She suddenly sobered. 'What a lot of nonsense I'm talking. What chance have either of us? I imagine there must be hundreds of women vying for the Captain's attentions.'

'Probably, but do you recall Major Willoughby who lived at High Tor then moved to London?' When Jessamy nodded Louise continued. 'Well, he must have had every eligible woman in the city after him, and why not? He was not only a handsome devil but was wealthy. And who did he marry? A sixteen year old girl with a face as plain as the back of a hansom cab. I forget her name.'

'Arabella Dawson. She certainly was plain, she didn't even have one feature to recommend her. She had mousy hair, a long nose and mean little eyes. Perhaps she has a beautiful nature.'

'*Not* with features like that. So, as I say, there is no accounting for taste. I think we have as much chance of attracting the Captain's attention as anyone else.'

Jessamy gave a deep sigh. 'He'll probably be miles away by now.'

But the Captain was not miles away. He arrived after Louise had gone to the warehouse and Jessamy was alone in the shop. Her father had been called to a child with convulsions and Alistair was busy unpacking boxes in a shed at the back.

When Jessamy saw Montague's splendid figure framed in the doorway hot colour rushed to her cheeks. He closed the door and came forward, smiling. 'Miss Jessamy, how are you?' His smile played havoc with her emotions.

'I'm very well, Captain Montague. Papa is out at the moment, attending to a sick child. He should be back soon.'

'I came to see *you*,' he said softly. In the dimness of the shop his eyes appeared a darker

62

blue, giving him a sensuous look. Tremors went through Jessamy's body.

'To—see me? For what reason?'

'You were in my dreams last night, a butterfly, flitting from bush to bush, evasive, tantalising. I had to ask myself if the dream had some significance, if perhaps you had flown away.'

Jessamy felt a swift disappointment. The night before he had shown a natural charm, this morning it was contrived, his phrases an exaggeration. She said slowly, 'How many women feature in your dreams, Captain Montague? How long did it take you to think up the dream sequence?'

His surprise seemed genuine. 'It's rare for me to remember a dream. This one was quite vivid and made a deep impression on me.' After a pause he added, with his devastating smile, 'But I must be honest and admit that I did have to see your father this morning, on business.'

Before Jessamy could think of a reply her father returned. He greeted the Captain, pleasure in his voice. 'How good to see you again, Fabian, but what has brought you here? I thought you were planning a visit to London.'

'I was, then I dreamed last night of your lovely daughter and I had to call and see if she was still here.' He related the dream and Chadwick gave Jessamy a smiling glance, which embarrassed her. She excused herself and went into the back room.

There she moved things around. By relating the dream, he had reduced it to ordinary conversation and yet deep down it was something she wanted to mull over, even though she had accused him of banality. She stayed in the back until her father called to tell her that Captain Montague was leaving, but she simply gave him a brief goodbye and had the satisfaction of seeing a puzzled look in his eyes.

Louise usually called for Jessamy when she left the warehouse and they would walk home together; but today they did not meet until the afternoon, when they set out to visit their grandparents. Louise made the excuse that she had been busy and late leaving. Although Jessamy mentioned the Captain's visit to her cousin she sensibly refrained from telling her about the dream.

The grandparents lived away from the moorland and after crossing the busy main road, the girls cut through a wood. The sky was heavy-looking and a farmer they met earlier had said, 'There's blankets of snow up there ready to come down, probably before nightfall.'

Louise stumbled over a tree root and began to grumble that she was sick of visiting her grandparents. Her grandmother wouldn't stop talking and she hated Beacon Hall, it was so cold and draughty. Louise was wrong about her grandmother. The old lady did more listening than talking, loving to hear all the gossip, but

64

Jessamy did agree with her about the Hall. It was old, built in Elizabethan times. Draughts came up through the floorboards in various places and through breaks in the walls. Her grandfather would invest money in properties but would never pay for repairs to his own house, probably because he had never been one to feel the cold. Jessamy said, 'It's not so bad if the fires are built up, which they usually are for parties.'

'But not for general visits,' Louise snapped.

This was true and as every birthday in the family had to be celebrated at Beacon Hall, parties occurred quite frequently. Jessamy enjoyed them, and usually Louise did, too. All the family attended, and friends were also invited. Although Jeremiah was insistent that celebrations must be held at the Hall, he contributed nothing in the way of food. The families always saw to this side of it.

When they left the wood there were two fields to cross and as they set out across the first one a few snowflakes were drifting aimlessly down.

'That's all we need to complete the visit!' Louise exclaimed. 'No doubt we'll be trudging back knee-deep in it.'

'Oh, Louise, for heaven's sake.' Jessamy stopped. 'Before we go any further will you please tell me what is wrong with you? You've behaved like a bear with a sore head for the past two days. What has happened?'

'Nothing.' Louise, her expression surly, walked on. Jessamy followed and catching her by the arm, demanded an explanation.

'I know you can be moody but your behaviour is out of all proportion. There has to be a reason so tell me, please.'

'It's nothing. Surely I can have a grumble if I want to. I'm not beholden to you for anything.'

'Doesn't our friendship mean anything to you any more?' Jessamy asked quietly.

'Yes, it does, but don't harass me. I'll tell you what's wrong in my own good time. Just accept it, will you?' Louise too had spoken quietly and Jessamy presumed her trouble had to do with Joseph Masterson. Perhaps Louise had not been too honest in saying he wanted to see her. There was no other reason she could think of for her bad humour.

CHAPTER FOUR

Beacon Hall was surrounded by trees. A three-storeyed lathe and plaster structure with small, diamond-paned windows, the jutting beam of the top floor over the jutting beam of the first floor seemed to Jessamy to give a look of protection to the one at ground-level. She liked the house in spite of the cold and loved listening to the stories her grandmother told of the people who had lived in it during Elizabethan times.

'They were a wild, drink-swilling, hunting lot according to a diary left there by a lady's maid in those days. They pushed food into their mouths with their fingers and the house was like a pigsty, with beautiful tables ruined by men and women dancing on them. They were just rabble, not ladies and gentlemen like us.'

This last remark was always accompanied by an impish twinkle in old Mrs Every's eyes, for there were no luxuries at Beacon Hall. The stone floor of the hall and the oak floors of the rooms upstairs were bare, carpetless, and all upholstery and curtains were shabby.

The elderly maid who opened the door told the girls their grandmother was expecting them. She was in the small sitting-room upstairs. Despite a sizeable log fire burning in the hall grate Jessamy could not repress a shiver as their footsteps echoed over the stone floor.

Their grandmother, Henrietta, called to them as they were going up the narrow oak staircase. 'Is that you, Louise, Jessamy? Come right in.'

When they went into the room they both stopped abruptly and looked about them. The floor was scattered with rugs and tapestries covered each wall. All were shabby but gave a surprising warmth to the room. Henrietta chuckled. 'I knew you would be surprised at such sudden *luxury*.'

She was tiny, with bird-bones, her eyes the bright curious ones of a robin. She always told people that she did not come up to her husband's heart but that she must have reached it somehow, because he proposed to her on their first meeting. At the moment Henrietta was dwarfed in the big armchair, where the once cherry-red upholstery was almost threadbare. A rug was over her knees, a shawl draped about her shoulders and her white lace cap, slightly awry, showed few brown strands in her grey hair.

Louise joked, 'Has Grandfather come into a fortune?'

'Well, between you and me and Farmer Brown's cow, he picked them up at an auction sale. At least, that is what he told me. I suspect that someone had thrown the lot out. Come and give me a kiss then you can tell me your news.'

With the greetings over the girls pulled up a wooden stool each and by then a younger maid had brought in tea. The old lady said, 'Now then, your grandfather will be here soon so we must get our gossiping done or we shall never get a word in edgeways.'

Henrietta smiled as she spoke because actually Jeremiah said very little; he observed, and listened under the pretence of napping.

With the tea poured Henrietta said brightly, 'So, what have you to tell me? Who is expecting a baby, how many couples have been betrothed and more important still, who has been kissing who they ought not to be kissing?'

'Grandma, you're terrible,' Louise exclaimed, with an anger unwarranted knowing it was just a game with the old lady.

'It's not terrible, my love.' The words were spoken mildly. 'News of other people and a little bit of gossip thrown in is food and drink to me, being unable to get about.'

Their grandmother had suffered two miscarriages after the birth of her last daughter and they had left her more or less an invalid. But she never complained and Jessamy was cross with her cousin for her outburst. Louise, obviously ashamed of herself began to talk about Captain Montague, explaining that she and Jessamy were having a contest, scoring marks according to the attention he gave to each one. Their grandmother laughed and clapped her hands. 'Now this is interesting. But is this paragon of a man not married?'

'Papa says not,' Jessamy replied. She laughed. 'But he will probably have a wife in every port, as the saying goes.'

'Not all men are polygamous. Look at your grandfather, who has never even glanced at another woman.' There was a faraway, dreamy look in the old lady's eyes. Louise gave Jessamy a wry smile as though to refute this and Jessamy, for the first time, found herself disliking her cousin. She could so easily destroy some-

69

one's illusions with a snide remark.

'Oh, I've just remembered, Grandma,' Jessamy exclaimed. 'Clarabelle Hall and Eustace Bridle have just become engaged. They are so ideally suited and so very much in love. It's nice to see them together, he so caring of her and she—'

'She's like glue,' Louise exclaimed. 'Terrified she's going to lose him to someone else. After all, he is about her last chance. She must be twenty-seven if she's a day.'

It was the old lady who made the protest, pointing out that she had been twenty-eight when she married. 'And your grandfather was *not* my last chance, Louise dear. He was the one I fell in love with and wanted to marry and it was love at first sight for him. You *are* in a bad mood. What is wrong?'

Louise had the grace to apologise. 'Forgive me, Gran. To tell you the truth I just don't feel myself at one with the world at the moment.'

The old lady patted her hand. 'Not to worry, my love, it will pass. We women are strange creatures, made up of so many moods. One day we can be sitting up on the clouds and the next be in the depths of hell. Tomorrow is another day. The boys will be home then and they will cheer you up.'

Before any more could be said Jeremiah came in. He greeted his wife and then his granddaughters, saying he hoped they were both well.

'Yes, thank you,' they replied in unison and Jeremiah, tall, white-haired and austere-looking, drew up a chair, sat down, tweaked his trousers from the knees and looked around him.

'Well, have you had a good gossip?'

'There's a scarcity of it, it seems,' the old lady replied with her impish smile. 'Now in my young days—'

'Do you like my tapestries?' her husband interrupted, addressing the girls. 'I picked them up for a song.'

Jessamy studied them for the first time. The colours were so faded it was a moment before she made out that most of them were hunting scenes, with one biblical scene. She said, 'They do keep out the draughts.'

Jeremiah raised his hands as though in horror. 'Great heavens! A young girl like you complaining about draughts. I bought them because your grandmother said the room was chilly.'

Henrietta gave him an indulgent smile. 'You are so thoughtful, Jeremiah. Old bones do get chilled if one is unable to exercise them.'

'Perhaps, perhaps, but this is not to say I agree with turning rooms into hothouses.' He crossed his arms and closed his eyes. 'You ladies go on with your gossiping, I shall take a nap.'

They all knew he was listening, which restricted their choice of subject. They discussed the families and trade then Henrietta said, her impish twinkle very evident, 'Oh, by the way, I understand the old squire has taken unto himself another mistress and has ensconced her in an apartment in London.'

At this her husband's eyelids flew open. 'The old squire? It's the first I've heard of it.'

'Why, Jeremiah dear, it's only hearsay. I thought you were sleeping.' He got up, hemming and hawing, saying it was impossible to sleep where women were gossiping and left the room.

When he had gone there was subdued laughter from all three with the old lady saying, 'He's a sly one, your grandfather. He enjoys a bit of gossip as all men do, but would they admit it? Not a man jack of them. Now, what else have you to tell me?'

Jessamy, knowing that her grandmother liked to hear about good deeds too, told her about the maid of one of her father's customers, an orphan who had got into trouble. Not only was the boy in question going to marry her, but the mistress had told the girl she could keep on with her job until the baby was born, as they would need the money.

'A true Christian,' Henrietta said. 'That is a rarity these days. Oh yes, indeed,' she added, when Jessamy protested at the 'rarity'. 'People go to church and pray and put money in the box, but for one reason only. To pave their way to heaven. How many of them would do what that mistress has done for her servant? They would push her into the cold to fend for herself. She had sinned, hadn't she—what else could she expect?'

Louise said, 'And would you look after a servant who had got herself into trouble, Grandma?'

'*I* would, but your grandfather wouldn't.'

'But he's a pillar of the church,' Jessamy exclaimed.

'There are many pillars of the church who have turned out to be rogues. What about Mr Braithwaite, who absconded with all his employer's money so he could live a life of sin in London.'

Louise gave a wry smile. 'Who could blame him with a nagging, miserable wife like his.'

Henrietta chuckled. 'Who indeed? But that doesn't stop me from making my point, that many people are not what they seem.'

Jessamy, recalling her cousin saying that all the family had secrets, glanced at her, only to find that Louise was watching her. Jessamy lowered her gaze, not liking the way this conversation was going. She said, 'I think perhaps we ought to be going, Grandma, before it gets too dark and we bump into trees in the wood.'

Henrietta begged them to stay a little longer, saying that the stable boy would see them safely through the woods with a storm lamp. But Louise rose to her feet, too, saying she would have to go as she had forgotten to give her father a message.

Old Mrs Every gave in. Of course, she was being selfish. She would see them at the party the following Friday—she was so looking forward to it. The girls said they were, too, and after taking leave of Henrietta they left, without having seen Jeremiah.

It was dusk and snowflakes were still drifting aimlessly. Louise said, 'Pray heaven I shall not be indisposed in my old age and have to depend on silly gossip to keep me going.'

Jessamy replied quietly, 'None of us knows what is in store for us and it's little enough of our time to give to Grandma. I didn't want to stay the way the talk was going, but I don't regret going to see her, I never do. I think she has a great deal of courage, but then, she has a maxim: "If it's impossible to change what has happened in life, then one must endure it with as much cheerfulness as possible".'

Louise made no reply and they walked in silence until they came to the main road, when Louise admitted that she had lied about having to give her father a message. She had simply wanted to get away from Beacon Hall. Normally, Jessamy would have gone home with Louise to stay overnight, but in this case felt she must wait to be asked.

They passed the warehouse, shops and the Highwayman's Arms and when they came to the pharmacy, Verity could be seen in the shop talking to Alistair MacKay. Louise went in with Jessamy, without saying a word yet, once inside, she became a different person, bright and smiling. Yes, she told her mother, they had had an enjoyable afternoon. Grandma was always such good company.

Jessamy could only stand aside and stare. This girl was not her Cousin Louise, she was a stranger. Louise never put on false airs. Could it be because Alistair had not taken his gaze from her since she came in? But then other young men had shown admiration for her and yet Louise had never acted in this way. Even Verity was eyeing her daughter in a puzzled manner. Then Verity said they must go, she would just say goodbye to Chadwick who was in the back room.

Alistair turned to Jessamy. 'So you have both had an enjoyable time while I have been slaving away making up love potions.'

'Don't let the customers hear you say that,' Louise teased, 'or you would be pestered for weeks. Love potions indeed! There are no such things.'

'Of course there are. I could name six. But I won't.' Alistair's eyes were full of laughter. Jessamy felt wooden. If only she could understand her cousin's behaviour.

Chadwick emerged with Verity and after some small-talk said to his daughter, 'I shall tell your mother you will be staying overnight with your aunt and uncle.'

'Yes,' she answered unsure whether she

wanted to stay if Louise reverted to her morose mood.

Louise, however, remained in a happy state, chatting brightly and making her mother enquire teasingly if she had had anything to drink at her grandmother's, to which she replied, 'Only the milk of human kindness, which made me feel good.'

'Splendid,' declared Verity. 'I only hope its effects will remain.'

It did until bedtime when Louise fell silent again, but before Jessamy could complain about her change of moods Louise sank on to a chair and looked up at her with a woeful expression. 'I've been trying for some time to follow Grandma's maxim, but it's become increasingly difficult. How can one always be cheerful with something pressing on one's mind?'

'What is pressing on your mind, Louise?'

'I can't tell you, it's a secret.'

There was such despair in her cousin's voice that Jessamy dropped to her knees and took Louise's hands in hers. They were ice cold. 'Louise, since our earliest childhood we've been as close as sisters, sharing our every secret. Why can't you tell me now what is wrong?'

'It's not just *my* secret and I have promised I wouldn't tell anyone else, not ever.'

'Do you mean it's something you could keep to yourself for the rest of your life? Is Joseph Masterson involved?'

76

'It is something I could keep to myself for ever, but if you want to help me, Jessamy, *please* don't ask any more questions.'

Jessamy, who had an avid curiosity about most things, knew it would be a torment to remain in ignorance, but at the same time she respected the fact that Louise had made a promise and must keep it. However, she did not stop speculating and reached the conclusion that it must have something to do with Joseph Masterson. Perhaps they had done wrong together and Louise was in trouble. No, not Louise, she had said that girls who got into trouble were stupid. At least, girls in their own class. It was different for a girl in service, who was perhaps raped by her master. Then she would be terrified to tell anyone in case she lost her job. Louise had told Jessamy what happened when a couple were married. Jessamy had thought it a shocking, shameful thing and said so; her cousin replied that according to what she had heard from two friends of hers who were both married, the act could be quite pleasurable, when one was used to it. Jessamy had refused to accept this, until she had begun to feel strange tremors in her body when thinking about certain boys. And more recently, she had experienced a powerful and pleasurable sensation when she met Captain Montague. Is that what happened, when one fell truly in love?

Louise had warned Jessamy there was a

possibility that a man might want to do this thing to her before she was married, but she was not to give in, not on any account. If she did, and got into trouble she would be an outcast. People would always remember her as the girl who had sinned—even if she subsequently married and had ten more children in wedlock, they would still think of her and speak of her, as the sinner. No, Louise would never have allowed herself to be put in such a position.

At that moment, Louise got up and began to undress. She had undone the buttons on the bodice of her dress when she paused. 'Jessamy, will you help me over this awful period, help me to keep up my spirits?'

Even without the desperate pleading in her cousin's voice Jessamy would have agreed. 'Of course, Louise. And it will help that the boys will be home tomorrow afternoon. They always cheer us up.'

And so they did. From the moment of their arrival the house seemed to take on a new life. They teased the girls, bandied jests, had wrestling bouts and boxing matches, until Verity had to scold them.

'Now stop it, the three of you. You are acting like children instead of young men. Sit down and stay sat down for the next fifteen minutes—or else.'

'Or else what, Mama?' This from Christian, who was the eldest. He was solemn-faced but

78

his eyes were full of laughter. Christian was Jessamy's favourite. He was long-legged, had grey-blue eyes and golden hair, hair that was ruffled after their antics.

'Or else what, Mama?' echoed Francis and Rupert. There was a year between the two younger boys, but both Francis and Rupert were of a more stocky build, with round faces and dark hair.

Verity, who was standing smiling at them, said, 'I'll have to think up a punishment, perhaps bar you from Andrew's birthday party next Friday.'

Christian now wore a cheeky grin. 'Grandfather would not permit it. You know how he is, with every member of the family having to attend each celebration. I know what we shall do. We'll all get out of your way for a while, Mama, and take the girls for a walk.'

Louise said she was not in the mood to go walking and the two younger boys also demurred. Christian held out a hand to Jessamy. 'I know I can depend on you to walk with me.' She got up at once, needing to talk to her cousin.

Most of the time, Christian dressed immaculately but when he went walking in the winter he always wore an old black cape left at the Highwayman's Arms by a traveller many years before. The brothers had used the cape in plays they performed and finally Christian laid claim to it. As well as the cape, he wore an equally ancient cap that had once belonged to a shepherd. Jessamy teased him. 'You do know you look incongruous, don't you?'

For answer he took the long scarf from her hand, wrapped it twice around her throat, looped it at the front and kissed the tip of her nose. 'But I know you would still love me, even if I were in rags. Shall we go?' Jessamy laughed and followed him.

The night was calm, but the air frosty, with the stars twinkling pinpoints of ice. Christian linked his arm through hers. 'So, what has been happening this week—anything new?'

'Oh, yes, many things.' Jessamy told him about her father's new assistant, Alistair MacKay. Christian wanted to know all about him, where he had come from, how old he was and whether he was attractive.

'Yes, he is. And then we had a surprise visit from a Captain Montague, a friend of Papa's. A most interesting man who has travelled the high seas and seen so many wonderful things.' She began to describe him but all Christian was interested in was when he could meet this sea captain, who might persuade Uncle Bertie to let him take up a seafaring life.

'It's not your father who needs persuading,' Jessamy said, 'it's Grandfather. You know his plans for all of you boys.'

Christian dismissed this. He was his own man and would not allow anyone to dominate him. At that moment Jessamy could see

Jeremiah in him, in the severe lines to his face and the stubborn thrust to his jaw. They would go to the docks tomorrow he said, and see if they could find the Captain.

'We won't,' Jessamy spoke firmly. 'For one thing you know Mama's feelings about the dock area, but for another, I feel Captain Montague would not welcome you. I'm sure he will pay another visit. Wait until then.'

However, this would not do for her cousin. Tomorrow it was, and if Jessamy would not come with him he would find the captain on his own, and introduce himself. He asked her to describe him.

Rather enjoying herself, Jessamy gave a full-blown description of Fabian Montague. He was the handsomest man she had ever met. He was big, powerfully-built, a Viking. And such eyes! Never had she seen any so blue. Then, after a pause she gave a deep sigh and said, 'I fell head over heels in love with him at that first moment of meeting.'

Christian stopped abruptly. 'Now, just a minute! You are my girl, always have been and I won't have any interloper coming between us.'

Jessamy's head went up. 'I am my own person, just as you are, Christian, and I will not be dictated to by you or anyone else about who I fall in love with.'

'Jessamy—you can't do this to me. I look

forward to coming home to see you every week-end.'

'I look forward to seeing you, too, Christian but as a brother, nothing more.'

'A brother! Jessamy, you are being cruel, cruel!'

Jessamy, suddenly realising that Christian was making a jest of it, walked on. 'I *don't* enjoy melodrama at this time of day.'

'It's not melodrama, my beautiful Jessamy. I love you, love you.' He caught her to him and flung his cape around her. He was laughing and she had begun to laugh too, when the warmth of his body against hers and his strong arms holding her close made exciting waves go through her, causing her laughter to die. Christian, also sobering, held her away from him, saying with a sort of wonder, 'I do love you, Jessamy. I think I always have.'

Taken aback by this declaration, Jessamy was silent. Was it possible for a man to arouse such strong emotions in a girl, even though he was not the one she would want to marry? She was fond of Christian, very fond but...she drew back. 'I think we ought to walk, don't you?'

'Jessamy, I— Yes, perhaps it would be wise.' He linked his arm through hers again but kept glancing at her. After a while he said, his tone light, 'I think I rather like being in love, or should I say, realising that I am in love with you. It gives me a goal to strive for.'

When she asked what goal he replied, 'Marriage, of course.'

'Marriage?' She pulled away from him. 'What audacity! I have no intention of marrying you or anyone else. And how dare you assume that I would *want* to marry you. I told you that I think of you as a brother.'

'Ah, but that is at the moment. Once you've become accustomed to the idea that you belong to me, then you will accept it.'

Jessamy stopped and stared at him. 'I thought a while ago that you resembled your grandfather in your stubbornness and now I know you've inherited another bad trait—you want to dominate everyone. Well, Christian, as I told you before, I am my own person and do as *I* want. Is that understood?'

'I understand, dear Jessamy,' he said, in an airy way. 'But I'm prepared to wait, years if necessary.'

'Good. And by then I shall have married someone else.'

'You won't, you know.' His tone was teasing again and she accepted it. After all, this was Christian who could be in a bad mood one minute and sunny the next. He began to talk of countries he would like to visit and she listened, not even suggesting that he would need to run away if he was determined to go to sea. By the time their walk ended he had made up his mind quite definitely to go to the docks the next morning and said he hoped

83

Jessamy would change her mind. Jessamy had almost decided to risk it when she learned that as Captain Montague was making a prolonged stay in the area, Chadwick had invited him to the party at Beacon Hall. Christian could make his approach then...

CHAPTER FIVE

Arriving at Beacon Hill for a party, Jessamy would normally be caught up in the scene—the chatter, the colour of the dresses, all the greenery decorating the old walls and the lamps casting a warm glow over everything. It never failed to impress her how large that section of the family seemed to be when they were all together. There were still many relatives she had not even met. Her grandfather had come from a large family and so had her grandmother, but those relatives lived in different parts of England.

Louise had paused to talk to two of her other cousins, but Jessamy moved on, brooding about all her aunts and uncles present having secrets, as well as her own parents. Jessamy's gaze went from group to group. She watched her Uncle Edward and Aunt Grace, both pleasant people but who at this moment seemed solemn and withdrawn. They had three sons, Alvin, Gervase and Andrew and two daughters, Anne and Rebecca.

Next to them were Uncle Digby and Aunt Dorcas, the 'Dismal Dees', both so prim and proper that Jessamy wondered how they could possibly have any guilty secrets. Dorcas looked as if she would be horrified should a man so much as touch her cheek. But then, the couple had six children... Their sons were Matthew, Mark and Luke and they had been disappointed that a fourth boy had not come along to be named John. Then there were Rose, Felicity and Grace, all nice young people, not a bit like their parents.

Talking to her grandparents were her Uncle James, who ran the wheelwright and saddlery business, and his wife Catherine, with their children, Robert, Paul, Peter and their daughter Hannah. Their other daughter, Lillian, whom Jessamy disliked so, had not arrived or at least, was not in view.

Chadwick and Uncle Bertie were in a group of other men, while Verity and Esmeralda were just walking over to talk to her grandparents. The boys, Christian, Rupert and Francis, were with young friends, chatting and laughing.

With a sudden urge to come out of her corner and have some fun, Jessamy was about to make a move when her Cousin Lillian appeared. She was wearing white which, with her flaxen hair, fragile looks and demure expression, gave her a virginal look. Jessamy had been told once how well-known actors or actresses always make a dramatic entrance and knew that this was exactly what her cousin was doing. Although Lillian had not been announced, there was a sudden silence as if someone of great importance had just arrived. Then she was being greeted with affectionate remarks... She was late, where had she been? No party was complete without her... She looked so beautiful... And didn't white become her, what charm.

Lillian assured them all in her gentle voice that she had been here all the time. She had discovered a slight tear in the frill on her dress and a little maid downstairs had stitched it for her. Then Lillian fluttered her lashes and added that she had not imagined anyone would miss her.

Christian came up to Jessamy then and gave her a quick hug. 'Where have you been hiding yourself? Your father told me you were here somewhere.'

'I was, observing you all.'

'And what conclusion did you come to?'

'That the Every boys are all very attractive.'

Smiling, Christian tapped the tip of her nose. 'And so is one very special young lady in the family. *Very* attractive.'

There was a sudden stir near the doorway and when Jessamy looked up she gripped Christian's arm. 'It's Captain Montague!'

'Excuse me, Jessamy,' Christian hissed, and

86

dashed towards him.

Jessamy stood tense, aware of the pounding of her heart. Lillian had made an entrance, an arranged one, but the casual way the Captain had arrived made a greater impact. Christian had already greeted him and was now leading him to meet the grandparents. The chattering had died away and the silence that followed was somehow uncanny. Women and girls edged forward to take a closer peek at this new and adventurous-looking arrival. Jessamy saw him bending over her grandmother's hand and Henrietta's pleased smile at meeting someone entirely new. After welcoming Fabian, Jeremiah began introducing him to those of the family who were nearest. And of course, Lillian was in the forefront—she would be! At this Jessamy experienced a new kind of rage, which she could only put down to jealousy and made an effort to control it.

The men too, had gone quiet as though resenting the competition of this commanding male presence. Some of the women and girls fluttered fans, although the coolness of the room did not warrant it. Jessamy saw Fabian greeting her parents and was glad to note that although her mother's cheeks were slightly flushed, Esmeralda gave no outward show of admiration. Then Jessamy saw Lillian moving closer, and although she had already been introduced to the Captain she stood there, obviously awaiting an opportunity to attract his attention. However, to Jessamy's surprise, after looking around him, Fabian made a beeline to where she and Louise were standing. The other guests parted to let him through.

'Miss Jessamy, Miss Louise, how good it is to see you both again.'

'And nice to meet you again, Captain Montague,' replied Louise, with all the aplomb of a duchess welcoming a guest. Jessamy, on the other hand, was only able to murmur a greeting, for the Captain's gaze holding hers, brought a weakness to her limbs.

'I didn't think I would be able to come this evening, but here I am,' he said warmly.

At that moment, Jessamy became aware of Lillian hovering nearby and was taken aback by the look of venom in her eyes. Christian approached and said, 'Captain Montague, my grandfather asks if you will come and have a drink and meet some friends of his.' He agreed and both men excused themselves, with Fabian telling the girls he would see them later. Jessamy noticed that Lillian followed the two men and Louise followed the direction of her gaze.

'I'm beginning to think you were right about our dear Cousin Lillian,' she said thoughtfully. 'See how determined she is that our handsome Captain will notice her.' Then she exclaimed, 'Just look at her, inveigling her way in! The impudence of her.' Lillian was being introduced to some newcomers with the Captain, as though they had arrived together. 'I must say,' Louise continued, 'she doesn't take after her parents in any way.'

This was true. James was inclined to stoutness, while Catherine was tall and lean. Both were dark-haired, dark-eyed. None of the offspring of the Every sons resembled their parents, yet some of the cousins of different families were as alike as twins. None, however, looked like Lillian. Some were fair, it is true, and quite attractive, but not one of them had her deceptively gentle smile and ingratiating manner.

Jessamy noticed then that quite a few new people had arrived while she had been busy observing the family. It had been agreed that the family would meet first at seven o'clock, and friends could arrive any time afterwards. More people were being ushered in and greeted. Christian came over to the girls and began grumbling about how the Captain would be leaving soon and how he had missed the chance to talk to him about wanting a seafaring life. 'Grandfather has whisked him away to the library with his friends, heaven knows why, but I expect it will be to discuss business.'

Jessamy felt mean, but was glad that Lillian had not made further contact with Fabian. It was just as well he was leaving. Perhaps he would call at the shop before he was due to sail.

With a sudden lightening of spirits she turned to Louise and was about to say, 'Come along, let's enjoy ourselves,' when she noticed her cousin staring at Joseph Masterson, who was standing a few feet away laughing with their cousin Rebecca. Jessamy said, 'By the way, how did you get on with Joseph?'

Louise turned her head slowly and murmured, 'Pardon?' then, 'Oh, I—'

There was a terrible bleakness in her eyes and when she said no more Jessamy laid a hand on her arm. 'What is it, Louise?'

'I—was rude to him. I didn't mean to be. I like Joseph, I like him very much.'

'Then tell him you didn't mean to be rude.' Louise shook her head, turned quickly away and disappeared among the groups of people.

Jessamy was about to follow when she found herself caught up by her Cousin Andrew. 'Jessamy! You haven't yet wished me a happy birthday.'

'Happy birthday, Andrew. I couldn't see you anywhere.' Jessamy laughed. 'I thought you must be in the kitchen breaking off tiny pieces of icing on your cake. Do you remember how you used to do that when you were small?'

'I certainly do.' He pulled a face. 'But no chance this time, not with all the dragons around in the kitchen. Do you know how many candles there will be on my cake? Eighteen! I'm ready to go into business. I can't wait.'

His exuberance was infectious. He took hold of Jessamy's hand. 'Come along, you have some admirers, friends of mine, they're dying to meet you. They think you are the most beautiful girl they've ever seen.'

Jessamy laughed. 'Andrew, you still tell fibs.'

'It's the truth, honest. Come and you'll see.'

She was introduced to three young men, two of whom were extremely shy and the other as exuberant as Andrew. The third one flattered her, said how he had noticed her the moment he arrived and asked Andrew at once who she was. '*At once*,' he repeated. More young men came up and for a few minutes Jessamy felt flattered at their attention.

Then came the ceremony of the cake being carried in, followed by a retinue of young maids bearing platters of food, which were set on trestle tables near the wall. The candles were lit then Andrew, after having a silent wish, blew the candles out in three attempts. All the guests began to sing 'Happy Birthday'.

When the singing ended, Jessamy felt a tap on her shoulder and she turned to face Captain Montague. 'I have to leave now, Miss Jessamy, but I just wanted to say *au revoir*. I've invited your parents, your aunt and uncle and Christian and Louise to have dinner with me at the Highwayman's Arms next week, and I hope that you will also be there.'

'Yes, yes, thank you, Captain Montague. I shall look forward to it.' He gave her a slight bow and left, leaving Jessamy with a madly beating heart. She went to look for Louise and found her sitting beside Joseph Masterson. Their heads were almost touching and Jessamy made no move to disturb the pair. Whatever misunderstanding had been between them seemed now to have been resolved.

On party nights it was the rule that the men served the ladies, and with each family contributing to the food there was a great variety of titbits and cakes. Christian served his grandmother and Jessamy and brought them the titbits first. On the plates were small pieces of succulent beef on squares of crusty brown bread; a piece of game pie; cheese and egg tartlets, a piece of ham rolled around asparagus; small rounds of deep fried sausage and sage. When Christian asked if that was sufficient his grandmother raised her hands and said, 'Heavens! this is just about what I eat in a day.' Louise, who had a healthy appetite, grinned and said that was enough, she must leave room for the cakes, to which the old lady remarked with feeling that it was good to be young.

When Christian brought the cakes he piled Jessamy's plate high and although she insisted she would simply never be able to eat them all, she consumed a square of strawberry shortbread, one piece of apricot and cream sponge, a portion of iced chocolate cake with a butter cream filling and a coconut snowball. And declared afterwards that she would be unable to move for the next half hour at least.

After the meal the family always had a traditional game of charades. Jessamy, who enjoyed working out a conclusion to the answer, completely forgot her own problem and the family secrets until Lillian came up and sat at the other side of her grandmother.

'Why, I thought you had forgotten about me, Lillian,' said the old lady, and Jessamy thought she detected a slight note of asperity in her grandmother's voice.

'But I greeted you earlier, Grandma dear,' replied Lillian. 'Have you forgotten?'

'No, Lillian, I do not forget anything, even though I am getting old. I think you probably intended saying something to me, but were distracted by the men.'

Lillian gave a trilling laugh that grated on Jessamy. 'Who couldn't be attracted by the attractive Captain Montague?' She patted the old lady's hand. 'I must go, Grandma, but I shall be back. Aunt Grace is waving to me.'

Grace, so far as Jessamy could see, had her back to them and Henrietta was obviously aware of that too, for she said, 'I see no reason to make an excuse to escape. 'Then she added, 'I can't stand that child. She's two-faced.'

Jessamy, who had never guessed that her grandmother felt that way about Lillian, wanted to hug her. Then the old lady gave a conspiratorial smile. 'But don't tell anyone I said this or I would have a pack of wolves at my door. They all think she's wonderful.'

Jessamy nodded. 'Yes, I know.' She leaned forward. 'I don't like Cousin Lillian either. I would like to tell you why, Grandma, but I can't at the moment. Perhaps some day when we're alone.'

'Come any time, Jessamy dear.' Normally the old lady's eyes would gleam at the hint of gossip but her expression at that moment was gentle. She gave Jessamy's hand a squeeze then said, 'Now let us talk about something else. Shall I tell you some more about the Exhibition?'

Although Jessamy must have known every square yard of the great Crystal Palace Exhibition in 1851 and all that it contained, she never tired of her grandmother repeating the story because she brought it all so much to life. No matter what part of the Exhibition she described, she always began with the journey to London. It had been her first experience of a train and she described the crowds, the hissing gaslamps and the smell of oil, and then their arrival in the big city and the excitement.

'There were so many people, Jessamy, it was unbelievable. There was a party of us, Jeremiah's brothers and their wives. They were all staying at an hotel, but we were to stay at a lodging house.' Henrietta chuckled. 'You know Jeremiah, he won't spend a penny when a halfpenny will do. It was one shilling and sixpence a night, including breakfast. The bed was lumpy, but the room and sheets were clean. Anyway, I didn't mind where I slept as I was just so overwhelmed by the feeling of adventure. After all, we had been married only a few months and although I was not exactly a *young* bride I was certainly impressionable. We all met the following morning and it was really the *big* adventure.'

Henrietta went on to describe the road to the Crystal Palace, with its never-ending line of wagons, carriages, barrows, carts and omnibuses, all moving slowly. The pavements were lined with vendors selling souvenirs of the Exhibition, small paintings of the Crystal Palace, medals and kerchiefs. Barrow boys sold oranges, nuts, apples, ginger beer, lemonade and orange drinks. Although Henrietta was thirsty with all the dust, Jeremiah wouldn't buy any drinks but fortunately, one of her sisters-in-law let Henrietta have a bite of her apple—and that quenched her thirst.

The old lady was interrupted at this point by Jeremiah, who announced that dear Lillian was going to play the pianoforte. Henrietta pulled a face. 'We shall have to continue the story later.'

If she was honest, Jessamy had always enjoyed the music but this evening, because of recent events and her cousin's posturings before she settled herself at the instrument, it struck discords in Jessamy's mind before Lillian had even started. She began to ask herself why her grandmother thought Lillian two-faced. Something must have occurred for her to say such a thing. Her cousin began to play some chords as a lead-up to the actual tune and Jessamy, looking at the faces around her, saw rapt expressions on the majority.

In spite of feeling out of tune with the world Jessamy found herself moved by the rendering of the haunting song, *Greensleeves*. Even Lillian herself seemed genuinely touched by the music, making Jessamy wonder if there were two characters inside the virginal-looking figure in white.

Lillian played only the one song, but promised another later. There was enthusiastic applause. Afterwards, all the young people were drawn into playing games.

Hide and Seek was first. Jessamy went to the place where she always hid—a large cupboard connecting her grandfather's dressing-room to the bedroom he and her grandmother shared. Although everyone knew about this cupboard Jessamy had once discovered that by pulling a short pair of ladders down at the end one could place objects on a high shelf. And it was on these ladders she always stood, covered by various articles of clothing. The only time she made herself known was when the seeker was the person she wanted to find her. Then she would open the door a fraction and someone would shout, 'Got you!'

This time, Jessamy had hardly had the opportunity to get into the cupboard before she heard women's voices. The women came into her grandparents' bedroom and one of them said, 'Well, you know what they say, like father like son. Jeremiah has always been a bit of a rogue.'

Her companion replied, 'Yes, I know, but Edward has always seemed so devoted to Grace.'

The first woman gave a derisive laugh and remarked that any woman who trusted her husband these days was a fool. For a few seconds Jessamy thought that the women had gone then one of them said, 'Here's my shawl, I knew I had brought it.' After that there was silence but Jessamy waited, trying to think who the women had been but she was unable to identify the voices.

Edward was the uncle she liked best next to her Uncle Bertie. What had he been doing wrong? He was such a kindly man, caring and loving towards his wife and family. And her grandfather, why had they spoken of him as a rogue? Although he was tight-fisted he was known as a scrupulously fair man who, if he gave his word on anything, never failed to keep it.

The women had been talking as though there was actually another woman in her uncle's life. Suddenly feeling suffocated among the clothes Jessamy opened the door, came out into the room and the next moment her shoulders were being gripped by Christian, who laughed as he demanded a forfeit. His lips touched hers lightly.

When Jessamy drew away he said, 'I should not really have demanded a forfeit, should I? You were not actually hiding. Why not?'

'I—I was hiding but I heard two people talking and—' she raised her shoulders in a helpless gesture and Christian eyed her with concern.

'What is it, Jessamy? What were these people saying?'

'They were suggesting that Grandfather and Uncle Edward were rogues.'

Christian chuckled. 'Grandpa is, he's a businessman, always out for his pound of flesh, but as for Edward, no, I could not believe that Edward would overcharge a penny, not even if he was sure he would get it.'

Jessamy hesitated, wanting to follow it up, but not quite sure that she would be doing the right thing. She said tentatively, 'Judging by the conversation between the two women I think they were suggesting that Uncle Edward was—having an affair.'

'Edward? Never. He's not the type. You can put that right from your mind, Jessamy. What you've been listening to was gossip. You know how much gossip there is in any family and ours is no exception. Forget it. Come along, we'll get back to the others.'

Jessamy agreed but when they went back to

the drawing-room and she looked around her it seemed that wherever women were standing talking together there was something secretive about the way their heads were close, nodding. She could almost imagine them saying, 'Well, would you believe it... Imagine that!'

Christian had been right when he said there was gossip in any family, but now that Jessamy thought about it, it was only recently that it had caused trouble in her family. As she had told Louise, there was *some* member of the family dropping the poison...she wondered again if it could be Lillian.

They were now organising a game of Hunt the Thimble, the thimble to be hidden somewhere in the drawing-room so that the older people could take part, too. But the only way in which the older ones would participate was to whisper suggestions to the youngest ones of where the thimble might be.

Louise, looking glum, came up to Jessamy grumbling, 'I'm going home, I don't want to play children's games.'

Jessamy teased her. 'What do you want to play then? Postman's Knock so Joseph Masterson can call you out?'

Louise gave her a scathing look. 'Don't be stupid. The last thing I want is to be kissed, and certainly not by Joseph Masterson.'

'Why, what's happened? What's gone wrong?'

'Perhaps it would be better if you asked me

what had gone right. Nothing has recently.'

'But you and Joseph seemed to be having an amicable conversation a while ago.'

'It was *not* amicable.'

'Louise, I do wish you would tell me what's the matter. You haven't been yourself at all lately.'

'No, I haven't, have I? I don't feel myself. But there's nothing that you or anyone else can do.' Louise went wandering off and Jessamy was just wondering if she should follow when someone touched her arm. It was Joseph Masterson. He too was looking at Louise's retreating back.

'Jessamy, can you tell me what's wrong with Louise? I came early especially to have a talk with her, Andrew told me I could, but I don't think I've had ten civil words from her since we met.'

There was a bewildered, hurt look in Joseph's eyes that were usually so merry. Normally too, he had a lively manner, a charm that drew girls to him. Jessamy had never really liked him for the way he would show interest in one girl then drop her when someone new came along, but at that moment, for some reason she felt sorry for him.

'I don't know, Joseph, what's wrong with my cousin. Louise's moods have been so changeable these past few days. One time she seems in the depths of despair and then the next she's smiling, happy. Or at least, she seems so.'

'Is there—I mean do you know if there's anyone else she's interested in?'

'Not as far as I know and we are a lot together.' Joseph looked so miserable Jessamy said to console him, 'She does talk about you.'

His expression became eager. 'She does? What does she say?'

'Well, earlier she told me that she had been rude to you and regretted it. After that she admitted she liked you, liked you a lot.'

His expression became radiant. 'Oh, that's wonderful. Thanks, Jessamy, you don't know what this has done for me. I must go and find her.'

He had moved away when Jessamy called him back and told him he was not to repeat what she had said, or it could upset her cousin.

He laughed. 'Don't worry, I shall be the soul of discretion.'

Jessamy watched him weaving his way among the groups of people and felt completely puzzled. She had thought Joseph Masterson was responsible for her cousin's changing moods —but apparently not. So, who could it be? Then, seeing her father beckon, she went over to him. Verity was with him. Chadwick laid an arm across his daughter's shoulders. 'We haven't seen very much of you, my love. Are you enjoying yourself?'

'Oh, yes, it's a lovely party. I've been here

and there, talking to this one and that one, you know how it is.'

Verity, who was searching the room said, 'And I haven't seen Louise since shortly after we arrived. Have you seen her, Jessamy?'

'Yes, she did say she might go home.' Jessamy lowered her voice and added, 'She said she didn't feel like playing children's games.'

'She's been behaving so strangely lately,' Verity mused. To Chadwick she said, 'Perhaps she needs a tonic. Can you give her something?' He agreed and by then they were announcing that the game of Hunt the Thimble was to begin.

Jessamy found it impossible to concentrate on anything for the rest of the evening. Her mind was not only on Louise, but on her father and Verity and on her mother and a friend of her Uncle Edward and his wife.

Every time she saw her father and aunt they were together and in Jessamy's sensitive state there seemed to be an intimacy between them. Once, her father put his hand over Verity's and she smiled up into his face. Another time he was looking down at her, smiling into her eyes.

Jessamy also began to see a similar intimacy between her mother and the man she was with. Esmeralda's cheeks were slightly flushed, and she looked quite coyly at her companion who, although not especially attractive, was tall and had a soldierly bearing.

What was happening? Jessamy had a feeling

of her own safe world dissolving. Or could it be that she was letting her imagination run away with her because of what she had over-heard while hiding in the cupboard? Someone once said that if you start a small rumour, in no time at all it will reach gigantic proportions. Wasn't this what she was doing? Seeing evil in her father and Verity being together?

Jessamy was to stay with her aunt and uncle that evening. When they arrived back from the party they found a note from Louise saying she had gone to bed with a headache, and asking not to be disturbed.

But when Jessamy went up to her cousin's room, she was not there—nor had the bed been slept in...

CHAPTER SIX

Jessamy's first reaction was to let her aunt know that Louise was missing, but then, realis-ing the worry it would cause she decided to wait, in the hope that Louise would return. She waited so long, getting colder and colder, that she finally got undressed and got into bed. The maid had put the warming pan over the sheets earlier but any heat there might have been had gone. Jessamy shivered uncontrollably. Where *had* Louise gone?

So many possibilities went through Jessamy's mind that they all became a jumble. She drifted into a semi-doze. It was still dark when she was roused by feeling something icy-cold touch her feet. It was Louise, but when Jessamy spoke to her there was no answer. Jessamy drew herself up in the bed.

'Louise, where have you been? I've been worried sick. I hesitated about telling your parents you were not in your room. Perhaps I should have done.'

'I was out walking. Yes, and you needn't say humph, as if you didn't believe me. I had to be alone to think. And don't ask me why because I won't tell you. Right now, if you don't mind, I want to sleep.'

'Lucky you! I am wide awake.'

'I'm sorry.' Louise turned over on her side. Jessamy sank back into the pillows and finding it utterly impossible to sleep, tortured herself going over all the unpleasant incidents of the evening.

Dominating them was her cousin's behaviour. Jessamy sighed. If only she could forget all this and go to sleep, but her lids felt as if they were glued open. Jessamy then found herself thinking of everyone at Beacon Hall gathering around the piano and singing softly to Lillian's rendering of *Just a Song at Twilight* before the party broke up.

Just a song at twilight,
When the lights are low,
And the flickering shadows,
Softly come and go...

There had been no venom in Lillian's eyes then. She had been as deeply moved as the rest. Jessamy could hear the haunting melody now, as though from the next room, and she began to cry, big tears rolling slowly down her cheeks. If only her life could go back to what it had been before Lillian had said that awful thing...

She roused the next morning to the smell of bacon cooking and was surprised she had slept. Louise was still sleeping and did not wake as Jessamy washed and dressed. When she was ready to go downstairs she met Verity on the landing, stifling a yawn.

'Oh, good morning, Jessamy. I feel half-dead. I was too energetic last night and I drank too much wine. How is Louise?'

Jessamy told her that Louise showed no signs of rousing and Verity said it was perhaps best not to disturb her. Breakfast was a quiet affair, with Verity saying at the end of it she thought a good brisk walk on the moors would restore her sagging spirits. She told Jessamy she would walk with her as far as the shop, pick up the tonic for Louise from Chadwick and then go on to see Bertie before taking her walk.

'It was a job to get your uncle out of bed this morning and usually he's up before dawn.' Verity laughed. 'Needless to say it was not from the wine your grandfather provided, that was nonexistent. Captain Montague brought a number of bottles and excellent wine it was, too. What a fascinating man. I'm so looking forward to our evening with him at the Highwayman's Arms on Monday.'

The sky was beginning to lighten when she and Verity left the house. The morning was mild for the time of year and Verity grumbled —she needed a wind to blow her cobwebs away! She went on to talking about Dorcas' husband, Digby, saying with a laugh that trying to make friends with him was like knocking your head against a brick wall, when a woman who had come out of a cottage ahead gave them a wave and then limped down the path to the gate.

'It's old Mrs Minnot,' Jessamy said. 'Perhaps her rheumatics are playing her up and she wants some medicine.'

Before they reached her Mrs Minnot was calling, 'Glad I've caught you, Miss Jessamy, I've had a fall. Me knee's all colours of the rainbow.' Jessamy went to the gate and asked what had happened.

'Fell down the stairs, I did.' She pulled up her skirt; her leg was bare, her knee swollen. 'Perhaps your Da can give me something to rub on it.'

'You go back into the house, Mrs Minnot, and I'll bring some witch-hazel to put on it.

That will bring out the bruise. I won't be long. Can you manage?'

'Yes, yes, don't let me keep you.'

When Jessamy and Verity walked on Jessamy said, 'She's a nice old soul, lives on her own but wants it that way, as she's very independent. Papa never charges her for medicine but she always pays him in kind. She'll knit him a pair of socks, a scarf, make him a fruit tart or some gingerbread. I admire her. People like that are the salt of the earth.'

Verity chuckled. 'You sound just like your grandmother. But I know what you mean. There are the other kind—the moaners, the get-something-for-nothing type. I can't stand them. Digby's like that. He's tightfisted like your grandfather, but has none of Jeremiah's other qualities, like his ambition to build, to increase his assets and his determination to work hard for what he wants. Digby was a sniveller when he was young and yet when he grew up, he was quite a lady-killer. Can you imagine that?'

'No, I can't. I would have thought it highly unlikely.'

'Oh, yes, he had half the girls in the area after him. And in fact,' Verity lowered her voice as though they could be overheard, 'there were quite a few scandals in connection with his little peccadilloes.'

Jessamy tensed. Was this one of the secrets of which Lillian had spoken? If so, she had no

107

wish to know. She changed the subject and said, 'The main road gets busier every day, doesn't it?'

When they went into the shop Alistair MacKay greeted them with a smile. 'Morning ladies, lovely morning. The master is in the back. Did you want to see him, Mrs Every?'

Verity nodded and left them. Jessamy then told Alistair about meeting Mrs Minnot and told him she was going to take some witch-hazel to her. And when Alistair suggested something else, Jessamy eyed him coldly. 'In this case *I* am prescribing.'

He gave her a mock bow and there was a twinkle in his eyes. 'Yes, Ma'am!' Jessamy was annoyed, more with herself than Alistair. Digby's 'peccadilloes' had upset her. She really must stop being so sensitive.

'I'm sorry,' she apologised, 'it's the effect of the party.' She went to get the bottle of witch-hazel then left to see Mrs Minnot.

The old lady's cottage was one of a row of six, each one as neat as the next. Her front door was open and Mrs Minnot called to Jessamy to come in before she had a chance to knock. The door opened straight into the living room, and although it was sparsely furnished it was homely, with rag rugs fashioned from scraps of cloth in many colours. There were crocheted antimacassars in multi-stripes on the backs of the shabby armchairs, with matching cushions on the seats. Around the mantelpiece was a

108

piece of dark red velvet with a bobble fringe and on the mantelpiece itself were numerous small ornaments, souvenirs brought home by Mrs Minnot's late seagoing husband.

Even the fire added to the cosiness, with the sparking logs sending a shower of 'red soldiers' up the chimney. Mrs Minnot insisted on Jessamy sitting down to a cup of cocoa first, before attending to her knee, then she sat down herself, ready for a chat. Jessamy accepted the invitation, even though she knew that the old lady would start reminiscing about how she had been widowed when she was thirty and how she learned of her husband's drowning the day before she gave birth to her sixth child.

'A lovely man was Jimmy, always cheerful, and there was nowt to be cheerful about in them days going to sea. Tied to the mast and flogged for any little thing...but when he came home, oh, Miss Jessamy, it were wonderful.' The old lady's face was alight with pleasure. 'I would hear him shouting before he started up the rise, ''Maggie, I'm home!''. I would come running out and he would start running and when we met we'd stand like two softies looking at each other. Then he'd lift me up and swing me around and when he put me down we'd both be crying...with happiness. Oh, they were lovely times, worth all the waiting. Then he would bring out the presents, combs and ribbons for me and once he brought me a lovely shawl like cobwebs. I was afraid to wear it in case it got damaged.

'There would be toys for the children, things he had carved out of wood, dolls for the girls and soldiers for the boys.' Mrs Minnot was silent for a moment then she sighed.

'At first when I lost him I used to say I wish we'd never met then I would never have known all the pain of losing him, but now I think of the lovely times we had together and I wouldn't have missed them for the world. It's life, Miss Jessamy, all the ups and downs. You can't have one without the other.'

'No,' Jessamy said. When the old lady had first started talking she had felt a sadness, but now she was relaxed for the first time since the night before. There was nothing one could alter—life was mapped out for everyone.

Jessamy drank her cocoa then stood up. 'Well now, I think I had better take a look at that knee of yours.'

Mrs Minnot pulled up her skirt and proudly displayed it. 'Worst bruise I've ever had, and I've had plenty in me life.'

Jessamy soaked a pad of linen, placed it on the knee, wrapped it around with a bandage to keep it in place and pinned it. 'There. I'll look in at midday on my way home to soak the pad again. It must be kept soaked for a day or two to do any good.'

When Jessamy left she was thoughtful. People led such different lives. Mrs Minnot, for example, worked charring in the big houses, working long hours, but she had once said, 'The Lord's been so good to me. He let me keep me health, otherwise me and the kids would have ended up in the workhouse.'

Jessamy wondered then if she had been foolish in trying to sort out other people's problems —problems that she *could* have imagined. A wind had sprung up and she stepped out suddenly, enjoying it. She would think no more about Louise but would get on with her own work, of medicine and healing.

When she reached the shop she heard voices and as she opened the door, saw Christian sitting on a high stool and his two brothers standing straddling a chair each. Chadwick, elbows on the counter, was laughing with them. The boys all got to their feet when they saw her and her father straightened.

Christian said, 'Hello, Jessamy, we've been waiting for you. We've had an invitation from Captain Montague to visit him today on his ship, which is now out of dry dock.'

Jessamy glanced at her father and Chadwick nodded, smiling. 'If you would like to go you may, Jessamy.'

'But Mama? You know how she feels about my visiting the docks.'

'I think I can assure her you'll be in good hands. Louise will be coming, too.'

'Oh, then in that case—' Jessamy suddenly paused. 'Mrs Minnot—I was going to resoak the bandage on her knee at midday.'

'You'll be back by then and if not, I shall call on her. Now off you go, here is Louise.'

Louise burst in, all smiles. 'I'm ready!' Jessamy stared at her. Why the sudden change from last night? Then she thought, why worry, she's here, looking happier and we are all going to the docks to enjoy ourselves.

They all walked sedately until they had turned into the road that led to the wharf then Christian and the boys began to run, jumping about. Jessamy said, 'Silly fools,' but she was smiling. When they came back to the girls Jessamy pointed to the hill at the end of the road.

'When I was young and was always running away to go to the wharf that hill seemed like a mountain to me. The awful thing was that I was always caught before I could get round it.'

Christian laid an arm across her shoulders. 'Poor Jessamy. Well, I can guarantee we will get round it very soon.'

Jessamy smiled up at him. 'We've been round it a number of times since and I'm always amazed that Mother never got to know about these visits to the docks.'

When they did round the foot of the hill it was like being in another world. There were vehicles of every kind on the wharf, emptying goods and loading others. Men were everywhere, shouting orders and a tug hooted on the river, giving a mournful sound. But Jessamy felt no melancholy—she was here to enjoy herself! As they passed the sheds, voices coming from inside had a hollow sound in those that were partially empty.

Sudden gusts of wind brought different smells, the aroma of spices and oranges, the pungent smell of tar, the stink of rotten refuse and the tangy smell of seaweed. There were many ships in port, mainly merchantmen, the majority being loaded or unloaded. There were swarms of men, speaking in many foreign tongues. Christian was just about bursting with excitement. 'One day I'll be a Captain, sailing the seven seas,' he declared.

Francis teased him. 'You were seasick when we went out in a rowing boat once.' Christian protested he had not been seasick, just queasy, for the sea had been rough. Rupert, his youngest brother, protested equally strongly that the sea had been like a millpond. At this Christian glared and both boys burst out laughing, with Rupert saying, 'Oh, Chris, if you could see your face, it would turn the milk sour.'

Then Christian was laughing too and punching out playfully, first at one and then the other. Louise snapped, 'Oh, stop it, for heaven's sake. It's like being out with naughty children.'

Jessamy said, 'I suggest we simmer down. If anyone sees us who knows our parents, the report of our behaviour would not be exactly favourable, would it?'

They agreed and Christian began to look for the Captain's ship, the *Abercarsis*. Rupert and Francis, however, were more interested in the seamy side of the docks. At one time, villagers had lived there, but now the area had been converted to eating-houses and groggeries. And up narrow streets, painted ladies waited to offer their favours. Even in daylight there were plenty of prostitutes, with drunken sailors hanging on their arms. The din coming from the groggeries of bawdy shouting, singing and sound of men fighting almost blotted out the sounds of creaking cranes, the hammering coming from the ships and the sound of men giving instructions.

Jessamy's gaze went beyond the docks, where twelve miles upriver lay the Newcastle docks and then to the fishermen's cottages which rose in tiers on the hillside. At one time the cottages had been outstanding because of the cleanliness of their whitewashed walls and climbing roses. Now each one was covered with the stone dust from the quarries and the creepers were choked by dust.

'There's the *Abercarsis*!' Christian shouted. 'Over there.' He pointed. 'Can you see it? Come on.'

The ship was no different from any other merchantman lying at anchor, but to Jessamy there was something special about the *Abercarsis* because Fabian Montague was in charge of it. Crewmen were swarming all over the ship and when Jessamy saw the Captain shouting to a group of them her heart began to beat a lot faster. Away from his ship, Fabian was a commanding figure: on it, he assumed the authoritative air of an admiral. They all stood watching him and when Jessamy glanced at Louise she saw that her cousin's face wore a rapt expression. Christian moved towards the gangplank saying, 'Follow me.' Rupert tugged at his sleeve. 'Don't you think we should wait to be invited aboard?'

Christian grinned. 'We could wait all day. Do you want to hand over your visiting card to one of the sailors?' He walked on and the others followed. When they were halfway up the gangplank the captain hailed them. Christian raised a hand acknowledging him, then Fabian was at the top of the gangplank with one of his officers by his side.

'Welcome aboard.' He shook the hand of each, then introduced them to his first officer, who was assigned to show them around the ship later, but at the moment Fabian was in charge and invited them to his cabin for coffee.

Although they lived so close to the docks it was a first visit to a ship for all of them and Louise and Jessamy were no less interested than the boys. What struck Jessamy most forcibly was the cleanliness: the decks were so white one could eat food from them, and the brasses shone. They negotiated a ladder to the lower deck, with the Captain going first to see them down safely. Jessamy's foot slipped on a lower rung and when she felt strong arms around her waist lifting her down the last two steps, she felt a thrill go through her.

The walls of the cabin were panelled in oak and the furniture was also of dark oak. The impression was sombre, and yet it seemed right not to have any colour or fripperies. There were several photographs on the walls, all seeming to be of officers, and the only small painting was an autumn scene in various shades of brown.

On a linen mat on the table were set fragile-looking cups and saucers with a Japanese pattern and matching coffee pot, cream jug and sugar basin. Steam came from the coffee pot and after Fabian had invited them to sit down he poured the coffee.

Although Jessamy was used to the masculinity of her grandfather's library, this masculine atmosphere was somehow different. Fabian seemed different too, not stiff, but rather as if he were conscious of being in charge. 'So,' he said when they had been served, 'and what have you all been doing this morning?'

'Seeing the sights,' Christian said with a grin. 'The seamy side.'

The Captain raised his eyebrows. 'The young ladies too?'

Christian said quickly. 'Oh, I didn't mean that we had been among the—well, the drunken men, or been up the side streets where—

no, we kept on the fringe, as it were.'

Louise, looking affronted said, 'And why shouldn't we see the seamy side? I don't want to be wrapped in cotton wool or be blindfolded, and I'm quite sure that Jessamy feels the same way.'

Fabian smiled wryly. 'Bravely spoken, Miss Louise, but drunken men fighting are no respecters of persons. They would knock you down if you just happened to be in their way.'

There was a sudden quiet and even Louise looked subdued. The Captain seemed quite at ease, however. To break the silence, Jessamy admired the cups and saucers. 'They're so fragile-looking and such a delicate blue. Did they come from Japan?'

'Yes, they did. They were a gift from a colleague of mine who married a Japanese girl. She's beautiful, so gentle.'

This prompted Christian to say, 'I would very much like to travel to these various countries. In fact, I've wanted to have a seafaring life for a long time. What are my chances?'

Rupert said, grinning, 'My brother is seasick in a rowing boat.'

Christian looked really angry. 'Rupert, will you keep your foolish remarks to yourself.' He turned to Fabian. 'I felt queasy that day but the sea was rough.' Then he glanced at his brother as though daring him to refute it.

Fabian, who had not yet touched his coffee, sugared and stirred it. 'Why not persuade your father to let you go on a trip as a passenger? Then you will get a feeling of whether you want to take up seamanship as a career.'

Christian was happy again. 'That is an excellent idea. I'll have a word with him. When are you sailing?'

'Next Wednesday if all is completed. But why not wait until the better weather? As it happens, our passenger list is full this trip.'

'You take passengers?' Jessamy asked in surprise.

'Yes, eight. You will be shown the passenger accommodation.' Fabian smiled. 'Just in case you fancy taking a trip some time.'

Christian's expression had changed to one of gloom. He had really set his heart on going right away. Was there a chance that any of the passengers might cancel? The Captain said it was possible but added that he still thought Christian would be wise to wait until the winter was over.

Christian protested. 'But don't you see, if I go when the weather is rough I shall know what kind of sailor I would make.'

While Fabian was talking to Christian, Jessamy was mulling over the fact that there would be passengers on the ship. Passengers meant company—the Captain would sit with them in the dining-room. When he had spoken of the stillness in the night-watch and his feeling of solitude she had had the impression of a lonely man.

Had Fabian just been seeking sympathy? He enjoyed telling stories. Was he looking for praise, admiration? She saw him now through different eyes and felt disappointed. Was he just one more person in her life who was not what he seemed? Her pleasure in the visit to the ship had disappeared. All she wanted now was to be somewhere where she could sit and think things over quietly.

CHAPTER SEVEN

When they left the ship Jessamy, Louise and Christian were quiet, with Francis and Rupert doing all the talking. They too, they said excitedly, had a sudden yearning to take to the sea. They talked about all the countries they could visit, for the Captain had impressed them on this score. It was then that Christian spoke, warning them that going to sea was not all visiting foreign countries. They would have to work—and work hard. At this Francis laughed. Look who was trying to put them off this wonderful life!

Christian began reproaching them like a father and an argument ensued. The three of them dropped back, arguing, and Louise and Jessamy went ahead. Her tone dry, Louise said,

'I blame dear Captain Montague for causing this upset between the boys. All this talk of visiting foreign countries...he should have discouraged them from wanting to go to sea.'

'I thought he gave very sensible advice. He did suggest to Christian that he ask your father to let him try a voyage as a passenger, before attempting to take up a sailor's life. And remember this, Louise. Christian did warn the lads that going to sea could be very hard work.'

Louise gave a derisive laugh. 'You know why, don't you? He doesn't want them to spoil his chances. You can imagine Papa's reactions, can't you, if the three of them declared they wanted to go to sea. Our Christian, like Fabian Montague, is a wily bird.'

'Wily?' Jessamy queried.

'Call it charm, if you like. He draws people to him. Did you see all the women at the party last night, their eyes nearly popping out. I bet they all went to bed last night dreaming of having him for a lover.'

'Louise!'

Louise laughed and then she suddenly became morose again. 'Men! Who do they think they are, anyway? The majority of them bring only misery to women's lives.'

Jessamy teased her—how could she say such a thing. Where would they be at parties, without men. Who would they dance with— each other? How unbearably dull.

The boys caught up with the girls as they

120

reached the shop. Now they were all chuckling. As Louise opened the door Chadwick came forward, beaming. 'Well, it certainly sounds as if you enjoyed your visit.'

'It was excellent,' Christian declared. 'Uncle, I want you to do something for me. Captain Montague suggests that I take a sea voyage as a passenger and see how I like the experience. I need you to persuade Father to let me go.'

Chadwick pulled forefinger and thumb over his chin. 'Well now, Christian, that might be a problem. When your father and I were talking last night he mentioned bringing you into the business and training you to take over a new branch of it. It's something your grandfather wants him to do. He does own some property on the quayside.'

'*No!*' Christian's expression was mutinous. 'I'm not interested. He can train Francis or Rupert for the work.'

The boys protested. They wanted seafaring lives, too.

Louise said to Jessamy, 'Oh, let's go into the back room, I can't stand all this bickering.' She opened the door then stopped abruptly as Alistair MacKay looked up from a ledger.

'Good day, ladies. Did you enjoy your visit to the good ship *Abercarsis*?'

'How could we do otherwise with the eligible and handsome Captain as host?' There was a saucy twinkle in Louise's eyes.

Alistair replied in equally light vein. 'Alas,

I am not a captain of a ship. I am, however, eligible…'

'Mmm.' Louise walked around him. 'Yes, a personable young man, but he lacks that— Oh, what is the word I want? *Charisma*. Yes, that is it. An attractive word, don't you think?'

'It's something one is born with,' Alistair replied regretfully, 'so, as I seem to lack it I shall have to look for a young lady who will love me for my goodness of nature, my generosity and my gentle caring of her.'

'Stop!' Louise begged, 'or with such qualities I shall be swooning at your feet, imploring you to marry me.'

They were all giggling when Chadwick came in, bringing their playacting to an end.

'Shall we get some work done? Jessamy, will you bring me some corn ointment. I'll take it to Amelia Weston and call on Mr Tilder at the same time to lance his carbuncle.'

When Chadwick had gone the girls burst out laughing, with Louise gasping, 'I can't think of anything more suitable to kill romance than to mention lancing a carbuncle.'

'Dear Papa,' Jessamy said, wiping her eyes. 'Perhaps Mama is right when she says that he thinks only of his work.'

The door opened and this time it was Christian who looked in to remind Louise they should be on their way to the warehouse and to tell Jessamy he would call for her later to go for their usual walk on the moors.

However, later on Jessamy found a note from Christian saying he would be unable to come. *'Father was busy when I wanted to talk to him about a sea trip, but told me I could speak to him this afternoon. He hates to have any of his plans thwarted and I feel I'm in for a "rough passage". If I can get away at a reasonable time I'll find you on the moors, but don't depend on it. Yours, Christian.'*

'I don't mind going on my own,' Jessamy said to her father as she went to get her hat and coat, 'but Christian's good company.'

'Don't stay out until dark, Jessamy, it could be foggy later.'

She promised and left. She had not gone more than about two hundred yards when she heard someone call her name. When she turned she saw Alistair MacKay sprinting towards her. He had pulled on a hat and was trying to shrug himself into an overcoat. He was not even slightly out of breath when he reached her. 'Your father suggested I walk with you, Jessamy, that is if you want company. I would certainly enjoy a walk.'

'Then come along.' At that moment Jessamy was not sure whether she welcomed Alistair's company, but once on the moors she took pleasure in the way he talked about the scenery at home.

'There's something so invigorating about the wildness, and a feeling of awe at the grandeur of the mountains in the background.'

'I know exactly what you mean. They are just hills yonder, but look at the beauty of them.' The tops were lost in the clouds but below, wraiths of mist drifted over the slopes. 'Aren't they lovely, and isn't it wonderful to be out in a storm? There's something so primitive about it, with the rain deluging and thunder crashing.' Jessamy smiled to herself, wondering how Alistair would have reacted had she told him how she always had an urge to run naked over the moors in a storm.

Alistair chuckled. 'It seems we are kindred spirits. Not many people like being out in a storm.'

'I know. Aunt Verity often comes walking with me but if a storm seems to be brewing she scuttles back home. It's useless to tell her she's missing a wonderful treat.'

Alistair looked down at her. 'We must share a storm some time.'

'Lovely. It could be fun.'

They came to the first of the large houses and Alistair waved a hand towards it. 'I wouldn't mind living there,' he laughed, 'but I shall probably end up in a cottage. We live in two cottages at home, which were knocked into one. It's cosy.'

'Even with two cottages you must be crowded with such a large family. Or are some of your brothers and sisters married?'

'Yes, the majority are, but then there are grandchildren. We are always overflowing at birthdays and New Year, but it's wonderful to be together. I miss them!'

There was a nostalgic note in his voice and Jessamy realised how little she knew of her father's new assistant. He was in lodgings but she was not sure where. When she asked, Alistair told her he was living with an elderly couple, a Mr and Mrs Davison at St Peel. He added, 'They're very kind and Mrs Davison is a good cook, but they have no family and I think they are often lonely. I feel sorry for them.'

The sun had gone in and Jessamy gave a sudden shiver. When Alistair asked if she was cold she said, 'No, it was just someone walking over my grave.'

He raised his hands. 'That is what my mother says. Why? Would it matter if someone did walk over your grave? You would be long since dead. It's the greyness of the moors affecting you.'

Jessamy shook her head. 'Oh no, I love the moors in all their moods. And it's never wholly grey. There are always colours in shrubs, even in the stones themselves.' She traced a finger over the nearby rockface. 'I can imagine someone dabbing several colours on the rocks and then smudging them all in, so that you get a faint marbling here, a streak of rust there, a brown—' She pointed higher up to where several tiny ferns were growing out of a fissure. 'And how many shades of green
125

can you see in that? Isn't nature wonderful?'

'Och, and ye're a girl after my own heart,' Alistair teased. There was a sudden flapping of wings as a curlew rose from a bush and went soaring, its mournful cry hanging on the still air. They watched it until it was out of sight then walked on. Then up popped a rabbit and they stopped again and watched it as it observed them from bright eyes, one ear cocked, nose twitching. The next moment it was away, disappearing down a burrow.

Alistair laughed. 'Fascinating creatures. I used to watch them for hours when I was young. I hated it when we had rabbit stew, which was often, but I was sensible enough to know I would starve if I didn't eat it. We had to live off the land.'

They came to another of the big houses. A carriage was waiting outside, the driver standing by the open carriage door. A woman came out, holding up her skirt. She was young, with a rather arrogant air. She was halfway to the carriage when a man in naval uniform came out, and called a goodbye to someone inside.

The next moment Jessamy's heart began a wild beating as she recognised Captain Montague. He reached the woman, helped her into the carriage and climbed in beside her.

'Well!' Jessamy exclaimed. She came to a stop.

'What's wrong?' Alistair asked.

'That man, it's Captain Montague.'

'So?'

Jessamy realised then how affronted she must have sounded. 'I was surprised at seeing him here.'

'Why? Most of these houses are occupied by people connected with shipping.'

'Yes, I know. I suppose it was because we had seen him on his ship this morning and he didn't mention that he visited anyone on the moors.'

'Should he have done?' Alistair's voice was teasing. 'You like the Captain, don't you?'

'He's an attractive man and I did like him at first, but I feel he has misled us all.' Jessamy told him how Fabian had described his feeling of aloneness then added, 'I discovered that the ship takes passengers, Alistair. They would sit at his table—he would socialise with them during the evenings. How could he ever be lonely?'

Alistair said quietly, 'Haven't you heard the expression that one can be lonely in a crowd, Jessamy?'

Jessamy felt a sudden rush of guilt. How could she be so insensitive? Here was this young man, far from his home and loving family and he had not even been invited to her house for the evening. Her father might have wanted to do so but Esmeralda would never have allowed it. If Alistair had been someone important, yes, but not an assistant at her husband's shop.

She said, 'Captain Montague seems to be such a man of the world I had never thought about him being lonely.' Then, wanting to change the subject she asked Alistair what had made him take up pharmacy.

'I suppose it all started when I was fourteen and my godmother took me to Edinburgh for a holiday. You can imagine my joy—I had never been further than the next village at home and the journey itself was an adventure.' He paused, a smile playing about his lips.

'The big buildings, the castle, all those people—I was entranced. I never stopped talking, asking question after question, and my godmother, being the kind of person she was, answered every one. She had been a teacher in Edinburgh before she married. And then—' His smile died. 'I saw the poverty everywhere, the misery of sick people who were dying for want of medicine, of care.'

'Did your godmother take you to show you this poverty, the despair of sick people, for a purpose?'

Alistair nodded. 'Yes, she did. Her grandfather had been a herbalist and she had seen the work he did healing people or helping those he couldn't cure. After that, the holiday was over for me. I wanted to get back home to gather plants and flowers, learn how to make infusions, decoctions and ointments.'

'Then why did you come to England? Why not stay at home and help people there?'

'I wanted a wider knowledge. My godmother was going to pay for me to get a better education, but she died before this could take place. Her last words to me were, "Help the poor people who are sick, Alistair, make it your goal". I promised and I was full of grief when she died. I had lost a friend.'

After a few moments' silence Jessamy persisted gently, 'But you still haven't said why you came to work with Papa. There must be many pharmacists in Edinburgh.'

'Well, for one thing, I had a contact and I also knew that your father having just failed to become a doctor, was bound to have more knowledge.'

Jessamy glanced at him in surprise. 'Papa, failed to become a doctor?'

Alistair stopped and said, distressed, 'Jessamy, I'm sorry, I thought you would know. I wouldn't have mentioned it otherwise.'

'It's all right, he probably didn't want to talk about it. It must have been a terrible disappointment to him.'

'Yes, indeed. I admire him, we've had a number of talks and I know what a dedicated man he is.' Alistair smiled at her, a gentle smile. 'And it seems as if you are going to follow in his footsteps. He speaks highly of your abilities.'

'But if Papa failed to become a doctor, what chance have I? There is so much opposition to women taking up any profession. As for becoming a doctor... Perhaps I'm just living in a dream world.'

'Oh, now, Jessamy, I'm surprised at you. You don't discard a dream because of opposition. Think of Florence Nightingale. No one could have suffered more from opposition than she did—and look what she achieved. Think of the number of nurses she recruited to go with her to the Crimea. I'm sure the nursing profession would not be what it is at the present time had it not been for this wonderful woman.'

Jessamy's head went up. 'Yes, like you I shall make it my goal. One day I shall come to your surgery and ask for a consultation with *Doctor* Alistair MacKay!'

'With what complaint?' he teased.

'Overwhelming admiration for a man with dedication.' Jessamy laughed suddenly. 'I know—we'll both be doctors and set up a surgery together.'

'And if I fail my exams I shall set up a dispensary for poor people.'

'If I fail mine, I shall join you!'

'Good. We have something to aim for, we shall help one another.'

They stepped out, both light-hearted, not saying much but with Jessamy feeling a closeness to Alistair, a very different feeling to the closeness she felt with Christian, but which she was unable to explain.

There was the plaintive baaing of sheep and a flock of them came ambling from behind two large boulders near a curve in the rockface. Alistair called, 'Yoo-hoo there!' and they began to run, their heavy fleeces swinging.

Jessamy scolded him. 'Shame on you, startling the poor things. You must have given them a fright.'

'It would stir their blood. I wish that was all I had to do, just cropping grass all day.'

'You don't. You have too much to do.'

A few wraiths of mist drifted over hollows and Jessamy could smell the dampness of the sea in her hair. Alistair said, 'I think a fog will come down soon. Perhaps it would be wise to turn back.' But Jessamy, reluctant to break off the rapport she had with Alistair, suggested they walk a little further, saying she knew every stone, every bit of turf on the moors and could lead him back blindfolded.

To this Alistair replied laughing, 'I once made such a statement to my cost. I was responsible for bringing out a search-party in the middle of the night to find myself and my two frozen brothers. I was never so foolhardy again.'

'Then I'll take your advice, Doctor MacKay! I don't think that Papa would be too pleased if such a thing happened, especially as he warned me that the fog could come down.'

Later, Jessamy was glad they had turned back. The fog became so thick in parts it blotted out every landmark and it was only the muffled sounds of traffic from the main road that guided them. When they actually reached the road, lights were on in the shops, but these were just a faint blur. Chadwick greeted them with a sigh of relief. 'I'm glad you're back safely. Give me your coat, Jessamy, and go and warm yourself by the fire.' To Alistair he added, 'I wondered whether you would catch Jessamy up as she's such a quick walker.'

'I hadn't gone very far, Papa. We've had a lovely walk and a long talk. Shall I tell you something? We've both decided to become doctors and share a practice—what do you think of that?'

Jessamy was smiling as she said it, but her smile faded when Chadwick answered quietly, 'Is that so?' and turned away.

Oh, dear how could she have been so stupid? And why had her father kept his medical training from her? His failure was not something to be ashamed of. There might have been a particular reason for it. Could this be one of the things her Cousin Lillian had mentioned? Had there been some sort of scandal? If so, what sort of scandal? Oh, heavens, she must stop this conjecture. She must forget secrets, get on with her life, keep on remembering her goal.

The shop door was suddenly flung open, the bell above tinkling madly. It was Louise. 'Sorry! I was glad to get out of that fog. What a night! It's thick on the moors.' Louise blew

132

on her hands. 'It's freezing fog.' She turned to Chadwick. 'Uncle, Mama wondered if you could spare the time to talk to Christian. Papa won't even consider letting him have a sea trip and we're afraid he'll do something stupid like stowing away on a ship. Jessamy, would you come too? Christian does listen to advice from both of you.'

Chadwick said, 'Poor Christian, I can understand how he feels, but haven't we all suffered from my father's strong will. We sons must abide by his orders and he's determined to have his grandsons follow in their father's trade.'

'It's not right,' Louise said vehemently. 'They should rebel.'

Chadwick, looking sad, raised his shoulders. 'And have our families suffer?'

For the first time Jessamy saw how tied her father was, how he was forced to control her mother's extravagant spending.

'Will you come, for Mama's sake?' Louise pleaded.

Chadwick said yes, of course. He gave orders to Jessamy to wrap up well and told Alistair they would not be long.

CHAPTER EIGHT

To Jessamy, one of the strangest things in a fog was the silence. It was impossible to hear any traffic from the main road and the only occasional sound was the mournful one of the foghorn on the point, and even that was muffled.

As they neared the house Verity opened the front door. The fog, as though eager for warmth rushed in, and dispersed. Verity called, 'I can hear your voices, but I can't see you.' Then in the next breath, 'Oh, there you are. What a night!'

They came up the garden path with Chadwick saying, 'This is one of the worst fogs I can remember—not fit for a dog to be out.' Verity laughed.

It was certainly good to get out of the cold and the dampness. Louise went straight to the fire in the hall and held out her hands. Christian appeared from the sitting room.

He said to Chadwick and Jessamy, 'It was good of you both to come but it won't do any good. Mother ought not to have sent for you.'

Louise was annoyed. 'Hark at the voice of doom. You should be glad we weren't lost in the fog and frozen to death.'

'Who has the voice of doom now?' Christian demanded.

Hats and coats were hung up then they went into the sitting-room, where Verity told them that Francis and Rupert had gone to their grandparents and would probably stay over-night at Beacon Hall. Then she added, 'And as Bertie won't be in until late we can have a quiet talk. Pull your chairs up to the fire.'

Christian, slumped in his chair, long legs stretched out said, 'It's not fair, it's just not fair.'

Chadwick leaned forward, speaking quietly. 'I think you must look at the situation from your father's point of view, Christian. He's paid for you to have a good education and you've had the best of tutors. Being a busi-nessman, he expects a return for it.'

Christian sat up. 'But I ask you, Uncle, is it just? Isn't it another form of slavery? The master cracks the whip and the slave jumps to do his bidding.'

'Now that is an exaggeration Christian, and you know it. Your father is a most caring man who has always done his best for his family. You yourself will have children one day and then you will understand what I'm trying to explain to you.'

'But Uncle Chadwick, should I not have a choice? I have no wish to work in the ware-house. I won't be able to give of my best. There will always be that yearning to go to sea.'

135

Chadwick talked of loyalty and Christian's expression became mulish. He mumbled that if he could not go to sea with his father's permission then he would go without it. Chadwick shook his head.

'I can tell you the experiences of several young men I know, Christian, all who were seeking adventure. If you become a stowaway you will be put to work—and I mean work! At the end of the voyage you will be glad to run away. You'll be unshaven, dirty, halfstarved. Who do you think will employ you? You would get no favours from Captain Montague. Nor from the crew because of your upbringing. On the contrary, the ordinary seamen detest stowaways, seeing them as parasites. You'd suffer, believe me.'

The talk went on but when Chadwick realised he was wasting his time he said he must go. Alistair would be expecting him. Jessamy could stay if she wished.

Christian was slumped back in his chair once more and when Louise said, 'Well, brother, do you still want to be a stowaway?' he looked up and grinned.

'Actually, yes.'

'You're mad,' Jessamy exclaimed. 'What you are seeking is adventure, but what you will get is degradation.'

'Far better degradation than a life of boredom.'

'Rubbish,' Louise snapped. 'You haven't the
136

faintest idea what Uncle Chadwick was talking about. You've always been spoon-fed, the blue-eyed boy. You think that everyone loves you and girls will fall at your feet.'

A slow smile spread over Christian's face. 'They do.'

Jessamy said earnestly, 'Listen to me, Christian. You like girls, you like parties, well—you'll have neither if you go to sea. But, if you stay and work here, and your father sends you abroad, then you'll have a lovely social life. But you will have to work your way up to it. Isn't it worth it?'

He raised his eyebrows. 'Could be. I'll have to think about it, won't I? Clever Jessamy. How about a game of backgammon?'

The fog had cleared by the next morning and Francis and Rupert arrived back in time to walk with them to church, where the Every family accounted for almost half the congregation.

In spite of going to services morning and evening and taking afternoon Sunday-school class, Jessamy liked going to church, but she especially enjoyed the walk with her cousins after the morning service. Sedate when they first set out, once away from the other churchgoers there was plenty of teasing and laughter.

Francis and Rupert had obviously spread the word about the visit to the ship because all the other boys were full of it. That was the life, one declared. Adventure! Why didn't they all take up a seafaring life, even try to get on the same ship? They appealed to Christian for his opinion and were taken aback when he informed them blandly he had given up all thought of it. 'Why?' asked Alvin, the youngest son of Edward and Grace, who kept the hostelry. 'I thought it was all settled.'

Christian gave all the reasons Chadwick and Jessamy had given him, after he had discovered that his father refused to pay for him to have a trip on the *Abercarsis*. He spread his hands. 'How am I to know whether I would take to a seafaring life? One has to start at the bottom and it's certainly not an easy life. No, I've decided to go into the business, learn all I can and then start up my own business.' They were not so sure about this until Christian said, 'Look, if I go to sea I won't see any girls for months and—' he paused and grinned, 'I like my girls.'

'And they like you,' said Alvin's sister Anne shyly.

There were groans from the boys at this and pleas not to make Christian's head swell any more than it did already. But after this there was a discussion, during which they eventually agreed that Christian could be right after all in aiming to have his own business one day.

Christian pressed home his point. 'Just think, once you've become established and made some money you could leave someone in charge, go to London, wine, dine, visit all the theatres, go to balls and—have any girl you want.'

'Yes, yes,' they said, carried away by the promise.

Jessamy found herself laughing. 'Do you know what I think? I think Christian would be throwing a chance away if he did decide to go to sea. He's a born businessman—a fellow after Grandfather's own heart. The only difference is that Christian does not have Grandfather's awful meanness.'

Louise glanced at her. 'But don't you think that Jeremiah's meanness is one of the reasons for his success?'

Jessamy shook her head. 'No, a lot of other things are responsible for success. Dedication, a certain ruthlessness, but charm has a part in it too and Christian has plenty of that.'

Louise suddenly chuckled. 'Shall I tell *you* something? You and our Christian would make a good pair. You would be the steadying influence, Jessamy.'

Louise and Jessamy had dropped behind and Christian stopped and wanted to know what they were talking about.

'Men in general,' Louise said. 'And you would not have been flattered if you could have heard what we had to say.'

'Oh, is that so,' said Rupert. 'Come on, tell us.'

'Well,' Louise began, but that was as far as she got. When they turned a corner in the

139

lane they came face to face with several more of their cousins, Lillian included. Jessamy tensed. The others, apart from Jessamy, greeted the party with pleasure, with Lillian coming in for special attention.

'Doesn't she look beautiful...'

'A joy to behold on this grey Sunday morning...'

'Especially after such a dreary sermon...'

Louise raised her eyebrows at Jessamy and gave a small sniff.

Lillian immediately singled Jessamy out for *her* attention. 'Jessamy dear, what is this I hear about you walking on the moors yesterday afternoon with a *very* attractive stranger? I also understand you got lost in the fog.' Her cousin's voice was sugary sweet.

Although Jessamy was furious she managed a bright smile. 'Why, Lillian, you've been completely misinformed. Mr MacKay and I were back long before the fog came down. He's Papa's new assistant and comes from the Highlands of Scotland. Papa thought he might enjoy some of our lovely moorland air.'

Louise said sharply, 'It's a pity that some folks don't have anything better to do than spy on a couple out for a pleasant stroll.'

'Yes, isn't it,' Lillian replied pleasantly. She turned to her companions. 'Well, shall we continue our stroll?'

The two parties separated and Christian confronted Jessamy. 'You didn't tell me you went walking with this Mr MacKay.'

Jessamy looked at him wide-eyed. 'Should I have done? I didn't think it necessary. Why on earth are Lillian and you putting such an importance on it?'

Francis laughed. 'Because they're both jealous. Actually, I was surprised at Cousin Lillian. Hadn't realised how—how—'

'How slimy she could be?' asked Louise. Francis protested, said he would not put it as strongly as that, but the quiet Anne agreed with Louise.

'Cousin Lillian behaved badly. She was awful —it was the look in her eyes, as if she *hated* Jessamy!'

Christian declared this to be rubbish. They were wronging Lillian, she was a dear, sweet girl. The rest of the cousins agreed.

'Have it your own way,' Louise shrugged, 'but don't say you haven't been warned. You'll find out in time what Lillian is really like. I'm just beginning to know her. If you have any secrets, keep them tightly locked away inside you.'

Rupert scolded Louise for being so melo-dramatic then added, 'You'd better not let any of the family hear what you said, Sis. Lillian is much loved.' To this Louise held up her hand, it was finished as far as she was concerned, she had had her say. But Rose, Digby's eldest daughter, attacked her.

'I think you are horrible to make such

accusations. You've obviously never seen Lillian with the older people, how protective she is, how kind, and as for the younger people—'

Louise interrupted. 'Let me say one more thing. Just don't let the *lovely* Lillian see you having an assignation with a young man or you'll find out what she's capable of.'

Rose flushed so deeply that Louise felt sure she must have secretly met a young man. Rose started to say something but Christian cut her short. 'That is enough.' He spoke in the authoritative tone his grandfather might have used, but being more kindly disposed towards people than his grandfather, he began to tell them about a little monkey he had seen the day before.

'It was on a handcart, pushed by its master, a tiny thing dressed in a red fez, trousers and a spangled jacket. It winked at people as they passed, raised its hat and did a little dance. People laughed and threw coins on to the cart.'

All his listeners, apart from Louise and Rose, burst out laughing. With Jessamy it was a relief to be free from tension.

However, Christian had not forgotten Louise's accusations and spoke to her again when they were on their way home.

There were just the three of them—Francis and Rupert were following a distance behind with Rose and Anne. He spoke quietly.

'You've been in a strange mood lately,

Louise, and I would be glad if you'll tell me if there's something wrong. If there is, I would like to help.'

Jessamy almost expected her cousin to flare up as usual, but Louise was subdued. 'I've felt off colour for a while, but Mama brought a tonic from Uncle Chadwick and I think it's doing me some good. I'm sorry I went on about Cousin Lillian, but I couldn't help it. I really saw her as she was for the very first time. But there, I won't say any more. Christian, if I do need help at any time I will tell you.'

'Good.' He squeezed his sister's arm. In the next breath he said, 'Do you know something, I'm famished!' And then Louise did laugh, and asked if there was a time when he didn't feel famished. And so they entered the house laughing and Bertie greeted them with a chuckle. Such merriment, had they forgotten it was the Sabbath?

This was one of the things Jessamy particularly liked about her uncle. Although he was a regular churchgoer he was never strait-laced, not like Digby, who would never allow any of his family to laugh on a Sunday. It was an insult to the Lord.

Verity came in wanting to know if they had enjoyed their walk. Christian said, 'Fine! We met, among others, three of Uncle James' brood—Paul, Robert and the delectable Lillian, who looked ravishing in silver-grey trimmed with fur. Now—what are we having for lunch?'

143

That evening, Christian brought up the subject of his studies to his father, saying he wanted to finish, he was ready to come into the business.

Bertie shook his head. 'Not yet, my boy. You have two excellent tutors who are teaching you specialist subjects to groom you for when you are ready to take over management. I want you to stay for just another six months. Yes, I know that Francis is coming into the business now, but in a lesser capacity. He will start from the bottom and work his way up. So will Rupert.'

The two younger boys protested at this. Why should they start at the bottom and Christian in a management position?

'There are several sides to this business,' Bertie said, 'all necessary to its success. I knew two years ago what each of you were capable of. You Francis, and you Rupert, are plodders and will get there eventually. Christian sees ahead. He has a way with people and a flair for languages. In time I may even want him to go abroad.' He looked at Christian. 'So now will you be patient and finish your studies?'

'Yes, Papa, although I still feel I'm ready now.'

Her uncle's tolerant attitude was something else that Jessamy admired about him. He had always allowed discussions, even when the children were younger and, although he was

144

stubborn and it was very difficult to change any rules once he had laid them down, it was usually possible to understand his reasoning. The talk after that was of business and ships. Jessamy was content just to listen and Louise seemed quite relaxed, too.

Verity came in, stifling a yawn. She was going to bed, she could hardly keep her eyes open. Then she said to the boys, 'I think you should all make a move as you have to be up early in the morning. Have you packed your bags?' They said they had and when they were on their feet Louise and Jessamy also stood up.

They said goodnight to Bertie and when they were all in the hall Christian drew Jessamy aside. 'I wish I wasn't going away. I'm jealous of that Alistair MacKay and of the Captain— you'll be dining with him tomorrow evening.'

'Not alone, Christian. Both our parents will be there and Louise. Anyway, I'm not in love with him, and neither am I in love with Alistair.'

'Are you sure?' There was almost a pleading in his eyes. 'You will wait for me, Jessamy, won't you? You heard what my father had to say tonight, I'm going to be a businessman, go abroad. I'll have my own business one day and perhaps own a ship.'

Jessamy laughed softly. 'Christian, don't push the years on. I want to enjoy the life I have now. I'm not thinking of marriage to anyone, no, not even to you, and if you are honest,

145

marriage is not really on your mind at the moment.'

He smiled then. 'It's on a lot of things...I want to take you in my arms and—'

'Come along, you two.' Verity was waiting for them on the landing. They went upstairs with Christian teasing his mother—had she always had *her* mother waiting around, spoiling young people's fun?

'You are lucky, son,' she said humorously. '*We* had Bertie's father to contend with. Talk about parental control! We would never have been allowed to go for a walk with our cousins after church, unless we were chaperoned. As for standing in the hall talking to each other alone! Unheard of, sinful!'

'I think you're exaggerating,' Christian teased Verity when he reached her. 'But I love you just the same.' He kissed her on the cheek and she patted his arm.

'I miss you boys every time you go away. I wish your father had let you finish with your studies, Christian. But there.' A mischievous look came into her eyes as she added, her voice lowered, 'Don't tell him I told you so.'

Christian promised and after giving Jessamy's hand a squeeze he left to walk along the landing to the room he shared with his brothers. Verity watched him for a moment then gave a sigh. 'I'm behaving stupidly. Anyone would think he was going away for months instead of a few days.'

Jessamy had always thought that Christian was her aunt's favourite and she was more sure now than ever of it. She kissed Verity then said, 'Louise will be thinking that *I* have gone home. Good night, Auntie, sleep well. Think of the lovely evening we have to look forward to tomorrow.'

'Oh, yes, dinner with Captain Montague. See you in the morning, love.'

They parted and when Jessamy went into the bedroom Louise was almost undressed. 'What on earth were you nattering on about?' she demanded.

Jessamy undid the buttons on the front of her dress then said lightly it was all about mother love, sons wanting to be free from the parental strings and the bad old days, when cousins were not allowed to walk together unless they were chaperoned.

'What are you talking about?' Louise asked in a peeved voice.

'Exactly what I said. Life can be interesting at times, can't it?'

'Interesting? When? All I can see is a dreary life ahead for the rest of my days.'

'What about tomorrow evening when we shall see the handsome Captain Montague.'

'Oh, him,' Louise said. 'You call that a treat?'

In spite of her words Louise, after pulling her nightdress over her head, stood silent and in the flickering light of the candle, Jessamy

147

was sure she saw a dreamy look in her eyes.

She said softly, 'I think we've been fooling ourselves about the Captain. He's someone I certainly want to meet again, and I'm sure that you do, too.'

'I don't care if I never see him again. What does really bother me is Cousin Lillian. Who told her you were on the moors yesterday afternoon with Alistair?'

'It could be anyone—does it matter? She's said much worse things to me.'

'I know and that's what gets under my skin.' Louise picked up her underskirts and threw them over the back of the chair. 'She's so smarmy and some of them this morning swallowed it up, hook line and sinker. *Dear sweet* Lillian. And anyway, what made *you* change your mind? You had plenty to say about her the other day.'

'I know. I think it was the sermon when the vicar talked about trying to love our enemies and forgive them their sins.'

'*Love Lillian?*'

Louise's voice was high-pitched and Jessamy put a finger to her lips. 'Shh, they'll hear you.'

'I don't care. *Love* Lillian! Yes, like I love Aunt Fanny and her seven sisters!'

Aunt Fanny and her seven sisters were imaginary figures conjured up by the girls when they were young. It helped them to let off steam after they had been reprimanded for some misdemeanour. Suddenly, Jessamy was laughing

148

and after a moment Louise was laughing too and they covered their mouths so that the rest of the family wouldn't hear them. Then Louise, sobering, said, 'If Aunt Dorcas was here she would be telling us that all this laughter would be followed by tears tomorrow.'

To this Jessamy answered lighly, 'Who cares? And anyway I prefer to think of Grandmother's saying "Be happy while you may".' She flung back the bedclothes. 'Come along, let's get into bed and dream the night away.'

Louise's short happy mood was already over, and she said she was more likely to have nightmares over Lillian, whom she felt like strangling. But nothing could take away Jessamy's pleasure at the thought of dining with the Captain the following evening. She climbed into bed and as her searching foot found the spot where the little maid had let the warming pan linger she thought how good life was. Of course, there were the good bits and the bad ones, but one must take the rough with the smooth—another of her grandmother's expressions. And who could be happier than Henrietta, despite being trapped indoors by her indisposition...

CHAPTER NINE

On the Monday when Jessamy walked home with her father at midday she felt happier than she had for some time. There was the dinner to look forward to, of course, but it was more than that. Louise had been laughing at breakfast; just like her former self and the atmosphere in her aunt and uncle's house had gone.

She told her father about Bertie wanting Christian to take a management role when he finished his studies, and Chadwick said he wished him luck. A man came out of a nearby cottage and Chadwick raised a hand in greeting. 'Good morning to you, Mr Midgin. Do I smell rain in the air?'

'Judging by my rheumatics when I got up this morning it could well be, but not until later in the day, I'm thinking. The missus was talking about coming to see you. She has a few pains in her chest.'

Chadwick said he would look in on Mrs Midgin later and see she had some medicine, then they parted. Curious to know why her father had failed to become a doctor, but knowing she could not ask him directly, Jessamy tried to get to it in a roundabout way. 'Papa,

Mr Midgin and other people address you as "doctor" and a woman at the party the other night was talking about her physician. What exactly is the difference?'

'A physician deals only in medicine, Jessamy, but a doctor can deal in medicine and surgery, if he is qualified for both.'

'Have you ever wanted to become a—doctor?'

'Yes, I have, but I failed my exams. I was foolish, Jessamy, immature and overconfident. Instead of attending to my studies, I ran wild with the other students and ruined my only chance of qualifying in medicine. Oh, how clever we thought ourselves.'

There was such bleakness in his voice that Jessamy said gently, 'Does it matter so much, Papa, failing your exams? You are an expert on so many medical matters and look how people sing your praises. Mrs Wright was telling Alistair that you're a miracle worker. She told him she couldn't walk for the rheumatics when she first came to St Peel and now she gets about, does her own work and—'

'Because she not only had faith, but perseverance. She takes a tisane of nettles three times a day, and has done so for months. Not that this will cure everyone, but then many people will not persevere. No, Jessamy, I am no miracle worker.'

'But, Papa, if you have made it possible to help cure one person of an illness, isn't it worth more than a piece of paper saying that you are a qualified doctor?'

He glanced at her and a slow smile spread over his face. 'You do my heart good, child. Your faith in me makes me feel that I *can* work miracles.'

'I'll always have that faith, Papa.'

When they arrived home Chadwick went round to the back of the house to see how some new plants from abroad were faring while Jessamy went inside. To her surprise, Esmeralda asked her what dress she was planning to wear that evening.

'I thought the pale green one with the darker velvet trimmings.' She made no mention of the fact it was because Fabian apparently liked it.'

'Ah, only I didn't want to wear anything that would detract from you. I thought of wearing my brown velvet.'

Jessamy said to Louise that evening, 'I nearly fainted when Mama said she didn't want to detract from *me*.'

To this Louise replied wryly, 'What she meant was, she didn't want you to look more attractive than herself. You'll see—she won't be wearing the brown velvet, but something much more exotic.'

However, Esmeralda did wear the brown velvet and Louise, her eyebrows raised, said to Jessamy, 'One does get surprises.'

When Captain Montague greeted Esmeralda, he bowed low over her hand and kissed it. 'You look charming, Mrs Every.' Louise nudged Jessamy, but Jessamy was not perturbed. The look Fabian had given her when he arrived was enough to keep her happy for the rest of the evening—no—for the rest of the week. It was a special look that had not been there when he greeted Louise or her mother. And while Chadwick was placing a white fur wrap about his wife's shoulders, Fabian said in a low voice to Jessamy, 'I've been looking forward all day to seeing you. Will you sit beside me at dinner?'

Jessamy whispered, 'I'm afraid I will have no say in the matter, Captain Montague. I shall have to sit where I am placed.'

He smiled and gave her an understanding nod. But when the carriage arrived he managed to draw Jessamy aside and say, 'You are wearing my favourite dress,' which had Jessamy feeling that nothing more wonderful could happen to her that evening.

Bertie and Verity, who were to meet them at the hostelry, arrived as Chadwick's party stepped out of the carriage. After exchanging pleasantries they all went inside. Jessamy and Louise had both visited the Highwayman's Arms a number of times before, but always during the day. They had never had a meal there. Now, as they entered the candle and lamp-lit room with its red wallpaper patterned in gold Chinese dragons Jessamy felt transported into another world. There was a cosmopolitan air. At one table were Orientals, all talking in their own tongue; at another were swarthy-skinned men, immaculately dressed, the diamonds in their rings winking as they gesticulated, their ladies elegant in evening dresses.

In alcoves were a few older men, their women from a different class. There were families, but overall there was a feeling of gaiety in the talk, the laughter. In front of the huge stone fireplace a side of beef was roasting on a spit, the appetising smell making Jessamy's mouth water. Young waiters were lined up to collect the thick slices of beef being carved by the chef.

The Captain and his party stood in the background while waiting for Edward who was keeping them a table, but they all, including Fabian, appeared to be interested in the scene. Then Edward arrived and shook the hand of each one as he welcomed them. Edward had a pleasant manner, kindly, concerned, not only for his family but his customers. He was on the portly side like Bertie, but he was not so fun-loving as his brother.

'I have a table at the far side of the room for you,' he said. 'It's quieter, but you'll be able to observe all that is going on.'

Bertie chuckled. 'Aye, and there's plenty of that, judging by that lot over there.' He indicated the alcoves where one man was 'walking' his fingers up the bare arm of his companion, while another was openly kissing his woman.

'Disgusting,' Esmeralda declared, to which Bertie replied in his amiable way, 'It's life, Esmeralda dear, you can't ignore it.'

'I can,' she snapped and motioned Edward to show them to their table.

As the party moved out of the light it seemed to Jessamy that some of the talk died away, especially when they reached the centre of the room. Jessamy realised it was the Captain who was the attraction. Fabian certainly did make an imposing figure, with his build, good looks and authoritative air, but he seemed quite unconcerned by the attention, chatting to Esmeralda as they negotiated tables.

'Here we are,' said Edward, pointing out a long narrow table near the wall. Then he added to Esmeralda, 'I've placed everyone as you suggested.' Jessamy and Louise exchanged glances, but made no remark.

It was the kind of table where all the diners would sit at one side only, facing the room, but where those in the middle of the table would have no contact with the ones at the end.

Then Fabian said to Edward, 'I'm afraid I don't like this arrangement, Mr Every. Conversation is part of dining out and with the chairs as they are placed we would have to shout at one another. Could we have some of them brought to this side?' It was all pleasantly said, but Edward looked a little worried, while Esmeralda appeared to be trying

155

to control her annoyance.

'But Captain,' she said, 'I understand there will be performers later—a juggler, a man balancing plates on sticks and—'

Fabian, smiling, interrupted. 'Then, Mrs Every, the ones with their backs to the room can turn their chairs around when the performance starts. And I'm sure it will not be commencing until after we have finished our meal.'

Edward confirmed this and a man was brought to alter the position of their chairs. And that his how Jessamy and Louise came to find themselves seated on either side of the Captain, facing the others. 'There,' he said, with one of his devastating smiles. 'Isn't that much better? Now we can all talk to one another.'

The talk at first was between Bertie and Fabian, with Chadwick and Verity obviously conscious that Esmeralda was in a temper at having her arrangements altered. However, when the wine was brought and poured, Fabian appealed to Esmeralda saying, 'I know you are a connoisseur of wine, Mrs Every. Will you tell me if you approve of my choice?'

For the first time since they had sat at the table Esmeralda seemed to relax. She tasted the wine and gave a nod. 'I do approve, Captain Montague. It is excellent.'

Jessamy noticed that her father and aunt were now relaxed and she was very much aware at that moment of how someone quite fragile-looking like her mother could dominate more than one person's life. Not that her father was downtrodden by her mother, but it was obviously important to Chadwick that Esmeralda's evening was made as pleasant as possible. Was that because he loved her so much? Jessamy had never really been able to assess the amount of affection between them.

The soup was brought: it was mulligatawny, and tasted excellent. The men had been discussing some Act of Parliament but later, while they were waiting for the next course Bertie said, 'How about some of your stories, Captain Montague? I was told the other day that the Indian natives of Peru more or less live on the leaves of the cocoa plant and are very strong.'

Fabian nodded. 'That is true. They climb incredible heights of over twelve thousand feet. It's said they have enlarged lungs to cope with the air at that height. I don't know, of course, if this is correct but then—nature does adjust to ways of living.'

'What started the cocoa trade?' Verity asked.

'I understand it goes back to AD 500 when cocoa leaves were found in the burial urns of many Peruvians. However, I feel sure its stimulant qualities must have been known long before this.'

Verity laughed. 'I could do with something to give me more strength.'

Fabian teased her. Then she must go to Peru,

157

he said, and climb the slopes, which in places were almost vertical. She would be allowed to stop every hour for a brief rest and change her 'chew' for a fresh one. After a pause he added, 'But you must also be prepared to have red-rimmed, sunken eyes, trembling lips, green and crusted teeth, and—' he chuckled, 'I had better stop there.'

They were all pulling faces with Esmeralda saying, 'I do declare you've put me off drinking cocoa for the rest of my life!'

'No, you mustn't. You enjoy it. It's very different from chewing leaves, wouldn't you agree?'

Bertie said, 'Ah, here is our roast beef. I know I'm going to enjoy this!'

The meal was succulent and Jessamy thought it was the best she had ever tasted. The syllabub that followed was approved by all. When they had finished dessert, Grace, Edward's wife, came up to greet them. The men jumped to their feet offering her a chair, but she thanked them and said she was on desk-duty as the woman who usually did this task had been taken ill. 'But I'll see you all later,' she added. 'You must come and have a drink in our own private room.'

The atmosphere was much less formal than when they dined at home and Jessamy kept thinking it was the best evening she had ever known. The Captain took pains to draw her and Louise into the conversation, and for once Esmeralda showed no disapproval.

When the performers were announced Fabian declared that this was where Jessamy, Louise and himself did a 'right-about turn'. He then asked the others to excuse them, to which Esmeralda replied, quite gaily for her, '*You*, Captain Montague, are excused anything!' The next moment she looked self-conscious at speaking so freely, that is until Bertie held up his glass and said, 'Eat, drink and be merry, that is my motto!' Then Esmeralda was laughing, and touched her glass to his.

Jessamy felt a little shocked. This was a side of her mother she had never seen before. She was behaving as freely as some of the women in the alcoves. She looked at her father and Jessamy's bubble of happiness began to dissolve. Chadwick and Verity were looking into one another's eyes and touching glasses. Oh, no, not her father, not her Aunt Verity, they were the pillars on which her life was built. If they crumpled she had nothing.

The three chairs were rearranged and as Fabian, Louise and Jessamy sat down a juggler was announced. Jessamy was aware of oranges being thrown into the air and caught, but her mind was elsewhere. Then when the oranges were replaced by knives and gasps came from the diners her gaze went to the various groups at different tables. They seemed to be respectable people out for an evening's enjoyment: the eyes of the younger people were rounded with wonder, while the older ones were smiling and ready to gasp as the act became more dangerous.

Jessamy's eyes went to the couples in the alcoves and she saw that these older men and their young companions all seemed to be caught up in the act and were watching with almost a childlike wonder. Was their evening out more innocent than she had imagined? But no, she had seen them earlier behaving quite differently... There was loud applause as the juggler finished his act.

'Good, wasn't he?' enthused Louise. 'My heart was in my mouth every time he flung those knives up. I was sure one would drop and stab him.'

Why had Louise not noticed anything going on between Verity and Chadwick? Jessamy began to wonder if she had exaggerated the whole incident.

Men were now carrying in a table with holes in it, where they later placed canes. Louise explained that plates would be put on top of each cane, one at a time, and the man would start spinning them. 'The most difficult thing he has to do is keep them spinning,' Louise said. 'Papa once told me about seeing this act.'

A tall, thin man in evening dress came forward to explain what Louise had just told her. Jessamy forced herself to watch, knowing if she continued like this her mood would be noticed. And she had to admire the expertise of the man. At one time he had all the plates spinning but when one started to slow there were cries from the audience. 'Watch the first plate, hurry, hurry!'

Time and again there were gasps and shouts, until at last the spinning plates were removed one by one then there was loud applause.

'That man will take some beating,' Bertie exclaimed. But then a clown came on with some performing dogs, the animals stealing the hearts of the audience. 'Ah, aren't they lovely...the dear little things... They seem to love their master.'

The dogs jumped through hoops, did somersaults and walked on their hind legs, for which they received a biscuit each. Jessamy glanced round at her mother and saw that her gaze was on the Captain's back. At that moment Fabian stood up and said lightly to Louise and Jessamy, 'Well, shall we join our other guests?' The chairs were turned again and Bertie called in his jocular way, 'Welcome back to the fold.'

When Fabian offered to pour more wine Esmeralda put her hand over her glass. 'Not for me, thank you, Captain. I think I've had enough, more than enough.' She spoke quietly and Jessamy wondered if it had been the wine earlier that had gone to her mother's head.

Edward came up then and invited them into their sitting-room. He smiled. 'We are free for an hour! Quite a change in this line. Grace and

I never seem to have a minute to call our own these days.'

They all went into a large room, which served as an office as well as a sitting-room. It was panelled in dark oak, with leather-covered chairs and dark brown linoleum on the floors. Louise had been in it before during the day, when it appeared sombre but in the lamplight, with the flames from the blazing fire casting dancing shadows on the walls and glinting in the crystal glasses and decanters on a side table, it seemed very cosy.

Edward offered drinks, but only the men accepted. Jessamy and Louise were given fruit drinks, without having been given a choice.

Grace addressed Fabian. 'I wonder whether you know, Captain Montague, that you are responsible for our boys wanting to go to sea? Alvin, Gervase and Andrew were full of it, talking of nothing else yesterday afternoon.'

Edward added laughingly, 'I really had to put my foot down and warn them of dire consequences if they kept on talking about it.'

Fabian spread his hands. 'You are robbing them of an interesting future. It is a healthy life and would make men of them.'

'True,' Grace admitted, nodding.

Edward scolded her. 'Don't listen to him, my love. Captain Montague has a way with him, all the boys said so.'

Fabian sat back and crossed one long leg over the other. 'Just let me ask you something, Mr

162

Every. Was there anything else you wanted to do when you were younger, other than run a hostelry?'

'Indeed there was. Would you believe that I wanted to be a shepherd?' They all laughed and Edward was chuckling, too. 'Yes, a shepherd!'

'What *was* the attraction?' Esmeralda drawled. 'It must be the most boring job I can think of, watching a flock of sheep.'

'No, it isn't. I used to go and sit with a shepherd when I was a boy during the school holidays, and it was a most rewarding experience. I was only twelve at the time and although I hated to go to church and to Sunday school I began to feel God all around me. The sheep became people to me. You'd be surprised at how every single one was different. Sometimes I would find several standing watching us and I'm sure they were weighing *us* up. Those animals have an intelligence that few people give them credit for.'

Bertie shook his head. 'No, I can't accept that, Eddie boy. I never could when you used to talk about them as people. I used to think you would end up a loonie.'

Edward looked from one to the other. 'Have any of you listened to silence? It's awe-inspiring.' His eyes had taken on a faraway look. 'You and the shepherd and his flock are the only ones in the world. You are enclosed, safe.' For a few moments Edward was lost to the people in the room, then he came to and gave a self-conscious laugh. 'Sorry, I really did let myself get carried away, but at the same time...I would not have missed that experience.'

Jessamy said quietly, 'I think that Captain Montague will understand what you mean. He told us of his feeling of aloneness during the middle watch when the sea and sky seem to stretch into eternity.' She stopped suddenly, like Edward, self-conscious. Then seeing her mother watching her intently she went on, with a slight feeling of defiance, 'I don't think I quite understood it then, but—' she looked at Edward, 'I do now, since you spoke of the silence. One experiences it in a lesser way, walking alone on the moors.'

'Exactly,' Fabian said. 'I think everyone in their life has an experience of this kind when we are very much aware of the vastness of the universe and how little we know about it.'

They all fell silent and it was Bertie who broke the silence, saying with a chuckle, 'Anyone would think we were at a wake.' He held up his empty glass. 'How about a refill, Eddie? Captain? Chadwick?'

The talk became general then, with the three women talking clothes, the men discussing commerce, and Jessamy and Louise listening.

Jessamy wondered now how she could have condemned Fabian Montague as a fraud. He *had* been sincere, she could understand that now. One could feel completely alone at times and not really want anyone else. Every now and then she would glance at her mother, who was more animated than usual, then at her father who was sitting next to Verity, but there was no more looking soulfully into one another's eyes. In fact, by now Jessamy had convinced herself she had imagined this intimacy between them. Verity was just saying that they really ought to be going, when there was a knock at the door. When Edward went to answer it there were some gabbled words before he left, closing the door behind him.

When he re-entered moments later, his expression was grave. He looked from Bertie to Verity. 'I'm sorry, but I'm afraid I have some bad news for you.'

Bertie, who had been puffing away on a cigar, took it out of his mouth. 'Bad news? Has something happened at the warehouse?'

'No, but apparently Christian left his school earlier this evening with the intention of going to the docks to try and stow away on a ship.'

'Stow away? That's ridiculous, he—'

'He's gone, Bertie.'

Verity, whose face had drained of colour, whispered, 'I don't believe it, not Christian.'

Fabian was on his feet. 'Three ships are due to leave on the tide, we might be in time to stop him.'

'Come on then, let's go,' Chadwick said.

Verity wanted to go with the men but Bertie

laid a hand on her arm. 'You stay, love, we'll come back here.'

When the men had gone Verity sank back into her chair. 'Christian wouldn't do such a thing, he was happy going back to his studies.'

'He wasn't.' Louise whispered to Jessamy. 'I knew what was going to happen, why didn't they?'

Grace said quietly, 'Try not to worry, Verity. I think they may yet be in time. I'll make us some tea.'

It was nearly an hour before the men returned and it was easy to see by their faces that they had been too late.

Bertie raised his shoulders with a helpless gesture. 'I'm sorry, Verity love.' He took her in his arms.

CHAPTER TEN

Three impressions of the evening at the hostelry remained vividly in Jessamy's mind the following morning: her mother, who had sat so wooden, seeming incapable of offering any comfort to Verity; her uncle Bertie, standing, the cigar between his fingers asking, 'What news? Has something happened at the warehouse?'; and later her mother insisting she come home to sleep, saying that her uncle and aunt would not want an intruder at a time like this.

An intruder? Jessamy thought it was about the most hurtful thing Esmeralda had ever said to her. She was family at her uncle and aunt's house. They had told her so, many times. *Close* family. They loved her.

Although it had been after two o'clock when they went to bed Chadwick was up at his usual time. Jessamy, who had been awake for the past hour, went down to have breakfast with him.

'I couldn't sleep,' she said. 'I'll come to the shop with you.'

Although Chadwick gave her an anxious glance he made no remark. In fact it was not until the porridge had been served that he spoke.

'Jessamy, you are not to worry over your cousin. Christian is not the first son to defy his father and he won't be the last. Whether he will take to a seafaring life remains to be seen.'

'I'll miss him,' she said. 'He's like a brother to me.'

'I know.' He reached over and laid a hand on hers. 'We'll all miss him. Your uncle and aunt especially. Bertie feels he's been betrayed.'

Betrayed? Did a son's welfare not come before business? All her uncle had thought about last night was whether something had happened to the warehouse. Jessamy pushed the porridge around the bowl with her spoon and looked up.

'And I expect that Grandfather, too, will think only of who will replace Christian in his plans if he does take to a seafaring life.'

Chadwick sighed. 'I suppose so. But the one I really feel sorry for is Verity.' Jessamy tensed. 'She looked dreadful,' Chadwick went on. 'Christian is her eldest and her favourite, although she would not admit it.'

'Think how lucky you are,' Jessamy retorted, 'having only me to worry about.' The next moment she could have bitten her tongue out when she saw the distress in her father's eyes.

'Oh, Papa, I'm sorry, that was a dreadful thing to say. I'm upset.'

'Of course you are, Jessamy dear. I think you had better stay at home today.'

'No, no, that's the last thing I want to do. I'm coming to the shop, I need something to occupy me.'

Chadwick smiled then. 'That is no problem. I had planned to do some infusions this morning.' He got up. 'Let me get you some bacon and egg.'

There was a frost and although Jessamy normally enjoyed the walk to the shop on such a morning, there was a chill inside her that had nothing to do with the weather, but she was glad to get into the shop all the same. Chadwick had banked up the fire in the back room the night before and the iron stove also gave out a warmth.

Before long Chadwick had the fire going and a kettle boiled.

Jessamy had just made some tea when Alistair arrived. As he closed the shop door he called, 'It's a nippy morning!' He came into the back rubbing his hands then, seeing Jessamy, he stopped. 'Good gracious, have I overslept by mistake?'

'No!' Chadwick laughed. 'No, you haven't. Jessamy was eager to get some work done. You've arrived in time, she's just brewed some tea.'

Alistair took off his coat and cap and hung them up. 'And did you both enjoy your evening?'

Jessamy, realising that her father was attempting to act normally, decided to try and do the same. 'The first part of it, yes. It was a lovely dinner, and good company, but we learned later that my cousin Christian had run away to sea. Quite adventurous! I'm sure he'll have plenty to tell us when he returns from wherever he gets to.'

Jessamy poured the tea and handed a mug to him and Alistair said, 'It takes quite a lot of courage to do that. It was a part of my boyhood dreams to go to sea...I think it is part of the dreams of a lot of children.'

At half-past nine Louise came in. Jessamy said, 'I wondered where you were. How are things at home?'

169

'It was like being in a morgue at breakfast. I was glad when Papa left to go to the warehouse. I would have liked to have called for you, but felt I couldn't leave Mama on her own, then your mother arrived.'

Jessamy eyed her cousin in some astonishment. 'Mama, out at this time in the morning? I can't believe it.'

'Neither could I but do you know she seemed genuinely concerned for Mama. I left them to their chat.' Louise paused then said, 'Jessamy, could I stay with you this morning? I don't want to go to the warehouse.'

'Yes, of course. We're going to do some infusions.'

'That's all right, I'll help.'

Although Louise would help gather plants in the spring and summer her heart was not in it, not like their other cousins who made it more or less a social occasion. But she brought the herbs to be weighed for the infusions and helped when they made up ointment. While they worked, Alistair talked about his life in the highlands.

When a woman came in later for something to ease indigestion she said she knew they were making medicines because as soon as she opened her back door she could smell them—and she lived over a mile away.

'And isn't it a beautiful fragrance?' Jessamy teased.

'Sometimes it is, yes,' said the woman, 'but

sometimes it smells like rotten eggs. Still,' she added, 'if you want to be cured it has to be endured.'

Word came from Esmeralda to say she would be staying with Verity for the day so Louise went home with Chadwick and Jessamy for lunch. And Jessamy was glad that her father made no mention of Christian, with the talk centring mainly on herbs. Afterwards Louise asked if she and Jessamy could take a walk on the moors, as she had something she wanted to talk over with her. Chadwick agreed at once. They had both worked hard that morning.

Curious to know what Louise wanted to discuss, Jessamy expected her cousin to confide in her once they left the house. However, they walked for quite a way in silence and when Jessamy became aware that Louise had gone into one of her sullen moods she said, 'What is on your mind?'

Louise raised her shoulders. 'I don't know now whether I want to talk about it.' When Jessamy pointed out gently the old adage that a trouble shared is a trouble halved, Louise laughed. It was a harsh sound.

'Sharing this won't halve it.' They had reached an outcropping of rocks and Louise sat on a flat slab. Jessamy sat down beside her and waited.

The wind was cold and the sky was heavy with snow clouds. Louise was silent for a long while then she said suddenly: 'I'm pregnant.'

For a moment Jessamy thought she must have misunderstood but then Louise turned her head. 'Yes, p-r-e-g-n-a-n-t. What lovely news for the family to gossip over.'

As the confirmation of all her worst fears hit her, Jessamy's heart began beating in slow, painful thuds. 'Are you sure, Louise? I mean to say, women do make mistakes.'

'This is no mistake,' Louise replied grimly. 'And don't start lecturing me. Also, don't start asking who the father is because you won't get to know, nor will anyone, not ever.'

Jessamy hesitated a moment then she said, 'Louise, you know when some women come into the shop and start whispering their troubles to Papa. Well, one time you said that a woman was asking for something to—well, to get rid of a baby. I don't know whether he gave her anything or whether he would give you—'

'He wouldn't, and anyway it's too late for that,' Louise snapped. 'I felt the baby give a tiny movement two days ago.'

Jessamy stared at her wide-eyed. 'But a baby has to be about four or five months before it moves, doesn't it? It would be too late to take anything. Why didn't you think about it earlier, not that I agree with such a thing, but—'

'I didn't *know* I was having a baby, or perhaps I tried to delude myself. I was still having my monthly periods, you see. People say it's not possible, but it is, isn't it? I've proved it. I didn't have any morning sickness either. I didn't have any change that would lead me to believe...although I think I suspected the truth, all along. I don't even look any fatter, well, just a little bit perhaps.'

Tears suddenly filled Louise's eyes as she went on in a despairing way, 'I don't know what to do, Jessamy. I can't even tell Mama, she has enough trouble to deal with.'

Jessamy sat beside her and put an arm around her. 'I don't know either, Louise, I've never met such a situation before. Would the—would the baby's father marry you?'

'Leave the father out of it, please,' Louise said in an anguished voice. She bowed her head and a big tear rolled slowly down her cheek and fell on Jessamy's hand. 'I would like to kill myself, but I can't because the baby would die too and it's not its fault. I'll probably end up in a nunnery or some such place until the baby's born. And I don't think I could bear it, being all alone.'

Jessamy put her other arm around her cousin and rocked her. 'You won't be alone. I'll go with you, I promise.'

'But you couldn't! There's the shop and anyway, your mother wouldn't let you. She would think that some of the stigma would rub off on you, and *that* she would not like.'

'Papa would let me go,' Jessamy said fiercely.

173

'He would understand, and he is the master in the house. And anyway, you would do the same for me.'

'I don't think so, Jessamy,' Louise said, a wryness in her voice. 'I'm made of more selfish stuff than you. I won't even keep the baby, I don't want it. It will have to be adopted.'

'Louise no! You couldn't.'

'I could and will. What sort of life would I have with a bastard child clinging to my skirts? And Mother? Does she have to suffer because of what has happened?'

Louise suddenly began to unbutton her coat and snatching Jessamy's hand placed it on her middle. 'There it is, the baby moving. Can you feel it?'

Jessamy felt choked at the wonder of it. A baby moving inside her cousin. A tiny live thing. Oh, how could she not want it? Jessamy was sure at that moment that by the time the baby was born Louise *would* want it, love it. After all, even though the baby's father was obviously married, Louise had loved him, otherwise she would not have done what she did. Perhaps she still loved him...

She said softly, 'It's wonderful, Louise. Thank you so much for letting me feel the baby's movements. I'm sure after you've been carrying the little mite for the next few months you'll want to kill anyone who tried to take it away from you.'

Louise got up and buttoned her coat. 'I

174

doubt it, but if you go on loving it, that will make up to it for what I lack. We'd better go now. I'll leave it for another week before saying anything about the baby but in the meantime, don't tell anyone. Not *anyone*. Promise.'

Jessamy promised but she felt full of grief that this awful thing had happened.

Louise decided to go home, saying her mother might feel she was neglecting her, and Jessamy, not wanting to go back to the shop just then made up her mind to go and see her grandmother. She had promised to tell the old lady all about the dinner at the Highwayman's Arms.

Henrietta welcomed her, arms outstretched. 'Jessamy dear, how lovely to see you. I want to hear all the news of Christian. Jeremiah has scared everyone away this morning with his bad temper. He doesn't want to talk about the lad, so I don't get the chance to, either.' She patted the stool beside her. 'Come along, sit down. I want to know everything that happened last night.'

Jessamy had wondered how she was going to talk to her grandmother without blurting out Louise's trouble, but with the old lady so eager for news she found it easy to start describing events at the dinner, concluding, 'But then, of course, we had the awful news that Christian had run away to sea.'

'What do you mean by awful news?' Henrietta demanded. 'I thought it the best news I had heard in a long while. Christian is a brave boy. He defied everyone, including Jeremiah, and did what he wanted, not what he was told to do like all the Every men. Now then, I want to know about the wonderful Captain Montague. Are you in love with him?'

Jessamy, taken aback by the sudden question said, 'I think most women are attracted to him.'

'I don't want to know what other women think about him, Jessamy dear. I want to know *your* feelings for him.'

'Well I, yes, I think I am. It's not only because he's so good-looking, it's something else. He has a charm, a power. Sometimes, although he hasn't touched me, I feel this power or whatever it is go right through me.'

'And it makes your skin tingle.' Henrietta hugged herself and gave a girlish giggle. 'I know that feeling, it's exciting, isn't it?' Her eyes twinkled. 'And dangerous. You do realise that, don't you?'

Jessamy nodded. 'Yes, that is why I try not to daydream too much about him.'

Henrietta's eyes widened in dismay. 'Oh, but you must daydream about him. That is part of the delight of being in love. I've been in love dozens of times and the joy has been the dreaming.'

'But you have only one real love,' Jessamy said softly.

'Of course, but that's a different kind of love.

176

The daydreaming is fantasy where everything is beautiful. The real kind is the one where you bite your tongue when your husband accuses you of allowing him to oversleep, who blames you if he can't find his cuff-links, or his tiepin and who shouts that you must get rid of your very excellent cook because once, only once, through no fault of her own, the meal is ten minutes late.'

Henrietta smoothed a wrinkled hand over the rug on her knees. 'And that's not all, Jessamy. You also have to bite your tongue when your husband is fawning over an attractive woman because you know if you mention it he'll deny it and if you harp on about it the evening will end up in a full-scale row.'

Jessamy smiled. 'You're funny and lovely, Grandma.'

'It's the truth, Jessamy. You must be prepared to put up with a hundred and one little things that irritate when you marry because men refuse to be put in the wrong. Nurse them, coax them, and give them a lot of love and you'll get on splendidly.'

Jessamy said, 'Mama is always saying that men are selfish. And I can't help thinking that Christian was a little selfish in running away. He didn't give a thought to the people he had left behind.'

'Of course it was selfish, but you must also remember it took a lot of courage for Christian to leave all those he loved to go to heaven

177

knows what. Stowaways aren't kindly treated. Your grandfather left home and if he hadn't—what would he be doing now? Probably mucking out byres and ploughing the land, things he hated. He was farseeing.'

Jessamy eyed her grandmother with interest. She knew that her grandfather originally came from farming stock, but she had never known how he made his first money. When she asked, Henrietta said, 'He went from village to village doing odd jobs, tackling anything from repairing a cart to thatching a cottage. Clever is my Jeremiah.' There was pride in the old lady's voice. 'He was a good-looking lad and had a way with him. Women liked him, so they gave him food, an extra copper or two. He saved every penny and when he had enough money he bought produce and took it to market.'

'Well,' Jessamy said, 'and I didn't know.'

'He was dedicated. He got up at four o'clock every morning winter and summer and bedded down in somebody's barn at ten o'clock at night. So you see, Jessamy, how true are the words ''Tall trees from little acorns grow''. Jeremiah can never really condemn Christian for leaving home, nor must you.'

When Jessamy sat silent Henrietta said gently, 'And what other worry do you have on your mind, my love?' Jessamy looked up startled and her grandmother laid a hand over hers. 'Is it Louise? I know what's wrong with her and

I'm surprised her mother doesn't seem to know. I've noticed how, like some pregnant women, she keeps smoothing her hand over her stomach, and I've noticed that look of despair in her eyes... Oh, it's plain for anyone with eyes to see. If Verity does know, she hasn't said anything—which is unlike her.'

'Aunt Verity doesn't know. Louise—' Jessamy stopped suddenly, appalled at what she had just blurted out. She burst into tears. 'I promised I wouldn't tell anyone.'

'And you haven't, Jessamy dear. I'm glad you know I know, it's wrong for you to have to share such a burden. There, there, now dry your eyes and we shall have a talk.' Henrietta held out her handkerchief. 'You'll feel better when we've sorted something out.'

Jessamy, calmer now, said, 'Louise thought she would be sent to a convent until she's had the baby. I promised I would go with her, but although I'll keep my promise I don't want to be shut away in a convent.'

'And you won't, my love, neither of you, not if Bertie and Verity are willing to adopt my plan. I can't say any more about it until I've spoken to your aunt and uncle but I can assure you it would not be like a penance. You especially, Jessamy, could actually enjoy your stay with Louise.'

The fact that her grandmother knew about Louise had taken such a load from Jessamy's mind that she left Beacon Hall feeling quite

179

light-hearted. She only wished she was able to tell Louise of her grandmother's plans for the coming months.

CHAPTER ELEVEN

When Jessamy arrived back at the shop Verity was there, talking to Chadwick. He said, 'Oh, there you are, love. We were wondering where you were. Louise said you had left her earlier.'

'Yes, I went to see Grandma. I promised I would call to tell her about our evening at the Highwayman's Arms.' After a pause Jessamy went on, 'She said she thought Christian very courageous to do what he did.'

Verity nodded slowly. 'And I think she's right. I had a long talk with your mother, who thinks the same as Gran, and I'm trying to accept it. By the way, your mother has invited Bertie and me, Digby and Dorcas and your Uncle Edward and Aunt Grace for dinner this evening. She thought it would make up for the unhappy ending to our evening last night.'

'That should be nice,' Jessamy said, marvelling at her mother's invitation. 'Will—er—Captain Montague be there?'

It was Chadwick who answered. 'No, he had to go to London. He left on the early train this morning. Your Aunt Verity wondered if you would stay with Louise this evening?'

'Yes, of course. I'll be glad to.'

Verity patted her arm. 'Thanks, Jessamy. I think that Christian leaving has upset her more than she'll admit.' She gave a wan smile. 'But as Bertie said at lunchtime, we've got to stop behaving as though we were mourning Christian. It's simply that he's turned out to be more adventurous than we imagined.'

After Verity had gone Chadwick said to Jessamy, 'I thought it very nice of your mother to ask them all for dinner. It will take Verity and Bertie's mind from thinking about Christian and it's rare for Edward and Grace to be asked out to dinner. I suppose people think they always have to be involved with the business. They do have a night free now and again, but as Grace said, they seldom are able to spend one together.'

The doorbell went and Alistair came breezing in. 'My goodness it's still parky out there.' He slapped his hands. 'Should be some snow before nightfall. Oh, hello, Jessamy. Back safe and sound?' He took a packet from his pocket and handed it to Chadwick. 'Mrs Mally thanks you for the medicine and has sent you some of her home-made treacle toffee.'

'Oh, thanks, but she shouldn't do it. I don't expect it.'

'No, but it gives the old lady pleasure. Strange, isn't it,' Alistair mused, 'how the poor people will offer gifts, but not the money-ed ones.'

Jessamy said, 'Because they've never known what it is to be short of anything. All that our wealthy female customers are interested in are products that will keep them looking younger.'

'And smelling sweet,' said Alistair with a grin. To Chadwick he added, 'while you were out this morning Mrs Wenthaven and her colleague were demanding to know why you don't stock French perfumes. And why don't you, Mr Chadwick?' Alistair said, serious now. 'We're constantly being asked for them.'

Chadwick nodded. 'Yes, I know. Actually I've been considering this very carefully. As a matter of fact, Captain Montague broached the subject last night. He has connections with a firm in Grasse and with a workshop of glass-makers who produce the containers. It's an interesting proposition.' Chadwick smiled. 'Yes, I think we shall be having some very sweet-smelling customers in the future.'

Jessamy said smiling, 'And a sweet-smelling daughter and cousins, too. We must have some samples.'

'But of course.' It was all so light-hearted that it was not until a few minutes later that she realised she might not be here when this new development took place. For the first time, it really came home to Jessamy what she would be missing if she went away with Louise. She would certainly miss the shop, the customers, the birthday parties held at her grandparents' and her walks on the moors. So many things...

When Jessamy arrived to stay with Louise that evening her uncle was his old amicable self. He teased the girls, saying mind they didn't get into any mischief while he and Verity were out. Verity, smiling, said, 'I can't think of any mischief they could get up to.' To the girls she added, 'Now don't stay up too late. We all had a very late night last night.'

When they had gone Louise said, 'Typical, isn't it? They were all gloom and doom this morning and now you would think that Christian had suddenly returned and all was normal again.'

Jessamy said, 'Now be fair, Louise. They are doing their best not to be miserable.'

'Well, it doesn't lift my gloom. Why couldn't we have been invited for dinner? Anyone would think we were five year olds, given a pat on the head and told not to get into mischief. Did they think we might sneak out for a secret rendez-vous with two strange gentlemen?'

Jessamy said quietly, 'Louise, stop it. We're going to be together for a few hours so let us make it as pleasant as possible.'

'I don't feel in a pleasant mood. And you had better think over your offer to come with me when I'm imprisoned in a convent for a few months. I will not be a jovial companion.'

'I don't expect you to be, but then neither do I expect you to be a misery guts for the whole of the time.'

Louise got up and picking up the poker stirred the logs on the fire, sending a shower of sparks up the chimney. 'I'm sorry I'm in this horrid mood, but I can't help it.' She looked over her shoulder at Jessamy and there was a bleak look in her eyes. 'And I really mean it, Jessamy, when I say you should think over your offer. There's no reason why you should suffer for my sins.'

It was then that Jessamy decided to let her cousin know about the talk with her grandmother. After all, Henrietta had been the one to tell her she knew what was wrong with Louise.

At first Louise was angry and accused Jessamy of having broken her promise, but when Jessamy insisted, 'I didn't tell Grandma, she told me about you,' and went on to explain that Henrietta had a plan in her mind as to where they would both stay, she began to look intrigued. Where could it be? Who would they be staying with?

They were in the middle of speculating, without getting very far, when the front doorbell rang. Louise said lightly, 'Two strange gentlemen callers, would you think?'

The visitors were Rebecca and Anne, the daughters of Edward and Grace. Dressed in brown velvet, with caps, necklets and muffs of fur, the girls were rosy-cheeked from the cold and both were giggling.

Rebecca, who was seventeen and the eldest said, her eyes twinkling, 'While the cat's away the mice will play. Papa said that Jessamy would be here and as Nanny had to go to bed with a very bad migraine, we escaped.' Anne, who was fifteen said it was exciting coming out on their own at this time of night, then added that they mustn't stay long.

Jessamy liked Rebecca and Anne and although Louise never mixed much with any of their girl cousins, she seemed to welcome their company tonight and played hostess.

Rebecca was the talkative one, always surrounded by admirers, while Anne was shy and looked to her sister for guidance, not even accepting a sweetmeat until Rebecca was nibbling at one. However, it was she who asked, concern in her voice, if they had heard any news of Christian.

Louise told her no and said she would rather not talk about him. She then asked Rebecca about a young man who had paid her a lot of attention at the last party and Rebecca asked if she meant Richard Staines. When Louise nodded Rebecca chuckled.

'I thought him quite wonderful until I met your Captain Montague. Isn't he just the most handsome man you've ever seen?'

Men were the topic for quite a while with Rebecca then when the grandfather clock began to strike Anne fidgeted. Should they not be going? It was another twenty minutes before

Anne managed to persuade her sister to leave.

'Come again, any time,' Louise called to them when they left then, closing the door, she leaned against it and declared that Rebecca was bound for trouble in the future. All she could talk about was men. Then she stifled a yawn and said she was ready for bed.

Jessamy felt wide awake but said she would go up with her. Louise seemed to go morose again as she undressed and Jessamy moved over to the dressing-table wondering what the months would be like spent in her cousin's company. There was a book of poetry on the dressing-table and picking it up, she opened it idly. She turned, holding out the book. 'What's this? I didn't know you liked poetry.'

Louise held out her hand. 'Give me the book, Jessamy, and I'll read you the first lines of a lovely poem by Tennyson, called *But Were I Loved*. See what you think of it.'

In a wistful, halting tone she read:

'But were I loved, as I desire to be,
What is there in the great sphere of the earth,
And range of evil between death and birth,
That I should fear—if I were loved by thee.'

When Jessamy remained silent Louise said with a catch in her throat, 'Well, what do you think of it?'

'I think it's beautiful,' Jessamy answered softly. 'How safe one would feel to have a love like that.' Christian drifted into her thoughts. Where was he now, how was he faring? If only he had been allowed to go later as a passenger on Fabian Montague's ship...but then he would have been cushioned to sea life. As a stowaway he would learn the rigours, the trials. Perhaps for him this would be a growing-up process.

An image of the Captain rose in Jessamy's mind. She could see him standing on the bridge of a ship, straight-backed, his stance authoritative. But his features were vague. Then, as the ship sailed away, the image became more blurred. How remote he seemed...

When the maid brought the hot water the next morning for the girls to wash she announced there had been a fall of snow overnight. It was about four inches deep, she grunted, making it sound a disaster.

Louise groaned and said not to mention the word snow. Jessamy got out of bed and went over to the side window, which gave a view of an expanse of moorland. The girl went out, closing the door quietly behind her. It was still dark and there was a pattern of lights from thinly-curtained windows. There were uncurtained ones and various patterns from swinging lanterns held by farmers and farmhands going about their chores. The sound of traffic was strangely muffled and the baaing of sheep quite nearby seemed to come from a distance.

Normally Jessamy would enjoy such a scene but for some reason she felt disenchanted, possibly because of Louise's baby. Louise's baby. How very much alive it sounded. But of course it was alive. It moved and it kicked. Jessamy looked towards the bed. Her cousin was hunched under the bedcovers. How awful it must be, knowing you are carrying a child that must be given away to strangers because it was shameful to have a baby out of wedlock.

Louise said, in a peevish tone, 'If you're going to get washed will you do it now and let me get back to sleep. I need another half hour, I hardly slept last night.'

Without a word Jessamy poured the water, and in less than ten minutes was ready to go downstairs. On the landing she met Verity who, after stifling a yawn said, 'I enjoyed our evening out last night but the wine is quarrelling with something I ate.'

Jessamy said, 'Louise has a headache. She said she thought she would have an extra half hour in bed.'

'Louise is having far too many headaches. I think she's just making an excuse this morning. She never did like the snow, not even as a child, as you know.' Verity stifled another yawn as they went downstairs then after apologising said, 'I really must pull myself together. I promised to meet your mother at your Uncle Digby's this morning. She wants some material for some new evening gowns.'

'Gowns?' Jessamy exclaimed. 'She has plenty already. It was only two months ago that she had the gold velvet made.'

As they went into the dining-room Verity said over her shoulder. 'Your parents were talking about going to London for a few days. Your father wants to do some business and your Mama—'

'Wants to look at the shops,' Jessamy finished for her.

'Well, you know how much she likes having new clothes,' Verity said in indulgent tones, as she helped them both to bacon and egg.

Jessamy felt angry. Why didn't her aunt see what was wrong with her own daughter instead of helping her mother to spend money her father could ill afford. She said rather stiffly, 'I know that you and Mama were good friends when you were young, but you don't as a rule help her to choose material for dresses.'

Verity, who had put the plates on the table said, 'Why, Jessamy, would you rather go with your mother this morning? I just didn't think.'

'No, no of course not, Mama would certainly never ask my advice.'

'She might, Jessamy.' Verity spoke earnestly. 'Esmeralda seemed a different person last night. No, before that. It was when she knew that Christian had run away. She's been so understanding.'

'Possibly because a son was involved. You know how she is about sons.' Jessamy was about to add that if she had run away her mother would not have bothered, but stopped herself in time. Not only was she wallowing in self-pity but she was upsetting her kind and generous aunt who would not hurt a fly. She said softly, 'I'm glad that you and Mother are good friends again. Enjoy yourselves and get Uncle Bertie to treat you to a new dress.'

Verity laughed. 'Oh, I'm all right. Your mother pays for dressing up, but me, well I look the same in whatever I wear.'

'You don't. You look lovely in blue. Now, you work on Uncle Bertie.'

Verity, still laughing said, 'I'll do that! I'll come out with you and call in at the warehouse.'

Verity and Jessamy had many things in common and one of them was their enjoyment of snow. They walked arm in arm, kicking their feet in the soft snow, revelling in it like children. Verity said that people living in cities missed so much. The snow soon got dirty whereas in the countryside it kept a pristine whiteness for miles around. Jessamy said she would like to visit London but didn't think she would ever like to live there. Verity said, 'Nor I, but your Uncle Bertie does hanker after a city life.'

Jessamy glanced at her in surprise. 'He does? I've never heard him mention it.'

'He wouldn't dare, would he?' Verity chuckled. 'Your grandfather would be at his throat. There are some things, Jessamy dear, that one keeps to oneself.'

The fun of the morning had suddenly gone

for Jessamy, knowing that soon now her aunt would learn about Louise, which was something that would have to be kept as secret as possible.

Verity looked in at the shop to say hello to Chadwick and to tell him that she and Esmeralda were going shopping. Chadwick said, 'So I've heard, but I warned Esmeralda that she cannot have a visit to London and a wardrobe of new clothes.'

Although Chadwick spoke lightly Jessamy was aware that his smile was strained. Verity left soon afterwards with a promise to put a rein on Esmeralda's spending and after she had gone Jessamy mentioned the London visit and asked her father why he had not spoken of it.

He spread his hands. 'I knew nothing about it until last night. I just happened to mention I would be going some time to replenish stock and the next thing I knew, your mother had it all arranged. And, of course your Aunt Dorcas suggested at once that your mother would need new gowns. Dorcas is worse than Digby for having an eye on business.'

There was very little time for much talk after that. They had a busy morning with a number of people coming in for medicine for coughs and colds. One small boy came in for some chilblain ointment, saying his sister should be at work but couldn't get her boots on. Chadwick tried to explain to him how the ointment was to be used, but the boy paid his threepence and was away.

After that there were a number of lady customers from the bigger houses. One or two came to buy medicines but a few, Jessamy suspected, came just for a chat to her father. Jessamy was always pleased to see that although Chadwick was courteous and attentive he never gave them encouragement in any way.

Then there were the women whom Verity called the Whispering Brigade. They wanted to speak to Chadwick privately, and after a conversation Chadwick would bring a packet from a cupboard in the room at the back, which he kept locked, and handed it over with quiet instructions. To Jessamy's query about these packets Verity explained it was to help women who suffered dreadful pain at the time of menstruation. Verity said that before she was married she had suffered dreadfully, but put up with it because she thought that every female was the same.

Later in the morning a burly workman came in asking if Chadwick could get a splinter out of his finger. 'Had it in for a week now, Guv,' he said. 'I'm tree felling at the Ransome place. I've had dozens of splinters in me time, but I've always been able to get them out—but not this bugger. Sorry, Miss,' he said to Jessamy, 'didn't see you there. It's a right one this, got itself buried in and I can't get it out. Had several goes wi' a knife but it were no good.'

The finger was about four times its normal size and badly inflamed. Chadwick tutted over it. Why on earth had he let the finger get into such a state? There was a danger he could lose it. Chadwick would have to lance it.

'Cut it off if you have to, Guv,' the man declared cheerfully. 'I'll still have enough fingers left to get on wi' me tree felling.' Jessamy had brought hot water and bandages and the man eyed her, smiling. 'You're a bonny one and no mistake. Your lass?' he asked Chadwick.

'Yes, now pay attention. This will hurt.'

The man boasted he was not afraid of a bit of pain, but he lost all his colour after Chadwick had lanced the finger and he saw all the pus oozing out. 'Oh, Gawd,' he mutteed, 'never seen owt like that afore.'

Chadwick bandaged the finger, gave strict instructions for bathing it, but said with a sigh to Jessamy after the man had gone, 'He won't do it—he won't ask for any time off to do it. And he should have done, because Ransome is good to his workmen. It was he who sent a note to say he would call and pay the bill.'

Alistair had just arrived, having had time off for study, when a small boy came running in to ask Chadwick if he would come quickly, his da was trying to kill his ma. Chadwick grabbed his bag and after calling Alistair and asking Jessamy if she could cope the two men left.

When they returned some time later Chadwick was shaking his head. 'It was just the build-up of a man who had been out of work for some time coming to the end of his tether. His wife nagged and he picked up a knife and slashed her arm.'

'But the wife took all the blame,' Alistair said. 'She admitted she nagged but it was through worry because they had no food in the house.'

'Oh, the poor souls,' Jessamy said, and offered to take some round.

Chadwick told her it was all taken care of. The cottage was near the warehouse and the men, hearing the woman's screams, had gone to see what was wrong. 'Bertie was there,' Chadwick went on. 'He's going to find a job for the man and he says Verity will see to the food and arrange to get some warm clothes and footwear for the children. All the little ones were barefooted.'

'In this weather!' Jessamy exclaimed. 'It's all wrong.'

'So what are you going to do?' Chadwick asked gently. 'Deny yourself a new dress and give the money to the poor? We are all guilty, Jessamy. It's only at a time like this that we realise our shortcomings.'

The shop soon became busy again, cutting short their conversation. Although some people were genuine customers, the rest only came in to gossip about the man who had attempted to kill his wife. These people left after a stern talk from Chadwick, who advised them not to make

194

melodrama out of the troubles of those less fortunate than themselves.

Jessamy wondered what the rest of the day had in store.

CHAPTER TWELVE

The shop was busy too during the afternoon, but made brighter by a visit from two middle-aged spinster sisters, the Misses Agatha and Mildred Dingley, for whom Jessamy had developed a great fondness. The pair lived on a pittance, with no living relatives but they had invented some for the purpose of playing games with Chadwick, who happily joined in the pretence.

At first, it had been imaginary uncles who could all speak fluent Latin and the sisters would mention the Latin names of plants to see if Chadwick recognised them. He pretended to ponder for a while and the sisters watched him, their faces alight with expectancy, like children.

Sometimes he would say, 'Well now, that one eludes me. Just let me think a moment.' At other times he would shake his head and pretend to admit defeat. Then Agnes, who was always the questioner, would turn to her sister with a gleeful smile. 'Did you hear that

Mildred? We've beaten the dear doctor. How good he is to take his defeat so splendidly.'

Mildred would nod and blink rapidly, but once she said to her sister, 'We really ought not to boast about our successes, Agatha. Doctor Every is a very clever man.'

Agatha heartily agreed with this then turned to Chadwick, saying in a confidential way, 'You see, Doctor, my sister and I were great dunces at school.'

When Chadwick said he refused to believe this there were happy smiles from the sisters and the game continued. After a while they switched from the Latin to the common names of the plants, asking Chadwick what plants had the nicknames of Gill-go-over-the Grounds and Lizzie-run-over-the Hedge. When he told them they were both names of ground ivy the sisters showed such disappointment that Chadwick resolved to pretend ignorance on some of the questions.

The sisters were both small but while they were dissimilar in features, they both wore their greying hair with little bunches of curls peeping from under the front of their hats; they were only ever seen in grey.

This afternoon, they had invented some new relatives. There was a sister who suffered from a nervous disorder: they thought they might buy her some blue betsy. Chadwick pretended to ponder and the sisters smiled up at him. Could this be tansy? No, it must be... He shook his head, looking baffled. He had forgotten for the moment.

'It's periwinkle,' the sisters chorused happily.

'Of course! A splendid herb. It's also excellent for inflamed throats, for drying up sores and wounds and healing the lungs. Did you know that it's a plant of friendship and faithful affection, too, and that if a married couple chew the leaves, their love will remain constant?'

Mildred beamed at him. 'Isn't that nice.' She studied their list. 'Now then, my brother-in-law has gout. We shall have some lady's tears—'

'—and a ladder to heaven,' Mildred offered eagerly.

Chadwick decided to let them score again and Agatha said, 'It's lily of the valley and it helps to ease varicose veins, bruises and sties and dropsy.'

Next on the list were three cousins for whom they wanted to purchase fairy clocks, priest's crown and devil's milk plant. One cousin had rheumatism, the second a liver complaint and the third was suffering from kidney trouble.

Chadwick waved a playful finger at them. 'You are wanting one plant for all three complaints. It is the weed that gardeners hate and physicians welcome—our friend, the dandelion!'

'You've won,' said Agatha with a warm smile. 'I'm so pleased.'

At this point Verity arrived, saying she could only stay a minute, she had just come to collect some ointment for a neighbour, but the sisters took their leave, promising to call again with some more 'teasers'—harder ones the next time.

'They're such darlings,' Jessamy told Verity, after explaining the games. 'They're satisfied with so little. And they went to all the trouble to learn those Latin names, which I find so difficult.' She was just about to add that she would *have* to master the names if she was ever going to be a doctor, when the doorbell rang and Fabian Montague walked in. Jessamy's heartbeats quickened. Was there any other man so handsome or with such presence?

To Chadwick's surprised greeting that he thought his friend was in London, Fabian replied, 'I was, but have been recalled to take over another ship.' He bade good afternoon to Jessamy and Verity, then added quietly to Verity, 'I'm so sorry, Mrs Every, that I was unable to do anything about Christian.'

'That's all right, Captain Montague. My husband and I have accepted that it was something our son wanted to do and we are trying to come to terms with it.'

They talked about events in London for a while then Fabian said he felt like stretching his legs after the journey. Would the ladies accompany him on a stroll? Verity said she had been out most of the day and really ought to go home. Perhaps Jessamy would like to go. She looked at her father, who gave his permission, saying some fresh air would do her good.

Alistair, who had busied himself while they were talking, brought Jessamy her outdoor clothes. Fabian, acknowledging Alistair with a smile and a nod, took Jessamy's coat from him and held it out, saying, 'Remember the snow. You must wrap up well.'

Jessamy slipped her arms into the coat and before she had even fastened a button Fabian had taken her scarf from Alistair and wrapped it around her throat. He then asked if she had gloves and as she drew a pair of red knitted ones from her pocket she felt a bubble of hysteria rising. She was like a child being dressed for an outing. But there was nothing childish about her emotions as Fabian, knotting the scarf, touched her face. Blood rushed to her cheeks and she hastily pulled on her knitted cap saying, 'We won't be long, Papa, perhaps half an hour.' To Verity she added, 'Tell Louise I'll look in later and see her.'

Goodbyes were said and Fabian and Jessamy left. Once outside he put a hand under her elbow and guided her in the opposite direction to the one she normally would have taken, but she made no protest.

The traffic had churned up the snow on the main road but at the side where they walked the snow was crisp underfoot. Jessamy had to resist an urge to stamp her foot on small frozen pools to hear the ice crack as she had done as a child. She said politely, 'You must be very disappointed to have been recalled from London, Captain Montague.'

'A little. I did actually go on business, but met friends last night. It was very pleasant and we had arranged to go to a theatre this evening. But there, business comes first. Ships cannot be held up because captains want to enjoy themselves.'

They were passing the Highwayman's Arms and Fabian glanced towards it. 'It seems impossible to believe it was only two nights ago that we were dining there. I so enjoyed the evening. I'm sorry I was unable to discover anything further about Christian, but at the same time I am glad that his parents have accepted his reasons for leaving home. If there were no adventurous spirits like Christian we would still be living in the dark ages.'

'How true. I had never thought of it in that way.'

They had left the main road and reached the path that led on to the moors. And then Jessamy forgot everything else for that moment. Although the moorland at the other side of the shops was normally her favourite area, she found herself caught up in the beauty of the scene. The frost on the outcroppings of rock had turned them into strange and lovely shapes that belonged to a child's fantasy world. It was not yet dusk, but the small church, which was known as the Church of the Fishermen, was already candle-lit, giving an extra beauty to the scene. She whispered, 'How lovely the moors are under their blanket of snow.'

'I agree.' Fabian looked down at her. 'I wanted this scene to carry away with me, Jessamy. Just the two of us and the purity of the snow.'

She found it difficult to weigh him up. The words were a little extravagant. Was he sincere or were these expressions something he conjured up to draw women to him? She had always thought that when she married she would like her husband to say nice things to her, to fuss her a little like her Uncle Bertie did to her aunt. But somehow they seemed wrong coming from this big man with the dominant personality. And yet big men could be gentle. Why should they not be poetic? Why should they not express what they felt? Wanting to change the subject she asked where his new ship was bound, and whether he would be carrying passengers.

'The Low Countries and no, there will be no passengers. Not on this trip. Just cargo.'

She looked up at him. 'Where do your family live, Captain Montague?'

He was a while in answering. 'I have no family, Jessamy. My parents died four years ago within a few months of one another, and

I never knew my maternal or paternal grand-parents. I was an only child.'

'Oh, how sad,' she said, full of warmth now for him. 'Although I am an only child I have so many cousins that I've never really missed not having brothers and sisters.' Although Jessamy felt she had no right to probe into his life any further there was one question she felt she must ask. 'Did you ever—marry, Captain Montague?'

He was silent for so long that Jessamy was about to apologise for the question when he said, 'I was engaged once, but Caroline decided she could not face a married life where her husband would be at sea most of the time. She went off and married someone else. I can understand it, of course, it is a lonely life for a woman.'

'But hundreds of women marry seafaring men,' Jessamy protested. 'They have children, a home to care for.'

'So you would not mind being married to a sailor?' Fabian asked, a suggestion of teasing in his voice.

'No, not if I loved him. I was talking to an old lady who lives on the other side of the moors a few days ago and she was telling me of the excitement of having your man come home and, although she lost her husband quite early in her marriage, she told me she would not have missed the life she had had with him for the world. She had her lovely memories, she said.'

Suddenly realising that in a way she was condemning the girl Caroline who had jilted Fabian, Jessamy quickly went on, 'But I suppose there are some women who need a man with them the whole time. I too can understand that. My aunt is a most loving person and she just hates to be away from my Uncle Bertie for very long.'

'Lucky Uncle Bertie,' Fabian said quietly, which had Jessamy thinking that without family there would be no one waiting for him when he returned from a voyage. And perhaps he was still in love with his Caroline...if so, he must be very unhappy indeed.

They had almost reached the church when he said, 'Shall we go in? Have you time?'

She told him yes, guessing now why he had wanted to walk in this direction. Nearly every man who went to sea visited a church before setting out on a voyage, to pray for a safe return and to ask for the care of his family while he was away. Jessamy felt deeply moved and when they went into the church, was aware of a different atmosphere. Because the little church was not old she had always thought it lacked the godliness of the old church at St Peel. Now she knew that the fault had been within herself. What had impressed her in the older building were simply the embellishments—the gilt, the centuries-old font, the exquisite carvings of the reredos and the impressive stone figures of a knight and his lady lying side by side, hands clasped in prayer. Even the chill, the dampness which emanated from the old stones had suggested an age coming back to Biblical times.

In this edifice, the embellishments were simple. A few small alcoves in the stone walls contained candles, the flames flickering in the chill air, and some small Biblical figures. The pulpit was made from a ship wrecked on that coast, the font was of stone. As a child Jessamy had been intrigued by the colours from the stained glass windows which were reflected on the stone slabs when the sun shone. Now as she looked up at the windows she thought she saw the water moving in the sea scene. Why had she been so blind that she had not seen the beauty of simplicity?

She walked on tiptoe as she went down the aisle with Fabian; his steps echoed in the empty church. They sat down in a pew near the front then knelt on hassocks, their heads bowed. Jessamy prayed for Fabian to come back safely, for Christian to return safely and for herself to be purged of the hatred she felt for her Cousin Lillian. When she raised her head she saw that Fabian's head was still bowed.

They both straightened then rose when the elderly vicar entered the church from the vestry and came up to them. He knew Jessamy and all the family and he was also acquainted with Fabian. The two men talked in low voices for a few moments then after the Reverend Belford had blessed Fabian the three of them walked to the door of the church together. Fabian put some money in the offertory box then he and Jessamy left.

The sky had darkened and as Fabian replaced his peaked cap he suggested they start on their way back. While they had been in the church the snow had perceptibly hardened and it now crunched loudly under their feet. Fabian said in a musing way, 'It's strange but each time, just before I go into that church I'm aware of a turmoil, yet when I leave I feel at peace.'

Jessamy glanced at him. 'Why? Do you know?'

He shook his head. 'Not really, but once I felt there had been a bloody battle there at some time.'

Jessamy gave a shiver. 'There was a battle on this spot but way back in the seventh century, I think. Do you have this odd feeling at any other time?'

'I'm aware always of a storm being imminent, even on the sunniest of days, but then so are farmers and other people. I'm quite sure I haven't any psychic powers. Jessamy, I—' He stopped, and taking her by the shoulders, turned her to face him. 'There's something I want to say to you.' He paused and the next moment his arms had fallen to his sides. 'No, I'm sorry, this is not the time.' They moved away, leaving Jessamy feeling frustrated. She glanced at him.

'Please tell me what you were going to say, Captain Montague.'

'Perhaps next time we meet.' He was staring straight ahead so she was unable to read his expression.

What had he been going to tell her? Was it something about her mother, or new information about Christian?

'You are not being fair,' she accused him. 'It's like being in the middle of a book and someone snatches it away. In the case of a book I might have been able to get the book back and to find out the end, but in your case you'll be leaving me soon and I might not see you again for months.'

'I'm sorry, Jessamy, I spoke on impulse.'

'That I doubt. I feel quite sure, Captain Montague, that you are not a man given to impulses. It's something you've given some thought to. Is it about my Cousin Christian?'

'Christian? No, I told you—I was unable to find out anything about his movements.'

Jessamy stopped. 'Very well. I shall wait here until you tell me what you were going to say.'

In the dusk she could see that although his eyes were serious a wry smile touched his lips. 'You are a very determined young lady and I'm not sure that I admire that trait in a woman.'

'Please stop evading the question, Captain Montague.'

'Very well. I've grown fond of you, Jessamy, something beyond my control. I would rather

206

it had not happened.'

The unexpectedness of his reply had Jessamy's heart racing unsteadily. Fabian ran a fingertip over her cheek saying softly, 'I know your every feature, my dear. I know your voice, your frown, your smile. Did you know that your eyes change colour with your moods? They are almost green when you are angry and a lovely tawny colour when you are speaking to children and to your grandmother. And your voice changes then too, it holds a gentleness, a warmth. It touched me.'

Bewitched by his words she searched his face, but in the quickly fading light she could only make out that his eyes seemed almost black. Jessamy felt a sudden ache for him—he had no one to care whether he returned from a voyage or not. But how did she feel about him? He could still rouse emotion in her, such as when he had touched her cheek, he was still able to make her heartbeats quicken, but there was not that feeling of being madly in love with him, as there had been when they first met. Was she unconsciously aware of a flaw in him that she was unable to name.

She said: 'Why me, Captain Montague? There must be dozens of women in your life, women who are very much attracted to you. At the party held at my grandparents the eyes of every female were on you.'

He inclined his head. 'Very flattering, but only you interest me, Jessamy. If I've offended you, I apologise.'

Perversely she made no move, not wanting it to end in this way. He had not pleaded with her to care for him, simply conceded to her wishes. But then she would have hated it if he had pleaded. She glanced at him. 'We could be friends, Captain Montague. I would write to you. Papa, I'm sure, would give me permission.'

'I would like that, Jessamy, I would like that very much.' There was a genuine warmth in his voice then that pleased her.

They walked on and after a short silence she said, 'A while ago, Captain Montague, you told me you had dreamed about me. Well, last night, while I was on the verge of sleep I saw you standing on a ship, but although your figure was clearly defined your features were vague and, as the ship moved away your face became more and more blurred.'

He smiled down at her. 'You know why, don't you? It's because you are constantly on the defensive as though you don't believe that what I'm telling you is the truth.'

Jessamy's cheeks flushed with embarrassment. It was as though he had read her mind. 'I'm sorry,' she said in a low voice. 'Put it down to inexperience. I don't meet many men outside the family or our circle of friends.'

'Please don't apologise.' He spoke softly. 'I like it that you weigh me up, it shows you are sufficiently interested in me to know what kind

208

of person I really am. I hope in time you'll come to accept that if I pay you a compliment it is not idle flattery. Will you remember that, Jessamy?'

'Yes, and I shall do my best not to try and analyse your ever word. Not that I think I did, it was just now and again that I questioned certain things you said to me, which I thought you might have said to many other women.'

'Oh dear.' There was a teasing in his voice. 'What a dreadful reputation you are giving me. No, Jessamy, I don't keep a little notebook of flattering remarks and quote from them.'

Jessamy was indignant and accused him of belittling her intelligence and he apologised and suggested they change the subject as they had very little time together and he did not want to spend it quarrelling. Contrite, Jessamy then said, 'Oh, I'm sorry, Captain Montague. When are you sailing?'

'On the morning tide. Fortunately, this will be a short trip, so I should be seeing you again in a matter of weeks.' He stopped suddenly and turned her to face him once again. 'Jessamy, what I was trying not to say is that I'm in love with you.' When she made to speak he put a finger on her lips. 'No, don't say anything, not now. I know I'm not being fair to you, but if you will write to me, maybe think of me now and again, I shall be so pleased.'

'Yes, I will,' she said softly, suddenly bemused that this much-admired man should have declared his love for her. It seemed to Jessamy then that the rosy glow from a lamplit window of a house nearby reflected the warm glow inside her. It was a love so different from that of parents or family, or the adoration of a young, inexperienced adolescent. This was a mature, virile, passionate man who desired her.

As she thought of the word 'desired' small pulses began to beat in her body. She felt excited. A girl had once told her that when a couple married all the secrets of actual love-making were revealed. Not that Fabian had mentioned marriage...and yet he was not the kind of man to tell her he loved her if marriage was not his intention.

His expression was solemn. Had he regretted declaring his love? 'You're so lovely,' he said softly, 'so tantalisingly lovely. Could you love me, Jessamy?'

She raised her face to his and whispered, 'I think I already do.' He lowered his head to hers and his lips warm and soft met hers. When Jessamy had been kissed in the past they had been stolen kisses, a swift touching of lips on lips or on cheek. This was a new experience, one that set Jessamy's blood racing and sent little shivers of ecstasy through her. Fabian had told her she was tantalisingly lovely, well she found the movement of his lips on hers tantalisingly exciting, stirring depths of emotion, stirring a need in her she had not known existed.

She began to tremble and Fabian, concerned said, 'You're cold, my darling.' Undoing his greatcoat he drew her close and wrapped it around her and she became aware of his heart beating wildly. He undid her scarf and pressed his lips to her throat, murmuring, 'Jessamy, Jessamy, I want you so desperately.'

Then the next moment he drew away, saying, his voice ragged, 'No, this is terrible. Forgive me.'

Jessamy, bewildered, searched his face. 'What have I done wrong?'

'You've done nothing wrong, Jessamy.' He fastened her scarf. 'I'm the one at fault. I lost control, something I've never allowed myself to do before.' He cupped her face between his palms, 'Don't look so upset, my darling. Your father trusted you with me and I was near to betraying that trust.' He kissed her gently on the lips. 'Come along, I'll get you back home. We'll walk quickly, keep you warm.'

As he buttoned up his greatcoat she said in a sorrowful tone, 'Does this mean that you don't really love me?'

'It means, Jessamy, that I not only love you but respect you. I was overcome with love for you. This must never happen again. There's a time for letting emotions run wild and that is when we are married. I shall speak to your father.'

'No,' Jessamy spoke sharply, all the beauty of their little interlude gone. 'I don't want to marry you. I don't like the way you turn emotion on and off, like a—like a machine.'

'Jessamy, don't you understand? Emotion is a powerful thing. It has to be kept under control, otherwise it could hurt, destroy. As I said, there's a time to indulge oneself, after marriage.' He paused then added gently, 'And there's nothing more that I want at this moment than for us to be married. But, Jessamy, I'm prepared to wait until you feel you want to marry me. Do you understand?'

She said, 'Yes,' but felt that he had behaved in a rather cold, clinical way and asked him to delay talking to her father until after his next voyage. He agreed, saying he thought it a most sensible suggestion.

At that moment Jessamy thought commonsense should be the last thing to intrude where love and romance were concerned. And yet, when Fabian drew her arm through his and smiled down at her before setting off back to the shop she felt a sudden pride that she was loved by this dynamic man whose sole thought was for her. Another man might have thought only of his own pleasure.

When they got back to the shop Jessamy asked her father for permission to write to Fabian and he said at once, 'Yes, of course. I know how much letters mean when one is away from home, in a way they're a lifeline.' Fabian, in a quiet voice agreed and then he said he must get back to the ship. And, although goodbyes were brief Fabian managed to convey in a handshake to Jessamy and a look in his eyes how sorry he was to be leaving her.

For a while Jessamy went about in a trance-like state, wondering how she could ever have thought she was not in love with Fabian. It was a wonderful feeling and she found herself longing to talk about it. What would Louise say when she knew about Fabian's declaration of love?

Louise? Jessamy came down to earth with a bump. How could she have forgotten her promise to her cousin to go away with her while she was carrying the baby? It would mean she would not be seeing Fabian when he returned from his voyage. Or indeed the next, or perhaps the next. There was one thing certain—she would not go back on her word to Louise. If only they both knew where they would be going. Somewhere sufficiently distant, no doubt, to keep the rest of the family from learning about Louise's disgrace. Jessamy would have liked to have gone there and then to see her cousin, but willed herself to be patient until it was time to leave the shop.

On the way home she said to her father, 'I'll just look in and see Louise. I won't be long.'

Louise was on her own when Jessamy arrived. When she saw her white, drawn face she guessed that her parents knew about the baby. Louise confirmed it. 'Mama asked me outright if I was pregnant. And I'm glad now they know. It's a relief.'

Jessamy sank into a chair. 'So, what is going to happen?'

Louise shook her head. 'I don't know. Mama and Papa have gone to see the grandparents. I suppose in due course we'll get to know the verdict.' There was a bitterness now in Louise's voice. 'I feel like a criminal waiting for a jury weighing up a sentence to fit my crime.' She broke into sobs.

Jessamy said gently, 'Don't torment yourself, Louise.'

'I can't help it. I keep wondering where I'll be sent.'

'Where *we* will be sent,' Jessamy stressed. 'I'll be with you, wherever it is.'

'Probably the other end of England, in some godforsaken hole, like lepers.'

'No, Grandma's plan will not be like that, I'm sure of it. She's a most understanding person.'

Louise gave an impatient toss of her head. 'Well, let's talk about something else, for heaven's sake. Tell me about your customers in the shop, anything to get my mind off this.' She laid her hand on her abdomen.

Jessamy suddenly made up her mind. 'Captain Montague called today and we went for a walk.' She told Louise about their visit to the church, the smalltalk they had made, about promising to write to him, but she did not mention that he had declared his love for her.

Louise said, 'Beware of our Captain, he's a charmer.' Then she added wrily, 'I don't suppose I would be saying this if things had been normal and *I* was the one he had asked to walk with him.' Before Jessamy could reply, Verity arrived.

CHAPTER THIRTEEN

Verity, who looked as pale and drawn as her daughter said, 'Your grandmother suggests that I write to Cornelius and Abigail Blake, distant relatives of hers who live in Berwick. She says she's sure you'll settle with them, they're lovely, caring people. I shall write to them tomorrow. We'll discuss the situation further when I hear from them.'

Four days later Jessamy was with her aunt and Louise when a letter came from the Blakes. Verity, after reading the letter, looked up frowning.

'Oh, we have a change of plan.'

'Dear Cornelius and Abigail don't want me,' Louise said wrily.

'Yes, they do, they would be delighted for you to stay with them but unfortunately they are leaving Berwick next week to help their daughter and her husband who have taken over a farm in Cornwall.'

'Cornwall!' Louise exclaimed. 'That must be hundreds of miles away. I wouldn't have gone there anyway.'

'Ah, but they want you to go. And so do the daughter and her husband. They would welcome you and do their best to help you to settle and be happy.'

'Happy?' There was a bitter note in Louise's voice.

Jessamy, who had been listening with mounting dismay, intervened, 'But Aunt Verity, I told Louise I would go with her wherever she was sent.'

'I know, Jessamy, Louise told me. It was more than generous of you but your parents, your mother in particular, do not want you to go so far away. They would have agreed to you going to Berwick, but even then your father thought you would be homesick.'

'But it's all right for *me* to be homesick,' Louise said, a catch in her voice. 'I'll be exiled.'

Verity went to her and put her arms around her. 'No, Louise, no, not exiled. We'll be in touch with you all the while. I'll travel with you and stay a few days and I shall be there when the—the baby is due. Believe me, dear, this is the best way. We desperately want you to be with people who will care for you and Henrietta assures us you could not be with much kinder or more caring people than Cornelius and Abigail.'

Louise gave a resigned sigh. 'So, I go to Cornwall. What are the family to be told?'

'That you haven't been well lately and are going for a change of air. They might not believe it but it's the best we can do.' Verity sounded utterly weary. She straightened and said to Jessamy that she would walk her home and let her mother know the latest news.

Once outside Verity said, 'Louise won't say who the father of the child is. Do *you* know, Jessamy?'

'No, she seems determined that no one shall know.'

Verity sighed. 'There's no one more stubborn than Louise when she makes up her mind to something.'

They walked in silence for a way then Jessamy spoke. 'Aunt Verity, I do think it's a shame not to let me go with Louise. Couldn't you persuade Mother to let me go? I can talk to Papa. Louise needs to be with someone of her own age and we understand one another.'

Verity said yes, she knew, but then pointed out all the things that Jessamy had admitted to herself she would miss if she left home, the family, the birthday gatherings, the shop and the work she loved. Then Verity added with a small smile, 'And you would also miss seeing our handsome Captain when he comes home from sea. He is, I know, very attracted to you.'

Warm colour rushed to Jessamy's cheeks.

Yes, she would miss seeing him, but she in turn pointed out to her aunt that surely sacrifices had to be made in the name of friendship.

Verity agreed and said they would see what her parents said.

But neither Chadwick nor Esmeralda would accept Jessamy going so far away and no amount of pleading on Jessamy's part could get either of them to change their minds. It was for her own good, her father said. She would, in time, have come to resent the isolation.

'So what about Louise?' she demanded. 'Has she to suffer misery for months because she makes one mistake in her life?'

Chadwick took her by the shoulders saying gently, 'In a matter of weeks Louise will have accepted the situation and settled down. She's that kind of person. Louise is adaptable. You'll see.'

To Jessamy's surprise her father was proved right. After what to Jessamy had been a heartbreaking parting with her cousin, the first letter she had from Louise was all brightness. For the first time in her life, she said, she knew the meaning of freedom. There was no one constantly to tell her what and what not to do. Cornelius and Abigail were an interesting couple, kind but eccentric. They kept their hats on in the house because, said Cornelius, God once visited it. Abigail's daughter and her husband were also very kind and respected

Louise's privacy.

The letter went on to describe the farm and the animals in such glowing terms that Jessamy began to wonder if Louise was trying to make her wish that she was there, too. But when Verity returned from Cornwall after a week she confirmed all that Louise had written.

'It's really amazing how she has settled,' she told Jessamy. 'She's up early every morning and you know what a sleepyhead Louise has always been in a morning. Cornelius and Abigail are delightful people and so are Daisy and Edward, the daughter and son-in-law. I really have Henrietta to thank for recommending them.'

Jessamy missed Louise terribly. There had seldom been a day when the two girls did not meet. Then came another letter from her cousin that actually had Jessamy feeling envious of Louise. The letter began, *'Guess what? No, you'll never guess. Cornelius and Abigail deal in herbs and herbal medicines. They have a van and go on Saturdays to nearby villages selling them. And they not only deal in herbs but Cornelius makes and carves small picture frames and Abigail paints pictures to go in them. I do wish you could be here, Jessamy, you really would like it...'*

When Jessamy told her father about Louise's new life and said how she wished she could have gone to Cornwall too Chadwick said gently, 'Have you forgotten, Jessamy dear, why Louise is in Cornwall? Don't be envious of

219

her. Just be glad that she has so much to interest her.'

Although Jessamy felt ashamed for having envied Louise it did not stop her from thinking of the different kind of life her cousin was leading in Cornwall.

But then a letter came from Fabian Montague one morning and all else was forgotten. It arrived before breakfast. Jessamy, feeling all trembly inside, ran up to her room to open it. When she read, *'My darling Jessamy,'* she closed her eyes momentarily. Her first love letter. She read on.

'Last night I walked in a vineyard in France at midnight and in spirit you were there by my side, Jessamy. The high-riding moon cast a glow over the earth and the stars were so low I plucked one for you, which I enclose in the letter.' (It was a star-shaped piece of silvered cardboard.)*'I longed to hold you in my arms, to kiss your eyelids, your adorable mouth, your beautiful throat...'*

Although Jessamy knew that the phrases were extravagant she gave a shiver of pure ecstasy as she imagined his lips moving over her body. She had started on the next line which said, *'I have written to your father asking for permission to marry you—'* when she heard her father call to her to ask if she was coming down to breakfast, he had something to tell her.

Jessamy hastily folded the letter, put it in her dress pocket and went out on to the landing. 'Coming, Papa.' She forced herself to walk

220

sedately downstairs and to go into the breakfast room solemn-faced, but when Chadwick told her he had a letter from Captain Montague Jessamy beamed at him.

'So have I.'

'Indeed. Then you will know he has asked permission to court you. Sit down and I'll get you some breakfast, then we must talk.'

Jessamy, a little alarmed at noticing how serious her father was said, 'You do approve, Papa?'

Chadwick lifted covers off silver dishes on the sideboard, speared kidneys, bacon and sausages on to plates and returned to the table. 'I would be pleased to accept Fabian as a son-in-law and I feel quite sure your mother would too, but I do think you must give this matter a great deal of thought. You have an ambition to become a doctor. Not that I approve of you, or any other girl, taking up such a profession, and certainly not one who has marriage in mind.'

'But Papa, Fabian goes away for long voyages. I would have plenty of time for study.'

'And what happens if by chance you become qualified? Are you going to be attending to patients while your husband eats alone? A wife's place is at home, with her husband and children.'

Jessamy's chin went up in a stubborn thrust. 'Then I will give up the idea of becoming a doctor.'

221

'Jessamy dear,' Chadwick spoke gently, 'this is easily said. Marriage is not something to be treated lightly. It's for life.'

'I know, Papa, know that I could give up everything just to be with Fabian. I love him, I had not realised just how much until I had the letter from him. I could forget about being a doctor, settle down, have children.'

'We shall have a talk with your mother this evening. Incidentally, your mother and I will be going to London at the weekend. We shall probably be back on the following Wednesday. Mr Blackwell will take charge of the shop until I return.'

Jessamy, suddenly miserable said, 'All the joy I had at receiving Fabian's letter has gone. You don't want me to marry him.'

'Shall I tell you something, Jessamy,' Chadwick spoke sternly. 'Your very immature attitude tells me you are not ready for marriage. We shall say no more for the present.' Chadwick, who had not finished his breakfast, wiped his mouth with his table napkin and threw it down, proving to Jessamy just how angry her father was. He got up, pushed his chair back into its place and said, 'I shall see you at the shop. Perhaps you would like to speak to your mother before you leave.'

Speaking to Esmeralda at this stage was the last thing that Jessamy wanted. She got up from the table and went to the window, feeling there was more to her father's anger than the letter from Fabian. It could be, of course, that he did not want Esmeralda to go to London with him.

To Jessamy's surprise when she sat down with both her parents later to discuss Fabian Montague's proposal, Esmeralda was on her daughter's side, pointing out to Chadwick that he had been the one to stress that Jessamy was a young lady, not a child, and old enough for marriage. 'And after all,' she added, 'the Captain would be a most suitable match. He's sensible, comes from a wealthy background. What more could one ask for one's daughter?'

A stubborn line came into Chadwick's jaw. 'From childhood Jessamy has had an ambition to become a doctor. Now she dismisses it as unimportant, showing that she's not so much in love with Montague as in love with the idea of being married to an eminently attractive suitor.'

Jessamy protested strongly at this. 'I may be young,' she said, 'but I weighed up Captain Montague before he ever hinted at marriage. I felt he was a lonely man, without family. I also found him a caring person. Perhaps I was a little excited that he should have fallen in love with me, but I not only feel that I could love him enough to make sacrifices, but that I respect him, which you, Papa, have always said is important in marriage.'

'Jessamy.' Chadwick leaned forward, his expression earnest. 'I withdraw what I said earlier about you behaving immaturely. But I must point out that ambition is not easily dismissed. It can eat into one. I failed my exams because of my own stupidity, but it's something I shall regret to the end of my days. If you marry—and don't have a chance to study to become a doctor—resentment could build up in you and destroy your marriage.'

'Papa, not so long ago you told me you had no wish for me to become a doctor.'

'Only because I know of the resentment you would suffer from men in the profession, from fellow students. They could make your life a misery, as they have done with other women.' Chadwick paused then went on, 'I would accept you and the Captain becoming engaged, Jessamy, if you would both be willing to wait a year before contemplating marriage.'

When Jessamy said she would be prepared to wait her mother gave a whimsical smile and asked, would Captain Montague want to wait?

Chadwick replied, his manner terse, 'He will have to.' And that was the end of the conversation. But Jessamy was sure that Fabian would persuade her father to shorten the time of the engagement.

This was a time when Jessamy especially missed Louise. She told Alistair about Fabian's proposal within minutes of his arriving at the shop and Chadwick remarked a little wrily that from now on the talk would be about weddings and all they involved.

Alistair congratulated her and declared that the Captain was a lucky man. A customer came

224

in then and no more was said.

Later in the day, Jessamy went to Beacon Hall to see her grandmother who, although declaring she was getting a fine man, agreed with Chadwick that it was wise to have a year's engagement. 'But why?' Jessamy asked. 'I won't change my mind about wanting to get married. How long were Mama and Papa engaged?'

'That was different,' Henrietta said quietly. 'Your mother was older, seven years older than you are, Jessamy, and that seven years makes a difference.'

'Grandma, you once said that age does not make a person mature, that a seventy year old person can still behave like a child and that a child can have a wisdom beyond his or her years.'

Henrietta laughed and said she would have to try and remember her own sayings in future. Then, more seriously she added, 'But Jessamy, your father is right, you must be sure that you won't hanker to fulfil your ambition to be a doctor before an engagement ring is put on your finger, much less a wedding ring.'

Jessamy said firmly, 'I am sure, Grandma. As well as wanting to be a doctor I've dreamed of getting married, having my own house and children. Being married to Fabian has won and I won't allow myself to regret it.'

'So be it, child. May God grant you happiness.'

225

Mr Blackwell came to the shop early on the Friday morning before Chadwick and Esmeralda left for London. Jessamy liked the old man, for he was jolly and full of stories about the early days of pharmaceutical work. She had remembered names from her childhood by his description of the people. One woman had stayed in her mind, Queen Hatsheput of Egypt who in the year 1500 BC had sent botanists out to seek medicinal plants. Mr Blackwell had described the Egyptian garments she would have worn then said, 'I wonder why she was called Hatsheput? Perhaps she forgot where she'd put things.' Jessamy had thought this very funny.

She remembered a man called Dioscorides, not so much because in the first century of our era he had produced a book listing over a hundred names of plants, but because Mr Blackwell said that Dioscorides was 'full of whimsy'. Hippocrates, one of the earliest physicians stayed in her mind because of the Hippocratic oath that men had to take when they became doctors. She had pictured the men kneeling, heads bowed before this mighty man, who favoured balm, basil, horehound, ivy, rue and sage to cure many ills.

There were many other names but the person she liked best was Nicholas Culpeper, who was born much later in the 1600s. Although he treated wealthy patients, he spent nearly every penny he earned on caring for the poor.

'A wonderful man,' said Mr Blackwell, 'who died in penury. He had great faith in parsley to cure many ailments but perhaps he started to treat himself too late, for he died young of consumption.' Jessamy had shed a few tears for poor Mr Culpeper.

Esmeralda had said to Jessamy the day before, 'You'll be staying with your Aunt Verity and she will pop into the shop from time to time. I don't think it's right for you to be on your own with two men when your father is absent.'

Although Jessamy felt impatient with this way of thinking she simply accepted it. It was no use causing an upset when her mother was so obviously excited about going to London.

When her parents were ready to leave for the station the following morning Jessamy thought she had never seen her father look so handsome or her mother more beautiful, Chadwick was wearing a silver-grey suit with a darker grey astrakhan-trimmed topcoat, while Esmeralda was in a deep blue velvet costume that emphasised the blue of her eyes. She carried a muff of squirrel, while draped casually around her shoulders was a matching stole. Verity, who had come to see them off said, 'There could not be a more handsome pair in the whole of London. Enjoy yourselves and don't worry about a thing.'

A friend came to collect them in his car and after Verity and Jessamy had waved them out of sight Verity gave a deep sigh. 'I wish *I* was off to London with Bertie. I've never been there.'

'Someday you will, I'm sure,' comforted Jessamy.

Normally, Jessamy missed her father when he was away, but this time she found herself enjoying the easier ways of Mr Blackwell and Alistair. On the Saturday afternoon Mr Blackwell teased Alistair, using the Scottish dialect, after Alistair had complained that life was all work—in the shop during the day and studying in the evenings.

'Now d'ye not mind the words of the Elder Pliny, who said he worked during his sleeping hours?'

'Aye, I do,' replied Alistair. 'I also mind Paracelsus, who said the universities don't teach us everything. A good physician should be ready to learn from midwives, gypsies, nomads and brigands and others who live outside the law. They should travel, and learn.'

Mr Blackwell nodded. 'And there's truth in that. My father was bald when he was thirty and then he met a nomad who told him to make an infusion of parsley, nettle, rosemary and camomile and to massage it into his head daily for two or three months.'

'And did it work?' enquired Verity.

'It did! My father never had a thatch of hair, but he had a goodly showing and he kept it until he died at the age of eighty.'

When both Jessamy and Alistair looked at Mr Blackwell's thick hair he grinned and said, 'No, *I* use cinquefoil.'

'Cinquefoil?' Jessamy exclaimed. 'That is used for diarrhoea, as a mouthwash for sore gums, and—'

'—To keep my hair in good order. A gypsy once told me about it. Actually, I spent a lot of youth in the company of gypsies. Perhaps I wasted precious years going to college.'

Alistair, with an impish smile, said to Jessamy, 'How about living a nomad life and joining the gypsies?'

She laughed. 'I'm willing. Seen any in the neighbourhood lately?'

The old man threw up his hands in mock horror. 'Can you imagine the furore there would be. Will you promise me something? If I let the pair of you go off now to have a wander on the moors, you won't run off with the gypsies.'

'We promise,' they chorused and Alistair laughed when they were outside. 'What a lovely bonus. I hope I'm as amiable as Mr Blackwell when I'm his age. He's a wonderful person, and so knowledgeable. He's been checking some of my studies.' Alistair took a deep breath. 'Isn't this invigorating? I'm glad the snow has gone, for your parents' sake. It's so dirty underfoot in London when the thaw sets in.'

Alistair then enquired whether Louise was

settling down well in Cornwall. Jessamy said oh yes, and described the eccentric Cornelius and Abigail, wearing their hats in the house and selling herbal medicines and making the pictures to sell.

Alistair chuckled. They sounded delightful people and with a tonic like that, as well as the change of air, Louise should soon be well and home again.

It came forcibly to Jessamy then just how long Louise would be away and she felt suddenly bereft.

Alistair in turn told her anecdotes about odd characters in his own family. There was an elderly uncle who always stamped his feet three times before entering the house. Once, he said, to let his wife know he was home and to have a cup of tea poured for him. The second stamp was to warn the evil spirits to get out of the house, and the third to let the good spirits know it was all right to return to the house. Jessamy laughed and Alistair went on to tell her about the two great-aunts who each repeated what the other one had said, one prefacing the remark with, 'It's the truth she's telling you,' and the other with, 'I know that's the truth.' These descriptions were told in a loving way and Jessamy felt that Alistair was letting her share his family.

They walked for a way in a companionable silence then Alistair remarked on the clarity of the air and the distance one could see. He spoke of an uncle who had travelled with a party on horseback to California.

'He wrote wonderful letters,' he said, 'and I found them so absorbing. He spoke of the clarity of the air there and how deceptive it made distances: one would aim to be at a certain landmark in three hours and find it would take over a day.'

When Jessamy asked Alistair if he would have liked to have made the same journey by the wagon-train, he replied with great enthusiasm, 'Indeed I would. I know there were many hardships, some of them terrible, but think of the experience. Imagine a body of people travelling in close proximity for about nine months, think of the conflict of temperaments, the jealousies, the hatreds. And the wonderful feeling of friendliness, with neighbour helping neighbour.'

Jessamy felt surprised that Alistair had this adventurous spirit in him. He seemed dedicated to his work and was determined to be a doctor. She said, 'And you no doubt would have been attending to their medical needs.'

'Possibly, but I think it would have been exciting building a home, starting a farm and later a family.'

Jessamy gave a nod. 'I could get caught up in that kind of life, too.'

'I'm sure you could,' Alistair said softly. 'I remember how you offered to help me in my dispensary, although, of course, that would be a very different kind of life.'

'But interesting, nevertheless. There must be a great satisfaction in helping those who desperately need help.'

'I agree.'

They had walked quite a way when Jessamy suggested they go back in case Mr Blackwell had become busy. As they retraced their steps, Jessamy noticed her Aunt Catherine and Cousin Lillian coming out of a nearby house. She looked away, not wanting to talk to her cousin but Lillian had seen them, and hailed Jessamy. Catherine had paused to speak to someone in the doorway and after calling something over her shoulder, Lillian came hurrying up to Jessamy and Alistair.

'Jessamy, how *nice* to see you.' Lillian gave Alistair a sidelong glance and Jessamy introduced him. Her look was coy as she acknowledged the introduction. 'Why Mr MacKay, what a pleasure to meet you. I've heard so much about you from Uncle Chadwick, he's always singing your praises. Isn't it an exhilarating day for walking?' She laughed. 'And so much more exhilarating when one is playing truant.'

Furious, Jessamy said, 'Mr MacKay is not playing truant. Mr Blackwell suggested that we have a walk as there was little business.'

Lillian's eyes went wide. 'Why, Jessamy, you've misunderstood me. I was referring to myself when I talked about playing truant. I did promise Aunt Verity I would look out some cast-off clothes for the church charity, but this lovely weather drew me, so I came visiting with Mama. Oh, here is Mama now.'

Catherine, a woman with little in the way of looks and very little to say, came over. Jessamy introduced her to Alistair then Lillian said, 'Well, as we are all going in the same direction, may we join you?'

'Of course,' Alistair said. Lillian immediately went to his side and they moved off together, leaving Jessamy to make conversation with her tongue-tied aunt. But then Catherine mentioned Chadwick and Esmeralda's visit to London and there was such a note of longing in her voice that Jessamy gave her her full attention, asking if she had ever been to the capital.

'I'm afraid not, Jessamy. I've always had a longing to go there, but it's the business, you see. Your Uncle James is unable to leave it.' She paused then went on, 'Sometimes I think that too much time is spent on business, leaving husband and wife with very little opportunity to get to know one another.'

Jessamy glanced at her aunt, appalled. Catherine and James must have been married at least twenty-four years. If they did not know one another now, there was little chance of them ever doing so. She said, 'You'll have to try and persuade Uncle James to take you to London. Tell him how important it is to you.'

'Oh, no, Jessamy, I couldn't do that.'

'But why? I'm sure he would understand.'

Catherine said this was quite impossible. James had a business to run and there was no time for anything else. No time for anything else but business? Did they have time for loving?

Intent on her aunt's problem, Jessamy had been only vaguely aware of Alistair and Lillian but now, when she saw how attentively Alistair seemed to be listening to Lillian, she felt a twinge of annoyance. Would Alistair, like most men, be duped into thinking Lillian a wonderfully gentle and sweet person?

Jessamy had her question answered after they left Catherine and Lillian at their front door. When they walked away Alistair said, musingly, 'Why do you think your cousin went to such lengths to attract my attention? She's a very beautiful young lady and must have many admirers.'

'She has, but wants *every* man to admire her.'

Alistair replied sadly that this was unfortunate, as a man wanted to be the one to make the approach and Jessamy felt glad that Alistair had not been taken in by her cousin's wily ways.

On the Monday there was a letter from Chadwick saying that he would be returning on the Wednesday, but that her mother would be staying on for a few days with friends. He added that Jeremiah would meet him at the station and as they had some business to discuss he would probably stay overnight at Beacon Hall. He ended the letter, *'All news when I see you, Jessamy dear. Looking forward to seeing you, your loving Papa.'*

After reading the letter aloud to her aunt and uncle at breakfast Jessamy said, 'Why should Grandpa claim Papa's attention the moment he's home? We want to see him and hear all the news.'

To this Bertie replied, 'Because, my lovely Jessamy, your grandfather thinks he has first claim to all his brood. He will want to know what business your father has conducted, where he and your mother stayed and who they met. He is brimming over with curiosity, but then that is one of the reasons why he has successfully built up his enterprises.'

Later that morning Jessamy happened to be on her own in the shop when who should walk in but Lillian. Jessamy could not remember her cousin ever visiting the shop on her own and, guessing why she had come said, 'Hello, Lillian, this is quite a surprise visit. Mr Blackwell and Mr MacKay are busy at the back. Is there anything I can get for you?'

'Actually, I need some cream. My skin is very dry.'

Lillian's skin looked in perfect condition but Jessamy brought out several jars for her cousin to make a choice. Lillian's gaze, however, was not on the jars of cream but on the door that led to the back room. When Jessamy began to explain the merits of the various creams Lillian said, 'I heard that Louise has gone to Cornwall. Why so far away?'

'For her health,' Jessamy replied promptly. 'She was very rundown and the air is so healthy in Cornwall.'

'It's healthy here. Oh, I know that a change of air is supposed to be beneficial, but it seems to me there's another reason why they've sent her so far away.'

The sneer on Lillian's face made Jessamy fume but she was surprised to find her voice quite steady as she said, 'A reason? What exactly had you in mind?'

Lillian picked up a jar and moved it slowly over the counter in circles. 'Don't try to play the innocent with me. You know why a girl is sent away for months. Will our dear Cousin Louise have the child adopted?'

Jessamy met the hateful gaze steadily. 'You must be a very unhappy person, Lillian, for your mind to be so distorted. Do men realise this and could it be the reason why none have asked for your hand in marriage?'

Her cousin's face flushed with anger. 'For your information I've turned down numerous offers. I happen to be particular in the choice I make—I don't associate with shop assistants and the like.'

'I don't blame you,' said a voice from behind Jessamy. She turned to see Alistair framed in the open doorway. He was smiling.

Lillian banged down the jar of cream and without a word marched out. Jessamy laughed and said to Alistair, 'I compliment you on a perfect entrance, Mr MacKay. Lillian was so intent on being nasty to me that she obviously had not noticed you open the door.'

Alistair came into the shop and, serious now, said, 'You were right, Jessamy. Only an unhappy person would make such insinuations. Her mind is twisted. What has happened in her life to make her this way, do you know?'

Jessamy shook her head. 'I have no idea. She was unpleasant to me when I was young, but no one would believe it. Many members of the family speak of her as an angel.'

'Poor girl, how sad. She's sick.'

Jessamy could understand how a man like Alistair could see a sickness in her cousin, but Jessamy did not share his opinion. To her Lillian was just an unpleasant person who deliberately set out to hurt those she felt were in opposition or a threat to her.

Under normal circumstances her cousin's attitude would have festered with Jessamy but because of Alistair's attitude she was able to put Lillian from her mind. That night in bed, when she usually went over various happenings before settling for sleep, she thought not of Lillian but of the three men who had an importance in her life.

There was Christian, becoming a stowaway

to achieve his ambition of going to sea. But in spite of his declaration of love for her Jessamy knew that her affection for him would never be more than a brotherly love.

Then there was Alistair, whose ambition was to become a doctor—and he would achieve it, because he had the necessary dedication. Until that afternoon he had been just her father's very likeable assistant who teased her and seemed to enjoy her company. Now she felt that quite a strong bond had developed between them. It was something that was not easy to define, but she sensed that for both of them it was more than friendship. The bond could be, of course, their shared love of herbal medicines... but no, there was another ingredient, as yet unknown to her.

For Fabian she felt the kind of love she had only dreamed about. He was handsome, mature, passionate, greatly caring. Just imagining his arms around her brought tremors to her body. She lost herself in a world of fantasy, where she and Fabian were never parted, where they made love all over the world: in Japan to the sweet fragrance of cherry blossom, in Venice to the haunting song of a gondolier and in a tent in the desert, where there were no dust storms, no shortage of water, only beautiful starlit nights where they made love between silken sheets. These fantasies stemmed from Fabian's talk of his travels, but the silken sheets were part of Jessamy's imagination. She drifted into sleep before they reached the next port of call.

Jessamy did not return to reality until the following day, when an irate customer brought back a bottle of cough medicine instead of the one she had wanted to relieve indigestion. Jessamy was horrified to think she could have made such a mistake: she could have poisoned someone. Mr Blackwell said to Alistair in dramatic tones that many a person had been poisoned in the cause of love. Then he added gently to Jessamy, 'No harm has been done, but it would be wise not to dwell on thoughts of love while serving medicines.'

'Please don't tell Papa,' she begged. 'I'm sure he would bar me from the shop and that I couldn't bear.'

Alistair pointed out that the customer might inform him, then added, 'Your father knows that everyone in any profession makes one mistake and is forgiven because it's a lesson for the future.' Mr Blackwell nodded his agreement and Jessamy was happy again.

CHAPTER FOURTEEN

Jessamy did not see her father until the Thursday morning, when she was finishing breakfast. After greeting her briefly Chadwick read his post, said he had to see Bertie at the chandlery and after telling her he would see her at the shop later, left.

Bewildered by his distracted manner, Jessamy put on her hat and coat and went to see her Aunt Verity, but the maid said that the mistress was out. Jessamy went on to the shop and found Verity there, holding a whispered conversation in the doorway with her Aunt Dorcas.

'What is going on?' Jessamy asked, her heart thumping. 'Papa came home, read his post and disappeared. Is Mama ill?'

'No, no, of course not,' Verity said in a soothing voice. 'It's just some family business that's cropped up which has to be discussed. You go into the shop, I'll be with you in a minute.'

When Jessamy went into the shop Alistair came forward smiling. 'Good morning! You are early, Jessamy.'

'Alistair, what's wrong?' Jessamy explained

about her father's odd behaviour then finding her two aunts talking in a secretive way. 'Something has happened, but what?'

Alistair shook his head. 'I have no idea. On my way here earlier I saw your three uncles going in the direction of your grandparents' house, then your father passed about ten minutes ago and I was surprised when he didn't come into the shop.'

The door opened and Verity looked in, saying she would be back in about ten minutes. But it was half an hour before she returned and Jessamy by then was in a tearful state, sure that something terrible had happened. Had her mother suffered a serious accident and they didn't want her to know about it, or had something happened to Christian—had he been drowned at sea?

Mr Blackwell and Alistair kept trying to reassure her that it would be neither of these things, or she would have been told. Mr Blackwell suggested that perhaps her grandfather had lost money in an investment, and to Jeremiah this would be a catastrophe. When Verity did return and found Jessamy so upset she was contrite. 'I'm sorry, love, it was thoughtless of me. I couldn't say anything until this business had been discussed with the family. We'll go home and I can explain it all to you.'

Verity did not keep Jessamy waiting. Once outside she said bluntly, 'Every member of the family has received a poisoned pen letter, none

241

of the children, except for Lillian. We've all been accused of doing something underhand in the past.'

'Poison pen letters?' Jessamy exclaimed. 'It's something that would never have occurred to me, not in a thousand years. Who do you think is responsible?'

'That is something we don't know, but as you can imagine it's created a very unpleasant atmosphere, each one suspecting the other.'

Jessamy said, 'It's the sort of thing I can imagine Lillian doing. You say that she received a letter too, but then she would send one for herself, wouldn't she, to allay suspicion.'

'It's possible, Jessamy, but one cannot accuse anyone without proof. I only know that something like this could divide a family, with suspicions festering for ever more. Your grandfather is livid.'

'What does Grandma say?'

'Oh, she thinks it all highly amusing. She's been accused of having secret affairs when she was young, and she says how flattering it is to be thought of as a wicked lady.'

'And the rest of the family, what are they accused of?'

Verity gave a wry smile. 'That is something none of us will ever know. And I might stress that each insists that the accusation in his or her particular letter is a lie.'

'Papa? Did he—'

'Yes, Jessamy, and there was one for your

mother, too. Your father recognised the hand-writing on the envelope and tore the letter up.'

'Won't Mama be annoyed?'

'I would think she should be very pleased that her husband did not want to know what it contained. He destroyed it in front of your grandparents. By the way, Jeremiah decided that all your cousins should be told so that there will be no speculation should there continue to be an uneasy atmosphere, which I'm sure there will be.'

Jessamy did not see her father until the evening at Verity and Bertie's when he apologised for neglecting her. 'Your grandfather takes a very serious view of this,' he said, 'and is determined to get to the bottom of the affair. I doubt we will ever know who wrote the letters but he wants to discuss the problem when the family meet at Beacon Hall on Friday evening for Hannah's birthday celebrations.'

'And now,' Verity said brightly, 'we shall forget the whole wretched business for the time being and hear all about your London trip, Chadwick. Did you enjoy it, and did Esmeralda enjoy herself?'

'Immensely, we both did. We had so many invitations socially it was impossible to fulfil them all. And as I told Jessamy in my letter to her, Esmeralda was invited to stay for a few days more.' He laughed. 'Actually, the invitation was to stay as long as she wished, but one does not put on good nature. She agreed to return at the weekend.'

Although Chadwick appeared to be pleased about his trip and talked brightly about visits to the theatre, Jessamy had a feeling that her father was not altogether at ease. She wondered if the poison pen letters were to blame, or if there was some other factor...

In bed that night Jessamy found her mind going over all the members of the family: she was curious to know the secrets of their past. Who would have dreamt that the prim and proper Dorcas could be guilty of any indiscretions, or the stolid Catherine. Nor could she imagine her gentle Aunt Grace getting into any trouble. But then, people were deceptive. Who would have predicted that Louise would end up as she had, having stressed so often that she thought any girl who became pregnant was stupid.

Jessamy thought now of the lovely poem that Louise had read to her and when she lay wide awake, tossing and turning, she decided to get up and find the poetry books she had used at school. She lit the lamp and after creeping along the landing went up to the attic, where she put the lamp on a small chest and looked around her. Some of the items were shrouded in dustsheets, the lamplight turning them into ghostly shapes on the walls. The air had an icy chill and she drew the shawl she had thrown around her shoulders a little closer. Then she went towards the cupboard where discarded books were kept.

The door was stiff and as she pulled the door the cupboard tilted forward. With a heave she managed to push it back, but everything on the top shelf showered over her.

There were numerous miscellaneous items— old invoices, notices of bargain sales long since gone, receipts, notes on herbal medicines, letters tied with ribbons. Jessamy put them all in one large envelope. Next, she picked up a folder fastened with string and was about to replace this on the shelf when some pages dropped out of it. She picked them up, looked at the first one then, dropping to her knees sat back on her heels and studied several drawings of a baby about six months old. The drawings were expertly done, the artist having captured some wonderful expressions on the face of the child.

Further pages showed the same child at ages varying from about one year to eight; the last one showed a boy in a sailor suit with dark curls beneath a broad-brimmed straw hat. He was standing, his fingertips resting on a tree trunk, his expression wistful and endearing. Jessamy turned this last page over and saw in tiny writing the inscription, *Ralph, aged eight years.*

Another folder held drawings of country scenes in pastel shades. They were exquisitely executed, and all were signed with the initials *E.F.* Jessamy remembered her Aunt Verity telling her that day on the moor how, although her mother had not shown any talent for drawing at school, she had produced excellent work at home. Her mother's maiden name was Frobisher. But who was the child? Was it one of her cousins? If so, why should her mother concentrate on drawing one cousin only? Jessamy suddenly felt as though icy water was trickling down her spine. Was the boy a part of her mother's past?

Her father's voice startled her. 'Jessamy, what in heaven's name are you doing up there at this hour?'

She called that she was just coming down and after closing the cupboard door, picked up the lamp and went down the stairs.

'Papa, I'm sorry, did I wake you? I couldn't get to sleep so I went up to the attic to look for one of my school textbooks of poetry.'

'Look at you,' Chadwick scolded. 'You're shivering. Go back to bed and I'll bring you a hot drink.'

Although Jessamy insisted there was no need, he shooed her into her bedroom and went downstairs. When he came back she was under the covers and Chadwick put the beaker of hot cocoa on the bedside table. Warning her not to let the drink get cold and scolding her again for going up to the attic, he dropped a kiss on her brow and left.

Jessamy felt chastened. Her father was not himself; he seemed tired out after his London trip and worried about the scurrilous letters.

She should have considered the risk of disturbing him. But if she hadn't gone to the attic she would never have known about the drawings... Jessamy spent a restless night and wondered what the outcome would be when the family all met. Would the letter-writer betray herself or himself?

Beacon Hall on a party night was usually full of lively chatter and laughter, but on that Friday evening when Jessamy arrived with her father, Verity, Bertie, Francis and Rupert, there was just a low murmur of voices. In the sitting-room people stood around in groups with solemn expressions, which Jessamy thought boded ill for her Cousin Hannah's birthday celebrations.

When Jeremiah knew that all were assembled he took the floor and held up his hand for silence. He began by apologising for bringing up an unpleasant subject at such a happy time but said he felt that no one would know any peace until a few matters were cleared up.

'All of us among the older ones have received one of these dreadful letters. Only we know in our hearts whether the accusations are true—but even if they are, we must ignore them, cast them into the flames where the culprit ought to be!'

There was applause at this then Jeremiah continued, 'If you talk and complain among yourselves and continue to feel anger at the culprit then you are satisfying the perverted need of this person to destroy the unity of our family. Well, let me say here and now that no one will ever do that. And why? Because I know that you will not allow it. Unite! Put this scourge out of your minds and then we can all know peace again.'

At this the applause continued for some time and afterwards talk became more normal and heads were nodding as though Jeremiah had solved the problem. Later, the cake and food were carried in and Jeremiah made a short speech about the joy of birthdays, with Hannah looking suitably impressed.

Jessamy suddenly found herself surrounded by a number of her cousins, who seemed to think she knew more about the incident than they did. 'I don't,' she said. 'I'm as much in the dark as anyone else. In fact, because of the secrecy going on I was sure that my mother had had an accident in London and no one wanted to tell me.'

A few of the boys thought it all rather amusing and asked what their parents had been up to for them to merit poison pen letters. At this the girls made a protest. How dare they treat the matter so lightly. It was terrible to be accused of indiscretions that were all lies.

'We're told they're all lies, but are they?' said one.

At this Lillian came up to them and asked, smiling, if she could join in the discussion, Francis said, 'Yes, but tell me, why were you not here when Grandfather was discussing the unpleasant happening that's blighted the lives of our parents?' His tone was serious but Lillian answered lightly that an unexpected visitor had delayed her.

'Who?' he asked.

Lillian shrugged. 'Does it matter? The important thing surely is to find out who has made these awful accusations against our parents.'

'And against you too, I understand,' Francis persisted.

Lillian nodded slowly. 'Yes, I did receive a letter, but I simply tore it up. It was all lies.'

'Why do you think that only you, among the younger ones, were singled out for the letter writer's attention?' Jessamy was aware of a relentless note in Francis' questioning.

'I just can't imagine. I have no enemies.' Lillian was gazing at him with a wide-eyed innocence but when he asked whom she suspected, Jessamy was aware of a sly look in her cousin's eyes.

'Well now, it's difficult to say, but I would suggest it was someone who was inclined to be moody and who, at the moment, has all the time in the world for letter-writing.'

This brought some laughter and remarks such as, 'Well, that absolves me as a suspect.'

Jessamy knew full well who her cousin was hinting at but it was Francis who brought it out into the open.

'Why don't you say it was Louise you had

in mind, Lillian.'

She protested at this. He was wrong, it was an imaginary person she had conjured up, but Francis would not accept this. It was Louise she was hinting at and he was annoyed because, apart from the fact that Louise was not here to defend herself, she was not the kind of person to stoop to such an action.

When Lillian protested more strongly than ever that he was mistaken Francis appealed to Rupert and his other cousins, asking who had thought of Louise when Lillian described the kind of person who might have written the letters. Jessamy raised her hand at once then Rupert followed and, after a few moments all but Hannah had agreed with Francis.

Lillian was in a tearful state. How could they think such a thing of her, it was terrible. Hannah put an arm around her and soothed her. Francis said in a cold voice, 'When people are guilty of a crime they usually try and put the blame on someone else— and I'm *not* having it put on my sister.'

For the first time Jessamy saw a look of fear in Lillian's eyes, who no doubt realised that she had lost her angelic image. With a sob she said in a low voice, 'You are all wronging me. I'm entirely innocent.' And with that she hurried away.

Some of the group looked a little sheepish and Rupert said, 'Grandfather was right when he advised us not to discuss the letters. Look at the bad feeling it has brought between us.'

'No,' Francis retorted. 'It has cleared your sister from being blamed for them—isn't that worthwhile?'

Rupert and the others agreed, and there was some talk of their surprise that Lillian should make such an accusation. By the time the group split up Jessamy felt that justice had been done in exonerating Louise from all blame.

Despite Jeremiah's insistence that the poison pen letters should not be discussed privately, there was a lot of secretive whispering going on between groups and Jessamy was glad when the evening was over.

Esmeralda was due home the following evening and Verity invited Chadwick to bring her to their house, where they would all have a meal together. When there was a knock on the front door Bertie, a broad grin on his face, flung open the door crying, 'Welcome home.'

Then as Esmeralda stepped in looking radiant and wearing a beautiful new fur dolman, there was a sudden silence. She laughed. 'So, where is this welcome?'

Verity stepped forward and kissed her. 'You've completely stunned us.' Then, running a finger over the fur she added teasingly, 'Is it true that the streets of London are paved with gold?'

Chadwick, who had just stepped into the hall, shook his head, his expression wry. 'Unfortunately, no.'

'It's just that I'm lucky enough to have a wealthy relative on my side of the family, who insisted on buying it for me,' Esmeralda explained. 'Oh, I've had the most wonderful time, I've so much to tell you.' She turned to Jessamy. 'Haven't you a kiss for your Mama?'

'Yes, of course.' After Jessamy and the boys had greeted her and Esmeralda was divested of her hat and dolman they went into the sitting-room where, from then on, the evening belonged to Esmeralda. She described all the places she had visited, the elegant house where she had stayed, all the exciting people she had met and the excellent meals she had enjoyed, until Verity was saying she was positively green with envy.

It was not until they were home that Chadwick broke the news to Esmeralda of the poison pen letters: as Jessamy had predicted, her mother was annoyed that the letter addressed to her had been destroyed. Even when Chadwick explained his reasons for destroying it, Esmeralda was not appeased. No more was said then but when Jessamy was in bed she heard her mother's voice raised in anger and her father replying coldly that he had no wish to hear any more about the letters nor about her visit to London.

Jessamy was prepared to find a strained atmosphere between her parents the next morning, but any there might have been was dissolved when Bertie and Verity arrived early, with the news that Lillian had left home during the night. In a note to her parents she said that she was not responsible for writing the poison pen letters, but there were 'some people' who blamed her—and she could not stand being in such an atmosphere. She added that she was going to London, but left no forwarding address.

Esmeralda's sympathies were all with Lillian until Francis explained how she had practically accused Louise publicly of being the culprit. The news of Lillian caused a stir among the family. Some said, 'Poor girl, driven from her home by malicious gossip, she was such a gentle soul...' Others said there was no smoke without fire. If she had been innocent she would have faced them all, her head held high. What seemed to intrigue most of them, however, was the sin she had been accused of by the letter-writer.

Chadwick said firmly, 'I hope none of them ever gets to know.' But Jessamy was to learn the contents of that letter later, from her grandmother.

On the Monday word came from Henrietta asking Jessamy to come and see her. Jessamy had chatted to her grandmother for only a few minutes at Hannah's birthday party and guessed she wanted to know all the ins and outs of what was being said about Lillian leaving home. And she was right.

After greeting her, Henrietta waved her granddaughter towards a stool. 'Come along now, Jessamy dear, and tell me all the gossip. Your grandfather has forbidden anyone to talk about it but he's gone to London so we can talk to our hearts' content. What is being said? Who is suspected of this foul deed?' Henrietta gave a little chuckle. 'It's the most teasing thing to happen since Squire Hunt ran away with three serving wenches.'

Jessamy told her all she knew, describing how Lillian had hinted maliciously that Louise was responsible and Francis' reaction. Henrietta gave a quick nod. 'Good for him. I have no pity for Lillian whatsoever. She has a mean spirit and doesn't care who she hurts.'

Jessamy said, 'Everyone, of course, wants to know what was in the letter that she received. I think she wrote one to herself to put everyone off the scent that she was the culprit.'

'No, she didn't.' Henrietta spoke quietly. 'She did receive a letter and she came to ask me if there was any truth in it. The letter-writer had accused her of being illegitimate.'

Jessamy stared at her grandmother. 'Lillian accused *me* of being illegitimate—do you remember?'

'Indeed I do. The thing is that you were not, but she is. It was a case of the biter being bit. She was deeply shocked and said it would be impossible to go on living here. That was on Friday night just before the party broke up.'

When Jessamy asked who Lillian's real father

was, Henrietta shook her head. 'That must remain a secret and I must ask, Jessamy, that you keep this to yourself. I would not have told you, had not Lillian cruelly accused you of being illegitimate.' Jessamy promised.

Henrietta's sombre mood suddenly changed and she began to coax Jessamy to tell her any little thing she had heard that might lead to the identity of the letter-writer. Jessamy felt annoyed with her grandmother and told her so, pointing out that she was trying to get excitement out of other people's misery. At this Henrietta gave a deep sigh. 'Oh, Jessamy my love, I don't like this primsy side of you, you remind me of Dorcas. A little gossip gives a zest to my very dull life. Anyway, I'm sure that half of what was written in the letters would be pure speculation.' She laughed. 'I know my letter was, but most entertaining to read, all the same. I should like to know who concocted them. Probably we shall never learn the truth. Now then, what is all this about your mother returning from London draped in furs?'

Jessamy repeated what her mother had told them and this set Henrietta off speculating who was wealthy enough in Esmeralda's family to present her with such a gift, but she had not found the answer when who should arrive but Esmeralda and Verity... Jessamy left the women to their gossip.

CHAPTER FIFTEEN

That evening, realising she had been neglecting Louise, Jessamy sat down and wrote a five-page letter. By return she had only one page, which began by saying how pleased Louise was to be out of the awful atmosphere of the poison pen letters and how she was sure that the culprit would be Lillian. She went on to say she had milked her first cow and what an amusing experience it had been.

Remembering how she and Louise had enjoyed talking over all sorts of little bits of gossip, Jessamy felt disappointed at the contents but as she read on, she felt choked.

'I miss all the family, especially you, Jessamy, and wish all this business was over and we could tear to shreds all the people we didn't like. Write again when you can, I live for letters, especially your long newsy ones. With love, Louise.'

Louise had never ever signed 'with love'—which made Jessamy realise how much her cousin was missing family and affection. After that, Jessamy wrote every week to Louise, sometimes twice a week, and worried when her cousin was a long time in replying. She also fretted that people were still surreptitiously discussing the poison pen letters weeks after the event and speculating what the accusations could have been. 'They're like vultures,' she complained to her father one morning when she arrived at the shop. 'Mrs Moss pounced on me this morning asking if we had heard anything from Lillian. You should have seen her face—it was mean, gloating.'

Jessamy had hung up her hat and coat when she realised her father was silent. She turned to him and saw a grave look on his face. 'Papa, what is it?'

'Your Aunt Verity and Uncle Bertie have had news of Christian. He's in Africa. He had been terribly sick all during the voyage and then developed a fever. Apparently an English family took charge of him.'

'Oh, Papa, thank goodness he's been cared for. Poor Aunt Verity and Uncle Bertie, how worried they must be.'

During the afternoon Verity came to the shop, to say that now the first shock of the news of Christian was over both she and Bertie were hopeful that their eldest son would soon be on his way back home. She talked about the family who were caring for him. 'Mrs Taylor sent a lovely letter, telling us that we were not to worry, Christian was being attended by an excellent doctor. Aren't people kind?'

Chadwick said with a gentle smile, 'It's just a small return, Verity, for all the many kindnesses that you have shown to other people.'

257

This sentiment was echoed by many people when they learned about Christian, which made the situation seem so much brighter.

The following day when Jessamy came back from the midday break to see a familiar figure talking to her father, her heartbeat began racing immediately.

Fabian held out his hands to her. 'Jessamy.' The word was a caresss. 'I've been waiting to see you. No, not in the shop, on the voyage. It seemed endless.'

'For me too,' she said softly.

Chadwick asked with a teasing smile if he should offer tea or nectar and Fabian said, 'With your permission, sir, I should like to steal your daughter for a while.'

Chadwick readily agreed and Jessamy knew a joyousness as they left the shop. It was a glorious afternoon with the delicate greens of foliage unfolding and the gold of primroses by the roadside. She was with the man she loved, his very touch on her arm making her blood tingle.

When Fabian asked her which direction they should take she suggested her favourite part of the moors where there were the waterfalls, streams, tarns and massive crags.

The sun chased shadows over distant hills bathing the land with a golden glow. Fabian said, 'The last walk we had together, the ground was snow-covered, do you remember?'

'Yes, I do indeed. It was lovely, but then I enjoy the moors in all their moods.'

Fabian talked about the moods of the sea and Jessamy felt he was filling in the time until they were away from habitation and he could take her in his arms. When they reached the house where she had seen him getting into a carriage with a young lady she mentioned the incident. Fabian told her that the young lady was the daughter of a colleague then added, 'Helen is happily married.' The warm amusement in his voice had Jessamy annoyed with herself for having mentioned the incident. How gauche he must have thought her.

When they came to a tarn they stopped. The water was still, their reflections mirror images. Fabian said softly, 'How lovely you are, Jessamy.' He turned to her. 'You do love me?'

She looked up, searching the strong features. 'Yes, I do, Fabian. I won't ever stop loving you.'

'Jessamy.' He drew her to him and kissed her gently on the lips. 'And I could never love anyone as I do you.'

Just the gentle touch of his lips had brought a response in her and she wondered how strong passion could be with a more loving kiss. He touched her cheek. 'I have brought you a ring, but I must keep it until our betrothal celebration, which I understand from your father is to be held on Thursday evening. I'm told it will be a small family affair.'

Jessamy was about to say that only her Uncle Bertie and her Aunt Verity would be there when Fabian added, 'Later, of course, we must face the ordeal of a family celebration at our wedding.'

'Ordeal?' she queried, a little hurt.

'I was hoping for a quiet wedding, but I accept that family and friends have to be invited.'

Jessamy had a feeling that her courtship was starting off on the wrong note, but then Fabian took her by the shoulders and looked deeply into her eyes. 'Believe me, Jessamy, my love for you is the strongest emotion I have ever known. If it were not for convention I would carry you off now and keep you to myself for ever more.'

The words would have thrilled Jessamy to the core, had they been followed by a passionate embrace, but Fabian remained as motionless as the water in the tarn. If only he would sweep her into his arms. He had no reason not to. The moor was deserted, the only sounds being those of gulls and the joyous pattering of a nearby stream as it tumbled over rocks. When they walked on Jessamy wondered if she was wronging Fabian. She had been allowed to walk with him unchaperoned and he was gentleman enough to respect this trust.

But Jessamy, stifling a sigh, could not help wishing that he had cast convention to the wind and shown her just how much he loved her. She said, 'I think perhaps we ought to go back.'

'Must we?' Fabian asked softly. There was a sensuous note in his voice then that brought a familiar throbbing to Jessamy's body. She stopped and stood hesitant. There was a path that led to a secluded bay below and Fabian had glanced towards it. It was so tempting. Jessamy longed to feel his arms around her, wanted to know the strength of his passion. The next moment she was appalled at where her thoughts were leading. How could she have forgotten Louise's weakness and her dreadful fate. She said, a slight trembling in her voice, 'I really think we should be making our way back.'

'Yes, perhaps we should.' The accidental touch of his hand on hers was enough to send a pulse jumping in her throat and Jessamy realised then the strength of passion and how easy it would be to succumb.

As they began to retrace their steps Fabian chatted about another voyage he had taken but Jessamy was only partially listening. Her main thoughts were on marriage and what it would entail. Louise had told her a little of what happened when a couple married but had not gone into any great detail. She had heard of women who hated sleeping with their husbands and was unable to understand it. Surely if one experienced emotions as strong as those Fabian could arouse in her with just a touch, then lovemaking must be one of the most enjoyable and exciting things that could happen. Even now she was experiencing small, pleasurable tremors.

'Jessamy, where are you?'

She brought her mind back quickly to Fabian's teasing question and, because at that moment Christian came into her thoughts she said, 'You've travelled widely and been to so many countries I keep wondering if you were young when you first started to go to sea.'

Fabian told her he had travelled abroad with his parents from boyhood. 'My father suffered from a wanderlust and my mother insisted she travel with him. My father agreed but said if they had a child he or she would travel with them when old enough. And so, at seven years old I became a traveller. And loved it. Then when I was twelve years old my mother got tired of travelling and she and I came home. I was sent to boarding school, which I hated. When I was fourteen I ran away to sea.' Fabian spread his hands. 'And that is the story of my life.'

'Without embellishments,' Jessamy said smiling.

Fabian gave a schoolboyish grin. 'The embellishments would fill a tome.'

'I'm sure they would. They'll be something to talk about on cold winter evenings when we're old and grey.'

Fabian laughed heartily. 'Now isn't that a pleasant thought. We are not even married and here is my future bride talking about being in our dotage. That will be something to talk about during my voyages.'

'Don't you dare,' she teased. 'I said it without thinking.'

He touched her cheek. 'But the thought was there, my darling. At least I know you are prepared to be a loyal wife.'

My darling... The way he said it gave Jessamy a lovely feeling of togetherness.

Although Jessamy had been a little disappointed when her mother suggested a small betrothal party, she was pleased afterwards that it was kept to just the six of them. It was cosy, intimate, and her mother had been so lovely towards her. She had talked to her before Fabian arrived about how there would be so much to arrange later—a trousseau, a house to choose and furnish; if Jessamy needed any advice, Esmeralda would be pleased to help, but she was definitely not going to intrude in any arrangements that Jessamy might want.

Bertie and Verity looked much brighter these days. Bertie talked about Christian, laughing as he said, 'Who'd ever have thought he would have gone off adventuring, but there, this is Fabian and Jessamy's night, we can talk about our lad tomorrow and he should be home soon.'

When Fabian put the ring on Jessamy's finger she felt she could never be happier. The diamonds were closely set together in the form of a heart. He put his hand over hers as though making a pledge and said with emotion, 'You have my heart too, Jessamy dearest.'

Chadwick had risen to his feet to propose a toast when Eliza came in to say there was a visitor. Before she could announce who it was Paul, the youngest son of James and Catherine, burst in, his face ashen.

'Uncle Chadwick, I'm sorry to interrupt your dinner, but please can you come at once. Mother has had a stroke.'

'A stroke?' Esmeralda exclaimed. 'But I saw her this afternoon—she was all right then.'

'Yes, I know, but we've just had word to say that our Lillian has been found drowned.'

There was a stunned silence for a moment then Chadwick said quietly, 'I'll just get my bag, Paul.'

By the next morning it seemed that everyone from St Peel to St Cade knew about the tragedy. Among the family there was a general feeling that Lillian must have been the writer of the poison pen letters, and had taken her own life out of guilt. As it turned out, however, this was not the case.

After Chadwick had visited the sick woman, he sent for the doctor and then he, James and Jeremiah travelled overnight to London, to learn the truth about Lillian.

Eventually Henrietta received a telegram from the three men to say that Lillian had apparently been robbed and pushed into the River Thames. At this there were exclamations

264

of horror. Murdered? How dreadful.

A letter that followed on from the telegram described how the police had dragged Lillian's body from the river. Her handbag, from which her purse was missing, had been found on the river bank containing a letter from someone called Margaret. The writer, who had obviously received a communication from Lillian, wrote that she would be delighted to have Lillian stay with her for as long as she wished. A postcript added that her brother John was looking forward so much to seeing Lillian again. The heading on the letter said Pimlico, but there was no address.

In the newspaper report of the tragedy the police asked for information about the woman Margaret and her brother John: a substantial reward was being offered by the Every family which could lead to the arrest of the assailant.

Before the men were due to return, Jeremiah wrote and asked the family to meet at Beacon Hall so all would know the result of their enquiries. On the evening of their return, all three men looked weary and dispirited, but when Jeremiah stood up to address the family his back was ramrod straight.

He began by saying that in spite of a detailed search of Pimlico by the police and themselves, no clue had been unearthed regarding the identity of the mysterious Margaret and John. There were those who had come forward claiming to know them, but all were false reports from people hoping to win the reward. After this Jeremiah paused then went on, 'I want you to know every detail. You are family and have a right to know, but I warn you that these details are harrowing...Lillian could only be identified by her clothes and a locket she wore next to her skin. Her face was...unrecognisable.'

There was a gasp of horror at this and Jessamy had a feeling of nausea. Dear God, no person, however much she was hated, should have been treated in this way.

Plenty of questions were asked but no answers were found. James in tears said, 'Let us hope we have no more tragic news.'

But the following day, Bertie and Verity had word to say that Christian had died.

During the next month, Jessamy thought there could surely be no worse time. Every member of the family was in deepest mourning and going into each house was like entering a morgue. The worst was her Uncle James' house, where her Aunt Catherine, paralysed down one side after the stroke, wept silent tears of grief.

Jessamy visited Catherine, only occasionally at first as the woman's speech was slurred and it was difficult to understand her. But when her Uncle James told her how greatly Catherine looked forward to her visits, she went more often; with patient tuition, she helped her aunt to speak slowly and only two or three words at a time. This method worked, and gradually her aunt's speech improved.

Jessamy also visited Verity, who had become withdrawn, but had no success in getting her favourite aunt out of her apathetic state. Then a letter came from Mrs Taylor, who had cared for Christian, explaining that she had had a fall from a horse and had been confined to bed. Now that she was up and about again she wanted Verity and her husband to know how much Christian had talked about them in his more lucid moments. She wrote:

'He said once that if anything happened to him he wanted you to know how much he loved you both. He praised you as being the best parents in the world, and added that he also wanted you to know that he would not have wanted to miss the adventure of the voyage, in spite of being so ill. He had become a man.'

Verity and Bertie wept over the letter, but afterwards were more reconciled to Christian's death. It was God's will—and Christian at least had fulfilled his ambition, something few people achieved in life.

During this terrible period of sorrow, the two people to surprise Jessamy were her mother and Fabian. Esmeralda talked to her daughter more than she had every done in her life. Not about anything important, just relating small incidents, mostly of London, that had not been told before.

And Fabian, after Christian's death, had visited Jessamy as often as he could before sailing. He had been so gentle, so loving. The evening before he was due to leave he said, 'This will be a short voyage, Jessamy darling. I feel I ought to try and get a shore job so that we can be together always.' But Jessamy, knowing that the sea was in his blood and he would be unhappy away from it, said no, she was prepared to wait.

At night in bed she relived that last evening, when they had been alone together for a while. Fabian had held her close and passion flowed between them; for Jessamy it was so overwhelming she knew she would have found it difficult to resist Fabian, had he begged to make love to her. But Fabian kept his emotions under control; even though there had been a tremor in his voice when he put her away from him saying, 'I long for the time when I can hold you in my arms all night. Think of me, my darling, and know how I shall be wanting you. Oh, Jessamy, I love you so much.'

His kisses then had brought the demands of her body to such a pitch that she wanted to cry out, 'Love me properly, please?' but once more Fabian put her from him and, after drawing his fingertips gently over her cheek and searching her face as though to memorise her every feature, he left.

Afterwards, Jessamy was not sure whether she was relieved or sorry, not to have experienced the true meaning of the consummation of marriage.

CHAPTER SIXTEEN

Jessamy felt bereft after Fabian had gone. Even Alistair was not at the shop to talk to. He had had a fall and hurt his back and Chadwick had insisted on him staying away and resting, adding that his time would not be wasted, the lad could study.

Mr Blackwell was always good company and Jessamy knew she could have gone to visit her grandmother, but felt she wanted to be with someone younger. Yet in spite of this she ended up going to visit her Aunt Catherine.

Catherine's eyes filled with tears when she saw her niece and whispered she had something to tell her. But the next moment she turned her head away and refused to say anything.

Jessamy put her arms around her. 'Oh, come on, Aunt Catherine, you're doing splendidly. You can tell me later what it was you wanted to say.'

But Jessamy did not find out. When she mentioned this to Verity her aunt said, 'I've had a feeling all along that Catherine knows something about Lillian that no one else does. Still, she's a strange person and might never tell us.'

Two days after this conversation, news came from the police in London that had the family buzzing with speculation. The woman Margaret, with whom Lillian had intended to stay, told the police that the letter found in the dead girl's handbag had been written by her a year before. Lillian had never come for the intended visit, nor had Margaret heard from her since—but then she and her brother had been abroad for months, and only learned about the tragedy when they returned home.

James and Jeremiah went off to London to meet Margaret Weaver and her brother John, but came back without any more information that would shed further light on the mystery.

It was apparently during a holiday spent with relatives that Lillian had met the spinster and bachelor brother. The pair had been taken with Lillian's sweet and gentle ways but knew very little about her, except the fact that she was engaged to a wealthy young man. However, as Lillian had never mentioned such a person and as the relatives concerned said that Lillian had never gone out alone, James and Jeremiah presumed that the couple had misunderstood her.

When Verity and Jessamy went to see Henrietta the old lady's nostrils were quivering with the desire for news. 'Jeremiah says there isn't anything to tell, that Lillian was the soul of propriety. She might have been when she was with her relatives, but what about her having a secret assignment with some man?'

Verity looked doubtful. 'I don't see how she could. She would be sleeping with her cousin Blanche.'

'And Blanche, as I have been led to believe, is a dreamy young romantic. Lillian would soon get her involved in a secret meeting. I'm right, I know—you mark my words.'

Jessamy wrote to Fabian and to Louise, telling them of the latest development concerning Lillian, but she only mentioned to Louise her grandmother's suggestion of a secret assignation. Louise replied saying it was the sort of thing that their cousin would do. Not, she added, that she agreed with the death Lillian had suffered.

Louise had grieved terribly over Christian's death, admitting that although she loved him, she had always been jealous because he was the favourite with both parents. She said she supposed that the first son was always the favourite with any family—but it did not ease the hurt, nor her remorse for having been jealous of him. Verity and Bertie were dreadfully upset over this, saying they had not been aware of any favouritism. They promised to make it up to their daughter when she returned home.

The weeks dragged by. Jessamy found that all she was waiting for was Fabian's return, but when she did get a letter it was to say he would not be able to see her this time when he arrived in England. The ship would

271

be docking in London and would reload to go to India.

India? Oh, no, he would be away weeks and weeks. It was only the fact that Fabian seemed equally devastated by their long parting that kept Jessamy from being utterly miserable. Chadwick commiserated with her but reminded her gently that she could expect this if she was going to marry a seafaring man, while Alistair's consolation was to say it would be easier when she was married and had children to care for.

'If I don't have children then I shall study and who knows, I might in time become a doctor.'

Alistair shook his head and said he did not recommend it. When a man came home from sea he wanted his wife there—he *needed* her. This brought a retort from Jessamy that his was a typical male attitude.

'This is what Papa says, but some married women lead a professional life and are happy. An American woman called Elizabeth Blackwell became a famous doctor and ran a dispensary for poor people.'

'She is an exceptional case, Jessamy. She not only came from a wealthy family, but her husband was a doctor who understood her needs.' Jessamy gave up.

Late that evening, Bertie arrived at the house to say he had just taken Verity to the station. They had had word to say that Louise was ill

272

and it was thought that the baby might be born prematurely. Verity had caught the overnight train to Cornwall.

Bertie looked grey. Chadwick poured him a large whisky and made him sit down, saying, 'You must stay here tonight,' and Esmeralda said of course he must, he couldn't go back to an empty house.

He took a drink of the whisky then looked up, his eyes full of tears. 'Thanks, I'll be glad to. Verity said she would let us know as soon as she could.' Bertie's voice trembled. 'If anything should happen to Louise.'

'It won't,' Esmeralda said softly. 'She's in good hands, and Louise is strong. I know it will be all right.'

Jessamy was surprised to find her mother so gentle.

It was eleven o'clock the following morning when Verity telephoned Bertie at the chandlery to say that Louise was all right but the baby, a boy, had lived only two hours. She said that although it had all been very upsetting she thought it was for the best. Bertie agreed, so did Chadwick and Esmeralda but Jessamy felt grieved about the baby. Although Louise had kept saying she didn't want it Jessamy had wanted her to at least have a chance to love it for a time. When she voiced this Esmeralda said it would be the worst possible thing to get fond of a baby then give it away to someone else.

It was not until a letter came from Verity that

273

Jessamy learned that Louise had refused to even look at the baby, but she had wanted it to be christened John, her brother Christian's middle name. The local vicar had refused to christen the child because it had been born out of wedlock, but a vicar in another parish had christened it and he and Cornelius had managed to bury it in consecrated ground.

When Verity arrived home ten days later she was alone. Louise, she said, needed a little more time to recover. She had had a rather dreadful time. It was the beginning of July when hedgerows and gardens were a riot of colour that Louise came home. She had arrived unexpectedly and when Verity came to the shop to ask them all to come to dinner that evening, she was agitated. It would help to ease things, she said. Chadwick promised her gently they would be there.

When Jessamy and her parents arrived that evening Louise greeted them brightly, saying how lovely it was to be home again.

Jessamy hugged her over and over again and said, 'Oh, it's wonderful to have you back. I've missed you so much.'

'I've missed you too, of course, but they really were wonderful people and I did enjoy farm life.'

Louise looked well. Her skin was a golden brown and she talked more than Jessamy had ever heard her talk. But later she had a feeling of sitting with a stranger—this brightness was just a facade. Jessamy longed to have her cousin on her own but did not want to suggest staying as her mother had said they must go soon, Louise had been travelling many hours the night before and would be tired.

They were getting ready to leave when Louise said suddenly, 'Jessamy, why don't we have an early morning walk on the moor in the morning.'

'Lovely, I'll look forward to it. Will it be all right if I call at seven o'clock?'

'Splendid, I'll be ready.'

When they left Chadwick said, 'I don't know who was the most tense this evening—Louise, Bertie or Verity.'

Esmeralda said, 'Well, it must be a strain for all of them. I only hope that things soon settle down. Louise has certainly changed. She was never much of a talker and never a walker. I suppose she wants someone her own age to talk to.'

Louise was ready waiting at the door the next morning when Jessamy arrived. She was much more subdued than the night before. As they left for their walk she confessed to her cousin, 'I never thought I would get through last night without screaming. Don't misunderstand me, Jessamy, I did want to come home, quite desperately, but circumstances were different on the farm. I was never made to feel I had sinned.'

Jessamy protested strongly at this. 'Well, you

certainly couldn't say that you were treated as a sinner by your parents or mine. I thought they were all very sensible, simply treating you as someone in the family who had been away for a holiday. Yes, your parents were tense but so were you.'

'I know, I know.' Louise sighed. 'I shall have to learn to relax and try and settle down. Oh, how I hate the thought of meeting the rest of the family. I'm quite sure they all know why I went away. I keep trying to tell myself that I don't care what any of them think, but I do.'

Jessamy said in a low voice, 'I was sorry you lost the baby.'

'I wasn't.' There was a harsh note in Louise's voice. They walked in silence for a way then Louise stopped and sat on a bench of rock. Jessamy hesitated then sat down beside her.

'Louise, did you get to love the baby?'

'No, how could I?' She stared straight ahead. 'The relationship was all wrong.'

'Relationship?' Jessamy queried, puzzled.

'The baby was my brother.'

'Your brother? I don't understand.'

'*My* father was *my* baby's father. Is that clear?'

Jessamy stared at her with a mounting horror. It couldn't be true. Not dear, amiable Uncle Bertie.

Louise suddenly jumped up and going over to the rock-face thumped a clenched fist against it. Then she turned, and tears slid slowly down her cheeks as she said in a pitiful way, 'He was so tiny, Jessamy, and there was a sort of puzzled expression on his little crumpled red face.'

Jessamy, crying inwardly, went over and put her arms around her cousin, but could find no words to console her. After a few minutes Louise dried her eyes and said, 'I want to tell you how it happened, because I feel that I'm more to blame than Papa. But you must promise never to tell a soul.' Jessamy gave her solemn word.

They sat down again on the slab of rock and Louise told her story.

'It happened one night when Mama was away visiting her parents. I had had a nagging headache all day and although it wasn't bad enough for me to want to take any medication it did keep me awake. Eventually I came downstairs and heated some milk. Papa, having heard movements, came down too and, as always, being so caring, he offered to get me some medicine. I told him no, that in fact the headache was easing.

'We sat talking, Papa about his ambitions and perhaps because everywhere was so still, so quiet, there seemed to be an intimacy about it, such as when Papa would come to read me a story when I was in bed, as a child. I used to love those evenings, when I felt I had him all to myself, no Christian, Mama or the boys to share him with. I had always adored him.

Yes, I know I don't show it. Shall I tell you something? I think I've always been a little jealous of Mama and the way Papa fussed over her, loved her...'

Louise was silent for a while and when she spoke again there was a tremor in her voice. 'I think perhaps I was mostly to blame for what happened that night. I became a little sleepy and Papa picked me up in his arms and said laughing, "Come on baby, bedtime. I'll perhaps read you a story if you're good." I cuddled into him and when he laid me on the bed I asked him if he would hold me for a while. He said yes of course and he lay down beside me and held me. He asked me what was wrong, was I in love with someone?

'I had met a boy recently and was longing to see him. I told him yes but refused to say who the boy was, only that he did not seem to care for me. Papa said he understood my hurt, that he had once been in love with a girl when he was younger who did not return his love, and then he drew me closer.'

Louise paused and when she went on her voice was little above a whisper. 'Papa kissed me on the cheek, just little pecks at first, then he kissed me on the mouth and I...I responded. Oh, God, Jessamy, once we had started on that wave of emotion we couldn't stop. I never even thought of what could happen. You can guess the consequences.'

Louise began to cry again. Jessamy wanted

278

to hold her, but couldn't. The truth was so terrible—a sin in the eyes of God. How could she ever face her Uncle Bertie again?

When Louise became calmer she looked at Jessamy with pleading. 'Don't turn away from me, Jessamy, I couldn't bear it. You are my only friend.'

'I won't, Louise, I promise.'

Louise then spoke of the terrible shame and guilt she and her father had suffered. 'Papa brought the Bible in and we both swore it would never happen again. We also agreed that Mama would never know.' Louise shook her head slowly. 'I still can't believe the way I acted. Because of it I can never marry.'

Louise then begged Jessamy to try and not let it make any difference in her feelings towards Bertie. 'You've always loved Papa too. You know how kind and caring he is.'

At that moment, Jessamy felt too shocked to make any promises but she did say she would try. To this Louise replied quietly, 'Thanks for listening. I've kept this bottled up inside me for all these months but now I feel I can face Mama again without that awful urge to tell her the truth.'

Jessamy knew only one thing—that her life would never be the same again. She had known about the peccadilloes of husbands and wives but had not guessed at the stark reality of life—that loving someone could be a twisted, secretive, hateful thing.

Jessamy had a long wait for a letter from Fabian but when one did come she was over-joyed to hear he would be home soon. But he wrote, '*Unfortunately, we are docking in London and as I have some business to attend to, there should be two days delay. But rest assured, my darling, I shall be with you at the earliest oppor-tunity. When I do arrive I shall discuss with your parents an early marriage. We shall look for a house or a plot of land on which to build, then you can be planning furniture and furnishings...*

The rest of the letter was full of his love for her. '*I have so much love building up inside of me to give to you I ache with it.*'

Jessamy closed her eyes and held the letter to her. Would her parents agree to a wedding while the family were still in mourning? The girls would soon be in half-mourning. She would talk to her parents that evening.

However, it was not the wedding that Jes-samy sat down that night to discuss, but a poison pen letter...

CHAPTER SEVENTEEN

The letter came for Jessamy in the second post, after her father had left for the shop and her mother was still in bed. The envelope was postmarked London, and as she didn't recognise the writing Jessamy sat studying it for a few moments before slitting open the envelope.

'If you are planning to marry the delectable Captain Montague I would ask him first about the mistress he visits and keeps in luxury in a house in London.'

The tightness in her chest was so bad Jessamy felt she could hardly breathe. A mistress? *Oh, no.*

Relief came. The whole thing was ridiculous. Someone who obviously disliked her was trying to poison her mind against Fabian. But who? Could it be one of the family? Someone who had been to London recently. And Lillian, poor warped Lillian, was dead. Murdered and drowned.

Jessamy got up shakily, went into the hall to get a jacket and after calling to Eliza that she was going to the shop, left, heading instead for her Aunt Verity's house. Perhaps she could shed light on the wretched situation.

Verity and Louise were still at breakfast. 'You *are* early,' Louise said cheerfully.

Verity teased her. 'Did the mice in the wainscotting get you out of bed?' This was a saying between them.

Jessamy held out the letter to her. 'It was this that brought me here.' She watched her aunt's expression change from interest to puzzlement, then to consternation.

'Who could have written such a thing?' Louise held out her hand for the letter and Verity passed it over. After Louise had scanned it she looked up.

'So our Captain has a mistress. What man doesn't?'

Verity was angry. 'Every man doesn't have a mistress, Louise, but that is not the most important thing at the moment. It's the letter. Who wrote it? We presumed that such letters were at an end when Lillian died. And here we have another horrible insinuation. Who could have written it?'

Jessamy said hotly, 'The only thing I want to know is whether it's true that Fabian has a mistress. If so, I'm certainly not marrying him. I would take it as an insult. What puzzles me is how anyone in the family would know. I don't feel it's the sort of thing that a man like Fabian Montague would bandy around.'

'Why not?' Louise queried. 'I should imagine he would be proud to boast that he had a beautiful young fiancée and a beautiful mistress.'

Verity scolded her, said it was unseemly of a girl to make such remarks. Then she got up, suggesting that she and Jessamy went to visit Henrietta, saying that quite often the old lady had an idea about incidents such as this. To Louise she added, 'On your way to the warehouse call in and tell Uncle Chadwick where we've gone, but don't tell him the reason why. We shall have a talk with him later.'

Henrietta showed no surprise on hearing about the letter. She had actually suspected that something like this might happen. After all, she had never wholly believed that Lillian was responsible for the other spate of letters.

'Then who is it?' Jessamy enquired, eyeing her grandmother with some astonishment.

'Ask yourself how many of the family are jealous of you. Dorcas for one has been making her tongue wag about how her daughter Rose would have been a much more suitable match for the Captain. And, as you can imagine, young Rose is very ready to agree with her Mama.'

When Jessamy pointed out that neither her Aunt Dorcas nor Rose had been to London lately, Henrietta dismissed it as unnecessary. They had relatives there, didn't they? What was to stop either of them from asking them to post a letter from there and give a simple explanation.

Although Verity and Jessamy stayed for a while they made no further progress and

Verity said they had better go.

When Chadwick was told the reason for the visit to Beacon Hall he was shocked. Fabian Montague was an honourable man, how dare anyone vilify him in such a way.

Verity said a little wryly, 'The Captain is a handsome, virile man with appetites like any other man. He may well have a mistress, but the more important thing is this poison letter. Is there going to be another spate of them and if so, what can we do about it?'

'Ignore them, like we did with the others,' Chadwick stated firmly. 'It's the sensible thing to do.'

Jessamy spoke up. 'I have no intention of ignoring this letter.' She waved it. 'I want to see Fabian and I want to see him alone.'

Chadwick declared this to be out of the question. He and her mother would be present at the interview. He would send a letter to the Shipping Office asking Fabian to call as soon as possible.

Two days later, Fabian arrived at the house, his arms full of gifts and saying with a smile, 'I hope it's good news. Has Jessamy found a suitable house?'

He was handed the letter and after scanning it was a different person, stern, cold. Who had been dastardly enough to pen such words? No, he did not have a mistress. The young lady he had visited was his former fiancée.

'Caroline?' Jessamy echoed.

Fabian's expression softened. 'Please let me explain what happened.' He told Chadwick and Esmeralda first how he had been previously engaged, and how his fiancée had rejected him, fallen in love with someone else, then he included Jessamy in the rest of his story.

'Caroline married this other man and they went to live in Texas. Her family went out to visit them, and they and the husband perished in a fire.'

'Oh, how terrible,' Jessamy said. 'The poor girl.'

Fabian nodded. 'Exactly how I felt when I heard of the tragedy. Caroline came home to live with her only other relative, an aunt, and two months later the aunt died. She now has an older woman living with her as companion. I knew nothing of this until my trip before last. A letter was waiting for me, telling me what had happened. I went to see her and again when we docked at London this time. I felt it was a humane thing to do. I never dreamt that someone was going to misinterpret my motives. And who did? Who is responsible for the letter?'

Chadwick said they had no idea and probably never would know, then he added that speaking for himself, he was glad that Fabian had been able to give a suitable explanation. It had settled the matter.

Jessamy intervened then. 'I don't feel it's settled at all, Papa. I still need to know what

Fabian's feelings are towards Caroline.'

Esmeralda said softly, 'Now is that fair, Jessamy? Fabian has told us that he was once in love with this girl and love does not die in a few months or even years. He has a different kind of love for you, dear.'

Jessamy clenched her hands tightly. 'Could Fabian please answer for himself?'

Captain Montague asked permission to speak to Jessamy on her own. It was given and her parents left them.

He drew his chair nearer. 'I did love Caroline and for this reason I'm concerned about her. She's just a shadow of her former self. She's lost all reason for living. Can you imagine the shock it must have been to her to have lost everyone she loved?'

'I can understand her terrible grief, Fabian, but I have to know your exact feelings towards her. I couldn't marry you knowing that you might want to visit her regularly, making her dependent on you.'

'Caroline killed what love I had for her when she went off with another man. We actually had our wedding date fixed. However, that doesn't stop me from being sorry for her and I couldn't desert her at such a dreadful time in her life. It won't interfere with us, I promise.'

'It *will* interfere with our lives, Fabian, and it's foolish to think otherwise. If ever you were delayed in getting home I would assume you were with Caroline and I would wonder what was happening.'

'Nothing would happen. Can't you really understand Caroline's plight? She's suffered terrible tragedies. She's alone in the world and desperately needs friends. Look, come to London and meet her, Jessamy. Your mother could come, too. I'll pay all expenses. We could stay at her house—Caroline would welcome you both. Why not talk it over with your parents.'

Jessamy knew if her mother was told of a visit to London with all expenses paid they would certainly go; she also knew that she herself would like to meet this Caroline, to find out what sort of threat she would be to her marriage.

When the question of going to London was raised it was all settled so quickly that Jessamy felt sure her mother must have already discussed it with her father. It was a sensible idea. Chadwick affirmed: when Jessamy saw the state the poor girl was in she would understand that Fabian's motives for visiting Caroline were simply those of kindness. Jessamy felt about five years old. She wanted to discuss it with Louise and her Aunt Verity, but there was no opportunity. Everything happened so quickly. A telegram was sent to Caroline and the reply was enthusiastic—she would be delighted for them to visit. It was arranged they would travel the following day.

When Jessamy did see Verity her aunt said she thought it an excellent arrangement. It would give Jessamy a chance to assess Caroline and find out if she showed any tendency to lay claim to Fabian's attention.

Esmeralda was vivacious during the journey, as though she were setting out on a sightseeing tour rather than trying to settle her daughter's future. Jessamy found it difficult to join in the conversation, although she certainly could not complain that she was in any way neglected. On the contrary, Fabian was ever conscious of her welfare—was she comfortable, would she like some magazines?

The strange thing was that during the journey Jessamy felt detached from her mother and Fabian, at times regarding them as though they were complete strangers. And really, wasn't that what they were? Her mother had always been an enigma to her and this was what Fabian had become, too. He was talking and smiling, but what was actually in his thoughts? Was he hoping that in some way he could continue to see Caroline but ease Jessamy's mind that the girl posed no threat to her?

When they arrived in London Jessamy was astonished at the volume of traffic. She had thought the road from St Cade to St Peel busy enough, but the traffic here was chaotic! However, there were many places of interest to see on the way to Caroline's house near Hyde Park. Jessamy as well as Esmeralda noted every shop along Piccadilly, with Esmeralda declaring what a wonderful time they would have shop-gazing.

Fabian laughed, 'And spending, if I am any judge.'

Esmeralda gave him a coy smile. 'You know women, Captain.'

Caroline lived in one of an imposing row of five-storeyed houses with pillared entrances and wrought-iron balconies, on which tubs of red and pink geraniums were displayed.

'How lovely,' Esmeralda exclaimed.

A trim young maid ushered them in, saying Madam was expecting them. They were shown into a room, rather sombrely furnished, apart from a large emerald green velvet armchair, and it was from this chair that the most beautiful young woman Jessamy had ever seen rose to greet them warmly.

Caroline was tall and slender, with large dark eyes, expressive eyes. Her skin had the texture of a magnolia petal and her features could only be described as classical. She spoke softly as she greeted each one and although she gave the impression of having lived a full life there was an aura of helplessness about her that would surely draw men to her.

When tea was brought in, Esmeralda enthused about the position of the house and Caroline agreed that there were advantages in being near Hyde Park. Within minutes the two of them seemed to have established a rapport. When Caroline was talking Jessamy watched Fabian and noticed how he listened to her with an expression of gentle indulgence. Esmeralda drew Caroline out about London and she showed a wide knowledge of places and people. Jessamy said tentatively, 'So you do have quite a few friends here?'

A sad expression came over Caroline's face. 'I did have, but since returning home after the tragedy few people have paid a second visit. I think perhaps they are embarrassed and I don't quite know what to say. Or perhaps I am oversensitive.'

Fabian was annoyed. How dreadful of people to ignore her, just when she needed friends. Well, there was one thing—Caroline could always count on his friendship, and that of Jessamy and Esmeralda. Esmeralda made a quick response. Yes, of course. Caroline must come and visit them when she felt well enough. Jessamy remained silent. Why should her mother be so ready with an invitation for Caroline, when she refused to have any of the members of her own family to stay with them? What scheme had she in mind?

With this feeling of wariness Jessamy was unable to relax at first, and she was not really sure when she came to accept that Caroline was not a threat to her marriage to Fabian. Perhaps it was in the evening after dinner, when a fire had been lit in the sitting-room, not that it was cold but there was just an autumnal nip in the air. Caroline had suggested it, saying it would be cosy.

Caroline had a soft voice that Jessamy found

soothing. She talked of her early married life in Texas, saying how her husband had loved horses and how she had come to love them, too. They were temperamental, like humans. Some of them were difficult to train while others were very amenable. They became close like friends.

When Jessamy asked Caroline outright if she would like to go back to Texas at some stage she said, 'Oh, yes! That is my plan, when the worst of my grief is over. I have many good friends there who would not be just one-time visitors.'

It was this, Jessamy thought later, that had lulled her into a feeling of security.

'She is such a charming girl,' Esmeralda enthused at bedtime. 'One can understand Captain Montague falling in love with her.' Jessamy found herself bridling and reminded her mother that Caroline had jilted Fabian for another man—possibly because her late husband had been a wealthy ranch-owner.

Esmeralda made excuses for Caroline. Perhaps her parents had demanded that she marry a man in a higher position. Jessamy dismissed this, saying that although Caroline seemed a very gentle person she felt there was a strength in her—and then was surprised to hear herself say this. If Caroline was strong, determined... there might be trouble.

However, no trouble loomed on the horizon during the next few days. The party went to Rotten Row and watched the aristocracy riding.

Apparently Fabian and Caroline had ridden together in the past, but neither dwelt on this. Jessamy was entranced by the ladies in velvet habits riding side-saddle and looking so elegant. Later Caroline, Esmeralda and Jessamy went to look at the shops while Fabian made appointments with business acquaintances. Esmeralda bought a blouse for Jessamy and one for herself but was not extravagant in any way. Caroline made no purchases. She said that when she came out of mourning she would have to replenish all the clothes she had lost in the fire. She did not seem upset when she mentioned this and in fact, Jessamy was aware of a slight note of excitement when she mentioned new clothes.

Fabian puzzled Jessamy. He was loving towards her but she had a feeling that it was for effect rather than true emotion. She wished she could have a long talk with him, but wherever they went the four of them were together. They visited Buckingham Palace, but were not lucky enough to see any of the Royal Family; they walked along the Embankment and Jessamy was very much taken with the Houses of Parliament—such wonderful architecture. Caroline said the buildings were most impressive when seen in moonlight, and Jessamy envied her this experience.

Fabian wanted to book seats for a theatre, but when Caroline said she really felt unable to go because of her bereavement being so recent Fabian decided that none of them would go, which annoyed Jessamy. After all, they had come to be company for Caroline, so surely she should have been magnanimous enough to insist that her guests go without her to the theatre.

The next afternoon, for the first time, Jessamy found herself alone with Caroline. Esmeralda had gone to visit a friend and Fabian to see a colleague. Caroline said, 'I'm glad we can be alone for a while, Jessamy, I've wanted to talk to you about Fabian. Do you mind?'

'Not at all,' Jessamy waited, pressing her palms together to try and still the quick beating of her heart, guessing what Caroline was about to ask her.

'Jessamy, are you in love with Fabian?'

'Yes, I am. I would not have agreed to marry him otherwise.'

'I thought your parents might have arranged it, as you are so very young.'

'Not too young to fall in love with the handsome Captain, nor to feel privileged that he should have chosen me when he had the chance of so many other women. At first I thought he might have asked me to marry him on the rebound after you had thrown him over but—'

'I had no choice, Jessamy.' Caroline spoke in a low voice. 'My father had heavy gambling debts which he was unable to meet. My mother begged me to save him from having to face a

293

long prison sentence.'

'I'm sorry,' Jessamy said, but wondered if Caroline was speaking the truth or just saying it because of what had happened to her family. She paused then went on, 'Tell me, Caroline, why did you ask me if I loved Fabian? Are you trying to tell me that you are still in love with him?'

Caroline gave a small sigh. 'Everything in life seems to move on and change but love remains constant. I've never stopped loving Fabian. Please don't think I'm trying to take him from you. It would be impossible anyway. Before we parted he told me he would never forgive me for what I had done to him and I accept that. He has one big fault—he's an unforgiving man.' Caroline reached out a slender hand. 'I do hope I haven't upset you.'

'No, I think one must be sensible and talk things over.'

'So do I, and I'm glad you've taken it so well.'

Caroline then drew Jessamy out about her life and such was her sympathetic manner that Jessamy found herself confiding her ambition to become a doctor.

'A doctor?' Caroline echoed. 'Would Fabian approve? I understood he was intending to give up his seafaring life as he wants to settle down and have children.'

Jessamy looked up quickly. 'He did mention it once, but nothing was settled. If he did leave the sea then I would have to forget my dream of becoming a doctor.'

'Should a dream be sacrificed?'

'There is an urgent need for Fabian to have children. As you will know, he was an only child. We are a large family and Fabian would like a large family of his own. I wouldn't deny him that right.' And as Jessamy said it she knew she was relinquishing all thoughts of a career. By the time Fabian returned, she had told Caroline many anecdotes about the Everys. Fabian apologised for having been away so long.

'Don't worry,' Caroline said. 'Jessamy and I have been having a lovely intimate talk. Fabian, why don't you take Jessamy for a walk? Esmeralda has a headache and is lying down and I have some papers to sort out for my solicitors.'

'Yes, I will do later. I have some figures I want to jot down. I have had an interesting business talk with my colleague. It will only take about twenty minutes to half an hour. By then you might have completed your task, Caroline, and we can all go for a walk.'

He was out of the room before any reply could be made, and Jessamy, deeply hurt, stood up saying she would take a walk on her own.

'Men,' Caroline complained, 'how insensitive they are. I'll go and have a word with him.'

'No!' Jessamy spoke sharply. That was the last thing she wanted, having Caroline to plead her cause. 'I won't go too far. Excuse me.'

She took her hat and coat from the hall cupboard and the next minute was walking in the direction of the park, her vision blurred by tears. They could not even go for a walk without inviting Caroline. It would have been the first time they had been alone since their arrival in London. So much for not forgiving Caroline! He seemed obsessed with her. Well, it would have to end, one way or another...

CHAPTER EIGHTEEN

When Jessamy reached Piccadilly she stopped to get a handkerchief out of her handbag to wipe her eyes when her arm was grabbed. 'Jessamy, forgive me, how stupidly I behaved. Caroline really read me the riot act.'

Jessamy tensed. *Always Caroline!* She shook her arm free. 'I'm sorry, Fabian, it's too late for apologies. It's obvious you are still in love with her and she with you. She told me so.'

'Oh, did she? Did she also tell you that I told her I was no longer in love with her?'

Jessamy dabbed at her eyes then looked up. 'Aren't you fooling yourself? You couldn't even bear to go for a walk alone with me without suggesting that Caroline come along too.'

For the second time since she had met him, Jessamy saw a stern expression come over Fabian's face.

'Caroline will have our company for no more than a few days. You and I will be spending a lifetime together.'

'I doubt it.'

'Oh—so being courteous counts for nothing in your life, does it, Jessamy? I'm sorry, you put me in a quandary. Do I allow you to walk in the park alone, not a thing a gentleman would do in the normal way, or do I inflict my unwelcome company on you so that we can observe the proprieties?'

'Put like that,' she said, 'I shall have to accept your unwelcome company as I do wish to enjoy some fresh air.'

'It pleases me that you are able to enjoy something. Will you accept the support of my arm on our travels?'

The situation had become so farcical that Jessamy felt her lips trembling. She laid her hand on his arm and they set off, with Fabian making remarks about the weather and how fortunate they were that it was so mild. When he continued in the same vein she said, 'Can we please call a truce?'

'My pleasure, Ma'am. What subject would you like to discuss?'

Jessamy was about to reply lightly, 'Marriage,' when she stopped suddenly and gripped Fabian's arm. He glanced at her quickly

297

and asked what was wrong.

She nodded speechlessly in the direction of a couple who had stopped so that they could greet an elderly man who had hailed them. All three people were elegantly dressed.

Jessamy said in a strangled voice, 'The woman...it's Lillian. My Cousin Lillian.'

'Jessamy, what are you saying? Your cousin is dead.'

'Some woman is dead, her face mutilated, but she was not my cousin. Who could mistake that false, sweet smile. It's Lillian, I tell you!' Jessamy took a step forward and Fabian restrained her.

'Jessamy, you're becoming hysterical. You're trembling.'

'I'm not hysterical.'

The elderly man tipped his hat, the couple raised a hand each in farewell then moved away. As they passed within a few yards of Fabian and Jessamy, the woman glanced in their direction, then looking away quickly, laughed and said something to her companion.

'Did you see her?' Jessamy asked Fabian urgently.

He hesitated before replying, 'Yes, I did, and I must admit that the woman did resemble Lillian, but of course it's quite ridiculous to suggest it could be her. The police identified her body.'

'They identified her clothing and the handbag that was on the river bank.' Jessamy looked up at Fabian and said earnestly, 'Don't you see? Lillian must have arranged for some woman who had died to be dressed in her clothes.'

'Why?'

'Because she wanted to lose her identity. She had met some man in London and wanted a different life from that at home. Fabian, it all ties in. She must live around here somewhere. She's seen you, seen you visit Caroline and being Lillian she could not resist dropping the poison.'

Fabian refused to accept this explanation, it was pure fantasy on Jessamy's part, but nothing he said could shift her from her opinion. When he realised he was unable to move her he begged one thing, that she would not mention the incident in Caroline's hearing. In fact, he added, 'It might be best if you did not mention it to your mother, either.'

Jessamy agreed, but was determined to try and find out more if possible. The incident had at least drawn Jessamy and Fabian together again. Like her father, Fabian had a lot of charm and he soon convinced Jessamy that only sheer thoughtlessness had made him act the way he had by postponing the walk.

Caroline had visitors that evening, three men, friends she had not seen for some time. One was elderly, the other two about Fabian's age. Esmeralda was at her most charming. Jessamy was glad of the guests, for she could not get

Lillian out of her mind and there was so much talk that her quietness passed unnoticed.

It was late when the men left. When Esmeralda said how nice it was for Caroline to have such interesting friends, Caroline hastened to say they were not friends, just acquaintances, as though determined to make herself seem a lonely figure.

Jessamy lay wide awake in bed that night, her thoughts jumping from one thing to another. Would Fabian have come after her when she left the house, if Caroline had not scolded him for his behaviour? And if he had not come after her, she would have missed seeing Lillian... It all seemed fated. How could she find her cousin? It was certain she must live in the vicinity. But then she could search for weeks, or months even, for Lillian would definitely not be using her own name.

Jessamy suddenly decided she didn't trust Caroline. It was true the girl was responsible for sending Fabian to her, but why go to such lengths to deny she had friends? She wanted Fabian to feel sorry for her—and Fabian was very ready to give her sympathy. As long as he was in England he would visit Caroline, Jessamy was certain of that.

She fell into an uneasy sleep and dreamed she was walking across the moors at home. It was winter, and there had been a deep fall of snow, so fine that a wind sent it in small spirals that looked like smoke. Then ahead of her she saw a figure that she recognised as Fabian. He was sitting on the flat rock facing the big waterfall, but the water had frozen and hung in massive icicles.

She called to Fabian, but when he turned his head and recognised her he jumped up and hurried away. She tried to run after him but the snow became deeper and deeper until she was up to her thighs in it and was trapped. She was sobbing in despair when she heard someone calling her name then Alistair was there, lifting her out of the snow and holding her close. When she awoke from the dream the pillow was wet with her tears. What was the meaning of it? That Fabian no longer really wanted her?

Jessamy tossed and turned and eventually climbed out of bed, pulled on a dressing gown and went over to the window. There was a new moon, and she remembered her grandmother telling her when she was young that it was unlucky to see it through glass, but if she was outside and saw it and had a penny in her pocket, she was to turn the coin over and make a wish. It was all nonsense, of course, but she had always believed in it because some of her wishes *had* come true.

She was about to turn away and go back to bed when a movement caught her eye. A couple came from behind a potting shed at the bottom of the garden, their arms around one another's waists. The next moment Jessamy tensed and her heart became a wild thing. Caroline and Fabian! They stopped and Caroline lifted her arms and put them around Fabian's neck. His arms went around her then bending his head he kissed her on the lips. The kiss became impassioned and Jessamy, caught up in the lurid scene, felt sick.

She turned away and stood, her back against the wall. How could they? And in sight of her bedroom window. Fabian, besotted, would not know this, but Caroline would. When Jessamy looked out again, the garden was empty. Had they come into the house or were they making love in some other shed? With her mind suddenly made up, Jessamy went downstairs. She was icily calm by now. At the foot of the stairs she stopped and listened, and hearing the murmur of voices coming from the sitting-room, pushed open the door. In the glow from the embers of the dying fire Fabian stood gazing into Caroline's eyes. Jessamy began to clap and, startled, they sprang apart.

'What a charming scene,' she said. 'Beautifully staged. So was the scene in the garden, too. How you must have been laughing to yourselves, imagining me fast asleep in bed. Poor innocent Jessamy.'

Her voice suddenly broke and she turned quickly away. Fabian reached her before she got to the door. 'Jessamy, it's not at all as you imagine. We can explain.' When he tried to touch her she whispered, 'Don't.' Then she ran out and crossing the hall stumbled upstairs. Once in her room she paced up and down, not knowing what to do. She was beside herself with grief, with hurt at Fabian's deception. What was she going to say to her mother? Should she get dressed and depart, leaving a note for her mother? No, she must tell her face to face what had happened. But would she be believed? By now Caroline and Fabian would have concocted some story.

With a sudden decision reached Jessamy went downstairs again, and found Fabian and Caroline standing in the hall. She said, 'I have to talk to you. I don't want my parents to know the whole sordid story.'

'Yes, of course,' Fabian said. Caroline went ahead into the sitting-room and stirred the embers of the fire into a small blaze. Fabian brought a chair forward but Jessamy said she preferred to stand, adding, 'I'll tell you quickly what I have in mind. I shall simply say that I would rather wait two more years before getting married. And also that I don't want to choose a house yet. Papa and Mama will lecture me, of course, but I shall let them know that my mind is made up and that nothing they say will make me change it.'

'Jessamy,' Fabian spoke softly, 'don't you think that Caroline and I should have a chance to explain what actually happened?'

'No, because it would be a waste of time. I saw you both embrace, and your kisses were not the kisses of friends. Shall we leave it at that. I shall do my best to behave as if it was the truth I had told about the change of plan and hope you will help me to keep up the pretence.'

Caroline protested that Jessamy was not being fair, that a prisoner in court had a chance to speak in defence.

'But you are no prisoner, Caroline, you are as free as air and you cheated. Good night.'

Jessamy swept out and no protest followed her. She felt ill, but no matter what it cost her no one would ever know what she had witnessed.

Jessamy had dreaded coming down to breakfast the next morning, wondering how she could possibly cope with the strained atmosphere there would be between Fabian, Caroline and herself, but Fabian saved all this by announcing that much to his regret he had to return to St Peel right away.

Esmeralda, who had complained of not feeling too well when she came down, said, 'I think it might be just as well if we return home too.' To Caroline she added, 'It's been a lovely change. I have enjoyed our stay and I know that Jessamy has enjoyed it, too. You must come and spend some time with us.'

Caroline thanked her, saying she certainly would if she had time before returning to Texas, and explained she had decided to go quite soon.

This move was the sole topic at breakfast-time. Afterwards Fabian looked up the time-table for trains home and decided that he must catch one before lunch. When Jessamy, not wanting to travel with him, suggested that she and her mother catch a later one, Esmeralda said at once they would travel with Fabian. It would not take them long to pack. Her tone forbade any protest.

To give Fabian his due, he was responsible for the leave-taking going smoothly. Goodbyes were said, without Esmeralda becoming aware that there was no exchange of kisses between Caroline and Jessamy. Fabian kissed Caroline on both cheeks in the continental way as he had done when he arrived. Caroline seemed composed but when she whispered to Jessamy that she was sorry for what had happened there was a glint of tears in her eyes. They did not move Jessamy in any way.

Even the train journey passed very well, owing to two colleagues of Fabian travelling in the same carriage. Whether Fabian had arranged this Jessamy had no idea, but it did not appear to be something that had been contrived.

There were times when the men and Esmeralda were talking when Jessamy did not take part in the conversation, having asked to be excused because of tiredness, as she had not slept very well. They were sympathetic, they knew the feeling. And so Jessamy sat from time to time with her eyes closed, torturing herself by going over everything that had happened the night before, and regretting that she could not stay in London a few days longer to try and trace Lillian.

Chadwick was waiting at the station when they arrived, and he was full of pleasure at having his womenfolk back. How he had missed them—they could tell him all the news on the way home.

Esmeralda did most of the talking. Caroline was a lovely person and they had all got on splendidly. She would probably be coming to stay with them for a few days before returning to Texas. Texas, Chadwick queried, and Esmeralda surprised Jessamy with all the details of Caroline's ranch, how many horses they had, all about the food, living conditions and how rich these ranchers were. How tragic it was, she added, that Caroline should have lost not only her husband, but her family too.

Fabian had left them at St Peel with a promise to let them know what his plans were and from there they went home, where they were greeted by Verity, Bertie and Louise. Jessamy asked if Louise could stay with her overnight, knowing she would have to tell someone about Lillian or be ill.

And so it was told as they were getting ready for bed and Louise said, 'I knew you had something on your mind, but that was the last thing I expected. And I won't even suggest that you mistook some other person for Lillian, we both know her too well for that. But what a miserable, wretched character she is to live such a life of deceit. She deserves to come to a violent end.'

'But she won't,' declared Jessamy. 'You've heard Grandma say many times how evil people always seem to prosper.'

What bothered both girls was that they had no means of finding out anything else about Lillian. Louise did suggest asking their grandmother's advice about whether Jeremiah should be told and see if he wanted to follow it up, but Jessamy was against it—what sort of hornets' nest would it stir up? If their Aunt Catherine came to hear about it she might suffer another stroke, and a second one could be fatal. It was far better just to keep the secret to themselves.

When they were in bed Louise asked Jessamy how she really felt about Caroline and added, 'I want the truth, not Aunt Esmeralda's doting version of her.'

Jessamy was torn between sharing her grief and hurt and keeping a promise to herself never to repeat what she had witnessed between Fabian and Caroline. The sharing of Fabian and Caroline's deception won. Louise, outraged, shot up in bed.

'And you mean to tell me you want it to be kept quiet? How can you? How can you go on meeting Fabian face to face with other people there and live a lie?'

Jessamy said quietly, 'I'm sure I won't have to. I feel sure he will call to tell us that he's going back to sea. Later, this will give me the opportunity of saying I realised I didn't love him enough. I'm just going to let things take their course, Louise.'

Louise said she must be mad to allow Fabian Montague to get away with such behaviour but Jessamy said, better that than to stir up trouble that would spread around the family and for people to be pitying her for ever more. She begged Louise never to tell anyone the truth and Louise, reluctantly, gave her word.

A note arrived at the shop the next morning for Jessamy from Fabian and when she saw the bold handwriting her heart gave a lurch. It was probably the last one she would get.

Fabian had written to say he would be sailing that morning so would be unable to see her, but suggested she tell her parents the truth. It would be foolish to live a lie and say she wanted to prolong the engagement for two years, when she had no intention of ever marrying him. This, he said, he regretted, for he loved only her and always would. If only she had given himself or Caroline the chance of an explanation.

At that moment Jessamy regretted it too, but before long knew it would have made no difference, she would never have trusted Fabian again.

When she told her parents she had broken the engagement with Fabian because she felt she did not love him enough, her father was upset. It was just a phase, he said. She was being too hasty—given time, she would change her mind. Fabian was a fine man and he didn't deserve such treatment.

Her mother, surprisingly, was on Jessamy's side. It was far better to be certain than to rush into marriage then regret it. Esmeralda glanced at Chadwick as she said this and Jessamy wondered if her mother had regretted their marriage.

Chadwick said no more then but the next day he mentioned Fabian again, saying, 'I realise now it was a mistake going to meet Caroline. At the time I thought it sensible. I'm truly sorry that things have turned out as they have. Perhaps in time, Jessamy, you may be able to tell me what really did happen.'

She looked up startled and saw a hurt in her father's eyes. She touched his hand. 'I probably will, Papa, but for now I want you to help me to go back to normality. You are always saying that our lives are mapped out for us. I think so, too. I've accepted that it was not ordained that I marry Fabian. Someone else will probably come along.'

Chadwick smiled then, a sad little smile. 'I'm sure of that, my love. Perhaps your mother was right and you are too young for marriage. I only wanted to see you happily settled.'

Mr Blackwell arrived, greeting them with a cheerful, 'Good morning. What splendid weather—makes one feel good to be alive.'

'Indeed it does, Mr Blackwell,' Jessamy said smiling. 'Come into the back and I shall make you a hot drink.'

Although Jessamy did not realise it then, Mr Blackwell's bright and breezy manner was the start of a slow recuperation for her.

Alistair helped too towards her recovery. He only once mentioned Fabian and that was to say how sorry he was to hear of the broken engagement. When they went on their usual Saturday afternoon walk on the moors the talk was always of medicine, and Jessamy would listen to what Alistair had been studying the week before. If he made a mistake she would correct him from a book. In this way, of course, she acquired a great deal of knowledge herself.

These walks with Alistair became the highlights of the following weeks for Jessamy. The rest of the time she lived with a feeling of controlled anger that through Fabian she now distrusted what any man said to her. The birthday parties were something she now no longer enjoyed but merely endured.

Henrietta tackled her granddaughter about this one evening. 'Why do you look at people as if they were beneath you in station?' When Jessamy protested at this Henrietta said, 'You should just see yourself looking down on everyone as though they were your subjects.' Then more gently the old lady went on, 'I know there is more to your broken engagement than you've told us, but don't, I beg you, let it warp your life. No man is worth that.'

'I try not to,' Jessamy said in a low voice. 'But something in me has been destroyed.'

'Rubbish. You alone are responsible for the way you feel. Think miserable thoughts and you will be miserable. Think evil thoughts as Lillian did and you'll destroy yourself, as she has done.'

Jessamy, wondering just how much her grandmother did know about her cousin, said, 'Someone else was responsible for her death, an assailant.'

'I'm not talking about her death but her life, the way she lived it. She became warped, couldn't think good of anyone and that is how you will be unless you get some sense into your head. You are only seventeen, with years and years of life to live. Get on with it and stop brooding about what has gone.'

'I'm not brooding,' Jessamy snapped. 'I'm deeply hurt inside and wounds like that don't heal easily.'

'They won't if you keep moaning about them and telling yourself that yours are worse than anyone else's. Try mixing an ounce of determination with an ounce of commonsense and two ounces of hope and your wounds will have healed up without you realising it.'

Jessamy jumped up. 'How can you under-

311

stand? You just don't know what happened.'

'Hazarding a guess I would say that the charming Captain Montague was caught up in the past by meeting his former fiancée again. He gave her some attention because of her dreadful tragedy, and you were insanely jealous, as the young always are.'

'I had every right to be jealous. I'll tell you what happened and you can judge for yourself.'

The tale was told and Henrietta said wryly, 'The Captain was well rid of you! His life wouldn't have been worth living had he married you. Jealousy is a destroyer. You didn't even give either of them a chance to plead their case.'

'Because they would have lied, that's why.'

'Oh, so the Captain has been in the habit of lying to you, is that it?'

'No, no, but they couldn't have told the truth, could they? Well...I didn't think that they would.'

'You didn't *think* they would.' The old lady spoke softly. 'Take my advice, Jessamy dear, and don't attempt to get married until you can learn not to condemn without knowing the other person's side of the story. Now go along and join the others and enjoy yourself. And, Jessamy, don't think I haven't made all the mistakes that other people have in marriage. It's because of this that I want to save you these mistakes.'

'I know, Grandma,' Jessamy said contritely.

'And I'll take heed. Be patient with me.'

'I will, my love, now off you go.'

Jessamy had too many things on her mind to enjoy herself that particular evening, and was sure about only one thing—that she still had no wish to marry Fabian. She either did not have the right kind of love for him, or perhaps she would never feel fulfilled until she had done something else with her life, studied to become a doctor. She would work to that end.

As the days went by, Jessamy found herself becoming increasingly close to Alistair. There was a warmth she had never known with either Christian or Fabian and she had to ask herself if it was simply because she was missing the love of a man and Alistair happened to be closest to her at that time, or whether it was something more.

One day in the shop when he turned quickly, not realising she was right behind him, Alistair caught her on the cheek with his hand and was full of concern.

'Did I scratch you, Jessamy?' The touch of his fingers on her cheek sent familiar tremors through her. She said no, he had barely touched her but he moved his fingers lightly over a small part and she longed to press his fingers to her skin. She moved away.

A few days later she found he was watching her and guessed that he felt more than friendship for her and longed for Saturday afternoon to come so they could be alone together on their walk.

It was the first time that Jessamy found it difficult to concentrate on medical matters. Alistair, obviously aware of it, said, 'I don't think that either of us are in the mood for working this morning.'

'It's not really work,' Jessamy began, 'it's just that at times it's—' She broke off, having glanced at Alistair and found his gaze on her, the look in his eyes betraying his feelings for her. She looked away quickly.

Alistair said in a low voice, 'I'm afraid these Saturday afternoon walks will have to stop, Jessamy.'

'Oh, no, no,' she said, 'I look forward to them, they've become the highlight of the week for me.'

'And for me, Jessamy, and unfortunately that is why they must end.' He stopped and turned her to face him. 'I'm in love with you, have been I think since the first time I saw you.' He shook his head. 'I ought not to have told you, not just after your recent broken engagement. The Captain is a fine man. I always felt that he was so right for you.'

'He was all wrong. He's still in love with his former fiancée—but please don't mention this to anyone. My parents don't even know this. I told them I felt I didn't love him enough to marry him.'

'You may get together again.'

'I won't,' she said earnestly. 'I thought I was

314

in love with Fabian, but I know now I'm not.' She searched his face. 'You've become very close to me, Alistair. I would be lost without our Saturday afternoons. Please don't deny me these meetings.' Her voice broke and she turned and moved away.

Alistair caught her up. 'I long to hold you in my arms, Jessamy, but don't you see, it would be wrong. I'm just an assistant. I have nothing to offer, won't for years.'

'Just go on seeing me,' she pleaded. 'Let me be your girl. You could love me—properly.'

'Jessamy, Jessamy,' he said in a despairing note. 'You don't know what you're saying.'

'I do,' she whispered. 'I need to be loved. I feel like a lost soul. I have no foundation any more.' Her lips trembled.

He took her hands in his and said gently, 'This isn't like you at all. You've always shown such strength, it's something I've admired in you. This bad time will end one day.' She shook her head and he went on, 'If it will help we'll continue our Saturday afternoons. But no more offering love or—' he smiled, '—or I might be tempted, especially if you look at me like that.'

She gave a wan smile. 'I promise to talk about medicine only.'

'Medicine it shall be.'

CHAPTER NINETEEN

Afterwards, the more Jessamy thought about the offer she had made to Alistair, the more appalled she became. She had behaved like a street woman offering to let him love her. Her cheeks burned. What must he have thought of her? If only she could see him, explain. But then, what was there to explain? All she could say was that she had desperately needed a man's arms around her to hold her close.

Jessamy knew many young men but there was none she would have wanted to hold her. Only Alistair. He had admitted to loving her. How could she face him on Monday morning?

The following Sunday, Jessamy was about to leave for churcn when her Aunt Catherine's maid called. Would she go to the house, as her mistress wanted to see her alone. Jessamy glanced at the clock, said she was a little late and could she call in on the way back, but the maid said she thought it would be better if she were to come right away. Mrs Every had stressed this. The rest of the family had already gone to church.

Wondering, Jessamy set out with the young girl who by now seemed agitated. Jessamy had visited her aunt regularly and when she had last seen her on the Friday evening, she had seemed quite well. But when they arrived and went into the sitting-room she saw a great change in the woman.

'Aunt Catherine, what's wrong? Have you had a bad turn? I could have asked Papa to come. He went to the shop to get some pills for Mr Turvy.'

'No, Jessamy dear, it's you I wanted to see, alone. I have something to tell you.' Her aunt's voice was little above a whisper and Jessamy was worried, as she seemed suddenly so frail. Catherine motioned her to a seat. 'It's about Lillian.' Jessamy's heart gave a lurch. Had her aunt found out that Lillian was alive? Catherine's next words proved that this was not so. She said that everyone had blamed Lillian for the poison pen letters but her daughter had not been responsible. She paused then said, a tormented look in her eyes, 'I was the one who wrote them.'

'*You*?' Jessamy sat staring at her, stunned. Then she said, 'I don't believe it! You're not that kind of person, Aunt Catherine.'

'Circumstances can bring the worst out in a person. I was driven to do what I did.' Her voice was stronger and a bitterness had come into it. 'From the day I met James the family decided that I was inferior to him. He was educated, while I was nearly illiterate.'

'That's not true, Aunt Catherine. Uncle

James doesn't think so and I'm sure you're mistaken about the rest of the family.'

'You haven't heard them. I have. They were all so smug, all behaving as if they had the perfect marriage and I knew differently. But out of all of them, our Lillian was the most cruel.'

Jessamy's head went up. 'Lillian?'

Catherine gave a weary sigh. 'Yes, I knew that would surprise you. Everyone thought she was so sweet, so gentle. Even James never saw that side of her. Nor did her sisters and brothers. Very cunning, was Lillian. Even as a child she called me names to my face. Told me I was ugly and that James hated me—her own mother!'

'Oh, Aunt Catherine, why did you put up with it? Why didn't you tell Uncle James?'

'He wouldn't have believed me, thought the sun shone out of her. I wanted to get my own back on Lillian and that was what gave me the idea of the poison pen letters. I knew I could wipe that sweet false smile off her face by writing just three words... *You are illegitimate.*'

Catherine gave a cunning nod. 'And it was the truth. Oh, it shook her to the core. She couldn't bear it, she always thought she was so superior to anyone else. That was why she went to London. And I can tell you she was up to no good—she deserved all she got. Even though she was my own daughter, I have no pity for her, Jessamy.'

318

Jessamy wanted to ask who Lillian's real father was, but Catherine continued, 'After I had written Lillian's letter I went on to write the rest of the family. For one thing, they all had a secret and for another I knew by writing to everyone it would lessen the chances of anyone finding out who had written them. Oh, yes, I sent one to myself.'

'You sent one to Papa and Mama—'

'I like your father, Jessamy, but not one member of the family is blameless. He and Verity are in love, did you know that?'

'I guessed it, and I can't say I blame Papa as Mama has never given him much love.'

'She has her reasons. She, like me, sinned. She had a baby, a boy. Her parents insisted that she had it adopted. Esmeralda was jealous of Verity, especially when she and Chadwick became engaged. Then, although nothing ever happened between Chadwick and Esmeralda she got him in such a compromising situation that her father insisted that they marry.'

Jessamy felt that her stomach had tied itself into a knot. How could her mother have done such a thing? She got up. 'I don't want to hear any more, Aunt Catherine.'

'Sit down, you may as well know why your mother has never taken to you. She and Chadwick had a son, but the baby only lived a few hours. Esmeralda longed for a son to replace the two boys she had lost, and you can imagine how she felt when you were born, and lived.'

For the first time Jessamy saw a malicious look in her aunt's eyes. She said, 'I think you are enjoying telling me this, Aunt Catherine.'

'No.' The woman's expression became tormented again. 'I know I shall suffer for my sins, but I'll feel better, Jessamy, if you say that you forgive me. I think you can save me from meeting the devil.'

'But Aunt Catherine, I have no power to absolve you from—'

'Yes, you have. You have the power of healing in your hands.'

'No, no, I haven't.' Jessamy put her hands behind her back. 'You just imagine I have.'

'Jessamy, please, please, take my hands in yours. I beg it of you. It's a small thing to ask. I feel I don't have long to live and I want you at least to grant me forgiveness.'

Reluctantly, Jessamy brought her hands forward and took her aunt's hands in hers.

Catherine closed her eyes and whispered. 'That is wonderful. I can feel the warmth of healing. When I'm gone you can tell the whole family that I wrote the letters, but until then, dear Jessamy, keep my secret.'

Jessamy felt a rise of tears for this woman who had suffered such torment, quite unnecessarily—for no one had ever been heard to say a cruel word about her. Yes, she had been called slow, with very little to offer in conversation, and some had called her a bore—but there had been no real malice from any of the Everys. And what torment had she brought to others by her accusations?

Catherine fell asleep and a look of peace had come over her face. Jessamy stayed with her, her own mind going from one person to another. Who was Lillian's real father? What had her own father done in the past? What would have been her aunt's reaction had she told her that Lillian was still alive? Jessamy felt she would not have welcomed the news.

When James returned from church Chadwick was with him. 'Why, Jessamy,' her father said, 'I wondered where you were.'

She explained that her aunt had asked her to call and in an effort to keep things simple said, 'She had some pain and believed that I could take it away.'

'And you do, Jessamy,' her uncle said kindly. 'I didn't want to leave her but she chased me to church, and the family. They've gone for their usual walk.' James smiled. 'You've obviously done your aunt a world of good. Look, she's sleeping peacefully.'

Catherine died in her sleep that night, which somehow did not surprise Jessamy but shocked everyone else... She was getting on so splendidly, they all said.

At the funeral all the men stood together in groups talking. The women sat together with Dorcas saying in a disparaging tone that all men ever talked about was business, even with a death in the house. Then, in the next breath she was telling the women about some lovely material Digby had bought from abroad, satin with beautiful muted designs and colours, and saying they must come into the shop and have a look.

Jessamy had not seen Alistair since their last walk on the moor, and when she went back to the shop again she rather dreaded meeting him, knowing he would have had plenty of time to think over what she had said. When she did arrive she found Alistair on his own, as her father and Mr Blackwell had gone to look at some Eastern plants that Chadwick was trying to grow. Alistair commiserated with Jessamy about her aunt, saying how sudden the death had been and what a shock for everyone. She agreed, then after a pause went on, 'I was hoping to find you on your own, Alistair. I want to apologise for my behaviour when we met last. I felt deeply ashamed, offering to—'

'Say no more, Jessamy.' He spoke gently. 'I was very much to blame. I had no right to tell you I was in love with you. It was unforgivable, seeing that the Captain and you had just parted. You were vulnerable.'

'But Alistair, I shouldn't have—'

'No, I won't allow you to take any blame. I understood how you felt. When I first came here I missed my family so much it was like an illness. And let me say at once that I could not have been with nicer people than your family. It was just that we're a loving family. I

322

missed having that affection and giving it. Do you know what I mean?'

'Yes, I do.'

'I felt like a lost soul as you did. So, Jessamy, please don't apologise for anything. I was the one to blame.'

They were having quite an argument when Chadwick and Mr Blackwell came into the shop. Chadwick laughed and said, 'Seems we are just in time to act as referees.'

'There's no need,' Jessamy grinned. 'I concede—Alistair is the winner.'

Mr Blackwell chuckled. 'First time I've heard a woman giving in. Good for you, Jessamy. You'll make a good wife.' Then probably sensing a delicate situation he said, 'Well, I think I'll get on with tidying the window. Want to lend a hand, Jessamy?'

'Oh, yes please. We'll display some of those new bowls of pot pourri.' Jessamy felt grateful to Alistair for having made it easy for her to resume the friendliness there had been between them before the incident on the moor, although it did not stop her from wanting to love and be loved.

She had not told anyone yet of her aunt's confession but with a feeling she was carrying a load of someone else's worry on her shoulders, she decided to talk to Verity about it.

Verity was silent for a while then she said, 'Your grandmother did once say to me that she thought Catherine might have been responsible for the letters, but I was not so sure. And yet Catherine did always carry a grudge against everyone. She had got it into her head that we all felt superior and nothing would shift it. You see, her family were poverty-stricken and it was said that James only married her because he was sorry for her, but she was quite attractive when she was younger.'

When Jessamy asked who Lillian's father was, Verity shook her head. It was something Catherine kept to herself. She had had the baby before she knew James, whom she had met when he was away at college. Then Lillian was being brought up by Catherine's mother. When James brought Catherine home to meet the Every family he had introduced her as a young window with a two year old child. The family had believed this, because James had a quiet, persuasive way with him and Catherine had an honesty about her.

Jessamy was silent for a while then she said quietly, 'Aunt Catherine told me that you and Papa were in love, always had been. She said that Mama was responsible for your engagement being broken.'

Verity gave a small sigh. 'Yes, Jessamy, your father and I were in love. We are still very fond of one another but I can assure you there is nothing between us now. I love your Uncle Bertie dearly.'

Her aunt spoke with such sincerity that Jessamy was sure she knew nothing of what had passed between Louise and Bertie, and wondered if she would feel the same about them if she ever *did* know. Jessamy would have liked to know more about her mother's past but hesitated to ask. Then, knowing she would never settle if she made no mention of it she blurted out, 'Aunt Catherine told me about Mama having a baby adopted.'

Verity glanced at her and said wryly, 'She certainly made her tongue go. I think she could have spared you that.'

'Please tell me about the baby. Who adopted it?'

'Only your mother knows, but I can tell you that his adoptive parents are now both dead.'

'Is his name Ralph?'

Verity stared straight ahead. 'Yes. Don't ask me any more, Jessamy. I feel I ought not to have spoken about this.'

'Don't you think I have a right to know?'

'No, it can serve no purpose. It's a part of your mother's life that has gone. She's suffered all these years for her mistake.'

The weather turned sultry and for the next three days the sky was sulphur-coloured. Thunder continually rumbled throughout the day and night and sheet lightning became spectacular when it was dark. People complained of headaches and said if only the storm would break. Jessamy had never known such a terrible restlessness. At times she felt there was some strange spirit inside her wanting to break free.

On the Saturday after lunch Chadwick said to Alistair and Jessamy, 'If you two energetic young people are going for your usual walk on the moors you had better not go too far. This storm could break at any time and you could get drenched.'

Alistair laughed and said that a good shower of rain never did harm to anyone and Jessamy suddenly felt a surge of relief. She had been so afraid that Alistair would make an excuse to avoid walking out with her.

Once they were on the moors she felt a strange excitement in the storm-laden atmosphere. Although Jessamy felt she had seen the moors in all their moods there was something different this time. It was not only the stillness —for no bird sang, no little frogs croaked on the edge of small ponds nor did any creature rustle through the undergrowth, but there was an eeriness in the stunted bushes with their crippled branches that could have been demons in a child's nightmare.

The air was clammy and at times they walked into patches of heat that reminded her of dragons blowing fire. She said with a shaky laugh, 'This weather has my imagination running riot.'

She told him her thoughts and Alistair said, 'When I was a boy and a storm was brewing I used to have a feeling I would explode. And

326

when the storm did break I would run around lashing out at the trunks of trees with a stick and shouting wildly at the top of my voice. I suppose it was something primitive I was feeling, the elements being unleashed.'

Jessamy teased him. 'So if the storm breaks while we're out do I have to run away and hide in case you want to lash out at me?'

He grinned. 'I think you are safe. The least I would do would be to pick you up and carry you to my cave.'

Jessamy, feeling little shivers run up and down her spine answered lightly, 'Fortunately, there are no caves to run to.'

He grinned and said there was an alternative, but when she asked him what it was he told her she would find out if it rained, which had Jessamy wishing secretly that the storm might soon break. It seemed she was going to be denied her adventure, for although the thunder rumbled continuously and sheet lightning continued to give a wonderful display there was not a hint of rain in the air.

They had walked well past the big waterfall when Alistair stopped and said. 'Rain!' and held out his hand. On the back of it was a patch of wet. 'The storm's breaking.' There was a note of excitement in his voice. The next moment lightning zigzagged from sky to earth, followed by a rattle of thunder that sounded as though a massive boulder had been cleft in two. Alistair grabbed Jessamy's hand and started to run as raindrops as big as pennies bounced from the dry grass.

Within seconds the rain was deluging down, bringing a refreshing coolness, but as a wind suddenly sprang up the volume of water almost blinded Jessamy. As she drew her hand across her eyes and glimpsed a cottage through foliage Alistair shouted, 'There is our refuge.'

Jessamy was so astonished she made to stop and stumbled as Alistair raced on, pulling her with him. She yelled, 'It's Davy Feld's cottage. He's a tramp, he's filthy. I'm not going there.'

Alistair's answer was to tighten his grip on her hand and he did not speak again until he opened the door of the derelict-looking cottage. When Jessamy tried to pull back he said, speaking close to her ear, 'It's spotless inside.'

And to her astonishment it was. While she stood looking round, Alistair went to a cupboard and brought out a towel. 'Here, dry your hair. I'll find a blanket for you in a minute but first, I'll light the fire.' It was already laid and with a match put to the kindling, flames soon began to appear. Alistair went out and when he returned he brought in a knitted blanket with all the colours of Joseph's coat. He made to put it around Jessamy's shoulders and when she drew back, he put the blanket under her nose. 'Smell. As sweet as a nut.'

Jessamy allowed him to drape the blanket round her then she said, 'You seem very much at home here.'

'I am. Davy lets me study here some nights —often I stay overnight. He's a learned man who likes to explore the countryside. People misunderstand him because he's shabbily dress-ed, but as you can see, there's nothing here that anyone could find fault with. He's scrupulously clean, scrupulously tidy.' Alistair suddenly eyed her with concern. 'You're shivering, Jessamy. You ought to get out of those wet clothes. I'll go into the scullery while you take them off.' And without waiting for a reply, he left her.

Jessamy stood, uncertain what to do. Then, as her drenched clothes were clinging uncomfortably to her she removed her dress and petticoats. The logs had caught and flames were licking around them; Jessamy wrapped the blanket around her and sat on a stool in front of the fire.

Had Alistair assumed it would rain and made plans to bring her to the cottage? If so, she ought to be annoyed, but she could only think of it as an adventure. Just then Alistair shouted to ask if it was all right to come in. She said yes and he entered without any sign of embarrassment. He touched her hair, said it was still quite wet and taking the towel from her, began to rub it dry. Jessamy was surprised when this action aroused sensual feelings in her. She decided to enjoy them...

The sky had darkened when the storm had

built up. Thunder still crashed and the lightning lit up the room. Alistair paused in the drying of Jessamy's hair and said, a note of surprise in his voice, 'You don't seem frightened of the storm.'

'No, I find storms exciting.'

He gave a mock groan. 'This is really where a young lady should fling her arms around a young man and beg him to protect her.'

Jessamy laughed. 'Sorry, wrong girl.'

'No, right girl,' he said softly.

Jessamy looked up. 'Did Davy Feld know you might be bringing me here?'

'Och no, I doubt t'would cross his mind. It didn't cross mine until we talked about the possibility of rain. Jessamy, you have no need to feel afraid.'

'I'm not afraid, it just occurred to me that I'm sitting here without my dress and petticoats. If anyone were to—'

'Where are your clothes?' He clucked his tongue as he picked the bundle up from the floor. 'Now they'll no' be drying like that, will they?' He brought a wooden clothes horse from the kitchen and draped dress and petticoats over it, without showing the least sign of embarrassment.

When Jessamy remarked on it he laughed. 'You forget all the sisters I have. When the weather was fine at home all the garments were spread out over the bushes. I remember my mother once saying, ''There's no time for mock modesty when you've a houseful of lassies".'

'I'd like your mother,' Jessamy said, and Alistair replied that his mother would like her. They were two of a kind. He then put a kettle on the fire to make some cocoa and while they were waiting for the water to boil Alistair sat in a chair opposite to Jessamy and she became aware of him watching her through half-closed eyes. She asked, 'What did you mean when you said that your mother and I were two of a kind?'

'You're both honest, loving, kind. I remember once when I was a boy seeing my mother sitting in a chair in front of the fire. It was just an afternoon as this, stormy, with the room darkening and the firelight on her face. I seldom saw her idle and I told her she looked really beautiful. She said what a lovely thing it was to say and there were tears in her eyes. Later, she told me the only time anyone had told her she looked beautiful was after she had given birth to my eldest brother. She said she was sitting nursing him and my father had said to her, "I've never seen you looking bonnier".'

After a pause Alistair concluded, 'When I saw you sitting there I thought how wonderful it would be to come home to a wife and child.'

There was such a wealth of loneliness in his voice then that Jessamy felt deeply moved. She held out a hand to him. 'Alistair, I know that lost feeling.'

He came over and knelt at her feet. 'Jessamy, I'm sorry, I had no right to put you in this position. I thought it would be fun to bring you here, but now I know I did wrong.'

'No, you didn't,' she said softly. His face was upturned to hers and on an impulse she leaned forward and kissed him. The next moment his arms were around her and she felt the mad thudding of his heart. Her own heart began to race as he returned her kiss with some passion. The blanket fell away from her shoulders and his lips moved from her throat to her breast and thrill after thrill went through her. Then at a sound as though a thunderbolt had hit the roof, the passion of both was unleashed and Alistair drew her down on to the rug, his breathing ragged as he explored her body.

She ventured to caress him and he moaned. 'Oh, Jessamy, Jessamy, I adore you. I've wanted you for so long there were times when it was like an unbearable pain.'

Jessamy would not have understood this had she not now been experiencing an agonising sweetness of desire. Although she was still not quite sure how this would all end, there was in her a need to touch Alistair. He had stripped off and when the shawl slipped away from her shoulders, he began to undo the rest of her garments. With a quick breath she helped him then with an inborn instinct, ran her fingertips lightly up and down his spine, causing Alistair to draw in his breath.

When he touched her on the most secret part of her body she cried out. Then Alistair moved her hand to his thigh and she ran her fingertips over it, moving in circles, higher and higher. When she discovered his masculinity she was both alarmed and excited. Louise's description of a man making love to a woman had been very sketchy—and Jessamy had never seen a naked man before.

Penetration was a mixture of pain and joy. Alistair was moving and she found she was matching his rhythm, marvelling at the way nature worked. At first she tried to concentrate on what was happening, feeling it was important, but then concentration was lost when an exquisite ecstasy began building up so that her body was one big throb. She whispered, 'Oh, Alistair, Alistair, please don't stop.' But the ecstasy was dying away when she realised that Alistair was still, his face pressed to her shoulder. 'I'm sorry, Jessamy, I couldn't wait. It's unforgivable of me.'

Jessamy was at a loss to know what he meant. 'It's all right,' she said. When Alistair rolled away from her he put an arm around her and kissed her ear, whispering, telling her to give him a few minutes and the next time would be fine for her.

Within minutes he was kissing her passionately again, her eyelids, her throat and once again she experienced the delicious ecstasy. But this time it was different. Alistair took her into another world where she experienced a sun-burst of joy that surpassed any emotion she had ever experienced. When Jessamy asked him sleepily later if it would always be like that, he kissed her gently and said it got better and better all the time.

This remark had her wide awake and bolt upright. In a low, controlled voice she asked him how many girls he had made love to. He told her only one—and then he had been an adolescent and it was not love, just an experience.

Jessamy got to her feet, ashamed of her nakedness, hating herself for what she had done, hating Alistair for treating her in this offhand way. She must have been mad, especially when she knew what had happened to Louise. Would she be safe—would she escape the possible consequences? She dressed hastily, even though her petticoats and dress were not quite dry.

Alistair was upset and began to plead with her as he pulled on his own clothes. 'Jessamy, please don't regret what we've done. It was the most beautiful thing that has ever happened to me.'

All she wanted now was to get back home. Her fingers fumbled with the buttons on her dress and Alistair said quietly, 'Let me.'

She allowed him to do it but when he had fastened the last one she said, 'I'm leaving here alone. I'm going straight home. Tell Papa we were caught in the downpour and that I've gone home to change.'

Alistair protested she would be foolish to leave. Although the storm was dying away, the rain was still heavy. Then in the next breath he said, 'Please don't hate me, Jessamy.'

She was suddenly contrite. She had no right to blame him, for she had wanted him as much as he had wanted her. She held out a hand: 'We must talk, Alistair. Perhaps tomorrow.'

CHAPTER TWENTY

It was the following Saturday before Jessamy had the chance of a quiet talk with Alistair during their usual Saturday walk on the moor. It had been all right in the shop talking to him about general matters, but alone with him out-doors, she felt uncomfortable. Unable to bring up the incident in the cottage of the previous Saturday, she said brightly, 'I may have found you a recruit for your dispensary wnen you start one.'

'Oh, and who is that?'

'My Cousin Anne. I'm sure she would make a dedicated nurse as she wants to look after sick people. She called at home last night, wanting to borrow books on herbs, on medical matters.

We had a long talk. I told her that you hoped to open a dispensary some day and she asked eagerly if she could help.'

Alistair laughed. 'Jessamy, that is years off. And anyway,' he sobered, 'it's one thing to talk about running a dispensary, but where is all the money coming from? I would need a very big house, beds, other equipment—my needs would be endless.'

'Papa knows some monied people, they might help. I could write letters, you know. There are many people who are sympathetic to those less fortunate than themselves. I would help in the dispensary, too, even if it was just making beds and scrubbing floors.'

Alistair glanced at her. 'You could be married by then. I don't think that the Captain will let you go so easily.'

'I will not be marrying him. I've already told you—he's still in love with his former fiancée.'

'You say he is, but is he? Don't you think you're being a little unfair to him? Jessamy, this girl Caroline had suffered terrible tragedies. Surely it was a humane thing for the Captain to comfort her. He had once been in love with her, after all.'

'And still is, I'm sure. I did see them lovingly embracing.'

Alistair said, 'Let me explain something. I was once in love with a girl. She was my first love and there's something very special about first love. We fell out and she married someone

336

else. I didn't see her for several years and when I did she was grieving over the loss of her three year old child. I consoled her, drew her to me and kissed her. I still had a soft spot in my heart for her, but I no longer loved her and would not have wanted to marry her. Nor she me. She loves her husband and her other child. Can you understand this, Jessamy?'

Jessamy thrust out her chin. 'I can only understand that Fabian would have wanted to visit Caroline if she still lived in England, and quite frankly I don't think she ever had any real intention of going back to Texas.'

'But you don't *know* that, Jessamy. She told you she planned to live there, where she had friends.'

Jessamy sighed. 'Caroline is in love with Fabian—she wants him, she told me so. I think she would do anything to get him back. Well, I have no intention of competing with another woman if I were married. And anyway, I don't want to talk about it any more.'

'So be it. Will you test me on my homework?'

'Of course,' Jessamy said, the warmth back in her voice. 'Any time. I shall be learning, too.'

By the time they had finished the homework they were back on their former friendly footing, and Alistair was once more discussing opening a dispensary when he got his doctorate. He said, 'It might be a good plan to set up a practice and progress from there.'

Jessamy disagreed with this. He ought to try and start the practice earlier. They would find the money, she would see to that.

'We?' he queried, teasing.

'Why not? I'll need to work too, now I'm not getting married.'

'Oh, you'll get married,' Alistair said softly. 'I've no doubt about that. Perhaps not to the Captain, but you'll certainly have a choice of suitors.'

When Jessamy said she would only marry if she could find the perfect man and Alistair told her it would be a hell on earth she laughingly agreed.

Although Jessamy had been determined to put Fabian out of her mind she found it was not so easy and, unfortunately, as time went on it became a torment. Fabian would come into her mind at any time of the day. When she went to bed she would see his image, see the hurt in his eyes when she told him she had no wish to see him ever again. Then she began to dream about him, awful nightmares where he was drowning and she was unable to reach him. Once in the dream he was holding out his arms to her, swearing he had never loved anyone else but her. Then, a wave swallowed him up and when she awoke, full of anguish, the pillow was wet with her tears.

It was then she began to wonder if she should have listened to his explanation of why he had been embracing Caroline. When she told Louise how she felt her cousin said, 'If you're not prepared to eat humble pie and give him a chance to defend himself then forget him.' Louise then said she would leave Jessamy to enjoy her misery and left.

Jessamy was furious and complained to her father about Louise's remark, and was further annoyed when he said he agreed with Louise.

'You said over and over again that you were deeply in love with Fabian and that you would always love him, yet at the first hint of trouble you walked out on him. You really must learn to trust people.'

'How can I, when I learn that all the family have guilty secrets? Yes, even you and Mama. Why didn't you trust me and tell me what they are?'

Chadwick flushed. 'Listen to me, Jessamy. I should think that every family has skeletons in the cupboard, some small, some large. If they are left alone they will harm no one, but if someone starts rattling the bones then there will be trouble. Many a person has suffered agonies because someone sick in mind chooses to sit down and write letters making accusations, enlarging on some small misdemeanour that belongs to the past. Stop letting the accusation about Fabian poison your mind. Give him a chance to vindicate himself in regard to Caroline.'

Jessamy said she would think about it.

It was on her mind that day when she left the shop at dusk to go home. What bothered her was the thought that even though Fabian might have a reasonable explanation, if Caroline did not go to live in Texas the obstacle remained—Fabian would continue to visit her. The dusk was deepening and Jessamy was startled when a figure in black appeared from behind a rock. It was a woman, and she was heavily veiled. Jessamy was about to pass when the woman stopped and said, 'Hello, Jessamy.'

The voice was low, gentle, but it sent icy shivers up and down Jessamy's spine. She whispered, *'Lillian.'*

'Yes. Surprised?' The veil was lifted, revealing her cousin's hateful, mocking smile. 'I need some information, Jessamy dear, and I think you might be able to give it to me.'

Anger suddenly flared in Jessamy. 'I don't know how you dare return here after what you have done. You do know you were responsible for your mother's death?'

'I did her a good turn. She'll be happier where she is than she ever was on earth.'

'You are despicable—a cheat, a liar. Maybe you are even a murderer. You mutilated some poor woman's face and dressed her in your clothes to give yourself another identity.'

'I did not mutilate her face, it was already done when we found her. And you can save your sympathy, she was not only a prostitute but a thief. I needed a new identity.' Lillian had raised her voice. 'I was dying of boredom. I wanted some life. It was the only way I could get it.'

'So what are you doing here now? You say you need some information. Well, whatever it is you can get it somewhere else.'

Jessamy made to walk away but Lillian caught hold of her arm. 'I wouldn't leave if I were you, not until you hear what I have to say.' There was a coldness in her voice that struck a further chill into Jessamy. She waited.

'When I was living at home the family went to visit the Derwents on a Wednesday evening. Do they still go?'

'I don't know.'

Lillian gripped Jessamy's arm, making her wince. 'You do know, tell me!'

Jessamy freed herself and pushed her away. 'Don't you bully me. I have only to scream to bring people to their doors.'

'I wouldn't scream if I were you.'

Although Lillian spoke softly Jessamy felt sure there was a madness in her. She said, 'I don't know your family's movements. You'll find out if you go home.'

'Don't talk so childishly. Why do you think I want to know when they'll be out? I want to collect my jewellery. I left it behind when I went to London, thinking I would get plenty more from the man who loved me. And I did until,' she stopped and looked about her and for moments seemed detached from reality, 'he died, you see, and he died penniless. He was a gambler and he had sold all the jewellery I had with me. I need money desperately, I'm in debt.'

When Lillian stared beyond her Jessamy said quietly, 'But Lillian, would the jewellery you still own bring you enough money?'

A sly look came over Lillian's face. 'You didn't know that the green stones in my oval brooch were emeralds, did you, and the ones surrounding them are diamonds.' She nodded slowly. 'They are, Halbert gave it to me. You didn't know Halbert, did you? No, of course you didn't. He's the one who died.'

Jessamy started to look around her, not quite sure what to do. It was obvious that Lillian was deranged and needed help, but how? If she left her cousin she was quite likely to follow her and what then? What might she do in this present frightening state?

Then Lillian said, 'I'll come later this evening and watch to see if the family leave. If they do then I shall let myself in and get my jewellery. But if you warn them, then you or your precious Papa shall suffer...' The dusk had deepened but when Lillian held out an object Jessamy gasped as she saw she was holding a pair of long thin pointed scissors. Her mouth was dry and she found herself trembling. Could this really be happening?

Suddenly Lillian began to laugh. It was derisive laughter. 'Scared you, did I? That, of course, was what I intended. Don't you think I would make a consummate actress?'

Jessamy stared at her, dumbfounded. 'Why? Why all this play-acting?'

'To make you suffer a little more than you already have when you were forced to end your delightful relationship with the handsome Captain Montague.'

Jessamy's heart began to beat in slow, painful thuds. 'So it was you who sent the letter. Why?'

'Because, Cousin dear, he was the only man I ever wanted, really wanted, and I could have had him—had it not been for *you*.' A viciousness was back in Lillian's voice.

Jessamy felt suddenly calm. 'Thank you for telling me the reason. I can now make it up to Fabian for distrusting him.'

'Oh, don't think you'll get him back. You have the dear Caroline to deal with. She has her claws in him. But I'll soon get rid of her by sending a letter to the Captain about her dealings with men.'

'You don't need to get rid of her. She'll be leaving for Texas soon.'

'Is that what she told you? Well, I can tell you now she won't be going anywhere. She wants to have the welcome mat out when her man comes home from sea.'

'You seem to know a great deal about Caroline.'

'I have...friends.'

'You have friends, Lillian? You do surprise me.'

Jessamy was quite pleased with this last remark but regretted it when Lillian held up the scissors. 'And don't you tell anyone about this meeting or you'll know about it.'

Jessamy wanted to laugh at what seemed pure melodrama but knew if she did there would be hysteria in it. Lillian was about to drop her veil again when she said with the sweetest of smiles, 'Oh, yes, I knew there was something else I wanted to say. Have you ever wondered why your dear Mama enjoys going to London? It's not to meet her lover, oh, no—it's to see her bastard son. I don't suppose you know about him.'

Jessamy wondered how she found voice to say, 'As a matter of fact I do know about Ralph.'

Lillian seemed taken aback at this then, without another word she dropped her veil and, turning, seemed to melt away behind the rock in the ever-deepening dusk. Jessamy began to tremble uncontrollably. What sort of nightmare had she been led into? She stumbled to the rock and leaned against it. Lillian might have been play-acting part of the time but there was no doubt that she was sick in her mind. Who could Jessamy tell about her experience? Who would believe her? Louise would! She had accepted her story without question when Jessamy had told her she had seen Lillian in London.

Making an effort to pull herself together, Jessamy walked on to her aunt's house, looking behind her nervously. To Jessamy's relief Louise was alone, her mother having gone visiting.

'What's wrong?' her cousin asked at once. 'You look as if you've seen a ghost.'

'I have. I've seen Lillian.'

'Sit down and tell me about it,' Louise said in a matter-of-fact way, as though seeing someone back from the dead was an everyday occurrence.

When the story was told Louise sat biting on her thumbnail for a moment then looked up. 'I don't think that our cousin came back just to frighten you. I think it was conscience that brought her back.'

'Conscience? Lillian?'

Louise nodded. 'Yes. She knew she was responsible for her mother's death and she wanted to take it out on you. She threatened to injure your father, but not your mother. Why? Because you have a real father's love. She was brought up by a stepfather then suddenly found out that her mother was never even married to her father. And she doesn't know who her own father was.'

'Are you asking me to feel sorry for her? If so—'

'I'm asking you to try and understand her motives, Jessamy, and yes, I do feel sorry for her because her mind is obviously unhinged.'

Jessamy sat silent for a while, wondering if the experiences Louise had gone through had softened her. Then she said, 'It wasn't conscience that made her tell me about Ralph. And how does she know about him, when I only guessed by the drawings I found?'

'She probably found out as I did. I overheard the parents discussing him once.'

'You knew and you didn't tell me?'

'You didn't tell *me* that you knew about him. After all, it's not something to boast about. And what's more, I didn't learn about it until recently. It was when the parents were discussing the dissension that it's caused between your parents. Apparently after Ralph's adoptive parents died he found out who his real mother was and got in touch with Esmeralda.' Louise added gently, 'It changed your mother, Jessamy. She's become so much kinder, more compassionate. All these years she must have been longing to know how the son she had been forced to abandon was faring. Can you understand, Jessamy?'

'Yes,' she replied in a low voice then, not wanting to dwell on the fact that a bastard son was more important to her mother than herself she said, 'Are we to tell the family about Lillian? I do feel that Uncle James at least should know that Lillian is alive.'

Louise said she thought that her uncle had never really accepted Lillian's death, and yes, he and close family should be told.

346

The result of this was a lengthy discussion at Beacon Hall between the grandparents, the two girls, their parents and James, the main point under discussion being should the police be informed. All but Jeremiah thought it their duty to do so. His objection was that they had no proof to offer that Lillian was still alive. When there were protests that Jessamy did not lie, he held up his hand. 'I know that Jessamy didn't imagine she saw Lillian, but to the police it could be an imaginary experience of a girl who has gone through the distress of a broken engagement. I for one do not want Jessamy to go through endless questioning and be made to look a fool.'

They all saw the sense of this eventually and it was agreed they would keep the matter to themselves.

When the party left the Hall James said, 'Jeremiah was right. Although I have never really believed that Lillian was dead, I might have been disinclined to credit Jessamy had she not mentioned the brooch. It is a tawdry little thing that I once bought for Lillian from a pedlar. She treasured it, saying she would have a real one like it some day. She kept it locked in a little box. I'm sure she never even showed it to the family. She was a pretty little thing, but secretive. Perhaps we spoilt her when she was a child. It's terrible now to think that her mind is unhinged. I loved her like my own child, but now I feel I don't want to see her

347

again. She killed my dear Catherine.' His voice broke and Jessamy linked an arm through his in sympathy...

From that evening, Chadwick would not allow Jessamy to go anywhere unchaperoned, which made her feel restricted at first until Alistair became the one who was with her the most. He had simply been told that some odd characters were roaming the moors and the womenfolk had to be protected. Alistair had teased Jessamy about it, saying he couldn't afford to have her carried off, he would miss her listening to his answers on his homework and she pretended to be offended. Was that all the use she was to him? At this he said softly, 'My life would be empty without you, Jessamy. I don't know what I'll do if I do get the chance to go to college.'

'Nor I,' she answered quietly.

At the time it had been said sincerely, but when two weeks later she had a letter from Fabian, her whole world changed.

Fabian had written, *'Dear Jessamy, I'll soon be back in England and I cannot imagine returning and not seeing your dear face. I know how you felt about Caroline and I wondered if it would help us to get together again if I told you that she will be on her way to Texas by the time we dock. At least give me a chance to explain why I was so loving towards her. Please...I will try and understand if you have no wish to see me again. You will always remain in my heart, Fabian.'*

348

Jessamy cried over the letter and wrote back to say she would be looking forward to seeing him again...

CHAPTER TWENTY-ONE

Esmeralda insisted that Jessamy should meet Fabian at home when she and her father would be present and Jessamy gave in, but she would have preferred the informality of seeing him at the shop. As it turned out, however, she met him on the moor when she was on her way back to the shop after lunch.

When she came face to face with him colour rushed to her cheeks. 'Fabian, I, we thought—'

'I know I'm cheating,' he said softly, 'but I wanted for us to be alone, for a short while anyway. Later I'm willing to share you.'

Jessamy had imagined their meeting a number of times but had not reckoned on feeling so shy and awkward. She said, 'I'm sure my mother would never believe that I had not prearranged this meeting.'

'Then we can be fellow conspirators and keep it to ourselves.'

His rather mischievous smile put Jessamy at ease. She joked, 'I doubt whether we shall be able to—a rather gossipy neighbour of ours is watching us from behind the curtains.'

'Then I shall confess to waylaying you and trust to be forgiven.' He curved an arm. 'In the meantime, shall we walk?'

Jessamy hesitated. 'I was on my way to the shop. We're doing some infusions this afternoon.' Then she said, 'Perhaps I can be spared for ten minutes.' She slipped her arm through his and they walked in the direction of the shop, strolling in silence until they came to a wooden bench under a chestnut tree where, without a word, Fabian led her. When they were seated Jessamy gave a little shiver and when Fabian glanced at her she said, 'No, I'm not cold. It's reaction. I hadn't expected to see you until this evening. I was worried, nervous. Full of guilt, actually.'

'Would it help if I told you that I felt the same?' he said quietly. 'I was so delighted when I had your letter saying you would be pleased to see me, but worried in case you would refuse to accept my explanation why I was so closely involved with Caroline that evening.' He paused and when he went on, his tone had lowered. 'We were saying goodbye. Caroline told me she would be leaving soon to go to Texas and said it was unlikely we would ever meet again.' Jessamy tensed. 'And because of what Caroline and I had shared. Jessamy, and what she had suffered, our leave-taking was fraught with emotion. You do understand?'

'Y-yes, I think so.' She wanted to say, 'But

I don't trust Caroline.' Instead she said, 'I think it might be wise if we left it at that.'

'Jessamy, I want you to be absolutely sure. It's important for our future to succeed that you harbour no thoughts that I could still be in love with Caroline. Such thoughts can create a turmoil in a person.'

Jessamy, wondering, turned her head slowly. 'Have you ever suffered such a turmoil, Fabian?'

'Yes, in my adolescent days. I was madly in love with a girl who I was certain was seeing someone else.'

Because Fabian had stressed to Jessamy that she must be sure she accepted his explanation before contemplating marriage and because he had mentioned suffering torment during his youth she wondered if he was seeing her age as a setback. Surely if he was really in love with her, had been longing to see her again, grooming her for marriage should have been the last thing on his mind.

'Do you see me as an adolescent, Fabian?' she asked thoughtfully.

'An adolescent? Good heavens, no, Jessamy. I see you as a very sensible young lady, a very beautiful young lady, who I want as my wife.' He laid a hand over hers and added softly, 'And who, I might add, is driving me mad because I want to sweep her up into my arms and make love to her.'

Tremors of desire began pulsating in Jessamy's body. She got up, saying in a shaky

351

voice, 'I think we had better go.'

Fabian sighed. 'Do you see what I mean by wanting to be married? I can't wait to have you all to myself. It's a terrible ache at times.'

Jessamy, wanting to get the situation on a lighter level, smiled, 'You would have a long wait when you're at sea.'

'But then you would not be with me, tormenting me with your lovely eyes. Oh, Jessamy.'

His voice was ragged as he made to take her in his arms but she drew back then moved away. 'Papa will be wondering where I am.'

'Yes, of course, I'm sorry. Forgive me.' He laid a hand on her arm and smiled into her eyes. 'I used to pride myself on having an iron control, but I seem to have lost it since meeting you. Shall I tell you that on my last voyage I was lenient with a young sailor who had shirked his duties because he said he was madly in love with a girl and couldn't sleep for thinking about her. He had to be disciplined, of course, but the punishment was light.'

Two men came towards them then, turning left, they walked in the direction of a farm. Fabian said, a smile in his voice, 'How would you like to be a farmer's wife? I've more or less decided to leave the sea.'

Jessamy looked up quickly. 'No, Fabian, you can't, you would be too unhappy.'

'I would be more unhappy if I had to leave you alone for months,' he teased.

352

'All right, old man,' Jessamy exclaimed, 'you can sit alone at the hearth puffing away at your pipe and reliving the days of your youth, but don't expect me to be there sitting with you.'

Fabian laughed heartily. 'Oh, I love you, Jessamy Every, even though you blackmail me to get your own way. Well, I shall give some more thought to wanting to become a farming man.'

They had reached the path that led to the main road and he said, more seriously, 'Jessamy, would you accept an early wedding if your parents were agreeable?'

She hesitated without knowing why. She wanted to marry him, had longed to see him, to feel his arms around her, feel his lips on hers, moving sensuously, demanding.

'Jessamy, you are sure, aren't you?'

Fabian's worried query brought Jessamy to her senses. She stopped and looked up into the strong attractive face. 'Yes, Fabian, I am sure. It was just that the family are still in mourning, although we younger ones are in half-mourning. By the time the wedding is arranged and—'

Fabian put a finger to her lips. 'Say no more, my darling. We'll arrange something. And now I must get you to the shop. I can't afford to be in your father's bad books.'

Chadwick was delighted to see him and said he was glad that Jessamy and Fabian had had the chance of a quiet talk together. When he looked from one to the other in a questioning way Fabian smiled. 'Yes, Jessamy has agreed to marry me.'

The awful part for Jessamy then was when her father called Mr Blackwell and Alistair from the back to tell them the news. Both men congratulated them, Mr Blackwell giving them a beaming smile, but although Alistair was smiling too it could not mask his pain.

After Fabian had left with the promise to be at the house at eight o'clock that evening Jessamy wished she could keep out of Alistair's way, but as they were working on the infusions this was impossible.

It not until they were alone together for a few minutes that he said, 'Jessamy, I'm glad that you and the Captain are together again. It's right that you should be. You are definitely suited.'

Although the longing to see Fabian again had been like a fever with Jessamy, the closeness she had known with Alistair made her feel his hurt. They had made love. For the first time it struck Jessamy forcibly that she would not be going to the altar a virgin. Would Fabian know?

Alistair said, 'I think it might be best, Jessamy, if I leave here.'

'No, Alistair, no. There's no need to. We can go on working together.'

'It wouldn't be right, Jessamy,' Alistair said in a low voice. 'Not the way I feel about you.'

Mr Blackwell came bustling in saying to

354

Jessamy, 'Your Papa has gone out for half an hour and we're to make some cough mixture first, as all of Mrs Bentley's eight children are down with whooping cough. Now then, we'll need coltsfoot, horehound, marshmallow, ground ivy, elder flowers, and don't forget the mouse ear. We'll make a goodly batch, as the neighbours' children on either side are all coughing too, so we can be prepared for a lot more whooping. It's a wretched illness, poor little mites.'

Jessamy would have liked to be quiet and reflect but Mr Blackwell was in a talkative mood. He began to describe plagues of the past, how many people cholera had claimed and said what a good thing they were not living in the times of the Black Death.

Jessamy said, 'Mr Blackwell, do we have to talk about such a depressing subject?'

Alistair laughed, but Jessamy was aware it was forced. 'Jessamy's mind is on weddings.'

'Of course, but plagues, like weddings and whooping cough, are all part of travelling along life's high road.' He gave Jessamy a broad smile. 'So when is this wedding to be?'

She said that nothing had been settled and the conversation veered round to medicine, with Alistair remarking he thought that the stock of cosmetic creams was a little low. The strange thing was that when Jessamy was in bed that night it was not of Fabian, Alistair or wedding bells that she was thinking, but whooping cough and the Black Death. Not that there had been anything depressing at home when the wedding and the buying of a house had been discussed over dinner with Fabian. He said if Jessamy was willing he would like to buy a house on the moor, or have one built.

When Louise and Jessamy had a private talk the next morning, Louise said quietly, 'Are you sure you're marrying the right man, Jessamy? Don't let yourself be carried away by Fabian's looks and wealth. Alistair too is in love with you.'

'I know, Louise. I also know it's Fabian I want to be with. When he was away I longed to see him, it was a sort of fever. I'm fond of Alistair and could have loved him had not Fabian come into my life.'

'You're lucky to have two men in love with you.'

Jessamy was silent for a moment and then she said, 'I saw Joseph Masterson the other day. He speaks so nicely of you, said he thought at one time you cared for him, but that since you came back from Cornwall you have practically ignored him.'

Louise gave a weary sigh. 'Don't you see, Jessamy, I have to. I can't ever get involved again with a man, but I'm reconciled to it now. And Jessamy, would you try not to avoid Papa? It's becoming noticeable. We both hurt, both suffer for what we did. After all, the Lord forgives people their sins.'

'Yes, I know,' Jessamy said in a low voice, 'but I am trying. I don't feel quite so antagonistic towards Uncle Bertie as I did.'

Louise then said in a brighter tone, 'All right, so what was settled about the wedding? Is it to be a big affair?'

'No, Fabian got his way. We'll be married in church but only close family is to be invited. I'm to be married in white, the bridesmaids in lilac. You will be my chief bridesmaid and the others will be the eldest girl in each family.'

Louise then asked where the wedding reception was to be held and where Fabian and Jessamy were spending their honeymoon. Jessamy told her that the reception was to be held at Beacon Hall, on Jeremiah's orders, but the location of the honeymoon had yet to be decided, as had the date for the wedding. Fabian was going to make enquiries about houses for sale or land available for building and would let them know the result that evening.

When he arrived at seven o'clock, Fabian was all smiles. He told them he thought he had found the perfect house: a farming family had just moved out and left it vacant.

Looking dismayed, Esmeralda said, 'A farmhouse?'

'No, Mrs Every. A former gentleman's residence. A farming family moved in temporarily but have now gone south.'

Chadwick said, 'Tell me, Fabian, were you serious when you told me a while ago that you might leave the sea and take up farming?'

'There's nothing definite yet.' Fabian paused then went on, 'I thought perhaps we could all drive out tomorrow and take a look at the house. It's about half a mile past the waterfalls —it's three-storeyed, brick-built.'

'I know it,' Chadwick said. 'It's in a lovely spot.'

'I've drawn plans of some alterations I would like done.' Fabian brought a paper from his pocket, unfolded it and spread it out on the table. 'I want larger windows and I should like balconies with wrought-iron railings outside the first-floor windows. We will need a larger and heavier front door, and a terrace to run the length of the house.' He went on to describe how there would be a long curving drive leading up to wide, shallow stone steps and pointed to where he would have fountains spilling water into pools.

The alterations seemed endless and Chadwick said, 'Don't you think it would be wiser to have a house built to all your requirements?'

Fabian said no, it would take so much longer. He gave Jessamy a loving glance. 'I want to be married to your lovely daughter as soon as possible.' Jessamy blushed.

After the alterations, furniture and fittings had been discussed Chadwick looked at Fabian in a thoughtful way. 'If you did leave the sea, how would you fill in your days? You are not a man to be idle.'

358

Fabian admitted that he had a number of plans. He would like to have some animals, cows, sheep, pigs, perhaps chickens. He also had an ambition to breed horses. At this, Jessamy gave Fabian a sharp glance. Breeding horses...this was shades of Caroline. Was she never to be rid of the wretched woman! She waited, watching Fabian, who explained how he had made friends long ago with a boy at boarding school, whose father bred horses. Although Jessamy relaxed after this she could not help wondering why she had not heard Fabian mention this when they were staying with Caroline. Fabian got up then, saying he must go and left with the promise to take them to see the house the following afternoon.

After he had gone Esmeralda said she only hoped the house would turn out to be as attractive as the plans, but she doubted it. It was foolish to have all this conversion done. Fabian should have chosen a house which was ready to be furnished.

Chadwick said quietly, 'It's what Fabian and Jessamy want. They will be living in it and, after all, it's people who make a house into a home.' Esmeralda said no more.

Although Jessamy had seen the house a number of times before it had not made any impression on her, but visualising it through Fabian's eyes when the conversion was completed, she shared his excitement. He described how the land at the front would

359

be lowered to allow for the steps rising to the terrace. There would be lawns, shrubs, walks, rose arbours, sunhouses...

When they went into the house and found the hall and rooms dark Jessamy felt no disappointment, knowing how much lighter everywhere would be when the new windows were put in. There was a morning room, breakfast room, kitchen, laundry and store rooms on the ground floor; sitting-room, five bedrooms and bathroom on the first and second, and the servants' quarters on the top floor.

Before they had a chance to take in the view from the windows an exuberant Fabian had whisked them outside to show them the stables and the other outbuildings.

This was a Fabian that Jessamy had never seen before and when she mentioned it to her father later he said, 'You must remember that a ship has been home to Fabian for a long time. You can imagine how exciting it must be for him, to contemplate having a home of his own, a wife and perhaps children.'

Jessamy said softly, 'Yes, of course,' and vowed she would do her best to make Fabian happy.

She thoroughly enjoyed the next few days, accompanying Fabian to the house and listening to all his ideas about how the stables and outhouses were to be rebuilt and the paddock enlarged. He wanted two extra rooms added on at the side of the house, one to be used as a study and the other as a library.

Once, when the foreman said he would really need more men to complete everything in the time stated, Fabian waved his arm and ordered him to employ another hundred men if necessary, but the house at least must be completed by the end of October.

One day Esmeralda, Verity and Louise came with them. Verity was taken with the plans but Louise showed little interest. She left them once and Jessamy found her upstairs, standing looking out of the window. 'Hello,' she said. 'I wondered where you were. What do you think of the view?'

Louise turned slowly to face her. 'I still think you are marrying the wrong person. Fabian is a seagoing man who will hanker after that life if he ever leaves it. You are steeped in medicines and would miss that if you were at home day after day. Oh, you would still be able to go to the shop but not to work in it—Fabian has made that clear. He'll want you by his side all the time. So, there will not only be two people dissatisfied with their marriage, but there will be Alistair, eating his heart out for love of you.'

'Louise, I can't answer for Alistair. I only know he'll be absorbed in his work, he's that kind of man. Fabian will adjust and so will I. It's Fabian I want to marry. We both want children, we'll be a loving family.'

When Louise was silent it suddenly occurred

to Jessamy to wonder why her cousin was so worried about Alistair, also why she should doubt the success of her marriage to Fabian. She said: 'Tell me, Louise, which man are you in love with, Fabian or Alistair?'

Louise gave a wan smile. 'Your reasoning is wrong, Jessamy. It's simply because it's the reformed me, who wants to prevent two people making a mistake and avoid making a third one unhappy.'

Because Jessamy had been aware of a softening in her cousin's attitude towards certain things since the tragedy in her life she accepted the explanation, but hoped to prove to Louise that she was wrong in her assumption that her marriage to Fabian would turn out to be a mistake.

CHAPTER TWENTY-TWO

During the next few weeks, Jessamy lived her life at different levels. Fabian had gone back to sea, taking only short voyages, until the end of October when they were due to be married. There would be the excitement when he was due home and the sadness when he had to leave again. There was the pleasure of seeing the 'new house' taking shape, and the awful time when Alistair told her he was leaving to take a job in London. It was weeks after he had first mentioned making a move and she had been complacent, enjoying working with him, thinking he had changed his mind.

'London?' she said. 'Wouldn't you have preferred to work nearer your home?'

'I would have done, yes, but your father recommended me to a pharmacist there, whose apprentice had just left, deciding to take up other work. He accepted me as a stopgap; I've only a few months of my apprenticeship to serve. I hope I might get into the London College to train.'

He told her he would be working in the East End and that he had good lodgings to go to. Jessamy, who had been trying hard not to show her distress at his leaving said lightly, 'Well, we shall be able to come and see you when we come to London.'

'Yes, of course,' he replied, his manner so formal Jessamy could have wept.

When Alistair left she missed him, missed him terribly, so did Chadwick and Mr Blackwell. 'A fine lad,' Mr Blackwell declared, 'a worker, he'll go far.'

Jessamy's solace was in seeking the right furniture and furnishings for the house, her choice being walnut for the sitting-room and oak for the rest of the rooms. And because she had always liked the warm colours in Verity's house she chose a red Turkey carpet for the sitting-

363

room and matching red velvet curtains, with a deep pelmet edged with gold braid, which met with Fabian's approval.

The main bedroom had a deep rose carpet and chintz curtains and bedcover. Fabian had wanted the tester bed and every time Jessamy saw it she felt a little thrill, thinking of the nights she would be lying in Fabian's arms after their passionate lovemaking. Sometimes it was difficult waiting for that time to come and it was only due to Fabian's iron control that the consummation of their love did not take place before their marriage.

The honeymoon was to be spent in Paris. 'For as long as you wish to stay, my darling,' Fabian said tenderly.

Henrietta, when told about this looked wistful. 'You, Jessamy my love, have fallen on your feet. Imagine your grandfather saying such a thing to me. I would have swooned.'

'But your love for one another is deep, Grandma, and that is the important thing.'

'Yes, it is, Jessamy, but your Captain is the kind of man who needs a lot of affection. Keep telling him how much you love him. Now, how are the workmen getting on with the house? I want to picture it in my mind's eye, because I'll never be able to visit it.'

Jessamy described the sitting-room and the bedrooms then said, 'The new fireplace in the kitchen is huge, it will need a forest of logs to feed it and the new wood-burning stoves. We are going to have grounds to walk in, with rose arbours, and pavilions and all sorts of trees are to be planted. Fabian wants it to become known as The Montague Acres. It's all so exciting.'

Jessamy was to wear her grandmother's wedding dress, which had once been white, but the satin had become creamy with age. It was full-skirted, with a small bustle at the back. The veil had appliquéd satin leaves all around the edge. Jessamy had thought at first that she would not be able to wear the dress because of the smallness of the waist but, with a tight corseting and the dressmaker letting a fraction out at each side, she managed it.

The bridesmaids' dresses were of pale lilac silk, with tiny pink rosebuds scattered over the skirts. Dorcas had objected to the rose-buds as being too ornamental when the family were still in mourning but Chadwick said that if one was to believe the Bible then heaven was a beautiful place with many flowers. The rosebuds remained.

All the married women had agreed to wear black but with a touch of white if wished. The older men would be wearing black, but the younger ones and Chadwick, who was giving Jessamy away, would be wearing grey with matching top hats. Fabian's First Officer was to act as best man and both men would, of course, be in uniform.

It was an Indian summer and on the October

afternoon when Jessamy set out for the church in the carriage with her father it was sunny, the air balmy. She was to be married at the Fishermen's Church on the moor and people came out of cottages to give her a wave. One child threw a posy of flowers through the open carriage window. Jessamy gave a shaky laugh and said she felt like royalty. Chadwick gripped her hand and asked if she was nervous. 'A little, Papa, but happy, very happy.'

'I'm so glad, Jessamy, there was a time when—' he paused then said, 'Good heavens, look at all the people outside the church, 'where have they all come from?'

There was a surprisingly large crowd, with a sprinkling of men among the women.

Suddenly Jessamy froze, sure she had seen Lillian in the crowd, but when she quickly scanned the faces there was no one who remotely resembled her. She relaxed, annoyed with herself for even allowing Lillian to come into her mind on this special day. When Chadwick helped Jessamy down from the carriage a woman called, 'A proud day for you, Doctor,' and to Jessamy, 'We all wish you well, Miss Jessamy.'

She smiled. 'Thank you for your good wishes, I appreciate them.'

Francis, who was one of the ushers came hurrying up, saying in a low voice, 'The church is packed, there's not a seat to be had. Fabian is here with his best man. Jessamy, even veiled, you look beautiful.'

Jessamy acknowledged the compliment with a smile, then slipped her hand through her father's arm and walked with him into the church. As they entered, the organist began to play Mendelssohn's *Wedding March*, the notes soaring and reverberating through the small, stone-built edifice. Louise, who had been waiting with the other three bridesmaids, moved behind Jessamy and her father and the procession set off down the aisle. Jessamy stared straight ahead trying to compose herself, but as she saw Fabian, his expression warm and loving, she had to fight the threat of tears. This was a caring man who loved her. When she reached him he whispered, 'Jessamy' and gave her hand a quick squeeze. After that Jessamy was aware only of the words of the marriage ceremony, of Fabian saying in a strong clear voice, 'I do,' and eventually of him slipping the broad band of gold on to her finger.

When they went into the vestry he kissed her gently, then whispered, 'I promise to cherish thee, sweet wife, for the rest of your life.'

Jeremiah, who seemed to take it as his right to be the first to greet the newlyweds, stepped forward, saying to Fabian, 'Jessamy is my first granddaughter to be married. You've made a good choice, but she is a bit of a rebel. If you keep a tight rein on her she'll make you a good wife.' He then turned to Jessamy. 'You heard what I said, girl. Talk to your grandmother, she will instruct you on how to please your husband.'

Jessamy, giving a quick glance at Fabian saw he was having difficulty in keeping a straight face.

Then Esmeralda stepped forward and said coldly to Jeremiah, 'If you don't mind, I would like to offer congratulations to my daughter and son-in-law.' He bowed and waved a hand. 'Of course.'

When Chadwick had the chance to offer his congratulations he gave bride and bridegroom a broad smile and a wink.

All of Jessamy's uncles were in the vestry and when it came to Bertie's turn to greet bride and groom he was shy, awkward, and Jessamy, remembering all his kindnesses to her from childhood put her arms around him and gave him a hug. His face lighted with pleasure and there was a hint of tears in his eyes.

Moments later Fabian and Jessamy were leading the procession up the aisle to the soul-stirring strains of *Here Comes the Bride*.

When Jessamy had come down the aisle she had been aware only of Fabian waiting for her. Now she noted with surprise how really packed the church was. And was further surprised when they left the church to find eight naval officers forming a guard of honour, their crossed swords making an arch.

Fabian laughed and taking Jessamy's hand

they ran stooped under the arch to good wishes and some cheers from the waiting crowd. Jessamy, straightening said, 'My goodness, royalty could not have had better treatment.'

Fabian helped her into the carriage and Jessamy, smiling, raised a hand to acknowledge the good wishes of the people when for the second time that afternoon she tensed, thinking she had seen Lillian, but once more, as she scanned the faces there was no one even slightly resembling her cousin. Could she really be so mistaken? Once yes, but twice...? 'Jessamy, are you all right?' Fabian's hand was on her arm. 'You look pale.'

She managed a smile. 'I think it's excitement. I was up at five o'clock, I couldn't sleep.'

He laughed softly, 'What a lovely excuse for an early night.' Then more seriously he went on, 'Just think, Jessamy, tonight we shall be in London and later in Paris.' He took her hand, kissed it first on the back, then on the palm and Jessamy suddenly drew in a quick breath, thinking that if a kiss on her palm could arouse such delicious tremors what other delights could Fabian have to offer on their wedding night?

When they arrived at Beacon Hall Jessamy and Fabian went right away to see Henrietta, who hugged them and wept unashamedly with happiness. 'What a handsome pair you make. I wish you all the good things in life, *love*, the sense to forgive one another, to understand the

369

needs of the other and most important of all to be able to be friends and talk over the problems that arise in the lives of every married couple.'

Fabian said, 'That is sound and sensible advice, Mrs Every. I shall do my best to follow it.'

'Then you'll have a happy life together, that is, if Jessamy follows it too.'

Jessamy assured her she would then she and Fabian were called away to greet the rest of the family. Verity, laughing, said she had heard of Jeremiah's remarks, adding, 'What impudence that man has, giving not only advice to Fabian on how to handle you, but telling you to talk to Henrietta about the right behaviour for a wife.'

There was plenty of talk about Jeremiah's remarks but they were forgotten when it was known that he had undertaken to pay for the reception and he had certainly not stinted matters.

The tables were laden with food. As well as a three-tiered wedding cake there were gâteaux of every kind, trifles, beef, ham, tongue, game pies... And as well as champagne there was wine, port and brandy. Fabian and Jessamy cut the cake and before Chadwick had an opportunity to make a speech Jeremiah was on his feet. His speech was short. He said he had made an exception in providing the reception because Jessamy was the first of his granddaughters to be married, but the rest of the girls were not to expect the same privilege. Henrietta raised her eyebrows then smiled around at everyone as though to say her husband did not really mean what he had said. But there were sour looks from Dorcas and Digby and Jessamy could imagine the talk there would be afterwards.

Jeremiah concluded by wishing Jessamy and Fabian a happy future and asked that the guests would raise their glasses to the bride and groom. Later, with champagne flowing and so much good food, all grievances seemed to be forgotten, but Jessamy did hear her Aunt Dorcas say to her sister-in-law Grace, 'I see no reason why Jessamy should be singled out for Jeremiah's goodwill gesture. After all, Chadwick is well able to foot the bill. At least, one would think so, with the extravagant clothes that Esmeralda seems to be wearing lately.'

Jessamy ignored the remarks, especially as there was an air of goodwill afterwards. This could have been partly due to the fact that the officers who had formed the guard of honour had been invited to the reception and with the best man there too, the older women as well as the girls came in for a lot of attention. By six o'clock that evening the big room was buzzing with chatter. Verity, who came up to Jessamy said, 'It's about the first time I've found you alone. What a splendid occasion it is, no snide remarks or back-biting. Mind you, I think the champagne has helped.' She gave a

371

little giggle. 'I must admit to feeling slightly inebriated myself, but to be honest I'm rather enjoying it.' Verity looked around her. 'Have you seen Louise?'

Jessamy smiled. 'Well now, the last time I saw her she and Fabian's First Officer were having a heart to heart talk and I was told afterwards that they had gone for a short walk to get some fresh air.'

'Oh!' A look of pleasure came over Verity's face. 'Wouldn't it be lovely if Louise was the next bride. I was thinking the other day—' She paused as a maid came up, bobbed a curtsy to Jessamy and handed her an envelope.

Jessamy thanked her and said to Verity as she slit open the envelope, 'This must be the ninth or tenth greeting we've had since we came back from church. I wonder who this one is from?'

She unfolded the sheet of paper and as she began to read she felt the colour draining from her face. The walls seemed to be closing in on her then receding. Verity, alarmed said, 'Jessamy, what is it?'

'It's from...Lillian.' Jessamy could hardly get the words out. She held out the letter to Verity. 'Read it, please, aloud.' Verity drew Jessamy out of the room into the passage then, after a pause she began:

'I'm leaving for America, for good. Yes, you will not be seeing me again. But before I go I must congratulate you on your marriage to the

372

handsome Captain Montague. What a feather in your cap. I really am delighted because I've had the ultimate revenge. You've married the wrong man, Cousin dear. Caroline has not gone abroad. She's still here in London, no not at the house you visited but at a small but delightful residence on the the river at Putney, paid for by your husband. You poor fool, Jessamy. How naive you are. Don't you know the lines from Much Ado About Nothing:

> Sigh no more ladies, sigh no more,
> Men were deceivers ever;
> One foot in sea and one on shore;
> To one thing constant never.'

Jessamy felt unable to breathe. She looked wildly at Verity then, plucking up the skirt of her dress began to run, ignoring Verity's urgent plea, 'Jessamy, please, *please*, wait.' She ran down the stairs, across the stone flagged hall, desperate to get into the fresh air. The front door was open and she had started down the steps when she tripped and with nothing to cling to went hurtling on to the gravel path, hitting her head on a stone. She smelt the freshness of the damp grass before blacking out.

When Jessamy regained consciousness she became aware of people whispering and wondered where she was. Then she found she was in bed, which for some reason did not feel right. She opened her eyes and realised there were several people in the room, but was unable to make out who they were. Then a man's voice said, 'I think she's coming round, Chadwick.'

The next moment she heard her father say gently, 'You've had a fall, Jessamy, and Doctor Briscow is going to examine you. He will lift your arms, then your legs to see if you have any pain.'

Jessamy was puzzled. Why should Doctor Briscow examine her? Her father always attended to her if she was ill. Not that she had been ill for years. She felt some pain when her right arm and her right leg were raised but according to the doctor this was due to bruising. Then she was being lifted up and asked to drink something. Obediently she did so, and was laid back on the pillows. She was glad, she wanted to sleep.

When Jessamy next roused it was daylight and a shaft of sunlight lay across a dark blue bedcover. Blue? Then she became aware of two people sitting by the bed, a nurse and her Aunt Verity. As she moved her head they were both on their feet, the nurse saying, 'How do you feel, Mrs Montague?'

Montague? Remembrance came and with it panic. 'I don't want to see him, I won't see him!'

She tried to struggle up, but the nurse held her. 'It's all right, Mrs Montague, you don't have to see anyone. I'll just take your temperature and your pulse then I'll see about some breakfast for you.'

'I don't want any breakfast, I want to talk to my aunt.'

But no matter how much Jessamy railed the nurse was adamant, pulse and temperature first then...

Jessamy gave in, and when the nurse left to see about breakfast she turned to Verity. 'My marriage is over, Aunt Verity, no one could make me live with Fabian. He's deceived me, lied, lied over and over again.'

Verity took Jessamy's hand in hers. 'Now calm down, my love, or you'll have your temperature up and we won't be able to talk. Now listen to me. You must remember it was Lillian who was writing the letter. She could tell any lies to hurt you. Fabian absolutely denies that he bought a house for Caroline to live in. He said he had a letter from her saying she was leaving for abroad and giving him a date. He said he had no reason to doubt her.'

Jessamy shook her head. 'I don't believe him. I can't. I know that Lillian is a liar but in this case I feel that what she said was the truth. I wish I was dead.' Tears welled up and rolled slowly down Jessamy's cheeks. She looked at Verity and added in a pitiful way, 'Was it only yesterday in church that I thought Fabian was a kind and caring person?'

'He is, Jessamy, he is. He's beside himself

that this should happen.' Verity pulled out a handkerchief and wiped Jessamy's tears away. 'He wants to see you, you must talk.'

'No, I won't, don't make me, please.'

'Jessamy, love, you won't be made to do anything you don't want to.' Verity smoothed back Jessamy's hair. 'The nurse will be here in a moment with your breakfast, you must try and eat something or she'll have Doctor Briscow here again.'

But all Jessamy had to eat that day were a few spoonsful of gruel. Her mother came to see her but she refused to talk to Esmeralda, just lay inert staring at the wall. Chadwick came several times but had no more response. Verity sat with her and so did Louise but neither were able to rouse Jessamy from her apathy. Then in the evening Henrietta was wheeled in. She asked to be alone with Jessamy and the nurse left them.

Henrietta said, her tone brisk, 'I would have left you to wallow in your misery had I not known how stubborn you are and that your withdrawal could become a permanent thing. I've advised your husband to take you to the home he has ready for you, where you belong.'

At this Jessamy sat up. 'You had no right!'

'Neither have you the right to deny him the chance to discuss the present situation. Your Cousin Lillian, whom you detest, writes a load of lies and you believe them.'

'I believe her because Fabian deceived me

over Caroline once before.'

'That is not what you told me. You said he had given a satisfactory explanation as to why he had been loving towards his former fiancée.'

'I didn't really believe him then, but I accepted it because I loved him.'

'Rubbish! You agreed to marry him because he was handsome and could offer you a comfortable life.'

'That's not true!'

'Then if you loved him why have you made such a mockery of your marriage? Yesterday you stood at the altar and swore before God to love, honour and obey and that didn't mean just a matter of hours. It meant for life.'

'I didn't know then that he had a mistress,' Jessamy retorted.

'You don't know now that he has. And you won't even trouble to find out. Why don't you grow up, Jessamy? You're a married woman now and you're behaving like a spoilt child. The first little ripple on the pond and you turn it into a tornado.'

Henrietta raised her stick to tap on the door to let the maid know she was ready to leave then she lowered it. 'I'll say just one more thing. I don't want you in this house. I am not going to be accused of helping to break up a marriage of no more than hours, and I doubt whether your mother will want you back home. Think of the scandal and the gossip.'

Henrietta tapped on the door and when the

maid came allowed herself to be wheeled out without even a glance in her granddaughter's direction.

Jessamy flung herself back on the pillows, fuming. As always her grandmother had had the last say. Well, no matter what anyone said, she was definitely not going to live with Fabian. She would make plans to run away.

But even as Jessamy thought this she knew, with a feeling of despair, that there was no place to run to.

CHAPTER TWENTY-THREE

Jessamy spent a restless night, and during the wakeful hours came to the conclusion that her grandmother was right. She *had* behaved immaturely in denying Fabian the right to defend himself. She wanted to see him to apologise and fretted that she had to go through all the routine of pulse and temperature-taking by the nurse, then go through it again when the doctor came before she was allowed visitors. She said, 'I feel much better, Doctor. Can I see my husband? I would like to go home.'

He shook the thermometer, put it in his bag and snapped it shut. 'You can see your husband of course, Mrs Montague, but I think it wise to stay in bed for another few days. You had a bad fall and a blow to the head.'

'But I feel so well! I had a good breakfast and I would go by carriage.'

He eyed her over the top of his spectacles. 'Be patient. It's far better to be safe than sorry. I'll look in on you again this afternoon. Good day, Mrs Montague.'

'Fiend,' she said under her breath.

Fortunately for Jessamy's frustration Verity arrived shortly after the doctor left and when Jessamy told her of her decision about Fabian she beamed at her. 'Oh, I'm so glad. The poor man has been beside himself with worry. He's with Henrietta, shall I send him in? Incidentally, your grandmother didn't mean a word she said about asking you to leave the house. She did it to help snap you out of your apathy.'

Jessamy said she knew and Verity told her she would tell Fabian the good news.

With quickening heartbeats Jessamy waited and when there was a gentle tap on the door she had to take a quick breath to compose herself. She called, 'Come in,' and when Fabian entered and she saw the lines of worry on his face she felt ashamed of the way she had behaved.

'Jessamy,' he said softly as he came forward.

She held out a hand to him. 'Fabian, I'm sorry for all my stupidity. It was the shock of Lillian's letter.'

'Of course it was. I hope the wretched

379

woman meant it when she said she was going to America to live. And I must stress now that there was no truth whatsoever in what she wrote about Caroline. I can show you the letter she sent to me, giving the date she would be leaving England. If Caroline didn't leave then I have no knowledge of it. I hope you believe me, Jessamy.'

'I must if we are to have any life together.'

Fabian frowned. 'Does this mean you have doubts?'

There were still doubts in her mind, but knowing there would be no kind of marriage if she admitted it she said, 'I just want to forget the whole thing, Fabian. I'm so looking forward to going...home with you.'

There was a sudden joyousness in him. 'Oh, Jessamy darling, you have no idea what this means to me. When will you be well enough to make the move?'

She gave a shaky laugh. 'I would like to say now, but Doctor Briscow gave orders. Perhaps tomorrow.'

He said he would see the doctor. Her bed would be well-aired, she would be well wrapped up, would come to no harm. And before she could reply he was away.

Jessamy lay, wondering how she could have been so foolish. She had missed her wedding night because of her lack of trust.

Verity was with Jessamy when Fabian returned, jubilant. he had seen the doctor and

380

Jessamy was allowed to come home. He gave her a hug. 'At last, my darling wife.'

There was as much excitement in the rest of the house as in the bedroom. Henrietta was wheeled in and the little maid brought stone hot water bottles, her face shining. Jeremiah arrived, giving orders that Jessamy should be carried, as she had complained of backache... Fabian assured him that every care would be taken. Afraid that something might stop her leaving, Jessamy lied and said she no longer had backache.

Then Chadwick arrived, and quietly organised everything. He would carry Jessamy down and if Fabian would get into the carriage he would put her into his arms. Far better than trying to get her comfortable on a hard seat.

Henrietta, all smiles, waved from one window, the staff from another. Jeremiah came out to see them off and gave orders to the coachman to drive carefully. Verity and Chadwick were going with them. Jessamy felt emotional at the thought of going to her new home in her husband's arms. What more could a bride want?

Being so busy before the wedding, she had not been to the house for some time and when it came into view she gasped, 'Oh, Fabian, it looks lovely.' There were boxes of geraniums on the balconies, tubs of plants on the terrace, the brass lion-head knocker gleamed on the massive carved oak door and every window shone. Fabian said, 'Saplings have been planted at either side of the drive. In years to come we should be driving through the aroma of lime trees.'

Verity added, 'With a lovely sweep of lawns and fountains playing. That's right, Fabian, isn't it?'

'It is.' He smiled at Jessamy. 'There's so much to show you, so much to develop.'

'And plenty of time to do it,' Chadwick said. 'I envy you this place, Fabian. I would be in my element pottering.'

Fabian laughed. 'My dear father-in-law, you will be welcome any time to come and potter. Nothing would please me more.'

The carriage drew up at the steps and a young stable boy came running to attend to the horses. A groom followed and then the servants were out on to the terrace to welcome Jessamy—a plump cook, a housemaid, parlour maid and kitchen maid, who all bobbed a curtsy, with the cook offering a few words of greeting.

Jessamy thanked her and with a tremulous smile said she would meet them all later. Then Fabian carried her inside saying softly, with his cheek to hers, 'Welcome home, my darling.'

A fire blazed in the hall grate, there was greenery everywhere and vases of bronze and gold chrysanthemums.

Jessamy had intended to ask to be allowed to stay downstairs, but after Fabian had carried her to see the dining-room, the morning-room and the big cosy kitchen she had lost strength and was glad when he said, 'And now to bed.'

She sank into the warmed feather bed and closed her eyes, the lower part of her back one agonising ache. She forced back tears of frustration, having thought of the coming evening as their wedding night.

Verity said gently after Fabian had left Jessamy to get settled into bed, 'You're in pain, aren't you? Perhaps we ought to have listened to the doctor. I was just as anxious as Fabian to see you settled in your new home.'

Jessamy whispered, 'I'll be all right after a rest. I must be. After all, I want to be a proper—' Jessamy tried to move and winced.

'A proper wife? You must forget all that. You have the rest of your lives together. Fabian, I'm sure, is a patient man.'

He was. He was tender, held her in his arms when he came to bed, but at some time during the night he left her and slept in the dressing-room. Jessamy tried to tell herself it was sensible, but found herself thinking that if it had been Alistair, he would have stayed with her in case she needed anything. And was appalled that such a thing should have entered her mind. What had been between Alistair and herself belonged to the past.

When the next morning Fabian explained, smiling, why he had left her she was appeased. 'As you can understand, my lovely one, I was terribly restless and realising I was disturbing you and causing you pain, I just had to leave you. How are you feeling?'

'Like you, restless. My back is easier. Perhaps this evening we might spend the whole night together.'

He gave a mock groan. 'Don't, the thought torments me. I want to make love to you now.' Teasing her, he untied the cord of his dressing gown then quickly looped it as there was a tap on the door. It was the little maid with their morning tea.

She kept her gaze on the tray but after she had bobbed a curtsy and left Fabian said, 'Did you see the funny little smile playing around her mouth? I wonder what she was thinking.'

'Captain Montague, you have a wicked mind.'

He leaned towards her and said softly, 'You have no idea how wicked I feel when I'm with you.'

Jessamy could only think that with such a look her back just had to be better that evening.

It was, but not through any help from the doctor, who told her when he called to go on resting. Fabian was responsible for taking the pain away by massaging her whole back with oil he had brought from Japan.

Jessamy, a very willing patient, who was lying on her stomach in a somnambulant state murmured drowsily, 'Who taught you to massage like that?'

384

'A geisha girl, she was excellent. She once cured a backache I had had for several months.'

Jessamy suddenly raised herself and looked at him wide-eyed over her shoulder. 'A *girl* massaged you?'

'Yes, it's part of their—' Fabian paused then gave a little cough. 'I take it that you don't know about geisha girls?'

'No, I don't. Tell me.'

'Well, they're trained to it. It's...um...a profession, just a profession. Many men have bad backs, businessmen and others.'

'And do the girls massage the backs of women, too?'

Fabian grinned. 'Not that I know of, but they might. Now relax and let me continue with the treatment.'

Jessamy had put her cheek to the towel when she raised her head again. 'Do you know what I think? Massaging is a very sensual thing. And I also think there is a great deal I don't know about you, Captain Montague.'

'And do you know what I think, Mrs Montague? There's a great deal that I don't know about you.'

Jessamy, thinking about Alistair, felt her heartbeats quicken. She said, 'Shall we continue the treatment, sir?'

Fifteen minutes later Jessamy rolled over on to her back, then drew herself up in bed. 'It's a miracle! I do not only have a wonderful glowing feeling all over my body, but all my pain is gone.'

'Are you sure, Jessamy?' The eagerness in his voice had her holding out her arms to him and within seconds two hearts were thudding in unison.

Some time later Jessamy was wondering why it had all been so disappointing and realised it was because of Fabian's iron control in an effort not to hurt her. Not like Alistair's undisciplined passion, who, although disappointing her at first had more than made up to her a short time afterwards. But there, she must stop comparing the two men. These were early days and she should be grateful that Fabian had been so gentle.

It was Fabian who brought Jessamy her morning tea and as he stood looking at her solemn-faced she felt a sudden qualm. She said, 'I'm sorry if I disappointed you last night.'

'Disappointed? Indeed not, my sweet. You were warm and loving.'

'Then why are you so serious?'

'Because so many people want to come visiting today and I wanted you to myself. Selfish, of course. At least we can have part of the morning together. Your mother is calling about eleven, and in the afternoon there will be aunts and cousins.'

Jessamy held out a hand saying softly, 'We shall have the evening together. Late evening.'

'Jessamy—' he cupped her face between his palms, 'how I love you.'

He kissed her on the lips, gently, and Jessamy said afterwards, 'Fabian, you must stop treating me like an invalid. I feel well, very well.' She smiled. 'You were responsible, for that with your expertise of massaging... taught to you by the geisha girls.'

Fabian gave her a broad smile, 'Jealous?'

'Of course. *I* want *you* to myself.'

'I am all yours, my darling.'

His next kiss had a little more passion, but when Jessamy responded he drew away. 'After you've had your breakfast I shall carry you downstairs and show you the extended plans for The Montague Acres.'

'I shall walk round the land. I feel well enough.'

Fabian pursed his lips. 'We shall have to see what you can manage.'

Jessamy was surprised at just how much land there was. Fabian had the front already mapped out for where the fountains would be. At either side of the sweep of lawns there would be rose arboured walks and a summerhouse. At one side of the house, running from front to back, an extension was already in progress which was to be a study and small library.

At the rear, the stables were being rebuilt and the paddock enlarged. Beyond was pasture land, a forest, fields that met with purple and pink heather-clad hills, their tops shrouded in mist. Fabian said he understood that the forest was carpeted in bluebells in spring and Jessamy said yes, it was lovely. Fabian waved a hand to the left. 'There we shall have a stream, spanned by small bridges, and all around there will be beds of daffodils and crocuses.'

She said, half-laughing, 'Where are you going to have a kitchen garden? We must be practical.'

There would be one, he said, but it would be hidden by hedges. He stopped and put his hands under her elbows. 'I want you to see only beauty, my sweet love.'

Jessamy had a sudden feeling of being trapped. It was all too cloying. She drew away. 'I don't want to be protected from reality, Fabian. I'm not a hothouse flower.'

'Of course you're not. But what is wrong in having beauty around you?'

'Nothing, it's just that I feel we have so much while others live in poverty.'

'Oh, Jessamy, I know about all the poverty in the world, but it won't make any difference if I leave the derelict-looking stables, if I don't plant shrubs, trees, flowers.'

'No, of course not. I was perhaps being a little foolish. It was just that through the night when I lay awake for a time I had an image of the people standing outside the church the other day, many of them poorly clad, while I—' Jessamy paused and smiled. 'Take no notice of me, I've gone through all this before with Alistair. Oh, there's Mama waving.'

Jessamy was glad of the interruption, feeling

she might have gone on to talk about Alistair's ambition of wanting to open a dispensary for the poorer people and this would definitely not have been the right time.

Esmeralda, looking elegant and beautiful, showed a genuine pleasure in seeing Jessamy up and about.

'This is splendid. Your father will be so pleased. He was very worried about you. He'll be calling later.' Jessamy explained that Fabian had been showing her the land he owned and what he had planned and Esmeralda sighed and said, 'I hope you realise how lucky you are, Jessamy.'

Fabian disputed this, saying that he was the lucky one to have such a loving and caring wife.

It was a pleasant enough interlude, with Esmeralda showing an interest in all the improvements made to the house. But when she was standing looking out of the sitting-room window later she said, 'It will be a future generation who will benefit from all the changes you're making out of doors, Fabian.'

'That is part of the reason for the improvements. I want our children to enjoy it all.' He put his arm around Jessamy's shoulder. 'I know that Jessamy is looking forward to children, as I am. I want a large family, I was an only child.'

Esmeralda said, 'Don't be disappointed if children don't come along. I wanted several children, wanted sons, but—' She raised her shoulders. 'The good Lord decreed otherwise.'

Jessamy felt disturbed. She did want children but had reckoned to leave them with a nanny so that she could lend Alistair a hand in his dispensary from time to time. And with this thought she realised how vague her plans had been. He could be anywhere when he qualified, Edinburgh... She said to her mother, 'You must see the new bathroom, Mama, it's so attractive.'

Verity and then Chadwick arrived and after that there seemed to be a constant coming and going of visitors and at three o'clock in the afternoon Jessamy was so exhausted she was glad to lie down on the sofa. Fabian covered her over with a rug, dropped a kiss on her brow, asked anxiously if she would be all right, and when she said, a note of sharpness in her voice, that yes she would, he told her he would go and see how the workmen were doing.

Jessamy clenched her hands. She needed affection, but did not want to be cossetted. She must try and explain this. But after a while she slept and awoke feeling calmer. Tonight it would be all right. They were both perhaps a little on edge after the pallid lovemaking of the night before.

But it was worse because Fabian suggested that he sleep in the dressing-room so that Jessamy could have an undisturbed night's sleep. She had had such a tiring day.

'I am rested,' she declared in a controlled

390

voice. 'I slept this afternoon. Now I'm wide awake.'

Yes, he said, he realised that. She was tense, strung up, the doctor had warned him about it. They were symptoms after a blow on the head.

Jessamy, trying desperately to keep her temper, said she had been perfectly calm until Fabian had suggested sleeping in the dressing-room. Did he understand that she loved him, wanted him to make love to her? Properly, not trying to be too gentle with her.

But he had to be gentle with her, he said, the doctor had actually told him to avoid contact with her until she had fully recovered from her fall.

'The doctor!' she shouted. 'The man's a fool. He's never been married, possibly never loved a woman. What does he know about it?'

When Fabian tried to soothe her, Jessamy became hysterical. 'I thought you were a man,' she shouted. 'I thought of you as a tyrannical pirate who would take any woman he wanted. And what are you? A namby pamby, who'll do anything to avoid making love to me.'

Although in a hysterical state she was aware of his shock, then his anger. 'Stop it, Jessamy, you don't know what you're saying.'

'I do know, you're weak, a liar.' She began to cry hysterically.

He slapped her face then held her to him. 'It's all right. Now calm down.'

Jessamy gave a hiccupping sob, the hysterical bout over. He took her on to his lap and rocked her. Presently he laid her on the sofa, covered her up and told her he would be back in a few moments. She was just to lie still.

Jessamy, feeling ill, but knowing she had committed the unpardonable sin of calling a man a weakling, lay steeped in misery. How could she have said such a thing? Before long Fabian was back. He sat beside her and held her hand. Then she became aware of her father saying as he raised her up, 'I want you to drink this, Jessamy love.' She drank it and he laid her back on the cushion saying gently, 'You'll be all right. Try and sleep.'

She was aware of the two men talking in low voices, but could not make out which one was speaking.

'It's understandable...Lillian again...and on her wedding day...thoughts distorted... She's young, she'll get over it...' Jessamy slept.

She kept waking and sleeping and when she roused knew that Verity, Louise, her parents, her grandfather had been, but she had no conversation with them. Then one morning she began to wonder why she had not seen Fabian. When her father came she asked him and he said, 'He has sat with you, Jessamy, but you rejected him, you would not accept he was there.'

'It was guilt,' she said.

Chadwick smiled and laid his hand over hers.

'My clever daughter.'

'No, not clever, Papa. It's just that I've grown up. It's painful.'

'Yes, Jessamy, it is, but valuable. You'll never make the same mistake again. I doubt whether you'll ever experience another hysterical bout. You readily admitted the cause and women prone to hysteria don't.'

When Fabian came in later there was no fuss, no loving concern. He was quiet, withdrawn. When Jessamy apologised for the time she had been hysterical he said, 'You were ill.' That was all. Then he said he had to go out, Verity would be coming to visit.

Jessamy lay worrying that what she had said that night could cause a rift. Although he had accepted that she had been ill he had not accepted it as an excuse for calling him a weakling. This was understandable. It was a dreadful thing to say to any man, much less one as virile and with such an iron control as Fabian.

Although Jessamy had decided it was something she could not talk over with anyone, Verity got it out of her when Jessamy kept pulling at the lace edging on her handkerchief and asked gently what was worrying her. Verity said to give Fabian time. Yes of course he was upset, what man wouldn't be, but he did love her and he would not deliberately go on making her unhappy.

'Caroline said he was an unforgiving man.

He told her that he would never forgive her for what she had done to him.'

'I would ignore that, Jessamy. He's a loving man and I'm sure that it's just a question of time before he starts fussing over you again.'

But Verity was wrong. Fabian remained aloof with Jessamy, yet to a visitor he was smiling, talkative, joking. There came a day when she felt it impossible to go on in this way and was about to ask if they could have a talk, when he told her he had employed a steward to look after the estate while he was away.

Jessamy caught her breath. 'Away?'

'I'm going back to sea; I want to know there's a man in charge. He'll live in a cottage about a hundred yards away. His name is Stannard.'

She was suddenly calm. 'Aren't you punishing me too harshly for something hateful I said to you when I was ill?'

He stared beyond her, chin outthrust. 'You would not have said it, ill or not, had it not been in your mind. I want to get away from this atmosphere.'

Jessamy's mouth felt dry and it was moments before she was able to answer. 'You are the one who is causing the unpleasantness, and I'm sorry you feel it necessary to humiliate me. Everyone knew you had given up a seafaring life, so why are you going back? They won't blame you. You are so charming to everyone.'

'You are letting your imagination run away

with you.' He sounded impatient.

'Am I? Don't you think that people will find it strange when you rush back to sea without even bothering to take your new bride for a honeymoon? And it's not because of illness— I'm quite well again.'

'I'm sorry about the honeymoon. If only—'

'If! A small word, sadly overworked. If I had not had the letter from Lillian I would not have had the fall, or the subsequent hysteria that made me say what I did. If I had torn the letter up without reading it, things would have been different.'

'Yes, they would.'

'I suggest you ask yourself, Fabian, if you truly love me. I feel that if you did you would have allowed for the state I was in. But you won't, because you're too stubborn. You're used to giving orders that men dare not disobey and you find it impossible to bend. I feel sorry for you. And now, if you'll excuse me.'

Tears blinded Jessamy as she walked away, wanting Fabian to call her back, yet knowing that pride would prevent him.

On the day Fabian left, it was like saying goodbye to a stranger. All he said was that he would write—his expression cold. When her parents learned about the rift, Chadwick was angry. Fabian had no right to go back to sea, not after telling Jessamy he had left it for good. Esmeralda replied wryly, 'Unfortunately, it seems that a man has every right to treat his wife as he pleases.'

There was one thing, however, on which Chadwick and Esmeralda were agreed, that it would be wrong for Jessamy to come back and work in the shop, her own suggestion. She was a married woman now and must act like one. Jessamy pointed out that there was nothing to do at The Montague Acres, the staff took care of everything. She begged to be allowed to work out of sight at the back of the shop, making infusions, ointments, creams and pills. After all, there was a constant demand for their bowls of pot pourri, scented sachets and small scented cushions. She could do so much to help.

It was this that finally won Chadwick over and although Esmeralda did give in later it was with some reluctance. People would gossip about Jessamy's marriage, ask why was she working...Jessamy refrained from saying, so be it. The important thing to her was to be kept occupied.

Verity kept assuring her that everything would work out all right with Fabian, but Louise was scathing about the rift. In her opinion Jessamy was well rid of him. Who wanted a husband who behaved like a spoilt child? To Jessamy's surprise she found herself defending Fabian. After all, it was a dreadful thing she had said about him. It had hurt his pride.

'Hurt his pride my foot!' was Louise's sharp

comment. Which had Jessamy quickly changing the subject.

Although she kept to the back of the shop as much as possible, there were certain people Jessamy liked and for whom she emerged to talk. To their teasing enquiries as to why a lovely young bride like her was not at home looking after her handsome husband she always gave the same answer: 'Well, you know what seafaring men are like. The sea is in their blood and they have to be weaned gradually. I think this short voyage will be his last.'

'Ah, it's sensible you are, Jessamy,' said a Welsh woman she had known for years. 'My mam nagged my father to get a shore job and he did, a good job it was too, but he was like a caged animal and fretted himself to death.'

Then there was little Mrs Bennett, widowed a year after she was married, who mothered her slatternly sister's children, five boys and four girls. She brought them food, clothes and cared for them when they were ill. This time it was the eldest boy Johnnie she worried about. 'He's a lovely lad,' she said, 'and normally good looking, but his face is all spotty and there's him in love with a sweet little dairymaid.'

'It's acne,' Chadwick said, 'the bane of adolescent boys.'

'He keeps squeezing the spots, Mr Every, and it makes them worse. Can you give me some ointment for them?'

Chadwick shook his head. 'What he needs

is something to take internally to cleanse his blood. You can either make an infusion every day, or I can give you a bottle of medicine.'

She settled for the medicine then beamed at Jessamy. 'We saw your wedding, oh, what a beautiful bride you made—and your husband!' Mrs Bennett gave an ecstatic sigh. 'I declare he's the handsomest man I've ever met. I bet he spoils you.'

'A little,' Jessamy said, then asked about her nephews and nieces, which kept Mrs Bennett chatting, even after the medicine was paid for and she was ready to leave.

Then she leaned forward and said with a beaming smile, 'I hope you have lots and lots of children.'

When she had gone Chadwick said, 'There's a born mother who has to lavish her love on her sister's children—and they think the world of her.'

'She's lucky to have so much love.'

There was a tremor in Jessamy's voice and Chadwick said, 'Don't grieve, Jessamy dear. Fabian will come to his senses. You'll have his love and his children.' He smiled, teasing her, 'You can't deprive me of being a grandfather.'

'But does Mama want to be a grandmother? I doubt it.'

'Yes, she does,' he said gently. 'She would be very happy if you told her you were going to have a baby.'

'Then we'll have to see you both get your wish, won't we?' Jessamy turned and went into the back room.

CHAPTER TWENTY-FOUR

As the days went by Jessamy began to feel that she was becoming detached from people. Mr Stannard, the new steward, a stockily-built man, would call every morning to tell her of the work in progress and remind her if there was anything she required, to mention it. There was never anything, but she told him she would let him know if any problem did arise.

Jessamy even stayed away from Beacon Hall, knowing that her grandmother would probe, wanting to know the full story of what was wrong between Fabian and herself. Up to now she had told her what she had told everyone else—that Fabian, like most seamen, needed time to settle down to shore life. The person Jessamy felt closest to at this time was Louise, who often stayed overnight since Fabian had left, and who could sit in silence with her, both feeling at ease.

One evening when they were sitting relaxed in deep armchairs in front of a blazing log fire

Louise, a brocaded cushion clasped to her said, 'Joseph Masterson has asked me to marry him.'

Jessamy sat up. 'He has? What did you say?'

Louise turned her head and eyed Jessamy steadily. 'What would you expect me to say? If I didn't tell him what had happened our marriage would be a lie. If I did tell him he would probably turn away from me in disgust.'

'He might not. He's had—well, quite a fling himself.'

'It's different, a man having a fling and a girl having a baby.'

'But surely it isn't necessary to tell him all about that? You can't suffer for the rest of your life because of one sin. As Grandma says, God forgives so why shouldn't we forgive ourselves for what we've done wrong?'

'What you say makes sense but it's not easy because I feel I'll always carry the burden of guilt, which would not make for a happy marriage.' Louise's smile held sadness. 'I think I'll wait until you have children, then perhaps you'll let me share your pleasure in them.'

Jessamy felt a sudden coldness. If she and Fabian did not get back together then she might never have children.

From then on she found herself waiting for a letter from him. But when one did arrive she could have wept. It was short and simply said he hoped she was well and asked how she was getting on with Mr Stannard. He told her he would be home in several weeks' time and that was it. It was signed *Fabian*, with no mention of love, or anything to suggest he was her husband, a man who only a short time ago had promised to love and cherish her till death parted them.

The matter gnawed at her and eventually she decided to go one morning and have a talk with her grandmother. She walked with an urgency at first then gradually slowed her steps. It was a lovely morning, with a hint of frost in the air. The sun gave a glow to the russets and golds of the last leaves. When one fell, a frisky breeze sent it frolicking for a distance, lifting it up, as though giving it a last fling before letting it fall to earth to die.

No, not to die; she mustn't get morbid. The fallen leaf would be reborn. Her grandmother had told her so when she was small and worried that the leaves would be swallowed up by the Devil in hell.

Henrietta gave her a warm welcome as always. 'Sit down, my love and tell me all your news. Have you heard from Fabian?'

Jessamy handed her the letter saying, 'What do you think of this from a husband who not so long ago swore undying love?'

Henrietta, of course, wanted to know why he had sent such a cool letter and when she was told what had happened said, 'How would you have felt had he told you that you were stupid, had no brains and that he couldn't bear you near him?'

When Jessamy protested at the comparison the old lady said, 'It's a good comparison. A man's virility is everything to him. Decrying it is the biggest insult you could offer him.'

When Jessamy sat silent Henrietta went on, 'First Caroline jilted him, which must have been a terrible hurt to his pride then he fell in love with you, married you, was gentle because of your fall, only to have you shout insults at him! Can you really expect him to forget all this and be lovey-dovey towards you again in a matter of weeks?'

'But he knew I was ill, Grandma.'

'Yes, but as Fabian so rightly said, it must have been in your mind for you to have said such a thing. Go home, Jessamy dear, and write your husband a loving letter. He will be lonely, will look for a letter. Being away from you will heal his wounds.'

Jessamy was not entirely convinced, but knowing now it was up to her she wrote a long letter, telling her husband all that was going on at Montague Acres and saying he would see quite a change when he came home. She told him she thought Mr Stannard very efficient and that he never failed to call on her every morning. One thing she omitted to tell Fabian was that she was back working at the shop, but she wrote about the house and said it had wrapped itself about her (which was the truth). She loved it, it was her very own home. She enjoyed the comfort, enjoyed burying her toes in the sheepskin rugs, wallowed in the deep feather bed and the rose-satin covered eiderdown of goose down. And realised, with a feeling of surprise, that she was also enjoying a feeling of independence, with no one to tell her what she must or must not do. After a slight hesitation she signed the letter, *Your loving wife Jessamy* and after another pause, added two kisses.

When the letter was posted Jessamy again found herself waiting for a reply and this time, the waiting seeming more endless than before.

She was seldom without someone calling in the evenings. Verity was a regular visitor, but Louise never came with her these days. Sometimes she would bring Anne with her and at others, Rebecca, but Rebecca was more lively if the two girls came together on their own. Anne's talk then was always of medicine and Rebecca's of men.

On Friday evenings Jessamy always went to stay with Verity and the family. She enjoyed these occasions because Francis was at home and Rupert, despite now working long hours for his father, always came home a little earlier when she was there. On other evenings he often came home and went straight to bed, pleading fatigue. Verity had argued about this with Bertie, saying it was no life for a young man, but he was obdurate. Work made or broke a person. Although Jessamy had hugged her uncle on her wedding day and felt close to him again, she disliked him for this reasoning.

When Jessamy did eventually hear from Fabian he could not have been more brief. He thanked her for her letter, said the ship would be docking in London shortly but they might be doing a turnabout trip—he would let her know. Again the note was signed simply *Fabian*.

Jessamy sat numbed. If a man could remain so unforgiving it would be impossible ever to live with him. The letter had arrived just after breakfast and she sat staring at it. How could Fabian have changed so much? Had he ever loved her, really loved her—or had he married Jessamy to get his own back on Caroline, to feed his ego, to show her that *she* might throw him over but look, see how young and lovely his new wife was!

She read the letter again then raised her head slowly. This was not the first time that the ship had docked in London... Was Caroline still in London and was he going to see her? Although Fabian had told her he could never forgive Caroline for jilting him, seeing her again might have made him realise just how strong his love was for her.

Jessamy thought this would account for their lovemaking lacking the wild, undisciplined passion she had known with Alistair. Louise had told her she thought she was marrying the wrong man. And yet Fabian had tried to make their marriage work. She was the one

404

to spoil everything.

Restlessly, Jessamy got up and, folding the letter, pressed the edges firmly between finger and thumb. Lillian might have been right and all the time, Caroline was ensconced in a house in Putney, bought for her by Fabian...their love nest.

Jessamy snatched her hat and coat and ran outside slamming the front door in a frenzy of rage. Fabian and his mistress had made a proper fool of her—they could be laughing at her this very minute. 'Poor simple thing, she's so young...'

Louise, who was coming up the drive to visit her, stopped Jessamy in her mad rush. 'Where's the fire? Where on earth are you off to at this hour?'

Jessamy told her quickly about the letter and the conclusions she had reached concerning Fabian's relationship with Caroline. Louise pursed her lips and suggested her cousin was being a little too rash in her weighing up of the situation.

'You have no proof that he's seeing Caroline.'

'No, but I'm going to find out once and for all. I've decided to go to London. I'll go to the house where Lillian was living and if I don't get any satisfaction there I'll enquire at other houses. I'm sure *someone* will know what has happened to her.'

'And what if she's gone to America?'

'Then I'll have a proper talk with Fabian when he comes home. I'm certainly not going to live with a man who treats me as a nonentity. Take a look at this letter. That is the second one I've had signed just with his name. It's an insult. He's reduced me to the status of a farmworker—no, less than that!'

'Jessamy, don't get so agitated, we'll go and have a word with Mama. Something like this is best talked over calmly.'

Over a leaping log fire in the morning-room Verity read the letter, listened to Jessamy's complaints about Fabian and Caroline and her suspicions of their relationship then said gently, 'There are many hurdles in a marriage, Jessamy, and not all are easily overcome. You are just starting your married life. I agree that you got off to a bad start through no real fault of your own, but don't walk out on Fabian without attempting to talk things over.'

Jessamy was not convinced it would do any good but agreed to at least try and sort out their differences. When she arrived at the shop and her father said they needed some backache pills to be made she forced herself to say lightly, 'Just the job I shall enjoy doing.'

This was true. Although there was a machine to make the pills, Jessamy liked making them by hand. Rolling out the paste into thin strips then moulding the small cut-off pieces between her finger and thumb, was a soothing occupation. As she worked, her thoughts shifted from one thing to another. She recalled the first time she had seen Fabian and how he had reminded her of a Viking and then a wicked pirate. She relived their walk on the moor in the snow, the way he had wrapped his coat around her so tenderly and held her close; then a stark image intruded of herself at the window in Caroline's house, watching the two of them embracing in the garden in moonlight... She gave a little shiver. She had known then, with all her heart, that Fabian was still helplessly in love with Caroline. She should never have allowed him to persuade her otherwise, however much he had tried to hide it from himself.

At midday when Louise called to walk home with her Jessamy repeated Verity's advice then added, 'I shall talk to Fabian but I don't think it will do much good because Caroline is the one he loves. If she is still in London, and he lied to me, then I shall definitely leave him.'

'And where will you go?'

'I have no idea at the moment, but certainly not back home.'

'Well, don't get carried away and think that leaving home is a big adventure. It isn't. I was well cared for in Cornwall, but the homesickness at times was appalling. And anyway, could you really bear to leave the Montague Acres?'

'I only know that I couldn't live with a husband who only half-loved me and who had a mistress.'

'Plenty of women put up with it—they have to, because of children.'

'Well, I don't have children and I refuse to be reduced to the status of a chattel. I'll wait until Fabian comes home and if I don't get any satisfaction then, I shall go to London and make enquiries.'

As it turned out, Jessamy had the chance to go to London in an unexpected way. She was getting ready to go to the shop the following morning when her father arrived at the Montague Acres. Without preamble he said, 'Jessamy, would you go with your mother to London? A relative is very ill and she wants to be with him. She's so agitated that I don't want her to travel alone.'

Jessamy said yes of course she would go and asked what time they would be leaving. Chadwick told her that Esmeralda wanted to travel on the train leaving at nine o'clock but he had his doubts about her being ready.

Mother and daughter caught the train with only minutes to spare and were lucky enough to get a carriage to themselves. Quick goodbyes were said with Chadwick walking alongside the train as it moved off. Then he stopped and waved until they were out of sight. Jessamy, still feeling breathless, sat back, thinking how strange fate was. Here she was, on her way to London, without having had to contrive to make an excuse.

Esmeralda was sitting, staring bleakly out of

the window. When she made no attempt at conversation Jessamy said, 'Mama, you haven't yet told me who this relative is who is so dreadfully ill.'

Her mother drew her gaze away and eyed Jessamy steadily. 'He's my son.'

Jessamy pressed her palms together. Should she tell her mother she knew about Ralph? No, it would involve her Aunt Verity. 'Your son?' she said, and waited.

CHAPTER TWENTY-FIVE

'Yes,' Esmeralda said, 'my son.' She leaned her head back against the carriage seat. 'If I had had my way, you would have known about him years ago, but your father refused to allow it.'

And so Jessamy heard the story once more of how her mother had been forced to have her illegitimate child adopted. 'I adored him, Jessamy, to the exclusion of anyone or anything else. It broke my heart to part with Ralph—I wanted to die. When your father and I married I prayed we would have a son. We did, but he lived only a short time and I was sure that God had punished me for my sin.'

'Oh, no, Mama, God is forgiving.'

'Is he? Then why were you not a son?'

Esmeralda reached out a hand. 'Oh, Jessamy, I'm sorry, I've treated you so badly. I've loved you, too, but I could never show it. Something died in me when I lost my second son.'

'He was Father's son, too,' Jessamy reminded her stiffly.

'Yes, and I tended to forget that. I've behaved badly too towards him. But when I longed to love him he rejected me.'

'No!' Jessamy sat up. 'Papa has always been caring towards you, wanting only your happiness. He gave in when you wanted to go to London with him and he could ill-afford it. You bought expensive clothes when he needed that money to replenish stocks. The fur dolman you were wearing the last time you came home I presume to have been bought by Ralph.'

'Yes,' Esmeralda spoke eagerly. 'His adoptive parents were wealthy. It was only when they died that he learned who his real mother was. He contacted me and when we met he cried. He has turned into a lovely person, I want him so much to make his home with us, but your father won't agree to it.'

'You can't blame him, can you? Papa has always needed your love but you always denied him, first because of your obsession with Ralph, then through the continuous mourning for the second son. Did you ever give a thought to me, who was so desperate for your love?'

'Please don't condemn me,' Esmeralda said

piteously. 'Ralph could be about to die. He became ill when he was abroad and grew worse when he returned to England. The doctors think he may have been bitten by a poisonous insect.'

Jessamy weakened. Why should she condemn her mother? She herself had never been in that position. She said quietly, 'I hope Ralph will get well soon.'

When they arrived in London, Esmeralda said, they would go to St James' Street where Ralph had rooms and stay there. 'The housekeeper Mrs Beasley will give you your meals, Jessamy and get you anything you want, but she doesn't live in. Meanwhile, I shall go to the nursing home and stay there, all night, every night, if necessary. I do hope you won't be lonely—Ralph has plenty of books.'

'I'll be all right, don't worry about me, Mama.'

'I do worry. I don't want you to be on your own. I didn't even want you to come but your father insisted. If you do go out, you must take a cab.'

Jessamy sighed. 'Mama, I'm a married woman. Nowadays single women go out unaccompanied. They have secretarial posts, work in shops. But I promise, if I go out I shall take a cab there and back if that will make you feel any easier.'

'Yes, it will, thank you.'

The rooms in St James' Street were quietly

411

but expensively furnished. Mrs Beasley, a small plump woman with a pleasant but respectful manner, obviously already knew Esmeralda. She told her she had received Chadwick's telephone call and would see that her daughter was looked after. She then enquired in a low voice about her employer's condition. Esmeralda left soon afterwards for the nursing home, after kissing Jessamy and hugging her daughter. She might not return until morning.

Although Jessamy had been in London before she experienced a sudden lost feeling, probably because before, she had been with Fabian and her mother and they had stayed with Caroline.

Caroline. That was her first task this afternoon, to try and find out if she was still in London. However, this evening she would go and see Alistair—it was something she had decided on during the train journey.

Mrs Beasley made her a lunch of soup, smoked salmon and apple pie and cream to which Jessamy did full justice. Afterwards she told Mrs Beasley she was going out. Could she please have a key? Then the housekeeper could go home, if she wished. The woman looked worried. Would she manage?

'Yes, Mrs Beasley, I'll manage fine, thank you.'

'Well...if you're sure. There's cake and biscuits in the pantry and if you want to make yourself a cup of tea—'

Jessamy assured her she would find everything and at last the housekeeper left with the promise to be with her in the morning, early.

Once outside, Jessamy hailed a cab, her heart thumping. When they arrived at Caroline's house near Hyde Park she paid the fare and stood looking up at the windows as though expecting to see Caroline waiting for her. Then with resolute steps she went to the door and lifted the knocker.

A young maid came to the door and to Jessamy's enquiry said with a foreign accent, 'Madame 'as left thees house, but I saw 'er zee other day in Oxford Street wiz a gentleman. We do not know where she is living. I am sorry.'

Jessamy thanked her and left, feeling grief rather than anger that Fabian had behaved so deceitfully. He had lied again and again about Caroline. And yet his love for Jessamy had once seemed so genuine.

With hours to spare she wandered aimlessly, thinking what a mess she had made of her life. She had let herself be carried away by Fabian's good looks, his charm and maturity. And now she was tied to him! No, she was tied by the church but she would never live with him again, not even if he begged her to, which she very much doubted. She would have to make plans to leave, but at that moment felt completely at a loss.

Jessamy longed desperately for company, for

413

someone with whom she could discuss her problems, but there was only Alistair and it would be hours before she could see him, if she did see him...

She decided to go back to St James' Street but once in the cab, changed her mind. She would only brood, make herself more miserable. She would go to the National Gallery. From there she went to the Tate and then to the British Museum and realising she had hardly taken in a thing, returned to St James' Street.

The fire had been made up and after making a cup of tea Jessamy sat huddled over it sipping her drink. Her parents, of course, would want her to come home to live but that was something she would never do. She would go right away, start a new life. Louise had talked about homesickness, but she would suffer that, she would have to.

Realising she was getting more and more morbid, Jessamy stood up and looked at Ralph's books. There were several volumes of Shakespeare's plays, a set of *The History of England*, one of *Crowned Masterpieces of Eloquence*, some Waverley novels by Sir Walter Scott and many books on law. Was Ralph a lawyer, or studying to be one? Jessamy chose one of the volumes of Shakespeare and spent her time browsing through the plays and standing at the window watching the world go by. At eight o'clock she dressed then went out and

414

hailed a cab, feeling quite cosmopolitan at travelling alone at night.

Alistair lodged in a humble street where the houses had two rooms up and two down and the windows fronted on to the pavement. Every doorstep was sandstoned and looked so clean under the lamplight it was as though no one ever used the front door. At all but one house light showed through the thin, drawn curtains of the downstairs rooms. The exception was number six, where Alistair lodged, which was in darkness. Jessamy stood, nonplussed, disappointed. He could still be at the pharmacy she supposed, for he had said he often worked late—but as she stood there, she became aware of light in an upstairs room. It was the moving light of someone carrying a candle—a man. Could it be Alistair? Her heart began to pound.

Without further thought she lifted the iron knocker and let it fall. The light steadied then flickered as the person turned. The light next appeared in the fanlight above the front door and Jessamy held her breath for a moment as she heard hurried footsteps on the stairs. Then, as the front door opened she slowly released her breath as she recognised the sturdy figure, his hand curved around the candle flame.

A street lamp was just outside the front door and she waited for Alistair to recognise her. 'Jessamy?'

The uncertainty in his voice had her taking a step forward. 'Yes, I was in London and—'

'I don't believe it.' He looked beyond her as though expecting to see someone else.

'I'm alone. I wanted to see you.'

'My landlady is out.' He laughed suddenly. 'What am I saying? I was so surprised. Come away in.' After he had closed the door he said, 'There's no fire on in the kitchen, I'm afraid. I've just lit the one in my room, but it hasn't burned up yet.'

'It's all right, Alistair. I'm sorry I didn't let you know I was coming. Actually, I came on impulse. It's a long story.'

'Come upstairs,' he said softly. 'I'm really pleased to see you.' The room was small, the fire burning fitfully. Alistair put down the candle and holder then lit a small lamp. Smiling, he pulled up a cane chair. 'Take a seat, Ma'am, sorry I don't have an armchair to offer. I'll go downstairs and make you a hot drink.' Jessamy told him there was no need, but he was away. She looked around her. There were handpegged rugs on the linoleum-covered floor; a plump chintz eiderdown on the bed with a folded blanket laid across the bottom. At one side of the fireplace, where flames were now beginning to show from the slowly-reddening coals, was a table covered with books and papers. A small framed picture of a Highland scene adorned one wall and above the mantelpiece hung an oil painting of a cottage in a wood, very like Davy Feld's cottage where they had made love. Had Alistair painted it?

416

He came up then with two mugs of cocoa and pulled out a small table from the other side of the fireside saying, 'All home comforts!'

'Does your landlady look after you, Alistair? Do you get enough to eat? I think you've lost some weight.'

'Not for lack of food, Jessamy. Mrs Douglas could not have looked after me better had I been her own son. She's a kind, generous soul. She goes to her daughter's once a week and stays overnight but she makes sure there's a meal waiting for me.'

'And I've stopped you from having it.'

Alistair smiled down at her. 'You are a feast from the gods. I still can't believe you are sitting here and I'm not dreaming. Is the Captain with you in London?'

'No, he...went back to sea.'

'And left his beautiful bride on her own?' His tone was teasing. Jessamy decided to match it.

'Leaving me free to visit my favourite Scotsman!'

Perhaps her attempt at lightness failed, because Alistair was suddenly serious. 'What's wrong, Jessamy?'

'Everything,' she confessed, her eyes brimming with tears. With some coaxing from Alistair, she told him about the rift between Fabian and herself, starting with receiving the letter from Lillian on her wedding day, then up to her arrival in London with her mother to be with a sick relative, and concluding her discovery that Caroline was still in London.

Alistair was silent for a while then he took her hands in his. 'Poor Jessamy, you seem to have gone through the mill, but don't you think there's a simple explanation to all this? Your husband is a very proud man and would take your accusation very badly and aren't you jumping to conclusions, condemning him because a foreign maid tells you she has seen Caroline in Oxford Street with a gentleman? It may not even have been Caroline.'

'Alistair, it's not only that. What about the letters he wrote to me? They were so cold I might have been someone he detested. Could you have written such letters to me?'

'No, but you can't compare the actions of two totally different people. Caroline told you that Fabian is an unforgiving man. This could mean that he's oversensitive, and that hurts go deep.'

Jessamy sighed. 'I thought you would have understood but you men are all the same, making excuses for the other.'

'I'm not making excuses for your husband, Jessamy, just trying to rationalise. This is your marriage that's at stake, your whole life. You know how I feel about you, I want only your happiness and there are times when truth can be a kindness.'

'Fabian showed me no kindness or understanding when I called him a weakling after I

418

had been ill. All I had was an icy reception.' Her lip trembled. 'I think I had better go.' She got up. 'I ought not have embarrassed you by calling.'

'Jessamy, you haven't embarrassed me. I was surprised yes, but—' He took her by the shoulders. 'Now sit down, you are going to share my meal. It's some excellent boiled gammon and beetroot. There's enough for two.'

She tried to protest but he placed her firmly in the chair and told her to do as she was told for once. She gave a wan smile and said, 'Yes, sir.'

And so they sat down to slices of succulent ham, beetroot and crusty bread in a room that to Jessamy had become cosy and intimate, discussing the questions of whether women should have the right to take up work outside the home and whether a woman with spirit would make a better wife than one who never questioned a decision made by her husband.

Alistair said he would accept a single girl working and perhaps a married woman having an interesting hobby or helping her husband, like Jessamy's Aunt Dorcas, who had a flair for choosing the right materials and who had a good business head—which was news to Jessamy!

As regards whether a doormat of a wife or a spirited one made for a better marriage, he had reservations. There was a twinkle in Alistair's eyes as he said that a wife who was a doormat could make for an easier life but a dull one; that a spirited one would make life more interesting, but if she turned out to be a virago it would be hell on earth, unless the man was strong enough to control her.

'Like you?' Jessamy queried lightly.

'Of course.' He smiled. 'You have spirit but you would never be a virago. You have too much warmth, too much love to give.'

'Which no one wants,' she said, feeling suddenly forlorn.

'Jessamy, don't.' They had finished the meal and Alistair stood up, pushing his chair back. 'You know how I feel about you. I can't bear you to be unhappy.'

'But I am unhappy.' Jessamy stood up too. 'I'm sorry, Alistair, I'm not being fair. I had better go. Thanks for letting me talk to you.' She made to take her coat from the bed but Alistair gripped her arm.

'You can't go like this. You're like a lost child. Oh, Jessamy.' He held out his arms and she went into them with a little sob. He comforted her, stroked her hair. She would be reconciled with her husband, he was sure of it. He then drew away, cupped her face between his palms and kissed her gently on the forehead. 'Try and make it up with Fabian.'

'I don't think he will want to,' she said, a catch in her voice. 'If only...'

'If only what, Jessamy?' Alistair's voice was ragged. He put a finger to her lips. 'No, don't say it.'

There was a silence in which Jessamy was aware of the ticking of the clock, of coal shifting on the fire, of Alistair's gaze holding hers. Then his mouth covered her mouth and they were lost in a world of unleashed passion where each undressed the other with a frenzied urge to lie flesh to flesh. They were both breathing heavily. Alistair covered her face with kisses then her throat, while Jessamy murmured over and over again, 'I love you, don't leave me.'

When every garment was abandoned they dropped to their knees and then on to the rug, which was warm from the fire. Fire was in their blood and unlike the first time they had made love, Jessamy reached the peak of ecstasy at the same time as Alistair. Satiated and joyful they eventually lay still in one another's arms, with Jessamy unwilling to relinquish this wonderful world of make believe for the one of reality, where she had a husband on the high seas.

They made love again and were lying in that delicious state of euphoria between sleeping and waking when Alistair said idly, 'Is your mother staying overnight with her relative?'

Her mother? Jessamy sat bolt upright. 'No, and she could be back by now.' She scrambled to her feet. 'I must go—she would be frantic if she returned and I wasn't there.' Jessamy began to dress, her fingers clumsy in her haste.

Alistair, who had also started to dress, said he would hurry and go and find a cab. Then, after a pause he added, 'I'm sorry, Jessamy, I acted despicably.'

Jessamy stepped into a petticoat and pulled it up. 'Please don't be sorry, Alistair, I don't regret anything.'

He said no more then but after he had been out and came upstairs to say a cab was waiting, he said, 'Jessamy, this was a terrible thing I did. I'll never forgive myself.' He covered his face for a moment then let his hands fall. 'It must never happen again.'

'No,' she said, knowing that she would have gone into his arms again there and then, had he wanted. She picked up her handbag and gloves. 'I'm ready.'

Outside when Alistair said he would come with her she told him there was no need, but he insisted and deep down she was glad, not wanting to part so abruptly. They were silent for a while and the clip-clop of the horses' hooves on the road was like a death-knell to Jessamy, knowing now that Alistair was the man she should have married. It was not because of the wild passion they had shared. It was so many things, their love of medicine, the enjoyment of their walks on the moors, his effort at trying to persuade her that the rift between herself and Fabian would be over when he came home again. True, Alistair had made love to her but she could see now how she was really to blame, playing on his feelings for her—his regret at his own weakness, his determination that they should not meet again... Also there was that extra something between them that was indefinable.

They passed a late street-market, where the flames of napptha flares wavered in the night breeze. People milled around, their voices and laughter mingling with the raucous cries of the stallholders calling their wares. 'Juicy oranges, thirteen for a tanner! Luverly gripes, twopence a bunch, 'ere y'are ladies, they'll make yer 'air curl!'

Jessamy thought how much she would have enjoyed the scene if things had been different. Even the main thoroughfare with its lighted shops and buildings and the constant traffic of carriages, broughams, carts and wagons no longer gave her the feeling of adventure she had known on her way to see Alistair.

When they arrived at the house in St James' Street Alistair helped her down then turned to pay the driver. She felt awful, knowing how little money he would have to live on, yet sensing she would insult him by offering the fare. There was no light on in the flat and when she said, 'My mother isn't back yet,' he gave a sigh of relief.

'Thank goodness for that. Explanations would have been awkward. Jessamy, I'm not going to lie to you. I love you, always will, but this has to be the end of our meetings. I know you must love your husband or you would not have married him. Be happy.'

He touched her arm in farewell and was gone and once out of the light of the street lamp he was swallowed up in the darkness. She felt choked by the abruptness of their parting and had to fight back tears. Her mother must never know that she had visited Alistair. That would remain her own secret.

CHAPTER TWENTY-SIX

The fire in the sitting-room was still glowing and after Jessamy had taken off her hat and coat she sank into an armchair in front of the flames, reliving the time she had spent with Alistair and thinking how different her life would be, if only she and Alistair could go away together. Only seconds later, her mother arrived and as Jessamy got up to greet her Esmeralda burst into tears. 'Oh, Jessamy, Ralph is going to be married.'

Bewildered, Jessamy said, 'Married? I thought he—'

'He's much better. His fiancée and her mother were there.'

'But, Mama, surely you should be pleased that Ralph is getting married.'

'How can I be? He'll call his mother-in-law Mother. I'll be nothing again.' Esmeralda, her eyes swimming with tears, gave her daughter a piteous look. 'When Ralph first called me Mother I thought it the most beautiful word in the world. Today he introduced me as Mrs Every, a very good friend.'

'But surely he was protecting you. His fiancée and her mother would know he was adopted, know that his adoptive parents were dead. If he had introduced you as his mother then you would have been classed as the woman who had given away her child for adoption.'

'Oh, Jessamy, I hadn't thought about that. Ralph is a kind person. I was with him for a time on my own this morning and he said he was looking forward to meeting you. I promised to take you there in the morning, just for a few minutes. He is over the worst but the doctor won't allow more than ten-minute visits. It was when I went in the afternoon that I met his fiancée and her mother.' Esmeralda paused then said with a sob, 'I'll never be able to acknowledge my grandchildren.'

'Mama, you will be able to acknowledge mine. I am your daughter—surely that should mean something to you?'

'Yes, yes, of course, Jessamy. I'm sorry.'

Children...Jessamy's heart gave a little lurch. It had not occurred to her until then that she could be carrying Alistair's seed. If she was, what then? She was married to one man and would be carrying another man's child.

Esmeralda said, 'I must go to bed, Jessamy.

425

I'm just so tired.'

'I am too. It's been a long day.'

Jessamy had thought with so much on her mind she would not be able to sleep, but she slept heavily and was surprised when she was awakened by Mrs Beasley who brought her a cup of tea, saying, 'It's a real November morning, Ma'am. A misty, moisty morning, as the nursery rhyme says. Your mother will not be getting up for a while, she has a headache.'

Esmeralda had one of her migraines and said it would be impossible for her to go to the nursing home: Jessamy would have to go alone.

Jessamy, who had seen her mother really ill with a migraine and at other times shamming when something displeased her, had a feeling that the headache this morning was an excuse not to go and be simply introduced as a 'good friend' of Ralph's. However, as she was curious to meet her half-brother she agreed on the visit.

The nursing home was obviously for wealthy patients, and the staff were deferential towards a bejewelled woman in a fur coat. The nurse who took Jessamy to Ralph's room spoke in an apologetic tone when she told her she would be allowed to stay for ten minutes only, adding, 'Mr Denton is still rather weak and the doctor does not want him to get overtired.'

'I understand,' Jessamy said.

When they went into the room and the nurse announced to Ralph that Mrs Montague was here to see him, his face lit up.

426

'Jessamy, how wonderful to meet you! Do please sit down.'

He was propped up in bed and had a drawn look, but Ralph was not as she had pictured him. She had imagined him to have grown up dark-haired with finely-chiselled features, instead of which he was fair, with a round face, a snub nose and a rather endearing smile, much like the old sketches of him.

'I've heard so much about you, Jessamy, from your mother.' He looked beyond her. 'Is Esmeralda not with you?'

Jessamy explained about the migraine and he said, 'Oh, I'm so sorry. I think she was upset when I told her yesterday I was engaged to be married. She seemed to see Dorothea as a threat.'

'No, actually, it's your future mother-in-law. She felt she would take her place with you.'

'No, never,' he said softly. 'She will always hold a special place in my heart. She's suffered so much because of me and, unfortunately, for her own sake, I cannot claim her as my mother.'

'She understands this.'

'The awful part of it is that when I do marry we shall be living in America. My future father-in-law has offered me a partnership in his business over there.'

Jessamy said, 'I don't want to hurt you, Mr Denton, but it might be a good thing. My mother is obsessed with you and my father, who loves her dearly, has been neglected.'

'Then I hope she turns to him,' he said quietly, 'and please call me Ralph. We are related, after all. How I wish we had been brought up together, Jessamy. I had no brothers or sisters.'

'Neither did I. I would have welcomed a brother.'

He reached out and squeezed her hand, a simple gesture that made them both emotional. Afterwards Ralph looked exhausted and Jessamy was glad when the nurse came in to tell her that the ten minutes were up, otherwise she might have wept. Before she left, Ralph asked in a whisper if she would break the news gently to her mother that he would be going to America, and she promised.

Esmeralda was up when she got back and before Jessamy had time to take off her hat and coat she said, 'I want to go home, Jessamy. I feel that Ralph is already lost to me.' And Jessamy, deciding that it might be best to get all the hurts over now broke it to her that Ralph would be living in America and the reason why.

Esmeralda looked at her, stricken. 'America? Then I won't *ever* be able to see him again.'

'Someday, perhaps, but Mama, it's time to give some love to Papa. He's been so patient with you.'

But her mother was not listening, and for the next hour she brooded. Then she got up and said in a calm voice, 'I am ready to go home now, Jessamy. Are you willing?'

'More than willing,' Jessamy replied, wanting now to sort out her own life.

A telegram was sent to Chadwick to let him know they were leaving and he was there at the station to meet them. Esmeralda, who had said little during the journey, talked in the cab about Ralph's recovery, grief just visible under her bright facade.

It was not until the evening when her mother had gone to bed that Jessamy and her father managed to have a quiet talk about Ralph and he, like Jessamy, thought it would be a good thing that Ralph would be living abroad. 'Your mother and I might at last get down to a normal married life.'

Jessamy wondered then if her own life would ever be normal again. She longed to see Louise to tell her about Caroline but when she did see her, it was Louise who brought her troubles to Jessamy.

Jessamy was finishing her breakfast the following morning when Louise arrived. She said without preamble, 'Mama knows about the baby Papa told her, saying he was unable to bear the guilt any longer.'

'Oh, Louise!' Jessamy pulled up a chair. 'Sit down. What did your mother say?'

Louise sank onto the chair. 'She's locked herself in her room and won't come out. Papa has gone off walking somewhere and I just couldn't bear to be on my own any longer. I used to think of Papa as a big strong man, but he's weak. He's betrayed me in his desperation to get rid of his guilt.'

Louise looked up at Jessamy, her gaze tormented. 'I prayed that Mama would never know. I can't bear her to be hurt, can't bear that she will hate me.'

'Louise, your mother hasn't an ounce of hatred in her whole body. Given time—'

'Time won't alter anything. I've made my mind up to go away. If I'm out of sight Mama might be able to forgive Papa, but if I was there I would always be a reminder of what had happened.'

'Where will you go?'

'To Newcastle, to Cornelius and Abigail. They've left Cornwall.'

'But I thought their home was in Scotland.'

'It was, but some relative has left this house to them. When Abigail wrote recently she said cheerfully that it is large and rather dilapidated, but that they are gradually getting it shipshape and hope to rent rooms at a low rent to the needy. Perhaps they'll rent one to me.'

'Louise, when I talked about leaving Fabian you advised me not to do anything rash. Well, I ask that you make your peace with your mother before you go ahead with any plans to leave home.'

'I will. I couldn't leave otherwise.' Louise was silent for a moment as though deep in thought then looked up. 'You went to London with your mother, didn't you? Before all this awful business cropped up Mama told me that a relative was ill.'

Jessamy explained how she had taken the opportunity to find out if Caroline was still in London—and how the maid had confirmed that she was.

Louise, like Alistair, thought the maid could have been mistaken and Jessamy said, 'If she wasn't mistaken then that will be the end of my marriage—and then I might be asking your friends if they have a spare room for me.'

Louise gave a little twisted smile. 'I would welcome the company. Still, in spite of saying you married the wrong man, I can't believe that Fabian would be such a fool as to lie about Caroline.'

'I'll soon know when he comes home, which should be soon.'

'Let me know what happens.' With a sigh Louise got up. 'I'll go and see if I can make my peace with Mama.'

She was near to tears and Jessamy put her arms around her. 'I know you will. Your mother could never bear a grudge for long.'

'Oh, Jessamy, what a mess I've made of my life—and all because I wanted to be loved. I'll see you tomorrow.'

When she had gone Jessamy felt a bleakness, thinking that she, too, had made a mess of her life because she also had wanted to be loved. She found herself wondering if Fabian had proof that Caroline was abroad. If he wanted to make up the quarrel, would she? The answer was no. It was Alistair she wanted, for he was her kind of person. He would never have treated her in that cold way, left her on her own to suffer the slight. He would never have behaved like a sulky child, he would have reasoned with her. But even as Jessamy thought these things her heart ached, knowing that she and Alistair could never get together, not even live together—and that would certainly set the family tongues wagging—because he would have no means of supporting her until he had a practice. And that could be another four or five years. A bleak outlook indeed.

When Jessamy went to the shop her father said smiling, 'I have some nice news for you, my love. Fabian will be home this evening. A colleague of his called to tell me on his way to the docks.'

Unprepared for a confrontation with Fabian so soon Jessamy felt tense and had to force herself to say lightly, 'Well, what a surprise. I'll have to let Cook know.'

Chadwick beamed, 'Off you go! I know what you women are, you'll have a hundred and one things to do.'

Jessamy tried to protest, not wanting to mark time until Fabian arrived, but her father was already hustling her towards the door, saying that he and Mr Blackwell would manage fine.

Jessamy walked slowly along the path that

led on to the moor, one part of her wishing she could have had more time to prepare for meeting Fabian and the other, knowing it was best to get their future settled. The air was damp, wisps of fog hovered over hollows and the bleating of huddled groups of sheep sounded more plaintive than usual.

When she came to her parents' house Jessamy hesitated, wondering if she should call and see how her mother was after the London visit, then decided she was not in the mood to face Esmeralda if she happened to be in a depressive state.

There was no movement from any of her aunts' and uncles' houses and she was just thinking it was as though everyone had died when she saw little Mrs Dingley coming out of one of the small cottages ahead. The old lady raised her stick and hobbled towards her.

'Well, Miss Jessamy, ain't see you since you were wed. And a bonny sight you were, gal. I'm just on me way to see your pa. I promised as I would distemper the walls of me sister's parlour but I reckon I'll not be able to do it today. Me rheums are playing me up. I can manage if they stay at home…home being me knees, but they've decided to go a-wandering. Thought your pa might give me some of that willow bark medicine, did me good the last time they played me up.'

Jessamy smiled, seeing the 'rheums' as tiny figures having a bit of fun. She said, 'Your little wanderers might come home if you rested more.'

'The day I start to rest, Miss Jessamy, it'll be under the soil.' The old lady grinned. 'And that'll not be until I'm ninety. Nice to have seen you.'

And away she went, hobbling along with her stick, leaving Jessamy feeling ashamed that there was a woman, always cheerful in spite of being in pain from rheumatism while she was in the depths of despair without knowing for sure that her husband had been lying to her.

Trying to shake off her unhappiness, she still felt an ache when The Montague Acres came into view. If she had to leave she would not only miss the comfort of the house, but also the beauty of the gardens when they came to full glory in the summer.

Time dragged for Jessamy that morning and she was glad when Louise called in the afternoon to say that she and her mother had had a long talk. 'Do you know, Jessamy,' she said quietly, 'I don't think I realised until then what a wonderful person my mother is. She said she was so shocked at first she was unable to even think straight, but then she began to weigh everything up and found she forgave Papa because he had shown he had a conscience and regretted what had happened. She put no blame on me, which I thought wrong but when I told her this she said, "Your father is a man of the world and knows its temptations." '

434

'Louise, does your mother know that I know?'

'No, I thought it best to let her think that the secret was between the three of us.' Jessamy agreed and Louise went on, 'I told her I wanted to go away for a while and although she was upset at first she thought later it might be for the best.'

Louise stayed quite a while talking about the various happenings in their lives and when she got up to leave she said, 'I hope that the maid was wrong and that everything will be amicably settled between you and Fabian.'

Jessamy made no reply.

It was seven o'clock when her husband arrived home and by then Jessamy was very tense, not knowing how he would greet her. Fabian's manner was formal rather than cold. 'Hello, Jessamy. I hope you received the message that I would be home this evening.'

'Yes, I did. I'll let Cook know to start the meal. It is prepared.' He said he would take his bags upstairs meanwhile and have a wash. Jessamy made up her mind then that she would question him about Caroline when he came down. It was no good being polite to one another when this matter had to be faced.

When he came downstairs again smiling, looking completely at ease and saying it was good to be home again, Jessamy felt angry. How dare Fabian assume that she had forgotten his manner of leaving, the coldness of his

435

letters. She said abruptly, 'We must have a talk. There are several things I need to know. Shall we sit down?'

He pulled a chair up to the fire for her then sat down opposite, still looking at ease...or was he?

She said, 'I was in London a few days ago and I called at Caroline's house. The maid told me she had left but said she thought she was still living in London.'

Outwardly Fabian had not lost his composure, but there was a nerve beating in his right temple. 'As far as I knew she had gone abroad.'

'Can you swear on oath that you have never seen her since you, Mama and I stayed at her house?'

'I have no need to swear on oath. You are my wife.'

'What has our relationship to do with it? Either you have seen her or you haven't.'

He jumped up and walked to the window. 'I refuse to be cross-questioned.'

Jessamy stood up too, her eyes blazing. 'You've answered my question. Well, some wives might sit back passively and say or do nothing when their husbands take a mistress but I am not one of them. When you left to go to sea you were utterly indifferent as though I was a useless ornament to be cast aside. You sent me two letters that were so impersonal they could have been addressed to a stranger.'

She walked across the room with quick steps and spoke to his rigid back. 'I want to ask you one question only and I hope you will answer it truthfully. *Are you still in love with Caroline?*'

Fabian was silent for a while then, without turning he said on a note of despair, 'I am, God help me.' When he did turn his face was haggard. 'I tried to fight it, Jessamy, but Caroline is fire. I fell in love with you because of your innocence, an innate purity. I thought you could make me forget Caroline, but—' He raised his shoulders.

Jessamy wanted to protest, wanted to tell him about her lovemaking with Alistair—how he was fire too, alternating with tenderness, but she remained silent.

'I don't know what the solution is, Jessamy. Caroline wants me to go to Texas with her, but I don't want to desert you. Should we, could you, live a sham life with me, for the sake of your family?'

'No, definitely not. It's our lives that are in the balance, not those of the family.'

'I will provide evidence for you to get a divorce eventually. It takes a long time—a few years, I believe. I'm sorry to sound so brutal about it, but it's fact.'

'I don't think you're being any more brutal than you already have been to me. You have made me suffer.'

'Jessamy, I'm sorry. In a misguided way I thought if I made you hate me things would

437

be easier for you.'

'I don't see how hating you would achieve anything. What I desperately needed was to love and be loved.'

'Oh, Jessamy, what have I done to you?' His voice held pain.

'What you've done is to prevent us living our lives in a mock marriage, which for me would have been a hell on earth. I suppose I ought to congratulate you.'

'Don't Jessamy, please.'

'What do you want me to say? You married me, swore undying love and gave only a small part of yourself to me. You say that Caroline is fire. Did it never occur to you that *I* might have fire in me, too? But no, I never had the chance to show it. You were always making the excuse that I wasn't well, when all the time it was because you were...to put it crudely, burned out when you came to me. You humiliated me.'

'No, that's not true. It's difficult to make you understand that one can love a person in different ways unless you've experienced it. With Caroline it's an all-consuming emotion, with you it's a more gentle love. Perhaps some day you will meet a man who arouses this emotion in you, then you'll know what I mean.'

At this Jessamy felt ashamed of her outburst. How dare she criticise Fabian when she had gone to see Alistair, knowing she wanted him to make love to her. She had experienced with

438

him the joy that Fabian had found with Caroline. Jessamy wanted to explain this to Fabian but knew that Alistair must not be involved in any way in their affairs.

The maid came in then to say that supper was ready and although Jessamy said she was not hungry, Fabian persuaded her to sit at the table with him as there were business matters to be discussed. While he talked he served a helping for Jessamy too and she began to eat.

He discussed the basic things, such as the house, which he said she could stay in as long as she wished. He would go back to sea for a time and make his base in London until he decided what to do. He told her he would, of course, make her a substantial allowance and asked if she would object if he came to see Mr Stannard from time to time to discuss the estate. She said no and he then asked what her parents were to be told.

'The truth,' Jessamy said. 'And the reason for separating.'

Fabian agreed and afterwards told her that anything that needed to be done to the house or to the land would be dealt with by Mr Stannard. He then enquired after all the family and Jessamy told him what news there was, afterwards questioning him about his last voyage. To anyone coming in, they would have seemed like a normal, happily-married couple. So normal, that when Jessamy went up to bed she half-expected Fabian to come in and claim his conjugal rights. However, he went into the dressing-room and when she eventually heard the creaking of the bedsprings she wished, childishly, that she could have had the chance to prove that she could match any fire that Caroline might have.

CHAPTER TWENTY-SEVEN

When Jessamy went down to breakfast the next morning she found a message from Fabian to say he would not be back until the evening. She felt angry. He had promised he would go with her to break the news of their separation to her parents. She crumpled the note and threw it into the fire. Well, she was not going alone. After breakfast she would call and see Louise —she just had to talk to someone.

But when she called it was Verity who came into the hall. 'Why, Jessamy, come on in, Louise wasn't expecting you. She's gone to Newcastle for the day to see Cornelius and Abigail. Come into the morning-room.'

When they were seated in front of a blazing log fire Verity eyed Jessamy with anxiety. 'Something's wrong, isn't it?'

'Yes, Fabian wants a separation.'

Verity stared at her. 'Separation? I don't

believe it, can't believe it. They still speak of you in this area as the young bride. Whatever has happened?'

When Jessamy told her about Caroline her aunt shook her head. 'I don't know how he had the temerity to marry you then say he still loved Caroline. Really! The man deserves to be horsewhipped. What are your father and mother going to say?'

As it turned out, they were furious. Chadwick actually went white with anger. He would not allow such a thing. No man was going to humiliate his daughter—it was an insult. Fabian Montague was no adolescent youth to chop and change his mind, he was a grown man with responsibilities. He would stay married to Jessamy—Chadwick would see to that.

Jessamy, who kept protesting that she had no wish to live with Fabian again, eventually gave up and left her parents to their argument.

It was six o'clock when Fabian arrived back at The Montague Acres and when he saw her parents and Verity he greeted them quietly, saying he thought they might be present. Before Chadwick had a chance to say anything, Fabian apologised about what had happened, but was in no way subservient. In fact Jessamy found herself amused, and full of admiration, for the way Fabian handled the situation.

He explained very carefully that he had married Jessamy in good faith. He had fallen in love with her and still loved her, but heaven help

441

him (with a shrug)—it had not occurred to him that his old affection for Caroline could still be so strong. He had not been aware of it for some time, then she was constantly in his thoughts, tormenting him. Could they understand? (Heads nodded slowly.) He could have kept it from Jessamy, but would that have been fair? No, of course not, he would have been living a lie. He told Jessamy (with a warm loving glance) that he would be willing to live a sham marriage with her if she was agreeable, but she had refused, saying it would be wrong. (Heads nodded a little more vigorously.)

Fabian concluded by stating that he was willing for Jessamy to stay on in the house and he would see that she had a substantial allowance. By this time Chadwick was looking pensive and Esmeralda and Verity wore the indulgent expressions that parents have when they want to be tolerant over the misdemeanour of a favourite child.

The confrontation ended with Fabian saying sadly that he had certainly not expected this situation to arise, but that was life, wasn't it? At this point he sighed and looked so genuinely regretful that even Jessamy had to wonder if it was all play-acting. And how could she condemn Fabian, when she had so recently discovered that it was Alistair whom she truly loved.

Fabian left not long after this, saying he would see his solicitor and return when all the legal affairs had been settled. Although Chadwick, Esmeralda and Verity did not exactly claim Fabian as a hero, they all agreed he had behaved in an honest way, when he could have led a secret life with a mistress in the background.

The four of them sat silent for a while then Esmeralda said, 'Well, Jessamy, I think you had better pack a bag and come home with us.'

Jessamy said no, she would rather stay at The Montague Acres for a while and was in the throes of resisting her parents when Louise arrived, breathless.

'I've just got back from Newcastle. Papa said something about... Oh, I ran all the way... about Fabian wanting a separation. Is that right?'

When this was confirmed by Chadwick and she was told the reason why, Louise sank into a chair and blew out her cheeks. 'Well, whatever next? I always knew there was something strange about him but I never imagined this. Jessamy, what are you going to do?'

Esmeralda interrupted. 'Louise, what did you mean by saying you found something strange in Fabian?'

It was Jessamy who replied. 'I think she thought, like me, that there was a flaw in his character, but was not quite sure what it could be. But doesn't everyone have some flaw?'

There was a silence and her parents and her aunt looked anywhere but at one another.

Jessamy then asked Louise if she would stay with her for a few days and Louise looked up. 'Yes, of course, I'd be glad to, then I can tell you all about my visit to Newcastle.'

This seemed to be an opportunity for Chadwick, Esmeralda and Verity to take their leave, with her parents offering advice to Jessamy. If she felt she needed to talk to them about the situation then she must come to them at once. Chadwick added, in an attempt at teasing, 'We can always do with some help at the shop.'

Jessamy said she would remember that and they left. Louise gave a sigh of relief. 'Thank goodness they didn't hang on. I wanted to know *your* version of the separation.'

Jessamy repeated the full story but when she concluded that she could understand Fabian's actions, Louise was furious. Why was she so passive? Fabian was mean, deceitful.

Jessamy, who by this time had made up her mind to tell Louise about Alistair said quietly, 'So am I, but before I tell you why, I want you to promise not to repeat this to anyone.'

Louise, solemn-faced, said, 'You have my word.'

When Jessamy described her visit to Alistair's lodging and what happened there, Louise looked shocked. 'Oh, Jessamy, you fool! You know what the consequence of those few hours could mean. When are you due for—?'

'In three days' time.'

'And if it doesn't happen?'

'I'll have to go away, even if it's just for a week or two. I want to get out of the house.'

'Why not come with me to Newcastle? I know that Cornelius and Abigail will welcome you. I've already planned to leave home—Mama knows and has accepted it. She'll be coming with me to see me settled in. I don't see how your parents could object to you coming with me, for a change.'

'I would love to meet Cornelius and Abigail, but I don't know what Papa and Mama would say.'

'Jessamy, you don't have to ask them—you are a married woman now in your own right. Remember that.'

'Very well, yes, I would like to come for perhaps just a couple of weeks.'

Louise looked delighted. 'Good, but don't expect luxury. Cornelius and Abigail live in the dock area. Their house is very big, one of many that used to belong to merchantmen in the past until the families moved to Jesmond, a better-class district. Now they're tenements, but I love the place. Cornelius and Abigail live busy lives, too. When they can manage it they still go off to villages with a horse and wagon selling their herbs, medicine and other small goods. On Sunday mornings they even sell their wares on the quayside.'

'On a Sunday?'

Louise chuckled. 'Yes, the people come after church. All sorts of things are sold and there

445

are entertainers, jugglers and acrobats. During the week there are the big shops and the theatres. Newcastle is a lovely place. I shall have a three-roomed flat, with bedroom, sitting-room and kitchen. Abigail has told me she can get me some furniture quite cheaply.'

'How long are you planning to stay, Louise?'

'Until I need another change. I will go home occasionally, of course, such as Christmas-time, but I want to be free. So, will you spend a couple of weeks with me?'

Jessamy smiled. 'Yes, you have your first guest. I'll break the news to Papa and Mama.'

'That's it, tell them you're going. Be firm.' Louise paused, eyeing Jessamy in a thoughtful way. 'What will you tell them if you find you are pregnant?'

Jessamy winced. 'Don't! I'm trying not to think about it.'

'But you'll have to think about it if you are. Will you tell Alistair?'

'No, he must never know. He has to go to college—his whole career depends on it.'

'So you would let the family think that the baby is Fabian's?'

'No...oh, Louise, I don't know and I don't want to talk about it. It might never happen. It will be time enough if such a situation arises.'

For the next two days both girls were on edge, waiting for the third day to see what happened. Nothing did, and when the fourth day came and went without Jessamy's period

446

starting they were both sunk in gloom.

'It's not fair,' Jessamy wailed. 'Why should it be the women who suffer? Men can enjoy themselves, have as many partners as they like and nothing happens to them.'

'Other men just admire them their virility,' Louise declared scornfully. 'Mind you, worry can delay one's period. It may start tomorrow or the next day.'

They allowed a week and eventually became resigned to the fact that the worst had happened. Then Louise said they must put their plan into operation to go to Newcastle.

To Jessamy's surprise her parents agreed at once that a change would do her good, and when Jessamy went to see her grandmother she too said it was a good idea.

'Your husband has turned out to be a very disappointing person, Jessamy, but it is far better to find out now than to live with a man who is supporting a mistress in secret. Divorce is a filthy business with a lot of conniving and scandal attached to it but at the same time, you are young and could find a more worthy husband. Meanwhile, you have a lovely house and you will be getting a good allowance from your husband so that you will not be beholden to your parents.'

'Yes,' said Jessamy, feeling a dreadful fraud. She had to restrain herself from blurting out the truth to the old lady.

'It's a good job you didn't,' said Louise.

'Anything could happen—you could have a miscarriage.'

'Oh, no,' Jessamy said, alarmed and knew then how much she wanted this child who was going to cause so much friction in her life.

Her guilt grew worse until it felt like a lead weight she was carrying around. Eventually she decided she would have to tell Fabian she had been unfaithful to him, otherwise she would never know any peace.

When she confessed this to Louise, her cousin was horrified. 'You can't do it, Jessamy, you mustn't! Otherwise he might claim the baby, for he does want children. He could say you were immoral, incompetent to handle a child.'

Jessamy shook her head. 'No, Fabian would never do that, I know it. The thing is, I want the baby to have the surname Montague, and I can't do that without asking Fabian's permission.'

Louise sighed. 'Oh, what a tangled web we weave, when first we practise to deceive! I only hope you won't regret what you're planning to do.'

'I only know it's something I have to do, Louise.'

Two days afterwards, a boy delivered a note by hand from Fabian to say he would like to call on her that afternoon, if possible. She told the boy yes, then feeling that her legs would not hold her Jessamy sank on to a chair in the

448

hall, wondering what the outcome of the visit would be.

Although Louise had offered to stay with her Jessamy said no, this interview had to be between Fabian and herself.

By midday Jessamy felt surprisingly calm. She wore her hair swept up, as she did when going to a party, and a silver-grey silk dress with motifs in velvet ribbon shading from deep purple to pale lavender. Studying her, Louise said, 'If you are trying to win Fabian back I think you'll succeed. You look ethereal... desirable. Was that your aim?'

'No, definitely not. I simply want him to see me as a prospective mother who wants to keep her coming child and who looks capable of doing so.'

'I wish you success.'

When Fabian arrived it was impossible for Jessamy not to feel a pang of regret that they were to part. It was not only his good looks and commanding presence, there was something indefinable that she still liked about him. Yet she knew if they lived together for thirty years she would never feel the deep love for him that she had for Alistair.

'Jessamy,' he greeted her solemnly, bowing over her hand. 'You look lovely.' A maid had already taken his hat and coat and Jessamy motioned him towards chairs by the fire. When they were seated he said, 'There are one or two questions I have to ask.' He opened a folder,

449

studied a document then looked up. 'I feel this first question is unnecessary, but my solicitor says it has to be asked. Are you by any chance *enceinte*? I told Mr Dean you would have mentioned it if you were.'

The question was so unexpected that Jessamy felt slightly faint. The next moment she had pulled herself together, wishing rather desperately that it had not been asked. She sat up, head held high.

'As a matter of fact, I am, Fabian, but not by you.'

Fabian, whose gaze had been on the document, looked up startled. When Jessamy returned his gaze steadily he said, 'You do understand the question, Jessamy?'

'Yes, of course. I'm expecting a baby.'

He shook his head, a look of pain in his eyes. 'No, Jessamy, no. Not you, you're too honest.'

'Is my behaviour any worse than yours?'

'I suppose not, but I put you on a pedestal. To me you were purity personified...'

The phrase could have sounded dramatic but it didn't because it was so quietly spoken. And because his words hurt her she said, 'You were partly to blame, Fabian. I desperately needed to be loved, to be wanted and you had rejected me, discarded me, there are no other words to describe it.'

He stared at her. 'Are you saying that you let some man make love to you because of the way I behaved? Who is it?'

450

'That I can't tell you. I'm fond of him and he's always been kind and caring of me. He doesn't know about the baby and I don't want him to know. I would like to keep your surname for the child, if you are agreeable.'

'Would I have access to it?'

Jessamy's heartbeat quickened. 'I hope you wouldn't try to take the child from me.'

'No, Jessamy, I would never do that. I give you my word on it, will put it in writing if you wish. The child is yours. I should just like to see him occasionally, pay for anything he needs, education.'

'You speak of the baby as a boy. It could be a girl.'

'Girl or boy, I'll do all I can to help, and if it will save any embarrassment with the family, I'm willing to pass the child off as mine.'

'It's good of you but I—yes, I'll accept. Thank you.'

After that it was all business, with Fabian explaining these were just preliminary matters dealing with a settlement after they were officially separated. There would be other documents to sign later, when perhaps she would wish her father to be present.

He got up to leave then, seemingly quite brisk, but once he had donned his topcoat he lingered. 'Jessamy, you'll be all right? If there's anything you need you can get in touch with me through the shipping-office. I'm sorry that things have turned out this way.' He gave a wry

451

smile. 'I think I'm a little jealous of this unknown man. But there, we never know what fate has in store for us, do we?'

Jessamy saw him to the front door and he was halfway down the steps when he turned and came back.

'Jessamy, is it possible to make a mistake? Could the baby be mine?' She said definitely not and he raised his shoulders, accepting it.

When Louise knew of their conversation she said, 'He'll have that baby from you, I'm sure of it. I know you wanted it to have his surname, but I do think it was a big mistake to tell him you were pregnant.'

Jessamy however took a complacent view, positive that Fabian, with all his faults, would never give his word if he intended breaking it. Nothing else Louise said could make her change her mind.

At last Louise said, 'Well, we had better decide when we are travelling to Newcastle. I should imagine Mama will come with us to see us settled in.'

Jessamy said worriedly, 'I just hope that my mother won't want to come. Can you imagine her reaction—"Living on the quayside? Never! Not if I can prevent it".'

'I don't think she'll want to come,' Louise said. 'London is more her style. Anyway, don't let us imagine obstacles. Time enough to face them if we have to.'

Esmeralda did not offer to go with them for

the simple reason she had one of her bad, prolonged headaches. The girls had expected to go by train but Bertie had arranged for them to travel on a small motor van so Verity sat in front with the driver and the girls sat on boxes in the back and thoroughly enjoyed themselves.

Chadwick had said to Jessamy before she left, 'I'm sorry your life has been so upset, my love, so try and enjoy this visit. A change of company can sometimes get one out of the doldrums. Newcastle is an interesting place—there's the old castle to visit and other castles around the countryside, should you get the chance of any travel.'

Although Newcastle was not very far away Jessamy had been only once before and that was when she was a child. She had gone with her mother, her Aunt Verity and Louise. Jessamy, being adventurous, had kept darting from shop window to shop window and, getting more and more excited, had darted into shops, leading Esmeralda such a dance that she swore it would be Jessamy's first and last visit to Newcastle...and she had kept her word.

When Jessamy mentioned it now Louise laughed. 'I know, you went mad. I wanted to do the same, but was sensible, knowing what the punishment would be. I remember how a tight-lipped shop assistant caught hold of you and said to your mother that you ought to be locked in your room for a week and fed on bread and water. I remember thinking heaven help *her* children if she ever had any!'

Mention of children had Jessamy quiet for a while then she put the problem to the back of her mind. There would be plenty to contend with later, when her condition was known to her parents.

When they crossed the River Tyne on the road of the High Level Bridge Jessamy, remembering her childhood visit to Newcastle and the journey by train on the bridge above, felt a small surge of excitement. Soon, they would be meeting Cornelius and Abigail.

When they left the High Level Bridge they travelled down to the quayside and soon were driving along a narrow road of three and four-storeyed houses on one side and derelict shops and warehouses opposite. From this road, streets of similar houses branched off, with poorly-clad children playing in the gutters and men sitting hunkered on street corners in groups. Although many of the houses had a neglected look, others had an air of being cared for, with their windowpanes shining and net curtains stiffly starched. Such a house was the one they stopped at on the narrow road. 'Here we are,' said the driver. 'I'll get the bags down then I'll be off.' To Verity he added, 'I'll deliver what I have to, Mrs Every, and after I've been to see my daughter at Gateshead I'll pick you up at about six o'clock.' Verity told him that would be splendid, and he left.

When Louise lifted the heavy knocker and

let it fall it seemed to reverberate through the whole house but brought no response. She bent down and peering through the letter box informed them that the stairs were still uncarpeted, and that there was no linoleum or anything on the hall floor. The next moment she straightened as a child's voice called, 'Hey, lady!' A small boy came running towards them. Panting, he said, 'The Reverend and his missus are on their way.' He paused to get his breath. 'The 'orse went lame. 'Ere they are now.'

A tall thin man in a black suit and stovepipe hat, and a plump woman wearing a large hat, the brim laden with artificial flowers, were hurrying along the pavement. When they reached the group they greeted Louise and Verity with great warmth and when Verity introduced Jessamy, she received the same welcome. The couple said how delighted they were to meet Jessamy, they had heard so much about her from Louise.

Jessamy took to them at once. Cornelius, with his mop of silvery hair, had the most beautiful smile and she thought of him as a saintly man. Abigail had a wide beaming smile but was softly-spoken.

'Now come along,' Cornelius said jovially, 'We're keeping you standing here when I'm sure you will welcome a cup of tea.' He gave the boys some coppers, and thanked him.

Although stairs and hall lacked covering there was nothing bare about the room into which he led them on the ground floor. A welcome wave of heat came from a built-up fire, protected by a fireguard. The floor was closely covered with handmade rugs in many colours and patterns; the walls were distempered in daffodil yellow, but very little of this was visible because of all the photographs, pictures and small paintings adorning them. A pair of heavy plum-coloured velvet curtains at the window was so long that the hems were folded over. Two sofas and several chairs were covered in various materials, so that the whole room gave off an air of cosiness and gaiety.

Over cups of tea and home-made fruit cake Cornelius and Abigail enquired after various members of the Every family and Jessamy thought that Louise must have talked about them a great deal, because they knew all by name.

The time flew by and all too soon Verity had to leave. When Jessamy managed to get a few minutes alone with her she said, 'Aunt Verity, don't tell Mama the true position, will you, about the situation of the house and lack of carpets. I'm sure if she knew she would pester me to return home.'

Verity smiled. 'I'll tell them both that you're with two of the kindest and most caring people they could wish to meet—and that is telling them no lie.'

After Verity had gone Cornelius and Abigail talked about their working lives. As Jessamy let the gentle voices wash over her she knew that this was a house in which she could live and be content, but she also knew that her mother would never consent to her living in this area...especially when she was told about the baby.

In the meantime she would enjoy her two weeks of freedom.

CHAPTER TWENTY-EIGHT

Although Jessamy had lived in a dock area all her life she found this to be a new world, one in which neighbours were as closely-knit as families. They helped each other through illness, in times of death, they borrowed from one another when food was short and there were few who did not return eventually what they had borrowed. 'They're a proud people,' Abigail said one day, 'but pride will not feed their families. It's casual labour at the docks and men can be lucky or unlucky. The women do charring or washing, but this only brings in coppers and keeps the wolf from the doors. My husband and I hope to open a soup kitchen to help the local community, but we are not yet organised.'

Jessamy soon learned that Cornelius and

Abigail were indefatigable workers for the poor. From the herbs and medicines they sold a portion was put aside for their cause. Also from the paper flowers they made and the small paintings Abigail created, with her husband making the frames. Jessamy was in her element helping with the infusions, making up medicines and ointments. The old couple were delighted to have her expertise.

Abigail and Cornelius had furnished the flat upstairs for Louise. In the sitting-room was a mahogany table and four chairs, a matching sideboard and a sofa. There was a huge bed in the bedroom, a dressing table and massive wardrobe, and on the floor of each room were rag rugs. The kitchen had a black range with an oven and a sink with running water.

Louise said to Jessamy in a low voice, 'Not exactly to my taste but I must be grateful. I can always add my own touches later.'

On the first day after the girls had arrived, while Cornelius went to see about hiring another horse Abigail took them around the district, where they met women with black shawls wrapped around them and wearing men's caps. They all greeted Abigail with respect, and some asked her advice about sickly children or erring husbands. At every street corner men stood in groups, an aimlessness about them. All touched their caps to Abigail and the girls.

Further along they climbed steep, narrow

stone steps that led them eventually into the centre of the town, where a mixture of people were beheld, those who hurried about their business and the better-dressed ones who strolled along the streets, window gazing. There were also the wealthy in carriages, who when they alighted were treated like royalty, with shop doors being opened for them and chairs brought forward.

Although there was a constant stream of traffic as in London, there was not such a cosmopolitan atmosphere, or perhaps it was because London was the capital and one expected it.

Abigail took them to Northumberland Street, a busy shopping area and they went into Fenwicks, a popular store in which Jessamy and Louise joyfully explored the different departments. They tried on bonnets, bought one each then Louise purchased a pair of walking shoes. It was the first time Jessamy had ever bought something to wear without having the approval of her mother or her Aunt Verity. And Louise unconsciously spoiled her pleasure by telling her she should have bought some baby clothes. Louise had lingered in this department, a look of longing in her eyes.

When they got back Cornelius was home with the news that he had managed to hire another horse to give the poor lame Pegasus a rest. This one was called Charlie, he said, and was more robust than dear patient Pegasus.

Although Louise had her own flat (at Abigail's insistence) they ate with the couple. This was a holiday for the two girls, and they would not want to be bothered cooking. Neither confessed that they had never done any cooking before! They laughed about it later, with Louise saying, 'But I'll have to if I'm going to be a working woman, won't I?'

Jessamy had never thought about her cousin working in Newcastle and when she asked her what she had in mind Louise said that Cornelius and Abigail had asked her if she would like to help them in their work and she had agreed. 'I did make paper flowers for them when I was in Cornwall, you see and dressed dolls. Some of the neighbours make the cloth dolls and embroider their faces. It earns them a few coppers. Not many of them like to make the clothes, though. They take too long—they're fiddly, as Gran would say.'

That evening, Jessamy was initiated into making paper flowers and dolls' clothes. Louise was adept at both, especially the flowers, working at as great a speed as Abigail. Cornelius dyed the fine paper from plants and then cut it into strips and shaped these into petals, curling them over the blunt edge of a knife. The flowers were then wired to stalks of green, with leaves. There were beautiful shaggy chrysanthemums in white, gold, and bronze, roses in pink, yellow, red and white, and daffodils. All the flowers sold well, even though the roses and daffodils were out of season.

The dolls' clothes were made from scraps supplied by a friendly dressmaker. Some of the dolls wore only a simple dress with a piece of cord tied round the waist, while others wore a complete outfit of petticoat, dress, hat and coat. The outfits were tedious to sew but Jessamy liked making these the best: they were a challenge. She created the styles and they caused a lot of amusement, with Abigail saying, 'Now this one is destined to be a duchess or this one, I think, could be a Madame in a brothel.' Then Cornelius teasingly scolded her, telling his wife that he hoped the public would not interpret a doll as being representative of a brothel or they might find themselves languishing in gaol. To this Louise laughed and said that at least it would be just one more adventure.

The girls' next adventure was going to the quayside on the Saturday to see Paddy's Market, which mainly sold secondhand clothes. Women in bonnets and shawls were in charge, most of them older women. The goods were laid out on the ground and many of the items seemed too worn to find buyers, but they were selling.

'It's all some of them can afford to buy,' Abigail said. 'Many people who couldn't get work in Ireland came over here but only a proportion of them managed to get jobs. They're

461

lovely, warm-hearted people, who would give their last crust to a stranger if they thought that the person needed it more than they did.'

They stood listening to a conversation between two women, both Irish, one wanting to buy and the other to sell. The one wanting to buy a man's jacket said, 'Aw, away wi' ye, Mrs McNulty. Me man's being promised a job on Monday, but he hasn't a stitch to his back he can wear.' She held out some coppers. 'That's me last sixpence, and I'm starving me bairns to get the coat.'

'Mrs McCarne, I have t'live. A shilling it is and I'll take no less.'

The other woman sighed and her hand closed over the coins. ' 'Tis a hard woman ye are, Mrs McNulty.' When she seemed about to move away, Jessamy made to get some money from her purse but Abigail stayed her hand and shook her head.

The woman at the stall said, 'All right, ye can have it for ninepence.' And when this brought no response she came down penny by penny then finally took the sixpence and handed over the jacket.

Abigail explained afterwards that both women would feel they had done a good deal and that Jessamy might have offended the woman wanting to buy. These people had pride.

On the Sunday morning the girls went with Cornelius and Abigail to the quayside to sell their wares. Although they went early to get a good stand, vendors and prospective buyers were already milling around. The morning was cold with a frosty nip in the air, but excitement kept Jessamy warm. She could even forget the problems she would have to face later when her parents were told about the baby.

There was a constant movement of shipping on the River and on the quayside, with men bringing up boxes of fruit and other goods for their stalls. All of them greeted Cornelius and Abigail and eyed the girls with appreciation.

Cornelius and Abigail set up at an end stand next to a sweetmeat stall then, after Cornelius had unhitched Charlie and led him away Abigail lowered the side of the wagon, displaying jars of dried herbs, bottles of medicines, boxes of ointments, jars of cosmetic creams, packets of tear-off sheets of face powder and tiny boxes of rouge, these three last items always being bought in a secretive way, according to Abigail.

On the lower shelves were the dolls, small paintings and boxes of secondhand toys, which included tiny engines, carts, wagons, jigsaw puzzles, ludo, snakes and ladders and lead soldiers, some of which lacked an arm but were in demand nevertheless. The stall had hardly been set up before children were dragging a father or mother by the hand to come and see the toys. Following them was a small retinue of people wanting to buy dried herbs or a bottle of medicine. Abigail asked the latter to wait a few moments until her husband arrived.

And once Cornelius was there, business began but everything was done in a leisurely way. 'Now just a moment, Mrs Peabody,' he said to a woman who was gabbling to him about her complaint. 'Tell me slowly—where is this pain?'

'Here, here, in me stomach, the pain is something cruel. Never slept a wink all night. An' don't tell me it's wind, I can't get any up.'

Cornelius reached for a bottle, poured some white liquid into a glass and after giving it to the woman to drink put his fingers on the spot she had indicated. He pressed, and the next moment she gave a great belch, which brought a gasp from the crowd. A man swore, 'That were a miracle! I'll have some, too.'

It was a good start to the day, so while Abigail and Louise dealt with the dolls, paintings, toys and paper flowers, Jessamy helped Cornelius to hand out various herbs and medicines.

'Something to get rid of your corns, Mr Todd? Some sundew will do the trick... Catarrh bothering you, Mrs Bell? Fennel tea should clear it.'

There was common tormentil for inflamed gums...white horehound for several people suffering from bronchial trouble...goutwort tea for eczema...parsley for a man suffering from boils...periwinkle for a woman with nervous disorders... And when one woman said she was
464

plagued with fleas, Cornelius offered tansy, saying that she would appreciate its lovely fragrance but the fleas would hate it—which brought a laugh and quite a number of buyers.

In fact, so much medicine was sold that Jessamy began to wonder if there was anyone among the crowd without a complaint.

At midday, when trade eased a little, Louise and Jessamy had a walk around the various stalls. At one fruit stall a man put a number of oranges, apples, pomegranates, bananas and a bunch of grapes into a bag and asked who would give him a bob for the lot. Many hands shot up with their shillings and Jessamy would have bought a bag, had not Louise pointed out that some bruised fruit was going into them. Abigail, who had just come up added, 'You have to know the honest ones. Come with me —these are conmen, only here this Sunday and you'll never see them again.'

There was a cake-stall doing a roaring trade, with the stall-holder selling the cakes off cheap because she wanted to go home. There were three performers juggling while doing somersaults; two clowns making people laugh with their antics and a gypsy woman with a parrot who said that the bird would tell a person's fortune for a penny. Louise and Jessamy held out their pennies. The bird dipped its beak into a box containing a card and brought one out. On Louise's it said, '*You are going to meet a dark handsome man. Don't turn him away.*' Jessamy's said, '*Stop worrying, everything will be in order in a few days' time.*'

Louise laughed as she handed her card back, but Jessamy read hers twice before relinquishing it. They were about to walk away, with Abigail teasing them when the gypsy woman said to Jessamy, 'You have the power of healing, don't waste it.' Then, staring at her she went on, 'You think you have made a mistake, but you've done the right thing. Time will tell.'

Jessamy, who had been tongue-tied for a moment, blurted out, 'How long?' and the woman said, her gaze steady, 'A few years. Be patient.' Then she turned to the people who were waiting to have the parrot tell their fortune.

Jessamy stood rooted, her heart beating fast. She wanted to know more but Louise pulled her away. 'Come along, it's all balderdash.' Abigail had stopped to talk to someone and the girls waited for her.

'But don't you see,' Jessamy said, 'she told me I thought I had made a mistake, but I had done the right thing—time would tell. It'll be years before I can get a divorce, four or five years before Alistair can become a doctor.'

'Jessamy, if you want to believe such rubbish it could also mean that you find out eventually you did *not* make a mistake in marrying Fabian.'

'No, you're wrong, I know it. The card said that I was worrying about something and I needn't. Perhaps I'm not pregnant, after all.'

466

'Oh, Jessamy love,' Louise wailed in despair. 'You're a dreamer. At times you live in a world of fantasy. You must stop it, come down to earth.'

Abigail approached as they were arguing about the validity of fortune-tellers and said, 'I think it's wise to just treat it as a bit of fun. The lady with the parrot has foretold some rather strange things which have proved to come true but on the other hand, she has also made statements that never came to anything.'

This prevented any more argument, but did not prevent Jessamy from hoping that she might not be pregnant after all...

One thing the girls did agree—it had been an exciting day. In the afternoon they browsed around the stalls selling secondhand books, jewellery, old porcelain and clothing. They saw a turbanned man throw a rope into the air which remained rigid, watched a boy climb up it and vanish into thin air. A sailor beside them said it was an illusion, he had seen it many times in India. Another man said the crowd were hypnotised by the turbanned man. Jessamy only wished she could tell her parents about the wonderful Sunday she had spent.

In the evening Abigail said that once the stock was replenished they would be going to Gateshead and to villages round about with the van—would the girls like to come? They consented, delightedly, but on the Wednesday morning when Jessamy got up at five o'clock

467

she was sick. Louise said sadly, 'Morning sickness, I'm afraid.'

At this point Jessamy was not sure whether she was pleased or sorry. She only knew after the next hour when she was still terribly queasy that she would not be able to go to Gateshead in the van. Abigail, who thought the nausea was caused by something Jessamy had eaten, gave her guest some medicine, but it only stayed the queasiness for a time. Louise wanted to stay at home with her but Jessamy said no, she would rather sit quietly on her own.

And so, with a promise not to be late, the three of them left. Jessamy, who was sick again, eventually stretched out on the sofa and pulled the crocheted blanket over her.

Although the sick feeling left her once she was on her back, her mind seemed confused and she found it difficult to sort anything out. She wanted to think over what the gypsy woman had told her but it all became jumbled up. Eventually she slept and was awakened by a dull thumping sound somewhere. It took her some time to realise it was someone knocking on the front door. At first she decided to ignore it then, thinking it might be someone with a message for Cornelius, she threw back the cover and got up. She pushed back her hair, glanced into the mirror as she crossed the room and winced. Heavens, what a sight she looked.

When she opened the front door she stood staring in disbelief at Alistair, as he had stared at her the evening she went to his lodgings.

'Jessamy, I'm sorry if I gave you a shock.' He spoke gently. 'Aren't you well?'

'It's just a stomach upset.' Oh, Lord, why did he have to see her looking like a washed-out rag? She forced a smile. 'Come on in. Who told you where I was?'

'It's a long story, a very long story.'

They went into the sitting-room and Jessamy found herself trembling as she folded the blanket. 'Sit down, Alistair, I'll make some tea.'

'Let me,' he said, taking the blanket from her. 'You sit down, I've obviously come at an awkward time. You just tell me where everything is.'

'Oh, Alistair, I'm such a mess, but I've longed to see you.' Tears welled up and ran slowly down her cheeks.

He took her hand in his. 'Now come and sit down. I'll get this tea made then we can have a talk.'

In the end they made the tea together, Jessamy smiling through her tears. She rinsed her face with cold water and after tidying her hair said, 'Now I'm ready to hear all your news. I know it's good.'

But Alistair would not talk until she had drunk some tea and then he answered Jessamy's question of whether he had been accepted by a medical college.

He nodded. 'Yes, at Edinburgh. I had hoped

for London, but I'm not grumbling.'

'I should think not. Oh Alistair, I'm so delighted for you. You've worked so hard—and I know your family will be proud of you.'

'They are. But something else has happened, too, Jessamy. A great-uncle who was a bachelor died recently, and he has left me a large sum of money to help me with my studies.'

'Alistair, that's splendid! I know how pleased Papa and Mr Blackwell will be for you. They had such faith that you would be accepted.'

'I have already written to your father. It was he who told me where you are staying and as I had to see some relatives who are living in Newcastle for a few months I thought your husband would not object if I called. How is the Captain?'

'Quite well, but he isn't with me. I'm just here for a couple of weeks to keep Louise company.'

Jessamy explained about Cornelius and Abigail with whom Louise had stayed in Cornwall, about their move to Newcastle and the business they ran. Then she said, 'I think I could take to a nomad life.'

Alistair laughed. 'I think your husband would have something to say about that.'

Jessamy hesitated a moment then told him that she and Fabian were separated.

He stared at her in astonishment. 'Separated? Whatever for?'

'Because he's still in love with the girl he was engaged to.'

Alistair shook his head. 'I feel utterly bewildered. How could he want to leave you?'

'Not everyone finds me lovable,' Jessamy replied, a catch in her voice.

'I do,' Alistair said softly. 'Oh, Jessamy. If only—'

She nearly told him then about the baby, but realised the extra problems it would cause. Being the father, Alistair would feel responsible for its care yet be unable to give the child his name. The baby would have to be a Montague, in order to get the stability of family background. And yet she wanted Alistair so much to know she still loved him.

'Fabian is talking of a divorce, but it will take a long time. I'm staying on at The Montague Acres for a while, anyway.'

'Could I come and see you, Jessamy? It wouldn't be often, perhaps every two months.' The longing in his eyes made her feel like weeping.

'I would like that, Alistair, but it wouldn't have to be at home. It could be here. Louise is going to live with Cornelius and Abigail for a while. She's restless, wanted to get away for a time.'

'It'll be easier coming to Newcastle,' he said eagerly. 'The train journey's straightforward from Edinburgh to the Central Station. Oh, Jessamy, it will be something to look forward to, something to break the constant studying. Not that I'm not looking forward to it, I am. As your father was saying...'

He talked about his aims, his future, his plans when he was qualified and Jessamy was so caught up in his enthusiasm that four or five years of waiting seemed no time at all.

Abigail had left a meal ready for her and when she told Alistair they would share it and he tried to refuse she said gently, 'It's tit for tat. Remember how I shared yours that night in London.'

They were both silent for a moment, remembering, then Alistair whispered, 'It was a lovely evening, Jessamy. I'll remember it always.'

'So will I. Tell me, Alistair, that painting you have of a cottage, is it the cottage where we sheltered from the storm?'

'It is.'

They had shared a wild passion, both at the cottage and at Alistair's lodgings, but there was a gentleness between them now.

They talked about all sorts of things. Jessamy described Cornelius, whom people addressed as Reverend but who had not been ordained. 'He's a saintly-looking man and he and his wife want to help the poor by providing a soup kitchen.'

Alistair said he thought it an excellent idea and decided it might be something worth considering when, in the future, he opened his dispensary.

He talked then about the dispensary and Jessamy offered suggestions for running it. They reminisced about their young lives, their dreams and their fears, with Alistair saying how he had always wanted to be a doctor but feared it would cost too much money and that it would never come to pass, an impossible dream. Jessamy told him how she had always wanted to have a husband and children, but was afraid her husband might think that twenty was too many.

They laughed softly together over this, with Alistair saying that although he came from a big family, he would draw the line at twenty.

The sky had been heavy all day and dusk came early. The room was warm and cosy, with flames from the fire casting dancing reflections on the walls. The pair sat silent for a while and Jessamy was aware that a bond had been forged between them that had nothing to do with passion. It was a closeness she had not experienced before. She only knew it was something that would go on until after death...she knew also that Alistair was aware of it, too, and would do nothing to sully it.

CHAPTER TWENTY-NINE

Jessamy did not mention Alistair's visit until bedtime when she told Louise, explaining the reason for his visit and saying they hoped to meet in Newcastle again in about two months' time.

Louise looked worried. 'Is that wise? You say you haven't told him about the baby, but he's going to find out, isn't he? You can't keep that a secret forever.'

'But don't you see, to all intents and purposes he, or she, will be Fabian's baby. I do have that protection and I'm grateful to him for that.'

Louise began to undress. 'I only hope you won't regret that you have that protection, Jessamy. It means you'll never be able to acknowledge Alistair as the baby's father.'

'I'll tell him once Fabian and I are divorced.'

Louise stepped out of her dress. 'Has it ever occurred to you that Alistair might meet someone else and get married?'

'He won't, I know him.'

'You thought you knew Fabian,' Louise said wryly.

'No, on looking back I realise I never knew

him. I don't think anyone does. Fabian is an island unto himself.' Jessamy stood a moment then began to undo the buttons on her blouse. 'So tell me about your day. Were you busy?'

'Frantically—we all but sold out. The dolls and the pictures had nearly all gone by the time we reached the second village. In the villages Cornelius always starts with a quotation from the Bible. The people seem to appreciate it.'

Louise went on talking about their sales but Jessamy's mind kept going back to the events of her day, how caring Alistair had been, how he had kissed her gently on the cheek before he left and saying how wonderful it had been seeing her. There had been times when she had felt a stirring of emotion, but was glad that nothing had happened between them for it would have spoilt her tender memories of the day.

Jessamy had no more morning sickness and might have thought she was not pregnant after all, had she not taken a dislike to tea. Cornelius and Abigail always drank coffee so she drank coffee, and no remark was made, but it worried Jessamy that her mother might notice her sudden dislike of tea and put two and two together. When Louise asked why this should worry her she said, 'Because Mama, knowing I was pregnant at this stage, might insist on Fabian continuing to live with me.'

'And you think that Fabian would agree?

You can put that from your mind. Look Jessamy, I'll come back with you when you're ready to leave. Together we'll fight anyone who wishes to oppose you. How's that?'

'Oh, thanks, Louise. Having you there will help me over Christmas.'

The girls took a tearful leave from Cornelius and Abigail with Louise promising to be back in the New Year. The girls were travelling alone this time but when they arrived at St Peel, Chadwick and Verity were there to meet them, with Chadwick saying to Jessamy, 'Your mother has one of her headaches so we're going to your Aunt Verity's for a meal.'

Louise whispered to Jessamy, 'Typical Esmeralda,' and then started talking brightly about the wonderful time they had had.

No one noticed Jessamy's dislike of tea and she was glad, wanting to delay letting the family know she was pregnant. They might start asking awkward questions, such as when the baby was due: it would have to tie in with a date when Fabian had been home.

As Christmas approached Jessamy began to worry how she would explain away Fabian's absence on Christmas Day, when the whole family met at Beacon Hall for a turkey dinner. But as it happened she woke on the morning of Christmas Eve with a sore throat, a raging headache and a fever.

Louise went to get Chadwick and after taking her temperature, he told his daughter she would have to stay in bed. He would bring over some medicine for her to take, and a special herbal gargle. Louise promised to stay with Jessamy and see she followed his instructions.

Jessamy slept for most of the day and by the next morning, the fever had abated. However, she croaked when she attempted to talk and her head still ached.

Chadwick and Esmeralda called early to see how she was. They wanted to stay but Jessamy tried to persuade them to go to Beacon Hall and with Louise adding her insistence they eventually agreed, with Chadwick saying he would call in after the meal to see how the patient was.

After they had gone Louise said, 'I'm glad to have an excuse not to go to Beacon Hall. I don't like all the gossip—I've grown out of it.'

Jessamy wanted to say she always enjoyed Christmas but felt too poorly. Later when Louise brought Jessamy her medicine she said, 'There's a letter for you with a Scottish postmark and a small parcel sent from London.'

Jessamy's heart beat a little faster. The letter would be from Alistair. Was the parcel from him too? Louise left her to open them.

Jessamy undid the envelope with trembling fingers. A card was enclosed. On the back it said: *'I do hope you have an enjoyable Christmas. Best wishes for the New Year, Yours sincerely, Alistair MacKay.'*

On the card was a drawing of a cottage in

a wood, a replica of the painting that had been on the wall of his lodgings.

Dear Alistair, so discreet, such simple words on the back but reminding her of their tempestuous lovemaking. Jessamy lay back dreaming about the past and it was some time before she remembered the small parcel. It was from Fabian—a brooch, a circle of diamonds inset with a glowing ruby. A note enclosed said: *'Dear Jessamy, I thought you might like to wear this at Christmas so that the family need not know yet of the break, for the baby's sake. I wish things had been different. Bless you both. Yours, Fabian.'*

After reading the note several times Jessamy panicked. Fabian was trying to be kind to her, but why? Because of the baby? Had Louise been right in saying he might want to claim it? She grew more and more agitated and was in tears when Louise came in. Louise soothed her.

'Listen, Jessamy, I was furious when I knew that Fabian wanted to go off with that woman, but deep down I think he is a caring man and it worries him that he can't fight this awful obsession for Caroline. I was stupid in saying he might want to claim the baby. Forget it, or you'll be ill again.'

When Jessamy felt calmer they talked more about the situation and she actually smiled when her cousin pinned the brooch to her nightdress saying, 'Your badge of defiance.'

Edward and Grace arrived with some of the

turkey dinner and Christmas pudding for the girls at midday, with Edward proclaiming that the meal would still be hot as the dishes were wrapped in several towels and a piece of blanket. He added that he had left the dishes with the maid. He then said, 'We've missed you both, young ladies. It's not the same without you.'

Grace said, 'Well, we must go, the rest of the family will be waiting for us to start the meal. Look after yourself, Jessamy, and you, Louise.' She kissed them both and departed with her husband.

Louise enjoyed the Christmas fare, but Jessamy had little appetite and only picked at it. She dozed later and was aroused when Chadwick arrived with Verity, announcing that it had started to snow—a white Christmas, after all.

Jessamy was always pleased to see Verity but felt hurt that her mother had not bothered to come. When she enquired about Esmeralda Chadwick said with a sigh, 'Poor Esmeralda. She had too much sage and onion stuffing and has indigestion. She'll call later.'

Jessamy doubted it but refrained from saying so.

Verity talked about Beacon Hall and how lovely it looked with all the decorations. There was holly everywhere, thick with berries. The Christmas tree was so tall this year there was just room on top for the angel. The cousins had decorated the tree and hung up the paper streamers. Then Verity said, 'Your gran missed you two girls, missed all your news. She told me to tell you that she has some news to give you for a change. Your cousins, Matthew, Mark and Luke are courting three sisters whose names are Margaret, Mary and Martha.'

'Courting?' Louise exclaimed. 'What does Aunt Dorcas have to say about that?'

'She said that the Lord had given the three girls looks, but missed out on brains.'

They all laughed and Chadwick said, 'Well, you know Dorcas, I don't think there's a girl born that she would think suitable for any one of her boys.'

They talked generalities for a while then Chadwick and Verity prepared to leave, with Chadwick promising to look in the next morning to see how Jessamy was.

After they had gone Louise was quiet and Jessamy asked her what was on her mind. Louise looked up. 'The cousins. One doesn't realise how they're all becoming of marriage-able age.' She gave a wry smile. 'I shall probably end up being the spinster aunt and godmother to all their children.'

'Rubbish! You'll marry and have a brood of your own.'

'Well now, you might be surprised at this, but—' The wryness had gone from Louise's smile, it now held a teasing. 'You remember the gypsy woman on the quayside saying that a dark handsome man would come into my life and I was not to turn him away? Well, I met him! It happened when I was at Gateshead with Cornelius and Abigail. He's Irish, his name is Flynn O'Rafferty.'

'Oh, Louise, that's wonderful. Tell me more.'

Louise laughed. 'There's not much more to tell. He deals in herbs, buying and selling. He has a lovely sense of humour, but I don't suppose I'll ever see him again.'

'You will, I'm sure of it.'

Louise shook her head. 'I'll be here, helping you look after your baby. You'll need support when you start studying to become a doctor.'

Jessamy stared at her. 'This is sudden, isn't it?'

'I just remembered the gypsy woman saying you had healing in your hands. Aunt Catherine once said the same thing.'

Jessamy felt suddenly much better, light-hearted. 'Oh, so now you believe in a gypsy's prophecy, do you?'

'I never have before, but it seemed too much of a coincidence, my meeting Flynn and the woman mentioning you had the power of healing. How could she possibly know such a thing? It gave me an eerie feeling.'

'So,' Jessamy said, 'if it's proved that I have healing in my hands, then Mr O'Rafferty could be your destiny.'

'It's time for your medicine,' Louise said

briskly, but Jessamy noticed a small smile playing around her mouth.

Jessamy was up the next day and from then on she was waiting for one thing only, to be with Alistair again. When she had been with him at Newcastle, four years had seemed no time at all to wait but away from him, every week seemed an eternity, especially when Louise returned to Newcastle.

Alistair did write once to Louise, saying he would like to correspond with Jessamy but was afraid to in case she and Fabian were together again. Jessamy wrote straight away that such a thing would never happen: she was simply waiting for the time they could be together for always.

The day she posted the letter to Alistair she had word from Fabian to say he wanted to call, as there were documents to sign. Would she ask her father to be present in case there was anything she wished to query.

Jessamy knew then she would have to tell her parents about the baby...and had the reaction she dreaded. There would be no separation, of course. Fabian had greater responsibilities now that a child was involved. It took Jessamy over half an hour to convince them that she had no intention of ever living with Fabian again and, if they persisted in harassing her she would leave The Montague Acres and live elsewhere. Fabian was perfectly willing to support her and the baby.

Her parents at last conceded to her wishes but Chadwick told Jessamy he felt she was making a big mistake. A child needed a father.

The afternoon the two men met they could not have been more affable to one another, and while Chadwick poured drinks for both Jessamy studied her husband. Nothing could take away his good looks but his face had a gauntness she had not seen before. Had there been some friction with Caroline?

When the two men got down to business Jessamy, not understanding the legalities, let it all wash over her. She only knew at the end of the discussion that Fabian had been more than generous in providing for her and the baby.

Chadwick was sensible enough to know that Fabian and Jessamy would want to discuss certain things alone and left them together. It was now Fabian's turn to study Jessamy.

'Well, Jessamy,' he said with a sad smile. 'We are partly severed. I'm not sure I like it.'

'Why? Have you changed your mind about Caroline?'

'No, that I will never do. It's just that she now wants to stay on in London and I was rather looking forward to going out to Texas and dealing with horses.' He shrugged. 'But then it is a woman's privilege to change her mind.'

'She might change it again,' Jessamy said, 'because she loves horses, too.'

'And you love children,' he answered quietly, the sadness in his eyes more evident.

Jessamy felt a sudden ache for him. Did Caroline not want children? This would be terrible for a man who had been an only child and looked forward to having a big family. But then, the choice was his. He wanted Caroline, so much so, Jessamy thought, that he had been willing to destroy her life. She hardened her heart.

In time all the family grew to know about the baby, but only those close to Jessamy knew about the separation. Fabian was still going to sea and some of the women condemned this, while others said it was his livelihood and a sailor did not give up a seafaring life just because his wife was having a baby.

Jeremiah made quite a fuss of Jessamy. She would be giving him his first great-grandchild and he warned her with a smile that it had to be a son. She wondered what he would have said had she told him it was Alistair MacKay's child.

Jessamy lived for letters from Alistair, which were sent to Louise and forwarded with her own letters. They were always short and about life at the college. He had made several new friends whom she hoped she might meet some time.

Louise's letters spoke of her life with Cornelius and Abigail and trips round the countryside with the van. In one letter she said, *'I'm*
484

learning all about medicines and becoming quite interested. I hope that you are studying hard: you have every opportunity.'

Jessamy did have every opportunity, but until this letter came she had been leading rather a restless life, visiting Verity, Henrietta and old people who were not able to get about. Sometimes she went to the shop and worked in the back room, but she never stayed there for long.

When her grandmother remarked on her restlessness and Jessamy blamed her condition, the old lady pooh-poohed it, saying, 'A man's responsible for it. Now, who is he?'

Jessamy was so taken aback she felt that the red creeping from her neck to her face denounced her as a scarlet woman.

'M-man?' she stammered.

'Yes, a man, and someone you are obviously besotted with. You're dreamy-eyed half the time. Is the baby his?'

'Gran!' Jessamy jumped up. 'You're terrible, that's a dreadful thing to say.'

'But I'm right, aren't I? Calm down and sit down. I think you had better tell me about it. I'm not going to shout it to the world.' Her voice softened.

Jessamy walked to the window and stared at the forest beyond the fields. Her grandmother enjoyed a bit of gossip but she had never known her repeat anything that she did not want anyone to know. So far, Louise was the only one who knew the truth. It would be a comfort to have another confidante, but...

After hesitating Jessamy turned slowly. 'Yes, Gran, you guessed right. It was like this...'

She told her story briefly, blaming herself for what had happened but Henrietta said, 'No, all three of you have behaved irresponsibly, without one of you having given a thought to the baby. A child needs to have a father. But there, I have no right to criticise, not having been in such a position myself. I can only suggest, Jessamy dear, that you stop living in a dream world and get down to the realities of life.'

Although Jessamy had felt a reluctance to confide in her grandmother she realised afterwards it was the best thing she could have done. Until then she *had* been living in a dream world, and although she knew she wanted to keep the baby it was something that seemed somehow to belong to the future. After the talk with her grandmother, the child had taken on an identity: it was a person, and she had a responsibility towards it. Once Jessamy realised this she was astonished at how indifferent she had formerly been towards her child. Was this because it had been created in sin? No, there was love involved and the baby would be much loved.

With her restlessness gone Jessamy settled down to some studying and wrote long letters to Alistair about what she had learned. One day she wrote, *'I've been reading about operations on the brain and am absolutely fascinated. I had no idea that an animal could still function after parts of its brain had been removed. I can understand you wanting to become a surgeon...'*

When Esmeralda called one day and saw all the books she said, 'Oh, Jessamy, why do you bother with medical matters? You'd do far better to learn how to handle a baby.'

'I'll be able to handle a baby when it arrives,' Jessamy said, trying to be patient. 'In the mean time I enjoy reading about the body.'

Esmeralda then began to talk about marriages that could be in the offing for the summer. Jeremiah had told Digby and Dorcas' three sons that he would set them up in businesses if they wanted to get married.

'You know why, don't you,' Jessamy retorted slowly. 'He's not content with owning sons and grandsons body and soul—he wants to take over great-grandsons, too. Well, I can tell you this, I hope I have a daughter.'

'Now, Jessamy, that's not fair. Your grandfather cares about his family and I have no regrets at having borne a son, even though it was under such unhappy circumstances. I feel I've lost Ralph now, but I knew such joy when he was mine for a while.'

Jessamy was angry, not only because of her mother's uncaring attitude towards her but because she insisted on playing the martyr over Ralph. And yet he wrote to his mother

487

regularly—tender, loving letters full of news about his life and promises of seeing her when he next came to London on business.

Her mother left shortly afterwards and Jessamy was still not over her anger when who should arrive ten minutes later but Louise. They hugged one another gleefully with Jessamy saying, 'Oh, what a lovely surprise! You couldn't have come at a better time. I was in such a bad mood after a visit from Mama. Here, give me your coat.'

Louise divested herself of it. 'Well, I hope I can put you in a better mood with an idea I have. It came to me last night and I could hardly wait until this morning to tell you.'

Jessamy laughed. 'I'm all agog. Sit down.'

They sat over the fire and Louise began, 'It's always irritated me that Grandpa thinks that all women are good for is tending to a man's wants and giving him sons and grandsons. He—'

Jessamy interrupted. 'It's amazing, but that is why I was in such a black mood.' She explained briefly about her mother's visit then said, 'But do go on.'

'Well, I decided to prove him wrong. You and I are going into business. We're going to have a string of shops up and down the country. Oh, not at first, we'll start with two. One at St Cade and one at Newcastle.'

A little taken aback, Jessamy repeated, 'Shops? What sort?'

'Selling herbs, scent and cosmetics. I've had a long talk about it with Flynn O'Rafferty.' Louise grinned. 'Yes, my fate, according to the gypsy woman. We've met quite a lot lately. He's so knowledgeable, Jessamy. He can arrange to get scents imported from France and phials and bottles from a firm in England.'

'But Louise, apart from the fact that I'm expecting a baby, the parents would never allow me to work in a shop. It takes a great deal of persuasion now to get Papa to agree to my working at the back of the pharmacy.'

'You wouldn't be working. We would be partners and employ assistants. And listen, Jessamy, as I keep reminding you, you are no longer bound by what your parents say. We'll be property owners who are going to own numerous shops and show Jeremiah Every that what *he* can do women can do equally well.'

Excitement stirred in Jessamy and a slow smile spread over her face. 'It would certainly be an achievement, but how about money? I am going to get a very good allowance from Fabian and I also have the two hundred pounds that Great-Aunt Philomena left me in her will.'

'And I still have mine—it's never been touched.'

They talked at great length, but Jessamy began to get cold feet, pointing out that she not only lacked a business head, but had planned in the future to help Alistair run a dispensary for poor people.

'Jessamy, that is four or five years away. Meanwhile, the money you earn from the business will help him to run more than one dispensary!'

And such was Louise's persuasive power that Jessamy found herself carried away and she agreed to the proposition.

Three days later Flynn came in person to The Montague Acres and brought them sample scent bottles to examine. 'Aren't they beautiful, now? See this.' He ran a finger lovingly over an emerald green cut-glass bottle, the tall cork representing a lady's head. Next he showed them an amber-coloured one with dark blue insets of hearts; there were flower-shaped ones with chased silver corks, star-shaped ones, cubes, a pyramid, the facets glinting rainbow colours in the sunlight.

There were also phials to keep in a handbag, one with shaded green stripes, another turquoise, patterned with silver birds; a delicate blue one studded with rubies...the variety was endless and both girls were fascinated. Jessamy said, 'I don't understand why Papa has never gone in for French scents and lovely bottles like this.'

'Because your mother thought it might bring the wealthy ladies in who would try to seduce him.'

'Louise!'

Her cousin laughed and Flynn chuckled too.

'It's true, not that Uncle Chadwick would have responded, but all men like some flattery.' She turned to Flynn. 'What about the perfumes and what names will they have?'

'They should be arriving in Newcastle shortly. We'll give some of them French names for those who can afford them, but we'll keep English names for the factory girls, so they can identify with them and, of course, those ones will be much cheaper.'

'What do you mean by identifying with them?' Jessamy questioned him.

'Well now, if you called one *Morning Dew* wouldn't a young lady now be seeing herself skipping happily over the dew-soaked grass, a thing I doubt she'll ever have done in her whole life. If we call another one *Sunset* she'll conjure up herself and a prince of men holding hands. And what more romantic name can you have than *Moonlight*?'

'Why, Flynn, you're a romantic!' She smiled up at the handsome Irishman. Although Louise had described Flynn to Jessamy, she had conveyed none of his charm. He was tall, with a presence. His thick brown hair had a tousled look, and there were laughter-lines at the corners of his dark eyes, which held a merry twinkle.

He grinned, 'I'm a businessman, Jessamy.'

'A good one,' she said, 'with excellent taste. I applaud your choice of glassware. Do you think we should buy some pot pourri bowls as well? Papa has some lovely ones and does a quick trade with them. Some are glass, some china and others papier maché.'

They had a long discussion about them, eventually agreeing on a choice and Jessamy felt more stimulated than she had done for a long, long time.

CHAPTER THIRTY

During the next fortnight or so, Jessamy's life took on a new dimension. She was intrigued by the devious way in which Louise and Flynn acquired two shops, one in Newcastle and the other in St Cade. They were bought in Flynn O'Rafferty's name, using his savings. The girls would pay him rent for a while and then when all the finances were sorted out, would buy the shops from him.

'In that way,' Louise said, 'no one will know that we own the properties.' When Jessamy asked what Flynn expected to get out of all this she said, 'Nothing at all,' and gave the reason.

'His mother was widowed when Flynn was ten years old. With five children younger than him and no money, it looked as if the family would all end up in the poorhouse, but his mother fought against it. She sold all the furniture apart from bare necessities, pawned her wedding ring, a gold brooch and a chain and set up a general store in her parlour. Their house was near a factory where people worked shifts. She was up at four o'clock every morning making bread and buns and cooking sausages—and she sold sausages and pease pudding and sandwiches to the workers. Flynn said his mother never went to bed before midnight, but as well as feeding and clothing her children she always found time to give them a quick cuddle.'

Louise paused and sat back. 'Flynn says he had a great admiration for his mother and admires us for *our* enterprising spirit. His reward in helping us will be our success. He's a really nice person, Jessamy. You'll meet him again when you come to Newcastle for Alistair's next visit. Flynn has rooms in Jesmond and says that Alistair can stay with him.'

For a moment Jessamy felt a swift disappointment. She wanted Alistair to herself when he did come, but she quickly realised that this would be impossible.

Louise brought out some papers. 'Flynn has listed the cost of everything we'll need to set up the shops and with our approval he'll order them. He's also worked out the wages for staff. We won't see any profit the first year, perhaps not even the second but we will, he assures us, in the third.'

'Louise…can you trust this Flynn O'Rafferty? He could be one of those conmen who take your money and vanish.'

'No, not Flynn. He's well-known and wellrespected.'

'Is there anything…romantic between you?'

Louise smiled. 'No, we're just good friends. Let's leave it at that, shall we? Incidentally, not even Mama knows about him or the shops so don't mention them, that is our secret.'

It was three weeks after this when Jessamy had word from Alistair to say he would be in Newcastle the following weekend. Louise came home two days beforehand to make it easy for her to suggest that Jessamy accompany her back to Newcastle for the weekend. Although Jessamy was uneasy about all the subterfuge it did not stop her from being in a fever of excitement at the thought of seeing Alistair again.

Then Louise said during the train journey, 'Isn't it time to tell Alistair about the baby?' and Jessamy's excitement died.

How would he react to the fact she was supposedly carrying Fabian's child? Would it turn him against her? He might not want to make love to her any more. Not that making love was something she could visualise at the moment, anyway, for what opportunity would they have? The most important thing remained—would he want to?

Jessamy could see how it would be distasteful

to a man, making love to a woman who was carrying her husband's child. But then if she told Alistair the baby was his he would do nothing but worry, and worry was the worst thing possible for a man trying to study. She appealed to Louise for her opinion.

'He should be told. After all, Alistair is responsible for your condition. What's more, he's no callow youth. I think he's been very careless. He knows all there is to know about bodily functions and he of all people should have had more sense.'

Although Jessamy hated Alistair to be blamed she knew that Louise was right and decided he must be told.

They arrived in Newcastle late afternoon and Jessamy was just enthusing to Abigail about how lovely it was to be back when Cornelius, who had gone to meet Alistair at the station, came in with Flynn O'Rafferty and Alistair by his side. Abigail had invited the Irishman to join them all for a meal.

Alistair said softly, 'Hello, Jessamy. I'm glad you could come. We have a lot to talk about, for Flynn has been telling me all about your project.'

Abigail, who had been bustling around, said with her beaming smile, 'Oh, it's lovely to be with young people. Sit down and make yourselves comfortable. I've cooked some fish and potato fritters.'

'Lemon sole,' added Cornelius, 'from the

last catch of the trawlers. You couldn't have them more fresh—you can taste the North Sea in them.'

Right from the start there was a festive atmosphere. Flynn described an amusing incident at the Central Station when a small, well-bred poodle in the arms of a very arrogant lady had taken a fancy to a scruffy-looking mongrel dog belonging to a tramp.

'That poodle went crazy wanting to get to the mongrel who eyed it with as much disdain as a wolfhound belonging to the Crown Prince of Russia.'

When Alistair teased him, asking what an animal belonging to the Russian royal house would look like Flynn did such a wonderful imitation that they all burst out laughing. Louise declared between chuckles that he had missed his vocation—Flynn ought to be on the music hall.

Flynn shook his head. 'No, I'm liking fine the vocation I have, especially now I have two such attractive young lady clients.' He gave Louise a broad grin.

There was plenty of lively chatter and when Jessamy glanced up at Alistair she found him watching her, a look of love in his eyes, and she felt a lovely warm glow.

Later, they all went for a walk along the quay. Jessamy had never been at the docks at night and she was impressed by the lighted ships and the reflection of them in the still, dark waters. On one of the ships some sailors were singing a hymn, baritones harmonising with tenors. 'They'll be practising for Sunday,' Cornelius said approvingly. Jessamy felt moved as she realised the singing was in a foreign language, by men away from their homes.

They didn't go as far as the groggeries and the bawdy houses but they could hear the noise, muted by distance.

As a narrow part of the road Cornelius and Abigail walked in front, Louise with Flynn behind them and Jessamy and Alistair bringing up the rear.

Alistair drew Jessamy's arm through his and smiled down at her. 'Happy?'

'Very. I only hope we have some time to be alone together. There are things I have to tell you.'

'About the project? Louise wrote and told me everything. I think it's an excellent idea. It'll give you something to have an interest in while we're parted. I was hoping it might have been possible for us to be together all the time, but I can't see your parents allowing you to come and live in Edinburgh.'

'No, that would be impossible for more reasons than one. Also, I might not even be able to come to Newcastle to meet you in the future.'

'Why? Oh, Jessamy, don't deny me that. I've been just living for this weekend. It was an agony waiting and it will be an agony when we have to part again. Why won't you be able to see me?'

'Because...' she took a quick breath. 'I'm having a baby.'

Alistair stopped abruptly and in the light of the street lamp she could see the dismay in his eyes. 'A baby? Oh, no! Does that mean you'll be going back to the Captain?'

'No. It's not his baby.'

'Not his? Then whose is it, for God's sake?' There was a pause then, 'It can't be mine.'

'Why can't it be?'

'Because I was, well—careful.'

'In what way?'

Alistair looked about him as though they might be overheard then explained in a low voice about withdrawal, and how he had withdrawn while it was safe to do so.

'But it obviously wasn't safe, was it? Fabian has not made love to me since that night, nor has any other man.' There was a catch in Jessamy's voice and Alistair put his arms around her.

'Oh, Jessamy, I know that. It never occurred to me that you—I'm just so angry at myself for getting you into this position. The thing is, what are we going to do?'

Jessamy drew away. 'I just don't know. We had better be walking on. The others might be waiting for us to catch up.'

They walked slowly, in silence, with Alistair's misery almost a tangible thing between

498

them. Jessamy ached because Alistair had not said he wanted the baby. Then, as though she had spoken her thoughts, he took her hand, saying, 'I want to take care of you and the baby, Jessamy. I must, I can't bear the thought of being away from you both. We'll work out something. I'll forget about college.'

'No, Alistair, that is something I won't allow you to do. No matter what happens you are going to become a doctor. We'll try and work out a plan.'

There was no further opportunity that evening for Jessamy and Alistair to be alone. When he was ready to leave with Flynn, Alistair's eyes held such a look of misery she longed to put her arms around him and tell him it would be all right. All he could do was squeeze her hand and say he would see her the next morning.

At bedtime Louise said, 'Well, Jessamy, and what did Alistair have to say? He looked anything but happy.' Her tone was sharp and Jessamy flared.

'How could he be otherwise, having that news flung at him during a walk. He was terribly upset, wants to give up his studies and look after us. We didn't even have time enough alone to work anything out.' Her voice broke and Louise was full of apologies.

'Jessamy, I'm sorry. You know how I feel about men in general but I ought not to take it out on you. I'll see that you and Alistair have

499

some time together in the morning. I'll take Flynn to the quayside then you and Alistair can come along later, just when you wish. Cornelius and Abigail will be leaving early. What do you think of Flynn now?'

Jessamy drew a fingertip across each eye. 'I liked him from the start, very much. In fact, I think it might be better if you had him as a partner.'

'No, that would be defeating the object. We two women are going to build an empire—I'm determined. And don't you see, Jessamy, it will be an interest for you while you're waiting for your divorce.'

An empire, Jessamy thought sadly and she could not even find a way to be with the father of her baby whom she loved dearly.

It was eleven o'clock the following morning when Flynn and Alistair arrived. Louise was furious, blaming Flynn. 'Don't you realise that Alistair and Jessamy have little enough time to be together?'

Alistair interrupted. 'I'm to blame. Flynn has had an idea that might enable me to leave college and be able to support Jessamy.'

'No,' Jessamy said. 'You are not leaving college. If you do, then that will be the end. I'll never see you again.'

Louise glared at Flynn. 'See what you've done? Come along, let us go and leave them to sort out their own problems.'

When Louise and Flynn had left Alistair

said, a stubborn thrust to his jaw, 'We are not going to be parted.'

This was the beginning of a discussion that lasted nearly an hour without a conclusion being reached. In the end Jessamy said on a weary note, 'I can only promise you one thing, Alistair, that I'll come to Newcastle as often as I can so that we can be together.'

'And how often will that be? Once every two or three months? I've been aching to make love to you ever since I arrived and what opportunity has there been? We can't even do it now, not knowing if someone will come in.'

She took him by the hand. 'We can. There's an empty flat upstairs.'

Louise must have been up before she left and put a match to the bedroom fire. The coals glowed. Alistair grinned.

There was no wildness in their lovemaking this time, it was all tenderness and caring, but Jessamy had as much satisfaction as the time she had spent with Alistair at his lodgings in London. Afterwards they lay content, Alistair's arm around her. After a while he said softly, 'I'm just going to let things take their course for the time being, Jessamy darling. But after the baby is born I want you to be with me, or near me in Edinburgh. If you have any bright ideas...'

She looked at him, sleepy-eyed. 'I did think that if Louise and I were to buy a shop in Edinburgh I might manage it.' Alistair shot up in

501

bed and Jessamy laughed softly. 'It's just an idea at the moment.'

'One which will have to come to fruition. Oh, Jessamy, I'm on fire...'

They arrived at the quay early afternoon, both feeling a little sheepish but they need not have worried, for Louise and Flynn were busy serving at the stall with Cornelius and Abigail. Flynn had a lively line of patter, praising the medicines. He held up a bottle. 'This is an elixir to benefit those suffering from rheumatic pains. In some cases it can cure them. Now, would you be looking at that lady over there in the plum-coloured hat? It cured her, didn't it, Ma'am?' The woman nodded, and Flynn went on, 'Several months ago she was a poor sickly creature, unable to walk a step. Three months after taking the elixir she was on her feet and hobbling along on two sticks. After taking the medicine for several weeks more she was able to throw one stick away. And after another two months she was able to walk unaided. A miracle? Yes, folks, the miracle of this elixir! And the cost? One shilling only—and the first two to hand me their shillings will get a bottle free!'

Hands shot up from all over the place.

Jessamy said to Flynn afterwards, 'Did it really cure that woman?'

'Well now, Miss Jessamy, I'll be honest with you. Not that particular one, no, but the Reverend told me of others he had cured.

502

They were not available at that moment, so I had to give the lady in the plum-coloured hat a little backhander.'

'But that's cheating!'

'Indeed no, it was the truth, twisted a little to help the people lose their pain. I knew that the Reverend would not lie to me.'

'No, he wouldn't—and he's looking at you a little bewildered. He does have his reputation to consider.'

'Indeed yes, I must explain my reasoning to him.' Flynn was as solemn as a judge, but Jessamy caught a twinkle in his eyes.

She said to Louise later, 'I still have a feeling that our Mr Flynn O'Rafferty is a conman.'

'No, he simply likes a challenge. So do you and I do, too.'

'At the moment I think I have too many to face. My greatest will be in persuading the parents that I want to live away from home. We'll talk about it later.'

Louise raised her eyebrows. 'That sounds interesting.'

With the future so uncertain the parting between Jessamy and Alistair was heartbreaking this time. They could only pray for guidance and give promises to write regularly.

Again it was bedtime before Jessamy and Louise had the chance to discuss Jessamy's earlier remark and by then, her voice was flat as she mentioned a business in Edinburgh.

'It's impossible, of course. I wish I had never

503

mentioned it to Alistair. It simply raised his hopes.'

'It's not impossible,' mused Louise, 'but it's certainly not something that is likely to take place before the baby is born. I would suggest, however, that you keep mentioning to the parents every now and then that you would like to make a home away from St Peel.'

'I think it would be a waste of time.'

'Jessamy, what's happened to your adventurous spirit? You were always the rebel. It's your whole future we're discussing, not a new dress.'

Jessamy sat up. 'Yes, you are right. Flynn was saying earlier that if a person wants something it's up to him or her to make it possible. He said hammer and hammer away until you've broken down all resistance. Once I'm home I'll have to keep dropping hints that I want to establish a household away from The Montague Acres.'

'That's the spirit. And to help it along, ask Fabian's help.'

'Fabian?' Jessamy looked at her cousin wide-eyed. 'I couldn't! He's doing enough as it is, accepting the baby as his own.'

'And won't he want to see his child settled in a happy home atmosphere?'

'I think he would be better pleased if I stayed on at The Montague Acres, where he can look in on the baby from time to time. He asked if he could have contact.'

'And can you see Caroline allowing such an arrangement?'

When Jessamy said no, she couldn't, Louise raised her shoulders. 'Well, then...?'

Jessamy returned to St Peel with a very different attitude, but whether she could solve her problems only time would tell.

CHAPTER THIRTY-ONE

Jessamy had been prepared for Esmeralda to cause some trouble when she learned about the baby, but was totally unprepared for the virago that she became in her condemnation of Jessamy wanting to leave St Peel. She stormed and raved, while Jessamy just sat and stared at her mother, her mouth dry.

Chadwick stood it for a few moments and then he got up and taking Esmeralda by the shoulders shouted, 'Stop it, stop it at once, do you hear.' When she continued her tirade he shook her hard. 'Sit down!' He pushed her into a chair. 'If you don't stop I shall put you out of this house and you'll never return. I've had enough. Do you understand?'

His words must have seeped through Esmeralda's anger, for her body went slack and she looked at her husband with frightened eyes. She nodded.

Chadwick took a breath. 'You've done what you wanted to do for years, said what you wanted to do without thought of Jessamy or myself. Jessamy told you she did not want to live with a man who had a mistress and I now agree with her. I put up with your coldness, your selfishness, your obsession with your bastard son for the sake of peace, but no more. From now on you'll do as I tell you, otherwise you'll go.'

He turned away and taking Jessamy by the hand said in a strangled voice, 'Come with me.'

He led her into the morning-room and she could feel his trembling. In the room he sank into a chair, put his hands over his face and whispered, 'Forgive me, Jessamy, for being so brutal. It had to be done to bring your mother to her senses.'

Jessamy was torn between her love for her father and pity for her mother. Her father had been angry many times in her life but never once had she heard him shout. Yet she knew there was a limit to a person's endurance.

Chadwick raised his head and she saw the agony in his eyes. 'Go to her, Jessamy, but don't allow her to think she's won, or you will be caught in the net forever.'

Jessamy, realising for the first time what her father must have suffered, gave him a hug. 'I won't, Papa.'

As she left the morning-room she met her

mother in the hall. Esmeralda said in a pathetic way, 'I have a headache coming on. I'm going up to bed.'

Normally Jessamy would have gone with her mother, seen her into bed, brought her medicine and fussed over her, but she said quietly. 'Bed is the best place. I'll see you in the morning.'

Jessamy and her father had a long talk. He apologised for his behaviour again, said he had put up with her mother's ways for years and now it had to end. He talked about Fabian again, saying that although he could understand and accept the love he felt for Caroline, he condemned him utterly for marrying Jessamy and giving his daughter all this pain. Chadwick himself would prefer her to stay near her family after the birth of his grandchild, but understood that she was now a grown-up, independent woman.

Jessamy was satisfied that the seeds at least had been planted, albeit with a lot of heartache and upset.

She had stayed at her parents' home overnight and was surprised when Esmeralda came down quite early the next morning. Although her manner was quiet, Esmeralda seemed less wrapped up in herself. She said, 'I was shocked when your father told me he would turn me out of the house if I didn't conform. I hadn't realised until then how badly I had behaved.' She looked then at Jessamy with pleading.

507

'Please don't expect me to change overnight, but I will try to alter my ways. Be patient with me.' They talked for some time of Jessamy's future plans, but came to no firm conclusion.

Alistair wrote more frequently now. He was full of hopes for their future after she had told him about the talk with her father. *'I thought I had always worked hard to achieve my goal,'* he wrote, *'but now I know about the baby I have a double goal. Oh, Jessamy, I can't wait for the day when the three of us will be together. Come to Newcastle as soon as you can.'*

When Louise had allowed Jessamy to feel the movements of her baby, Jessamy had been deeply moved, but when her own baby quickened her strong maternal instinct was overwhelming—and she wept at the joyousness of it.

She longed to tell someone, and rushed with her news to Verity only to be dismayed when her aunt said, 'I expected you to have quickened before now, Jessamy. But perhaps you and Fabian...'

She left it at that adding with a smile, 'It's a wonderful feeling, isn't it? So it will be a summer baby. Have you a preference, boy or girl?'

Jessamy said, 'No, all I want is to get it over with. I can't wait to hold the little darling in my arms.'

It was always difficult at times like this not to mention Alistair, and she was glad when

Verity began to talk about Louise, saying how well she seemed to have settled down in Newcastle. She did not dwell long however, on Louise, but began to talk about a new herbalist shop that was shortly to be opened in St Cade. 'I thought it might affect your father's trade, but he doesn't seem to think so.'

Jessamy, whose heart had begun a quick beating said, 'No, it shouldn't, for Papa's trade is well-established and he's far enough from St Cade for it not to affect him.'

'Your grandfather will be furious. He's been after buying up all the empty shops. I don't know how this one slipped through his fingers.'

Jessamy thought— Oh, heavens, if her grandfather ever got to know that she and Louise would eventually own this shop there would be ructions to pay. Far better perhaps for Flynn O'Rafferty to keep it and they could go on paying him rent. Jessamy decided she would go to Newcastle that very weekend.

When Jessamy told her about the shop Louise simply grinned. 'That is our eventual aim, after all, to let Grandpa know we are the owners—*when* we become successful. And there's no way he can find out beforehand because we won't buy the shop from Flynn until we have succeeded.'

Jessamy felt that her cousin had more faith in Flynn O'Rafferty's honesty than she had, but she let it go. The important thing at that moment was to see Alistair.

They were alone again on the Sunday morning but this time there was the added pleasure of Alistair being able to feel the movements of the baby.

'Oh, Jessamy, it's just so wonderful. I never imagined I would feel so much pleasure from such a simple thing. No, it's not simple.' He laughed. 'It's a magnificent thing. We have created a baby.'

'With the help of God,' Jessamy said piously. Then she looked up, startled. 'Oh, Alistair, do you think we'll be punished for sinning? I hope He won't let any harm come to the baby.'

Alistair wrapped his arms around her and nuzzled his cheek against her. 'Of course not and I hope He will allow us to create more children.'

'Greedy,' she teased him then suddenly caught her breath and submitted herself to the urgent demands of Alistair's caresses.

The day Jessamy returned to The Montague Acres, the first person she saw was Fabian, talking to Mr Stannard. Her first reaction was to go tense, wondering what had brought him here. The next was to wish that she would not always be impressed by his imposing presence.

She had hired a cab to bring her from the station and as she stepped out, the two men parted and Fabian came over. He swept off his hat, his smile broad.

'Jessamy, I had to see my steward. Now you are here could we have a few words?' She agreed instantly and invited him in, trying to appear calm.

When the maid had brought in coffee he said, 'You look well, Jessamy, if possible more beautiful than ever.' He then asked after the baby and when she smiled and told him it was very vigorous he said, 'It's obviously a boy,' then asked her in a more serious tone if there was anything she needed.

She shook her head. 'No, you've been very generous. I'm grateful.'

He looked distressed. 'Don't thank me, Jessamy. There are times when I hate myself for what I did to you.' He paused then said, 'I've persuaded Caroline to move to Newmarket, where we shall breed and train horses. I'll leave you the address of my solicitor. Will you let me know when the baby is born and also tell me if there is anything you need, anything at all.'

She promised and he said, an anguish in his voice, 'If only things had been different but...'

'It's fate,' she said. 'It had to be,' then was unable to say more for the tightness in her throat.

He kissed her on the cheek, then was gone. And suddenly Jessamy was angry. It had all been so theatrical. He had played on her emotions, wanting to hold her to him, to perhaps want to claim the child at some time. Well, she would fight him all the way. But in spite of her anger Jessamy could not help thinking that if

511

things had been different they might have made a go of their marriage.

Although during the next three months Esmeralda showed much more affection towards Chadwick and Jessamy, waiting for the baby to be born was a trial to Jessamy. At seven months she felt cumbersome and took her walks mainly on the estate.

With the spring the house and grounds had taken on a different appearance. There were budding leaves everywhere in delicate and deeper greens in the tubs on the balconies, in shrubs, trees and plants. Then there was all the colour of spreads of daffodils, the yellow and purple of crocuses, the carpets of bluebells.

Although Jessamy had not exactly made friends with Mr Stannard, who was a very withdrawn man, they did stop and exchange a few words when they met. He asked after her health, Jessamy would ask his opinion on what he thought the weather would do and that was that. But one morning when they met he touched his hat then said, 'Mornin', Mrs Montague. I had a letter from the master and he asked my opinion on keeping some animals—a few pigs, hens, ducks, a cow and perhaps one or two sheep. What do you think, Ma'am?'

Jessamy, taken aback said, 'Why yes. Yes, they would be useful, I suppose. It's something I must leave in your hands, Mr Stannard.'

'It's nice to have animals where there are children.' He coughed. 'A child. I'll be biddin' you good day, Ma'am.' And he went on his way, straight-backed, without even the suggestion of a smile. Children? Jessamy mused. There would be no more than one born at The Montague Acres, at least as far as she was concerned.

Louise spent most of her time in St Peel with Jessamy these days, partly to keep her company but mostly because Cornelius and Abigail had filled the house in Newcastle with homeless families. Although Louise said she knew that that had been their original aim, she needed at times to have some peace. She was still paying the rent of her flat and told Jessamy she was free to use it whenever she wanted to meet Alistair, but Jessamy fought shy of taking up the offer because of the change in the house. She cringed at the thought of Alistair making love to her with children charging up and down the stairs, yelling at one another. And yet she longed to see him. He kept writing and asking when they could meet and suggested they met in Newcastle at a museum, anywhere just so they could be together for a while. *'It's just so that I can touch your dear face, my darling, tell you how much I love you. Could you manage the short journey?'*

Jessamy was planning to do so when a remark from her grandmother brought a sordid touch to their affair.

'Jessamy, do you still see this man whom you love and eventually plan to marry?'

513

'I haven't seen him for a while. Why?'

'Because it occurred to me recently that if ever Fabian wanted to claim the baby he would be able to do so if he could prove you were having an illicit relationship.'

Jessamy found herself trembling. 'Surely not! He is the one to desert me for Caroline.'

'But if he wished he could claim in court that he left you because you had been unfaithful. A good barrister, according to your grandfather, can always twist a situation to fit in with his client's wishes.'

Jessamy sat for a while, head bowed, then suddenly she raised her head and stood up. 'Fabian Montague is not going to deny my seeing the baby's father. I shall think of some place where we can meet.'

Before Jessamy was back at The Montague Acres she knew exactly where their next meeting place would be—Davy Feld's cottage on the moors where she and Alistair had first made love. It was secluded, and if anyone wanted to spy on them that person would be visible from the upstairs windows. Jessamy was sure that Alistair could arrange for them to use the cottage. Their visits would be short and quite infrequent.

When Louise was first told of Jessamy's misgivings she was inclined to think that her cousin was making a mountain out of a molehill, but when the latter explained about the cleverness of barristers she changed her mind.

Yes, she said, it might be wise to use caution and offered to do all she could to help.

Jessamy wrote a long letter to Alistair and when a week went by before she had a reply, she realised why. He told her he would be with her the following weekend: it was all fixed for them to meet at the cottage. He would travel from Edinburgh, arriving at Newcastle when it was dark. A friend of Flynn's would drive him in a van to St Cade. *'Don't worry, my darling. We shall beat the courts, barristers and Fabian Montague. No one is going to keep us apart. I hope to be at the cottage about ten o'clock. The fire will be laid. Put a match to it as soon as you arrive. With all my love...'*

Louise grinned when she was told the contents of the letter. 'Dependable Flynn, he would do all in his power to get two lovers together. And I might add that you have a very resourceful husband-to-be.'

Jessamy smiled. 'I think so, too.'

Louise accompanied Jessamy to the cottage on the Saturday evening, stayed until the fire was blazing and left, saying with a laugh, 'I'll look out for spies.'

Jessamy laughed, too, seeing that her cousin was also affected by a sense of adventure. But when Louise had gone there was something eerie about sitting alone in a strange environment, with the tick of the grandfather clock interspersed with an owl hooting and in a sudden, uncanny silence, a rustling in the undergrowth. When a gentle tap came on the door she jumped up, her heart beating wildly.

'Jessamy!' She turned the lamp low and opened the door. The next moment they were in one another's arms.

For the first half hour they talked over cups of cocoa, weighing up every possible item that could arise and allow Fabian the right to claim the baby.

'I know barristers are clever,' Alistair said, 'but after all, he is living with Caroline. You did say they were going into business together to breed horses.'

'Ah, that's the point. In business, yes. He hasn't said he was living with her. Can you imagine Fabian in court—he can be very impressive with his play-acting. I imagine he could even weep if he wanted too, pleading that he wants his child and that I, unfortunately, am not a fit mother to look after it. Was I not, after all, having an affair with my father's assistant?'

'But they would have to produce proof and we won't give them an opportunity to do so. When we were at Newcastle you were staying with highly-respected people. From now on we'll never be seen together, but go on meeting here. It must always be secretive but I couldn't exist without seeing you, Jessamy. It would be hell.' Jessamy said it would be hell for her too, and they clung together.

But Jessamy still worried over the fact that

Fabian with all his wealth would be able to engage a top barrister and then Alistair said, 'And so would your grandfather. Jeremiah may have a reputation for meanness, but he would give his all, I know, to protect one of his own.'

It was this that finally quieted Jessamy's fears.

They made love and it was gentle, but later when they talked about being parted for weeks and weeks on end there was a surge of passion between them, a desperation not to be parted, especially as Alistair was leaving again at six o'clock the next morning. He had to, he said, for so much studying needed to be done. Exams were coming up.

He cupped Jessamy's face between his palms. 'Do you think I would willingly leave you, dear heart? My career is more important than ever because of our future life together.' He smiled. 'I can feel our energetic son kicking.'

'Do you want a son?'

'Well, let me say I would not be disappointed if it was a little girl who looked like you. Small daughters can wrap themselves round the hearts of their Papas.'

He talked a lot of nonsense after that, painting a picture of them coping with five sons and five daughters and Jessamy played up to him, her heart aching. Later they were serious, with Alistair saying there must be no tears when they parted. They both had to be strong to face the future, to help one another. She promised.

Alistair had arrived in darkness and left in darkness, which seemed wrong to Jessamy. There should be no stealth when two people loved one another so much. The only thing that kept her strong was their love, and knowing that the day would come when they could live together as a family.

Alistair had arranged to visit her again in six weeks' time but the baby arrived earlier than expected. At six o'clock on a balmy morning in the middle of July Jessamy began her labour pains. Because they were so frequent, Louise instructed a servant to ask Mr Stannard to take a horse and trap and bring the midwife to the house. Within an hour of the midwife arriving, Jessamy gave birth to a seven and a half pound daughter whose shrill screaming had the midwife saying, 'She's impatient, this one. She'll be trouble, m'dear, wanting all her own way.'

Jessamy whispered, 'At this moment she can have anything she wants.'

Later, when the baby was laid in her arms she felt so emotional she was unable to speak, but in her mind she was writing to Alistair, *'You'll adore her. Her dark hair is damp after her bath and lies in tiny curls. She's sucking avidly on her fist as though she has not been fed for days. Her eyes are blue now, but they may change colour. Louise says she resembles you, but I can't see it yet. I long for you to be with us...'*

It was the only time that Jessamy had alone with her baby that morning. Mr Stannard had informed her parents that their daughter was in labour and Esmeralda in turn had let Verity and Bertie know, also the grandparents.

Jeremiah held court as though he were the father of the child and for a time no one else could get a word in edgeways.

He told Jessamy it was a pity that she had not borne a son but then this was only his first great-grandchild. His tone implied that there would be other children. He then asked if she had now decided on a name for the child and Jessamy took a breath.

'Yes, Romaine.' There was a gasp from those in the room. This was not an Every family name.

It belonged to Alistair's family: his great-great-grandfather had run away and married a gypsy girl whose proud Romany family had disowned her. Jessamy, who had found the story romantic, had decided to name her baby after the runaway bride. She said, 'It was a name in a story that took my fancy.'

No more was said, but the baby came in for plenty of admiration. Esmeralda, to Jessamy's surprise, was quite sentimental over her first grandchild. 'I did hope it would be a boy but she's so beautiful, how could one not love her?'

Chadwick was emotional and there were tears in his eyes when the baby gripped his finger. 'Perhaps she knows I'm her grandfather,' he whispered.

The only sadness of that morning for Jessamy

was Alistair's absence and the look of pain in Verity and Bertie's eyes when Louise positively drooled over the baby.

It was Louise who arranged for Alistair to see his daughter a week later, sneaking him in the back way at midnight when everywhere was still. He cried unashamedly when he saw Romaine, and Jessamy and Louise wept, too. He asked to hold her and when the baby yawned he smiled through his tears. 'Oh, Jessamy, what a wonderful gift. I shall treasure this moment for the rest of my life.'

They talked in whispers and it was arranged that as soon as Jessamy was able to be up and about the three of them would meet in the cottage.

When the time for parting came they held one another tightly with Jessamy saying, 'I always remember your words that we must both be strong to help one another. It sustains me.'

'And me, too, Jessamy my darling. Just pray for the time when the three of us will be together.'

He said a silent goodbye to the baby, a touch on the delicate skin, then he was gone...

CHAPTER THIRTY-TWO

When Romaine was nearly two years old Jessamy took stock of her life since the baby had been born and came to the conclusion that a great deal had happened in that time. Some of it was good, some of it worrying. The worst time had been after the birth when Fabian had visited every week for six weeks to see the child and kept insisting that Romaine was the replica of a miniature of his mother done as a baby. He said he would find it and bring it, and did, but the only likeness as far as Jessamy was concerned was that both babies were dark-haired. It was then that she asked Fabian pointblank if he intended to lay claim to the child as his own.

He was shocked. No, how could she believe he would do such a thing? When she gave her reasons he explained that he had hoped deep down that the child might be his, as he wanted someone of his very own to love. But no, he would never, never try to take Romaine from her natural mother: Jessamy must believe him. She was touched by the thought that Fabian was genuine in wanting a child to love, but at the same time cautious that he could still be play-acting. Even when he stopped visiting both Jessamy and Alistair never risked meeting anywhere but at the cottage.

The sad times were their partings. Alistair adored Romaine and he was her favourite 'uncle'.

The child was a natural coquette with men and could wrap her grandfather and great-grandfather round her little finger. She was sullen one minute and sunny and malleable the next. At first she lived up to the midwife's prophecy that she was impatient and would want her own way. She threw tantrums but very quickly learned that coaxing was much less painful than being slapped. Her mother was determined not to tolerate a spoiled child.

Jessamy's approach paid dividends. By the time Romaine was a toddler she had many slaves, none more adoring than Esmeralda, Henrietta, Verity and Louise. And yet, if Romaine fell and hurt herself it was always for her mother she called.

In the two years since their initial investment the shops that Louise and Jessamy had set up had flourished and they had been persuaded by Flynn to buy another two—one in Gateshead and one in Wallsend. Although Jessamy was interested in them, she was not so involved as Louise. Jessamy had kept on hoping that her cousin and Flynn might marry but Louise just said, 'We're good friends, Jessamy, but nothing more and never will be.' The only thing that kept Jessamy hoping that they might eventually marry was that although Flynn would tease other girls he was never serious with any of them.

Louise practically lived at The Montague Acres now but the girls still went for odd visits to Newcastle to see Cornelius and Abigail and to take a look in the window of their shop, which was in The Bigg Market. They left Romaine with Esmeralda and Verity, meanwhile. The shop was small but it was well-stocked and did a good trade, especially on a Saturday. An elderly man and his two sons ran it, the older son always dressing the window, for which he had a flair. On one occasion he laid leaves on the bottom of the window, then had streamers of satin ribbons, shading from pale pink to deepest pink, swathing the coloured, cut-glass bottles arranged in tiers. The display attracted many customers. At this, the girls exchanged smiling glances with Louise saying, 'I don't think I could do a better job myself.' They shook hands with the man, feeling well pleased.

Alistair never accompanied them at these times as both he and Jessamy were still determined not to be seen together. Cornelius and Abigail had a houseful of people and by now had achieved their main aim of opening a soup kitchen for those in need. Every time Jessamy saw what they had accomplished she remembered her own and Alistair's wish to open a dispensary for the poor. She still studied medical textbooks and hoped that at some time in her future life she would be able to train as a doctor. It would have to wait until Romaine was at an age when she could be left in the charge of a nanny and not feel neglected.

By this time, Alistair had passed every exam he had sat with flying colours and had a well-known surgeon tell him that he was excellent 'scalpel material', a piece of praise which delighted and encouraged him.

He and Jessamy discussed his ambition to become a surgeon. 'It's what I want to do now more than anything, Jessamy. I see men losing a leg because of sheer inefficiency. A surgeon must be able to work quickly. Then there's the carelessness of dirty jackets, with some surgeons wearing one stiff with blood from previous operations. While some will wash their hands in water containing disinfectant, others ignore this precaution. In one hospital I visited where there were strict rules the mortality rate was quite low, especially infant mortality. At times I feel so frustrated, so helpless.'

Jessamy knew frustration the following year, when she had no contact with Fabian at all thus knew nothing about how the divorce case was proceeding. It was when she overheard a remark made by her grandfather to her father about Fabian that she wrote to the Captain's solicitor, asking him to forward the letter to Fabian. Three days later she had a reply from him to say he was coming to see Mr Stannard the following week and would call on her.

When Fabian did call he looked brimming over with health and seemed happier than when she had last seen him. He apologised for not having kept in touch but said he felt she still worried that he was trying to take Romaine from her.

She said, 'My worry at the moment is how the divorce will affect you. I heard my grandfather say to my father that you would be disgraced if you lost the case through committing adultery. I did not question this, wanting to hear it from you. Is it true?'

'Jessamy, if I were a Duke or an Earl or someone well-known in high society, I would be ostracised. As it stands, it will be an arranged divorce and afterwards Caroline and I finally plan to live in Texas, so whatever anyone has to say is of no importance to either of us. Even Caroline has lost interest in a social life, so you can stop worrying.' He smiled. 'Now tell me, how is dear Romaine?'

'She's a bundle of mischief but everyone loves her. Louise has taken her for a walk but they'll be back soon.'

Their talk after that was of horses and life at Newmarket and Jessamy was listening, fascinated, when the cries of a child could be heard. Jessamy got up. 'Oh, dear, Romaine is in trouble again.' She was smiling. 'She enjoys a little fuss.'

525

Romaine came running in, her hands held out saying, 'Mama, Mama, I fell, my hands hurt.'

Jessamy knelt down and kissed the palms. 'There, my love, they're better. Say hello to the gentleman.'

Romaine, a blue dress emphasizing the deeper blue of her eyes, pushed back her dark curls and buried her face in her mother's skirt.

When Fabian queried if she was shy, Jessamy laughed softly and said, 'No, simply showing off.'

Within seconds Romaine was on his lap and telling him about the animals. She even persuaded him to come and see them and Fabian, with a smile, said how could he refuse such a persuasive young lady.

Louise, who had just come in, went with them and Jessamy, watching from the window, saw a side to Fabian she had never seen before. He was acting the part of the Pied Piper, playing an imaginary flute and dancing as he led a single file of waddling ducks to the pond. Romaine rolled about, laughing at his antics.

When Fabian had gone, after receiving loving kisses from Romaine, Louise said, 'He's a surprising man.'

'Yes, he is,' Jessamy replied quietly. 'Very surprising.'

Although Jessamy never wavered in her love for Alistair she thought how complicated her life had once become through Fabian's inability to forgive. However, it was far better that they separated when they did than for her to live the rest of her life with a husband who had a mistress in the background.

There were times when Jessamy felt a strong surge of longing for Alistair to make love to her and she was frustrated that they were so far apart. Always when he came to the cottage he would tease her, asking if she wanted stormy love or gentle, but their first lovemaking was always wild after the long waiting. The gentleness came later.

When Romaine was coming up to her fourth year a difficulty arose when she asked who her Papa was. Jessamy was forced to say that Fabian was because only a few members of the family knew about the pending divorce. Outsiders did not even know of the separation, thinking that the Captain was away at sea.

It was about this time that Fabian took to visiting again, and he was not only astonished but delighted when Romaine called him 'Papa'. Jessamy had hitherto described him to her daughter as the gentleman who had played Pied Piper with the ducks.

Jessamy felt grieved that Alistair was denied being acknowledged as Romaine's natural parent, and Fabian was obviously aware of it too because he said gently during one of his visits, 'Allow me this privilege until the divorce, Jessamy, then I shall be out of your lives forever.'

When Jessamy told Alistair he said, 'We won't begrudge him this small thing. We have a lifetime ahead of us when Romaine will truly be *our* child.'

It was not until the date approached for the case to be heard that Jessamy understood the meaning of an arranged divorce. Louise told her, having learned about it from Flynn. To save Jessamy from appearing in court and listening to all the sordid details of adultery, Fabian had agreed to offer evidence that he had shared a room in an hotel with some strange woman. Louise pointed out that her cousin should be grateful to Fabian. The divorce was granted and the family were lucky that a ferocious storm was sweeping the country at the time, doing enormous damage. It occupied the front pages of every newspaper. All the case merited was a small paragraph tucked away in a corner of an inside page.

Afterwards Jessamy had a note from Fabian saying, *'Dear Jessamy, I'm sorry I put you through so much. Forgive me and be happy with lovely Romaine. Some day we may meet again, but only if you wish it. Caroline and I will be leaving for Texas in a month's time. Sincerely, Fabian.'*

Jessamy read the letter twice then putting it in her journal, locked it away.

She had sent a telegram immediately to Alistair, telling him that she was now free, but it was another week before they could meet, and then it was still at the cottage as their meetings must remain secret for a while longer. It would be another year before Alistair received his degree and only Louise, Henrietta and Fabian knew that Alistair was Romaine's natural father. Alistair and Jessamy clung together, Jessamy saying with despair, '*When, Alistair?* When will we be able to start a new life together?'

He stroked her hair. 'We've got through the past four years, so we can wait for one more. It'll be worth it, Jessamy. Don't desert me now.'

There was such a world of pain in his voice that she pulled herself together. 'Desert you? How could you ever think such a thing? I love you, Alistair and it's forever. You're right. Four years have gone by, this one will fly over and then...'

Alistair smiled as he held her away from him. 'And then my love, we shall have to start courting all over again.'

She laughed softly, 'It'll be something to look forward to, the two of us walking out. By then the family will have got over the fact that I'm a divorced woman. I'm sure that some of them regard me as a harlot, even though I was cited as the "injured party".'

The momentous day when Alistair qualified as a surgeon he came to see both Chadwick and Mr Blackwell, and Jessamy was present. Alistair was congratulated then Mr Blackwell said, beaming at him, 'My, but you've become a fine figure of a man, Alistair. I always said you would go far.'

Alistair had definitely changed. He had broadened and although he was not tall he had a similar commanding presence to Fabian.

The three men talked medicine and Jessamy observed and watched the changing expressions on Alistair's face, his concern as he discussed the poverty-stricken people, the depressed and the sick. The lightening of his manner as he talked about various cures that had been found in the past few years, and the Godsend of chloroform that could deaden pain during operations.

Once he spread his arms and said, 'There's a whole new world of cures out there waiting to be discovered. I want to experiment. There's so much I want to do, so many people to be helped.'

'And all the time in the world to do it,' Chadwick said softly. 'Concentrate on becoming the best surgeon, my boy. You had high praise from a top man for handling a scalpel.'

'Yes, well, we'll see.' Alistair looked at Jessamy. 'Would you care for a walk on the moors, for old time's sake? It's been a long while.'

'Yes, I would like that.' Jessamy stood up to get her coat and met indulgent smiles from her father and the old man.

It was autumn, and the leaves were turning.

In the late afternoon sun the moor had a burnished look. Alistair whispered, 'I suppose this is where I start courting you, my darling.'

She looked up at him. 'Oh, Alistair, how I've hated all this subterfuge. Sometimes I wonder how we've managed to keep our meetings secret.'

'I once read of a couple with warring families who met one another for ten years without anyone knowing.'

'What happened?'

'When they had their tenth child they couldn't keep it secret any longer.' Alistair was grinning and she slapped his arm. 'Oh, you!'

'No, honestly, they really did keep their meetings secret all that time. They confessed their secret and according to the records the families gave in to their getting married, but the families remained enemies.'

'How foolish of them, living their lives with hate.'

'I agree.'

They walked in silence for a way then Jessamy said, 'Alistair, I know you'll be looking for a practice. Have you any idea where?'

'I'm hoping for the East End of London. How do you feel about that? I've seen premises there that I think would be ideal for a dispensary.'

'You have? Oh, that's wonderful.'

He smiled. 'Don't get too excited. It will

need a lot of money spending on it.'

'We'll get the money,' she said eagerly. 'We'll beg, borrow or steal it. Is it a house?'

'Yes. At one time it was occupied by an aristocratic family, but you wouldn't think so to look at it now. It's known in the district as the house at Paradise Corner.'

'Paradise Corner? Oh, Alistair, it couldn't have a better name. We won't be able to make it a paradise, but to sick people it could seem a haven and that is what we'll try and achieve. I'll ask everyone I know for money. I'll ask Fabian, for a start.'

'Jessamy, you couldn't—that would be like rubbing salt into a wound.'

'No, it wouldn't. Fabian has his faults but he's generous. Flynn may help and there's my half-brother Ralph—I know he would like to contribute. So will Papa and I'll try and coax something from Grandpa.'

'Now wait, Jessamy, hold on a moment. You can't go rushing into this like a bull in a china shop.'

'Why not?' she said softly. They were beside an outcropping of rocks and, stopping in their shelter, she clasped her hands around Alistair's neck. 'We both have this dream to open a dispensary to help the sick poor. For five years I've been static, frustrated, needing something worthwhile to do, something to make me feel fulfilled. This is it. I want to start right away: give me one good reason why I shouldn't?'

532

He drew her close. 'I can't think of one.' He touched the tip of her nose lightly. 'All I want do at this moment is to enjoy the paradise of being here with you, of being able to walk and talk in the open. But tomorrow...'

He bent his head and their lips met, soft and warm. The past slid into the background and Jessamy thought, 'Yes, there is tomorrow and all the other tomorrows...' and gave herself up to this moment of paradise.